Joh

Practical Reflections on Select Passages of the New Testament

SALZWASSER VERLAG

John Bird Sumner

Practical Reflections on Select Passages of the New Testament

Reprint of the original, first published in 1859.

1st Edition 2022 | ISBN: 978-3-37512-986-6

Verlag (Publisher): Salzwasser Verlag GmbH, Zeilweg 44, 60439 Frankfurt, Deutschland
Vertretungsberechtigt (Authorized to represent): E. Roepke, Zeilweg 44, 60439 Frankfurt, Deutschland
Druck (Print): Books on Demand GmbH, In de Tarpen 42, 22848 Norderstedt, Deutschland

PRACTICAL REFLECTIONS

ON

SELECT PASSAGES

OF THE

NEW TESTAMENT.

BY

JOHN BIRD SUMNER, D.D.,

ARCHBISHOP OF CANTERBURY.

CHIEFLY COMPILED FROM EXPOSITORY LECTURES ON THE GOSPELS AND EPISTLES, BY THE SAME AUTHOR.

LONDON:

HATCHARD AND CO., 187, PICCADILLY.

M.DCCC.LIX.

ADVERTISEMENT.

The following Volume is in great measure a republication of certain portions of a much larger Work; from which I have selected some of the passages in the New Testament, which place in clear and strong light the nature and character of the Gospel, and exemplify its effect upon the hearts of those by whom it is received.

If an apology is required for adding another to the numerous works of a similar kind which issue from the Press, it must be found in the saying attributed to Luther, who compares the Scripture to a well-loaded tree, from which, however much has been already gathered, fresh fruit may be continually shaken down. However this may prove, I trust that nothing is contained in the Volume which is not the natural growth of Scripture; nothing added to, nothing diminished from that WORD, which is emphatically declared to be "truth," and which it has pleased God to reveal for the instruction and salvation of mankind.

CONTENTS.

PRACTICAL REFLECTIONS,

&c. &c.

I.

DIVINE NATURE OF CHRIST.

HEB. i. 1—4.

1. *God, who at sundry times and in divers manners spake in time past unto the fathers by the prophets,*
2. *Hath in these last days spoken unto us by his Son, whom he hath appointed heir of all things, by whom also he made the worlds.*

In this language St. Paul, himself a Hebrew, addresses his Hebrew countrymen. It was no new thing to them, as it was to the heathen disciples to whom his other epistles were addressed, that God had revealed himself to mankind. The Jews acknowledged, the whole nation boasted, that God had made his counsels known to them *at sundry times and in divers manners.* They had "Moses and the prophets," who *in time past had spoken unto them* in his name. But now in *these last days God had spoken to them* by one who was "more than a prophet:" by one who revealed what "prophets had desired to see, and had not seen:" by one who was not only to be heard, but to be adored: by one who had effected what none of the sons of men could ever have accomplished; for he had "taken away the sin of the world."[1]

It was hard for the Jews to understand this, when spoken concerning Jesus. They had seen him grow up amongst them "as a tender plant, as a root out of a dry ground;"[2] and they were slow to believe that he came, not as Moses, or Samuel, or Elijah had come, possessed of the power with which God endued them; but came in his own authority, being "equal to the Father as touching his godhead, though inferior to the Father" in the human nature which he had assumed.[3] St. Paul, therefore, reminds them, that God had *appointed him heir of all things:*—heir, that is, possessor, lord, governor;—that he had "been with God from the beginning," as Creator of the world: so that, when he came into the world, "he came unto his own;" and when "his own received him not,"[4] he whom they rejected was their Creator. Unless they believed this, they could have no due sense of what they owed to him, no knowledge of the value of his redemption. The apostle, therefore, proceeds to describe his greatness, as far as words can describe what it is impossible for the mind of man fully to comprehend or conceive.

3. *Who being the brightness of his glory, and the express image of his person, and upholding all things by the word of his power, when he had by himself purged*

[1] John i. 29. [2] Isa. liii. 2.
[3] Athanasian Creed. [4] John. i. 11.

our sins, sat down on the right hand of the Majesty on high;

4. *Being made so much better than the angels, as he hath by inheritance obtained a more excellent name than they.*

The ministry of angels was familiar to the Jews, and their history abounds with examples of its exercise. It might have been natural for them to regard Jesus as a created being, sent as one of the ministers of God to do his pleasure. St. Paul thinks it needful to guard against this error, by reminding his countrymen that the prophets, whose authority they acknowledged, had spoken of their expected Messiah in terms which could never be applied to angels. If any should affirm that Jesus was an angel sent from God to fulfil his will on earth, how would they account for the prophetic passage in the ninety-seventh Psalm, which, after describing in magnificent terms the advent of the Messiah, calls on all the angels of God to worship him?[5] Angels, no doubt, have a great office and dignity assigned them: they are spirits, ready to obey the command of their Maker: they are as a flame of fire, quick and prompt to execute his will. But they are not represented as possessing independent power; not as ruling, but obeying: whereas the Son is addressed, as seated on an eternal throne; as bearing the emblem of kingly majesty, a sceptre of righteousness; as having "a name that is above every name." His majesty is that of the Father himself, whose incomprehensible splendour was reflected in the

[5] St. Paul, it seems, so understood the words which are rendered in our translation, "Worship him, *all ye gods.*" He quotes from the Septuagint version.

Son, as *being the brightness of his glory, and the express image of his person, and upholding all things by the word of his power.* And so when the apostle Philip asked him, saying, "Lord, show us the Father, and it sufficeth us;"—we shall desire no more: —his answer was, "Have I been so long time with you, and yet hast thou not known me, Philip? He that hath seen me, hath seen the Father."[6] He has seen the Father, as far as it is lawful for mortal eye to behold him. He has seen him by whom the worlds were made, and who by *the word of his power*, by the exercise of his will, maintains the seasons in their order, the sun in his course, and so *upholds all things* which at first he made. For although his mercy and pity did cause him to descend from that glory which he had with the Father before the world was, he "was with God from the beginning, and was God."[7] To that glory he returned, when his purpose was fulfilled, and resumed his place *on the right-hand of the Majesty on high:* no created being, but the Creator of all things, whether in the heavens above or in the earth below: no angel, but the Lord of angels, inasmuch as, *being appointed heir of all things, he hath by inheritance obtained a more excellent name than they:* being "far above all principalities, and powers, and might, and dominion, and every name that is named, not only in this world, but also in that which is to come."[8]

Such, as we believe, is he, who *by himself purged our sins.*[9] St. Paul states this as the object for which he came down from heaven. To the offended justice and

[6] John xiv. 8, 9. [7] John i. 1, 2. [8] Eph. i. 21.

[9] καθαρισμον ποιησαμενος: having effected a purification.

holiness of the Father he offered a "full, perfect, and sufficient satisfaction;" so that it might become consistent with the divine attributes, consistent with the counsels of infinite wisdom, to pardon man's past disobedience and transgression.

For the state of the world, when God thus interposed, with the exception of one small nation, was a state of alienation from God: the thing made was ignorant of him who made it; the creature was estranged from his Creator. He, therefore, who had at first formed the earth for the use of man, and man to inhabit it, interposes once more. He who had said at first, "Let us make man after our own image, in our likeness;" now says again, Let us restore man to that image which he has lost, to that likeness which sin has defaced and deformed. "Hear, O heavens, and give ear, O earth, for the Lord, the mighty God, hath spoken:" hath spoken unto us by his Son, to whom "all power is given in heaven and in earth."[1] And if we hearken to his call, and obey his word, the revelation here made of his divine power is the strong foundation of our hope and comfort. He to whom we are taught to flee, he in whom we seek refuge from the wrath to come, is "God over all, blessed for ever;" and his greatness is our security. He who offers salvation is not, as some might pretend, and as the Jews especially might have supposed, a prophet endowed with authority to reveal God's will, but still a mere man of nature like our own: but is HE who, "was in the beginning with God, and was God." And there is solid comfort in the thought. True, he is man, with our nature to pity; but then he

[1] Matt. xxviii. 18.

is also GOD, with infinite power to save. Such is the ground of the confidence expressed by St. Paul; a confidence of which he desires to make all who trust in Christ partakers: "Who shall lay anything to the charge of God's elect? It is God that justifieth. Who is he that condemneth? It is Christ that died, yea rather, that is risen again, who is even at the right hand of God, who also maketh intercession for us, and is able to save unto the uttermost them that come unto God by him." The purpose to be accomplished, the work of man's salvation, was so great, that it could be committed to none other: and he to whom it was committed is so omnipotent, that nothing which he undertakes can fail.

II.

THE HUMANITY OF CHRIST.

JOHN i. 14.

14. *The Word was made flesh, and dwelt among us, (and we beheld his glory, the glory as of the only begotten of the Father,) full of grace and truth.*

ST. JOHN, in the verses which precede this text, had declared the DIVINITY of the Redeemer, saying, "In the beginning was the Word, and the Word was with God, and the Word was God."[1] He now testifies, with the

[1] The plainest reason why this essential Son of God is styled *the Word*, seems to be this: that as our words are the interpretation of our mind to others, so was the Son of God sent to reveal his Father's mind to the world.—*Whitby*.

same clearness, a truth which equally concerns us, his HUMANITY. *The Word was made flesh.* He who was God, took upon him the nature of man: the nature of frail mortal flesh. He did not cease to be what he was: he could not cease to be what he had been from eternity; but he became, what he was not before, man as well as God.[2]

Nothing is here asserted, which is not intelligible. There seems no reason why the nature which is clothed with flesh should only be such a nature as our own. God, we know, "breathed into man's nostrils the breath of life, and he became a living soul." That soul might have partaken of a nature different from that with which it was then endued. The mode in which God and man became one, we cannot explain; but we need not go beyond ourselves, and the union of soul and body in our own natures, to meet with that which we shall never comprehend: and there is nothing contradictory in believing that as the living soul and body constitute one man, so God and man are one Christ. "For with God nothing shall be impossible."

Further, what the Evangelist affirms agrees with what had been foretold, and with what the Jewish nation, possessing the oracles of God, had reason to expect.

God had declared to Adam that "the seed" or offspring "of the woman should bruise the serpent's head."[3] Jesus was the offspring of the woman, Mary; and was now manifested to bruise the serpent's head, and to destroy the works of the devil.

[2] As defined by the fourth General Council.—"He was so made flesh, that he ceased not to be the Word, never changing that he was, but assuming that he was not."

[3] Gen. iii. 15.

Moses had assured the Israelites, that in due time "the Lord their God should raise up unto them of their brethren a prophet like unto himself."[4] And now the Word was made flesh, and "born of a woman," among this people.

Isaiah had prophesied concerning a Saviour, in words which could only apply to one who came in fashion as a man, and yet who was in his nature more than man: whose generation was incomprehensible: whose appearance was frail and humble, yet whose power was divine.

The appearance, therefore, of Christ in the flesh did agree with the expectation raised by prophecy. And then we ask, thirdly, Was there a reason for it? Scripture explains the reason. Jesus "came into the world to save sinners," by dying the death of sinners. In the nature of God he could not die. He could not suffer except in that nature which had sinned. He could only bear the curse of the law in the nature which had incurred the curse by transgression of the law. Forasmuch, then, as those whom he came to redeem "are partakers of flesh and blood, he also himself likewise took part of the same; that through death he might destroy him that had the power of death, that is, the devil; and deliver them, who through fear of death were all their lifetime subject to bondage. For verily he took not on him the nature of angels; but he took on him the seed of Abraham."[5]

Therefore, according to God's determinate counsel, and for a reason which can be explained to us, "a body was prepared" for the Word:[6] the Son of God "was

[4] Deut. xviii. 15. See Acts iii. 22. [5] Heb. ii. 14—16.
[6] Heb. x. 5.

made of the seed of David according to the flesh,"[7] and *dwelt among us* in fashion as a man. "Without controversy, great is the mystery; God manifest in the flesh."[8] Great is the mystery: but how much greater is the mercy!

And now the Evangelist adds, *We beheld his glory, the glory as of the only begotten of the Father.* Though he showed himself in the nature and weakness of man, he also showed himself in the glory of Almighty God: that while we can approach and lean upon the one, we may trust and commit ourselves to the other. St. John says, "*We beheld his glory.*" St. John was one of those who enjoyed this privilege in a special degree. He was of that chosen party which attended Jesus on mount Tabor, when "he was transfigured before them, and his face did shine as the sun, and his raiment was white as the light."[9] The intent, surely, of that manifestation was to leave an impression upon the mind of the witnesses, which they should in time transmit to others. St. Peter used it for this purpose, saying, "We have not followed cunningly devised fables, when we made known unto you the power and coming of our Lord Jesus Christ; but were eye-witnesses of his majesty. For he received from God the Father honour and glory, when there came such a voice to him from the excellent glory, This is my beloved Son, in whom I am well pleased. And this voice which came from heaven we heard, when we were with him in the holy mount."[1]

Such is the clear assurance left to us, from those who spoke what they knew, and testified what they had

[7] Rom. i. 3. [8] 1 Tim. iii. 16.
[9] Matt. xvii. 1, 2. [1] 2 Peter i. 16—18.

seen. It has been handed down to us in uninterrupted order by successive generations of Christians. The apostles "related what their eyes had seen, and their hands had handled, of the Word of life,"[2] to the different assemblies among which they went, "preaching the word." And what was so witnessed and confirmed, the first companies of Christians received as true; and believed in Jesus as the Christ, the Son of God: so that Peter could affirm of them, "Whom having not seen, ye love; in whom, though now ye see him not, yet believing, ye rejoice with joy unspeakable and full of glory."[3] These, again, conveyed the word of truth to the generation that came after: the leaven was gradually diffused: the seed became a great tree, with its branches spread on every side, and "its leaves for the healing of the nations." But as the tree which may have stood for centuries, and which no man living has ever known except as a widely spreading and an ancient tree, was once a seed, and would never have existed at all if that seed had not been dropped into the ground: so with our Christian faith. The believers have multiplied; ages have followed ages; nation after nation has been added to the church: and the time seems far back since that church first began to be. Still there was a first seed; and that seed was planted when *the Word was made flesh, and dwelt among us, full of grace and truth,* and the apostles *beheld his glory.*

In one way, that glory has been evidently beheld in every age that has since passed. For in every age that has since passed, multitudes have been brought, through the preaching of the word, "from darkness to light,

[2] 1 John i. 1. [3] 1 Pet. i. 8.

from the power of Satan unto God:" multitudes have given up their sinful practices and their worldly desires, and have laid them at the foot of the cross, and have "received the gift of the Holy Ghost," so as to become "a peculiar people," living to the glory of God, and adorning the doctrine of the Saviour. Men "see their good works," see "their light shining;" and they behold in this a testimony, a glorious evidence of the Gospel. A testimony was given which it was impossible to resist, when, as Saul was on his way to Damascus, a light shone suddenly from heaven, "above the brightness of the sun," and struck the persecutor with blindness. But a few days after, Saul himself was a no less convincing spectacle, when praying for direction to him whom he had so lately persecuted, and preaching the doctrine which before he destroyed.[4] The voice which came out of the cloud was astonishing, when it said, "This is my beloved Son, hear him." But the dying voice of the christian Stephen was equally convincing, when, under the influence of the Holy Ghost, he knelt down and prayed, "Lord, lay not this sin to their charge!" "Lord Jesus, receive my spirit!"[5]

These, however, are exceptional cases. We need not go so far back, we need not appeal to extraordinary interpositions of divine power, to see proofs of the glory of Christ, or to be convinced by the evidence which it supplies. Every member of the fold of Christ bears about him testimony to his Shepherd's faithfulness, and truth, and power. No evidence can be stronger. When we see an individual of the Jewish nation, we see an undeniable proof of the truth of the Bible history,

[4] See Acts ix. 3—22. [5] Acts vii. 59, 60.

and of the prophecies it contains. So, when we behold a true and consistent Christian, we possess the same evidence of all that the Gospel says of the mercy of God, the divinity of Christ, and the power of the Spirit. What can be a greater miracle, than one who has his dealings here on earth, and his conversation in heaven: who is dead to the things with which he is daily and hourly conversant, and whose "life is hid with Christ in God?" Surely this is not natural: especially when we remember the temptations of that world to which he is crucified, and the corruption of that heart which he is subduing, and the rebellious lusts of the flesh which he habitually mortifies.

We have reason to be thankful, that these evidences of the glory of Christ have never failed. We may see them in those around us; nay, we may possess them in ourselves. Every one possesses this inward testimony, who, through faith in the Son of God, is renewed after the image of God in righteousness and true holiness, and enabled to escape "the corruption which is in the world."

III.

THE WORD, THE LIGHT AND LIFE OF THE SOUL OF MAN.

JOHN i. 4, 5.

4. *In him was life; and the life was the light of men.*

5. *And the light shineth in darkness; and the darkness comprehended it not.*

St. John had before declared that the eternal Word, whose incarnation is the subject of his Gospel, had been one with the Father from the beginning: and that "without him was not anything made that was made." He now adds, *In him was life.* On him life depended, and is by him imparted and communicated. "For as the Father hath life in himself; so hath he given to the Son to have life in himself. For as the Father raiseth up the dead, and quickeneth them; even so the Son quickeneth whom he will."[1]

But *the life* here spoken of is something more than that which was "breathed into man's nostrils, and he became a living soul."[2] *The life was the light of men.* It is the spiritual, and not the natural life which is the light of men. And this life is in the Son, and is by him shed abroad upon the heart. Accordingly, in one of his epistles, this same evangelist describes him as "the Word of life:" (i. 1, 3); "That which was from the beginning, which we have heard, which we have seen with our eyes, which we have looked upon, and our hands have handled, of the Word of life, that which we have seen and heard, declare we unto you." And justly is he so termed, who generates in the soul a new existence, springing up to immortality. He is to the soul, what light is to the body of man. If the eye be without light, how great is the darkness! But darker still is the soul, without that light which proceeds from the Son of God, and enables it to answer the purposes for for which it was created, and endued with understanding.

Some seeds of this divine life, some sparks of this heavenly light, had always been scattered in the world.

[1] John v. 26, 21. [2] Gen. ii. 7.

As it is in nature, before the actual rising of the sun, that certain beams of light are visible, and, however inadequate to all our wants, serve many useful purposes: so was it with that spiritual light which had now fully risen. It had long been glimmering in dim and partial rays, before the prophet's words received their certain accomplishment, before it could be said of Jerusalem, "Arise, shine; for thy light is come, and the glory of the Lord is risen upon thee." [3]

It was by that earlier light that some of the heathen, wiser than their fellows, and emerging out of the general ignorance, were led to "seek the Lord, if haply they might feel after him, and find him." As certain of their poets said, "For we are also his offspring." [4] Led by this light, they worshipped the powers which they perceived to be above them, though they worshipped they knew not what: so that Paul, as he "passed by and beheld their devotions, found an altar with this inscription, To the unknown God." [5] And much farther would that light have conducted them, if they had not too often quenched it, because they "did not like to retain God in their knowledge." [6]

Still, more particularly among the Jewish people *this life was the light of men.* Many had come to the light; had received life, had feared God, and wrought righteousness, "looking for glory, and honour, and immortality." It was by this light that "Abel offered unto God a more excellent sacrifice than Cain." It was by this light that Enoch walked with God: that Abraham obeyed the call of God, and left his country and his

[3] Isa. lx. 1. [4] Acts xvii. 27, 28.
[5] Acts xvii. 23. [6] Rom. i. 28.

kindred, looking for a better habitation, eternal in the heavens. It was by this light that Moses was enabled to refuse the pleasures of sin for a season, which he might have enjoyed at the court of Pharaoh, and "esteemed the reproach of Christ greater riches than the treasures in Egypt." It was by this light that many prophets and righteous men, "of whom the world was not worthy, died in faith, not having received the promises, but having seen them afar off, and were persuaded of them, and embraced them, and confessed that they were strangers and pilgrims on the earth."[7]

But still there was too just cause to say, as St. John goes on to add, *The light shineth in darkness, and the darkness comprehended it not.* The law was but "a shadow of good things to come,"[8] and could not be compared with "the very image of the things" which had now been manifested to the world. Prophecy was as "a light that shineth in a dark place;"[9] and even they who uttered it, desired to see the things which were now seen, and had not seen them; "inquired and searched diligently, searching what or what manner of time the Spirit of Christ which was in them did signify, when it testified beforehand the sufferings of Christ, and the glory that should follow."[1] The vast scheme undertaken by the Son of God, when he came to "give his life a ransom for many," could be but obscurely perceived and imperfectly understood, before the facts interpreted the predictions. The state of man, in regard to the things of God, in regard to present duties and future prospects, is exactly described in this expressive

[7] See Hebrews xi. 4, 5, 8, 26, 13.
[8] Heb. x. 1.
[9] 2 Peter i. 19.
[1] 1 Peter i. 11.

verse, *The light shineth in darkness, and the darkness comprehended it not.* Certain rays were discovered amid the general gloom, which glimmered, and shed forth a partial light, but did not disperse the darkness. There was not total ignorance, yet there was no clear knowledge.

It is a melancholy thought, that this representation too well describes even the present condition of too many in the world, who are now "without excuse." "The times of that ignorance God winked at; but now commandeth all men everywhere to repent."[2] The dim light, the uncertain knowledge of the Jewish patriarchs, could not be imputed to them as sin. But, alas! what must we now say for the wilful darkness of those who close their eyes against the light, which shines in all its lustre! The Redeemer himself has said, "If I had not come and spoken unto you, ye had not had sin: but now ye have no cloke for your sin."

He who was in the beginning with God, and was God, undertakes the salvation of mankind; proposes a mighty scheme, determined "from the foundation of the world;" gives intimation beforehand, by the mouth of "holy men of God, who spake as they were moved by the Holy Ghost:" sends rays of prophetic light as messengers to prepare the way before him, and warn men to be on the watch for the "brightness of his rising." Till at last "the Sun of righteousness" is fully displayed, "with healing on his wings;" and a voice goes forth from one end of the earth to the other, "Awake, thou that sleepest, and arise from the dead, and Christ shall give thee light."

[2] Acts xvii. 30.

And well may we expect that this voice should be heard. For observe the certain inference which we must draw from what the Evangelist reveals concerning the Christ, the Son of God. We learn from it the miserable and ruined state of man: so ruined and miserable, that the same power must redeem life, which had given life: the same divine person must create anew, who had at first created. He "without whom nothing was made that was made," now "comes to seek and to save that which was lost." Low, surely, was the condition, which must needs be thus relieved and raised. Utter, surely, must be the ruin which could only be thus recovered.. If he who comes to save, is he who *was in the beginning with God, and was God,* no other argument is needed to prove the depth of ruin and of misery. We see it in the majesty of the Deliverer. In the greatness of the Saviour we read the greatness of man's necessity. In the vastness of the sacrifice, we learn to calculate the weight of our debt, the burthen of man's sin. And we learn to measure from it, too, the extent of our obligation. Which will be greatest, the heinousness of guilt, or the extremity of loss, to those who put this mercy from them, "count themselves unworthy of eternal life," and "neglect so great salvation?"

IV.

THE RUIN AND RESTORATION OF MANKIND.

Rom. v. 18, 19.

18. *As by the offence of one judgment came upon all men to condemnation; even so by the righteousness of one the free gift came upon all men unto justification of life.*
19. *For as by one man's disobedience many were made sinners, so by the obedience of one shall many be made righteous.*

The fact here revealed to us, the entrance of sin into the world, God alone could reveal. He does not explain it to us: why it came to be so, we are not told: he merely declares the fact, that he "made man upright,"[1] and man became corrupt through disobedience: that he surveyed his works, and "lo, they were very good,"[2] and man amongst them: till sin entered into the world, and death by sin. He had issued a command, and required obedience from the creatures he had made; "saying, Of every tree of the garden thou mayest freely eat: but of the tree of knowledge of good and evil, thou shalt not eat of it; for in the day thou eatest thereof, thou shalt surely die."[3] When this command was disobeyed, *by the offence of one*, or by one offence, judgment *came upon all men to con-*

[1] Eccles. vii. 29. [2] Gen. i. 31. [3] Gen. ii. 16, 17.

demnation. This can neither be concealed nor denied: and it shows us, what men are so prone to disbelieve, the certainty of God's judgments. He issued his command to the man whom he had created, and said: In the day when thou transgressest the command, "thou shalt surely die." Adam disbelieved, and did transgress. Immediately was the sentence executed. Sin entered into the world, and with sin death: death, and all that leads to death;—so that every eye we close and every grave we stand by, nay, every pang we witness and every tear we shed, are proofs to assure us of the fact, that "the transgression of the law is sin," and that he who has given the law, will avenge the law; for "the wages of sin is death."

Here, then, is our condition: a miserable condition of physical infirmity, and spiritual ruin. "In Adam all died."

Yet in his judgment God remembers mercy. The goodness of God had been Paul's special theme in the preceding verses of this chapter. The admission of sin and death into the world, might seem to contradict this. Therefore, whilst he asserts the offence, and the consequent condemnation, he asserts also the mercy of God, and the gift by grace which is in Jesus Christ. We acknowledge that the sin of the father, Adam, has fallen in its effects upon his whole posterity. Still, observe God's goodness. If those sin, and suffer for sin, who sin through a corrupt nature, which nature they received corrupt: so likewise is righteousness imputed, through the mercy of the Gospel, to those who have not been previously righteous: nay, have been offenders. And in this respect, Adam, who transgressed, is the figure of him who was to come. For as by him all suffered loss, by the other all received a gain. *As by one man's disobedience many were made sinners, so by the obedience of one shall many be made righteous.* As the injury was by one man, Adam; so likewise the remedy is by one man, Jesus Christ. Therefore it was, that the birth of Christ was announced as tidings of great joy to all people; inasmuch as was born into the world "a Saviour, which is Christ the Lord." The Son of God had come, "to seek and to save that which was lost." In the dispensation of the Gospel, God has followed the same rule in mercy as in judgment. By Adam's disobedience evil came upon the whole world of sinful men. By the obedience of Christ a blessing is proposed to all. "God was in Christ, reconciling the world unto himself," and exempting from condemnation all that "repent and believe the Gospel." The effects of Adam's disobedience will not be fatal to them, unless they themselves continue disobedient. To as many as are conscious of these effects, and sorrowing for them: to as many as feel themselves to be labouring and heavy laden, labouring under the yoke of a corrupt nature, and heavy laden with the burthen of sin: to all such is the mercy offered, the invitation of Christ proposed; "Come unto me, and ye shall find rest unto your souls."

Comfort therefore may be derived, even from the contemplation of the ruin in which by nature we are involved. "If the Scripture has concluded all under sin," in that "all have sinned, and come short of the glory of God;" Scripture also assures us, that this our natural state was so pitied, that God actively interposed for our deliverance: "so loved the world," whilst in rebellion against him, as to send his only Son for our restoration. He has followed the same rule in mercy as in judgment. By Adam's disobedience evil came upon the whole world of sinful men. By the obedience of Christ a blessing is proposed to all. Every one, therefore, may reason with himself: *By one man's disobedience the judgment of God came upon all men.* We feel it in ourselves: in "the sin which is in our members:" in the sentence of death under which we live. But is there no hope? no way of escape? no "city of refuge," to which we may flee and be secure? The same Scripture, which tells us that by *the offence of one judgment came upon all men to condemnation,* tells us also, that *by the righteousness of one the free gift came upon all men unto justification of life.* So that if "sin hath reigned unto death, even so may grace reign through righteousness unto eternal life by Jesus Christ our Lord." In this way there is escape. By trusting to the righteousness of Christ, we may be accounted righteous in God's sight: nay, be admitted into his family, and by adoption reckoned among his children.

This, then, is the rock on which we should lay hold, and so cling to it as never to be shaken off. There is a deluge by which the world is overwhelmed, a deluge of sin and death: and its effects extend to all. Our business is, not to inquire how the waters should so prevail over the earth; but to seize upon the way of safety: to take refuge in the ark, which he himself has provided who rules the deluge. In thus offering the means of preservation, God has shown that he has a design of mercy. That is done for mankind to which the Psalmist trusts, and in which he rejoices: "God shall send from on high to fetch me, and take me out of many waters."[4] Our wisdom is, to profit by that mercy. We may be thankful that there is room for mercy, when there is so much room for judgment: that our offences, which are many, may still be blotted out: that if there is a "sentence of condemnation," there is also a "gift of righteousness:" and that if there is here a world of sin and death, there is also a world revealed to us where sin and death shall be no more, and where they who have accepted God's abounding grace shall reign in a life of holiness and happiness for ever.

V.

THE LAMB OF GOD.

JOHN i. 29.

John seeth Jesus coming unto him, and saith, Behold the Lamb of God, which taketh away the sin of the world.

THE character in which Jesus came, and the purpose of his Incarnation, had been revealed to the Baptist, though hitherto he had not seen his person. When, therefore, John saw him coming towards him, he points him out to his disciples in terms which at once explain

[4] Ps. xviii. 16.

a whole volume of type and prophecy. *Behold the Lamb of God, which taketh away the sin of the world.*

The purport is now disclosed of the fact which had been before declared, that "the Word was made flesh." It is disclosed in the description here given of Jesus, as *the Lamb of God.* He came to be the propitiation for sin. He came to furnish that which he alone could furnish, an atonement to the holiness of God for the guilt incurred by man.

Adam had transgressed the law which he was bound to obey, and involved the whole race of his posterity in corruption. And how could man be pardoned, and the holiness of God's government be maintained? "As by one man's disobedience many were made sinners," who could be the one, by whose "obedience many might be made righteous?" None of the sons of men could offer an atonement. They needed atonement; for they were themselves corrupt: they had nothing to pay: "No man can redeem his brother, or make agreement unto God for him." But the Son of God, the eternal, uncreated Word, consented to stand in the stead of that guilty race. "In the volume of the book it is written of him, Lo I come to do thy will, O God."[1] Being "without spot of sin," his innocence might be received as a free offering; and, taking man's nature upon him, he could suffer man's penalty.

This was determined from the beginning. And being so determined, it was foreshown in various ways. From the earliest times, the patriarchs are represented as offering sacrifice to God. As mankind were dispersed,

[1] Ps. xi. 7; Heb. x. 4, &c.

they carried the custom with them, though its purpose was lost and forgotten. But the whole is contained in the law given by Moses to the Israelites. It could not be mistaken, when the priest laid his hands upon the head of the creature intended for an offering, and made confession of sin over the head of the sacrifice;[2] thus prefiguring what was afterwards to be more fully explained, how the Lord had laid on one the iniquity of all.[3]

By the ordinances of the law, various animals were used in sacrifice; but none so constantly as the lamb. One was offered up in the temple every morning, and another every evening: and on the sabbath, two.[4] But it was the rite of the Passover which most evidently and remarkably typified that full and perfect sacrifice and satisfaction for the sins of all men, which was consummated upon the cross. The lamb slain as the passover was to be without blemish.[5] So was Jesus without spot of sin, neither was guile found in his mouth.[6] The lamb was to be "of the first year;" so Christ was cut off in the prime of his days, and slain by such a death, that, as was ordered in the killing of the passover, "not a bone of him was broken." The lamb was to be slain by the "whole assembly of the congregation of Israel." So it was on the principal festival of the year that "counsel was taken against Jesus to put him to death:" and the whole people made it their own act, by exclaiming, "Crucify him! crucify him!" "His blood be on us and on our children!"

[2] Lev. xvi. 21. [3] Isa. liii. [4] Num. xxviii. 3—10.
[5] Exod. xii. 3, &c. [6] See 1 Pet. i. 19.

And as in the manner of the sacrifice all was similar, so was the effect the same. The blood of the lamb sprinkled on the door-posts of the houses preserved the people of Israel from the messenger of destruction. And so the blood of Christ, sprinkled, as it were, upon the heart, is designed to exempt the sinner from the stroke of divine justice, and save him from "the bitter pains of eternal death." Thus was atonement made to the justice of God: who, in mercy to man's ruined and helpless state, has covenanted to receive the blood of one instead of the blood of many, and to be reconciled to the penitent offender for the sake of his dear Son.

Here, then, is the sense in which we behold Jesus as *the Lamb of God which taketh away the sin of the world*: taketh away the sin which is laid upon him by the faith of the penitent offender. The words of the Baptist show that he possessed the key of that mysterious worship which God had established in Judæa, and that he was empowered to disclose its meaning, hitherto concealed. He points to Jesus, and exclaims, *Behold the Lamb of God.* And behold, in him, the person so long prefigured by the sacrifices of the law. Behold the one righteous, designed in the counsels of God as a substitute for many sinners. Behold the true Paschal Lamb, who is offered for us, to take away the sin of the world: who by his death shall destroy death, and by his rising to life again shall restore to us everlasting life. "For as in Adam all die, even so in Christ shall all be made alive."

Thus it was, that Christ, by the sacrifice of the cross, fulfilled the law: explained the meaning of those sacrifices which the Jews had offered year by year continually; and removed the need of any further, any future sacrifice. The title of Jesus, as the Lamb of God, was addressed to the conscience of the Jews. The Jews acknowledged—it was part of their religion to acknowledge—that the blood of bulls and goats, i. e. of the sacrifices offered by the law, were means of expiation and purification. That which before was reckoned impure and unholy, became clean, was freed from its defilement, when sprinkled with the blood or ashes of the sacrifice. Yet what could these effect, considered in themselves? It was not possible that the blood of bulls or goats could take away sin. What then could these ordinances mean, except as prophetic types of something to come hereafter?—types of blood to be hereafter shed, and sprinkled, not externally on the body, but inwardly on the conscience? This indeed may well purge the heart from sin, by the testimony which it affords to the guilt of sin. Christ's blood, the blood of "that Just one," was shed "for the unjust."[7] And as the person under the law, when conscious of defilement, came for purification to the blood of sprinkling: so the man who is sensible of the stain of sin which defiles him, takes by faith the blood of the cross, and prays that it may atone for his guilt, as if his own blood had been shed.

No doubt, there are mysteries attending the whole of this dispensation, which we shall vainly attempt to solve. But we perceive its wisdom by its effects; and see how "the blood of Christ, who through the eternal Spirit offered himself without spot to God, may purge the conscience from dead works, to serve the living God."[8]

[7] 1 Pet. iii. 18. [8] Heb. ix. 14.

Pardon so obtained warns whilst it absolves. Sin is a heinous thing, if without shedding of blood there is no remission of sin. Sin is shown to be the ruin of the soul, if only the blood of the Son of God could save the soul from the condemnation of sin. So that the conscience, purged from the guilt of past dead works, is also delivered from the love or practice of sin: cleansed from all unrighteousness, to serve the living God, as the proper business of his creatures. The believer knows and feels that Christ died for him; that without Christ he himself was dead;[9] and that, being raised from the death of sin by the propitiation made, the victim substituted for him, he is no longer his own, but under obligation to devote his life to the service of the Redeemer. These are the cords by which the Gospel binds its disciple to obedience. It is not like a mere ordinance, which must be performed, but conveys no moral to the heart: but constantly affirms the truth, that "God commendeth his love towards us, in that whilst we were yet sinners, Christ died for us:"[1] and that such love must be repaid by all the obedience which he requires, and all the service which it is in our power to pay.

[9] See St. Paul's argument, 2 Cor. v. 14, 15.

[1] Rom. v. 8.

VI.

PURPOSE OF GOD IN THE GOSPEL.

JOHN iii. 16—19.

16. *God so loved the world, that he gave his only begotten Son, that whosoever believeth in him should not perish, but have everlasting life.*
17. *For God sent not his Son into the world to condemn the world; but that the world through him might be saved.*
18. *He that believeth on him is not condemned: but he that believeth not is condemned already, because he hath not believed in the name of the only begotten Son of God.*
19. *And this is the condemnation, that light is come into the world, and men loved darkness rather than light, because their deeds were evil.*

NICODEMUS, a man of authority in Jerusalem, had sought Jesus, under an acknowledgment that he was "a teacher sent from God." Jesus takes the opportunity of declaring the purpose on the part of God, for which he had been so "sent." It was a purpose of mercy. He had been sent to an idolatrous world—a world which had become idolatrous, because men had not "liked to retain God in their knowledge." He came to a nation which had misused the privileges it enjoyed, had rejected the counsels of God, and despised his reproofs: and yet he came *not to condemn the world, but that the world through him might be saved.* He brought an offer of reconciliation; and his first message was

Peace to this rebellious people:—"to the Jew first, and also to the Gentile." "Herein was love; not that we loved God, but that he loved us, and sent his Son to be the propitiation for our sins." *He that believeth on him is not condemned: but he that believeth not is condemned already, because he hath not believed in the name of the only begotten Son of God.*

If subjects are in a state of rebellion against their sovereign, and he sends an embassy, offering to receive them again to favour on their laying down their arms, those who refuse his offer, and reject his messenger, are *condemned already.* They are condemned by their act of rebellion; and "his wrath abides upon them:" their state of condemnation continues, because they have not accepted the terms of reconciliation. Such is the case of those who, like the Jews, reject the counsel of God against themselves.

These, then, were the terms in which the message of God was to be carried through the world. It offered salvation to as many as believed in Christ as the Saviour. It was to be addressed to mankind as in a lost or ruined state; it was to offer them deliverance from that state, for the sake of what Christ had done, on the condition of their becoming his disciples. The promise was, that as many as received the offer, and were baptized in the name of Jesus, should be placed in a new state towards God. Being justified by the atonement made for sin upon the cross, which they had embraced in faith, in reliance upon its all-sufficiency, they should have peace with God; and walking not after the flesh but after the Spirit, should be saved.[1]

[1] Rom. v. 1; viii. 1.

At first sight it may appear, as it has appeared to some, an unwarrantable condition, that this blessedness is made to depend upon the man's faith in the offer proposed to him: on his believing that Christ is willing and able to save him from the consequences of sin. Could it, however, be otherwise?

The Gospel is proposed to us as a remedy, which can only be received by being trusted. Jesus Christ is set before us as the physician, who has in himself, and who alone has, the remedy against sin, and against death, "the wages of sin." So that whosoever believes in him, resigns and devotes himself to him, has life, because he has the remedy against death; whilst one who "has not the Son of God, has not life,"[2] remains under condemnation, because he has not believed in the name of him who offers to reverse his sentence of condemnation, and to set him free.

It may illustrate this, if we suppose a land to be ravaged by a pestilence, threatening to overwhelm both young and old with general destruction. This is no far-fetched example; for sin is such a pestilence, and affects by its virulence the whole race of mankind.

Suppose, further, a physician to traverse this infected country, and promise an antidote which should preserve from danger as many as applied to him. Such is the offer of Christ. "He that heareth my word, and believeth on him that sent me, hath everlasting life, and shall not come into condemnation; but is passed from death unto life."[3]

Soon, probably, in that country there would be found three classes of persons. There would be some who neg-

[2] 1 John v. 12. [3] John v. 24.

lected all precaution, distrusted the physician altogether, and were satisfied to take their chance with others. There would be some who did not doubt the physician's skill, or the efficacy of his remedy: but finding that it required much care and self-denial, a change in their manner of living, and habits different from those around them, they would silently reject it, and prefer the unseen evil to the immediate trouble of the cure. Whilst a third class would be found so convinced of the impending danger, and so confident of the physician's skill, as to apply for his advice and obey his counsels, relying on his word and promise, at whatever pains, whatever sacrifice of present inclination.

And this third class, believing the physician, and acting on their belief, would be saved: whilst they who disbelieved, and they who acted as if they disbelieved, would be left to perish: would remain liable to the pestilence which sooner or later would lead to their destruction, because they refused the only remedy which could avert it and preserve them. No doubt their condition would be the more lamentable, because the remedy had come nigh them, and they rejected it. But neither the offer of the remedy, nor their refusal, would place them in their desperate state: it was their state before, as inhabitants of the country which the pestilence had entered, and where it raged. Like the sons-in-law of Lot, whom he warned to flee with him from Sodom: and "he seemed to them as one that mocked:"[4] they refused to listen to him. When the Lord rained fire and brimstone upon Sodom out of heaven, they were swallowed up in the

[4] Gen. xix. 14.

destruction. Yet they did not perish, as the penalty of rejecting his counsel; but rejecting his counsel, they perished together with their countrymen. And therefore our Lord, when he declares, that whoever believed on him should "not be condemned;" adds also, "He that believeth not, is condemned already, because he hath not believed in the name of the only begotten Son of God," who alone could avert his condemnation. "He that believeth not the Son, shall not see life; but the wrath of God abideth on him:"[5] he has not escaped it through the appointed way of reconciliation.

Without cavilling at the terms, we may well rejoice in the assurance, "He that hath the Son, hath life." There is a physician, who is come to seek and to save those that, without him, were abandoned to a devouring pestilence. There is an ark of safety, which we are invited to enter, and be secure; there is an all-powerful Guardian, who allays our natural fears, and meets our spiritual necessities, and sends far and wide his merciful invitation, "Come unto me, all ye that labour and are heavy laden, and ye shall find rest unto your souls."

[5] John iii. 18, 36.

VII.

BAPTISM OF JESUS.

MATT. iii. 13—17.

13. *Then cometh Jesus from Galilee to Jordan unto John, to be baptized of him.*
14. *But John forbad him, saying, I have need to be baptized of thee, and comest thou to me?*

It was part of the mysterious plan now about to be developed for man's redemption, that Christ should remain unnoticed in the province of Galilee till this time, when he was "about thirty years of age."[1] So it had been written, "He shall grow up as a tender plant, and as a root out of a dry ground."[2]

The Baptist was aware who he was who now approached him; *and he forbad him* with these striking words,—*I have need to be baptized of thee, and comest thou to me?* As much as to say, I am performing an office which assumes superiority in character and authority;—God has made me "great in his sight;"—has given me such authority over my sinful brethren. But comest *thou* to me, who art not one of these, and hast no sins to confess and repent of? Again: Comest thou to *me*, who *have need to be baptized of thee?* I have need to be baptized of thee, for thou art the "Lamb of

[1] Luke iii. 23. [2] Is. liii. 2.

God, which takest away the sins of the world;" and I am one of that world of sinners.

15. *And Jesus answering said unto him, Suffer it to be so now; for thus it becometh us to fulfil all righteousness. Then he suffered him.* [3]
16. *And Jesus, when he was baptized, went up straightway out of the water: and lo, the heavens were opened unto him, and he saw the Spirit of God descending like a dove, and lighting upon him.*
17. *And lo, a voice from heaven, saying, This is my beloved Son, in whom I am well pleased.*

That may be said here, which was said on another occasion, *This voice from heaven* came not for Christ's sake, but for our sakes. It was a testimony, first, of the blessing which may confidently be looked for and expected in the ordinance to which Jesus had submitted. The heavens were opened. As if to convey a promise and encouragement to as many as "receive him, and believe in his name." Their baptism is the entrance upon a new life on earth, which leads to eternal life above: opens to the redeemed and sanctified soul that inheritance in the heavens, which otherwise were closed against it for ever. [4]

So likewise the visible descent of the Spirit upon Jesus at this time, is surely a significant intimation that a like blessing is bestowed on those who are baptized in his name; and who, renouncing "the corruption that is in the world," devote themselves to God, as faithful

[3] The pronoun here is the plural, ἡμᾶς; in which form, it is observed, Jesus never speaks *of himself*.

[4] See Chrysostom *in loco*.

soldiers and servants of him who hath called them to this state of salvation.

But, further, the voice from heaven was the solemn testimony of God to the person and character of Christ. It directed those who heard it to the Saviour whom he had sent, and to the salvation which he had prepared for them. It was an assurance, first, that God was well pleased with the work which his beloved Son had undertaken, when he accomplished the prophecy, "Lo, I come, to fulfil thy will, O God." Lo, I come to offer that atonement which has been planned "before the foundation of the world;" that perfect and sufficient sacrifice for the sins of all men, that they may be brought back to the Father whom they have abandoned. With this sacrifice God was *well pleased.* It was agreeable to his HOLINESS that sin should be thus shown to be "exceeding sinful;"[5] that its dreadful consequences should be manifested to the world; as was most evidently shown, when the beloved Son, the only begotten of the Father, was lifted up upon the cross, that he might bear our transgressions and be bruised for our iniquities.

And, further, it was agreeable to the MERCY of God, that man, whom sin had ruined, should be delivered from destruction. He saw Jesus entering upon a course which all his disciples were to follow: he saw him submit to baptism, in token of that deliverance from the power of Satan, and that dedication to the service of God, which should hereafter "bring many sons to glory." He saw this, and was *well pleased:* for in this commencement of the ministry of reconciliation he foresaw the multitude of all ages and countries, who, being turned

[5] Rom. vii. 13.

from darkness to light on earth, should dwell "among the saints in light" eternally.

But there was another reason why God declared himself *well pleased with his beloved Son.* He was not only that "Lamb of God which taketh away the sin of the world:" but he was also, like the lamb by which he was prefigured, without blemish and without spot:"[6] he was "holy, harmless, undefiled;" "without sin," "neither was guile found in him:" a pattern of all righteousness. He took our nature upon him, first and chiefly, that he might "bear our sins in his own body;" in a body of that nature which had sinned. But he also set before us, in the same nature, an example of all that God approves, in manner of life, in love, in patience, in meekness, in long-suffering, in purity, in charity, in humility. And this character is pleasing to God: and the followers of this perfect pattern are pleasing to him also, when they faithfully imitate, and earnestly aspire after it. According to the frequent exhortation of the apostles, "Let the same mind be in you, which was in Christ Jesus:" who left us an example that we should follow his steps, and strive after holiness, "even as he who hath called us is holy."

Therefore the testimony here borne to Jesus concerns ourselves, and warns us to inquire how far we consent to it: how far our thoughts accord with *the voice from heaven:* how far our own minds are brought into conformity with the divine will. "The natural man receiveth not the things of the Spirit of God; for they are foolishness unto him."[7] But we, we Christians, are not of nature, but of grace: we are not to retain

[6] Ex. xii. 5; 1 Pet. i. 19. [7] 1 Cor. ii. 14.

the sentiments of the natural man; and we should ask ourselves, how far our mind agrees with the mind of God, who is *well pleased with his beloved Son.* "What think we of Christ?" Do we feel that his gospel,—the atonement it reveals, the covenant it offers, the promises of grace which it conveys,—afford us exactly that comfort which our hearts are in need of, and our condition requires?

This it will do, in proportion as we understand the holiness of God, the weakness of our own hearts, and the solemnity of the judgment which is to come. We find ourselves stained with the guilt of sin; but "the blood of Christ cleanseth from all sin." We are not sufficient of ourselves to do any thing as of ourselves; but he has engaged to "work in us both to will and to do." We are justly condemned as transgressors against the divine law; but "there is no condemnation to them that are in Christ Jesus." We are "born in sin, and children of wrath;" but he is revealed to us under the title of SAVIOUR. And we receive him as such. We receive him as "the author and finisher of our faith:" we welcome him, as "made unto us of God, wisdom, and righteousness, and sanctification and redemption." And, further, we look at him as the model by which, through the Spirit working in us, we are to form ourselves; as the example by which we are to judge and examine ourselves: "understanding what the will of God is, even our sanctification;" "proving what is acceptable unto the Lord, in all goodness, and righteousness, and truth;" and desiring to be "made perfect in every good work, to do that which is well pleasing in his sight, through Jesus Christ." He who declared himself well pleased with his beloved Son, has also declared himself well pleased with those who thus receive him: receive him as their Priest to atone, and their King to rule. For he says of them, "I will receive you, and be a Father unto you; and ye shall be my sons and daughters, saith the Lord Almighty."[8]

VIII.

MIRACLES.

JOHN xi. 11.

This beginning of miracles did Jesus in Cana of Galilee, and manifested forth his glory; and his disciples believed on him.

THESE words explain both the purpose and the effect of the miracles which Jesus performed. In this commencement of his "signs and wonders," he *manifested forth his glory,* when at his bidding the water became wine: and *his disciples,* who witnessed the miracle, *believed on him.* It was wrought with that intention. Proofs were needful of the authority in which he came. The people asked, as they had a right to ask, "What sign showest thou, that thou doest these things?" What sign dost thou give us, that thou hast a claim to

[8] 2 Cor. vi. 18.

our faith and obedience? And the natural answer was that which he himself alleged: "If I had not done among them the things which none other man did, they had not had sin;" they would not be condemned for disbelieving me.

It is only by some change in the usual course of nature, either by the communication of super-human knowledge, or by an interruption of the settled order of the universe, that a revelation can be proved to be of heaven, and not of men. For this purpose alone God has seen fit to interpose, and occasionally to permit a change in that arrangement of things which he established at the Creation. He did so in the case of Moses. Moses very naturally expected that neither the Israelites nor the Egyptians would attend to his summons. "He answered and said, But, behold, they will not believe me, nor hearken unto my voice: for they will say, The Lord hath not appeared unto thee."[1] And the Lord promised power, by which his mission might be plainly understood, when he assured him, "Certainly I will be with thee." The same power was with Joshua till the will of God accomplished the settlement of the Israelites in Canaan: the like power supported Elijah, when he recalled the people from their idolatry. And now the divinity of Jesus was manifested in the like manner. What we call the laws of nature, i. e. the principles on which God framed the world, were suspended at his command: water became wine: the sea was calmed: the provision of bread was augmented: the fig-tree withered away: fever, even death, was arrested in its course.

[1] Ex. iv. 1.

Thus the Creator did again what he had before done at the Creation. He visibly exercised that power to change the regular system of things, which he is constantly exercising to keep the system regular. It is not more surprising that a certain union of substances should produce wine, than that they should produce water: that the juice by which a tree is nourished should suddenly fail, than that sap should ever flow within its pores. It is not more surprising that the substance of a few loaves and fishes should be enlarged, till many thousands were satisfied with food, than that any substance should ever be produced where none existed before. It is not more surprising that the eye should be enabled to see, or the ear to hear, than that any ear should be formed for hearing, or any eye for seeing. It is not more astonishing that the blood should be restored to its natural circulation, or that the lungs should breathe again, than that blood should be "the life of man" at all, or that "the breath of life" should ever have been imparted.

If, then, it at first seems strange, that Jesus should perform these wonders and mighty deeds, we should look back to the beginning, when God created the heaven and the earth. What could be more strange than that God should say, "Let there be light,—and there was light." "Let us make man in our image,—and man became a living soul." But we are assured that God created all things by his Son: that by him the worlds were made; and that nothing was made without him who was now exercising his power: exercising his power to change or to suspend what he had at first ordained and established. The object was no light one; it was one which could not otherwise be fulfilled: it was to show that he who had now been born into the world was indeed "a Saviour, which is Christ the Lord." And St. John here, unintentionally as it were, alludes to the effect produced upon his own mind, and the minds of his brethren. *This beginning of miracles did Jesus in Cana of Galilee; and his disciples believed on him.*

Of the same nature was the testimony given by St. Peter, when he refers to the glorious spectacle which he and two of his brethren were permitted to see, when Jesus was transfigured before them.[2] "We have not followed cunningly devised fables, when we made known unto you the power and coming of our Lord Jesus Christ, but were eyewitnesses of his majesty. For he received from God the Father honour and glory, when there came such a voice to him from the excellent glory, This is my beloved Son, in whom I am well pleased. And this voice which came from heaven we heard, when we were with him in the holy mount."

Peter was well aware that there would "come in the last days scoffers," who would ascribe the history of the Lord Jesus to man's invention: treat it as a cunningly devised fable. To this he opposes the testimony of his own senses. Some say that Jesus was but a man: had no claim to be described as "the brightness of the Father's glory, and the express image of his person." But we were eyewitnesses to his majesty. "He was transfigured before us: and his face did shine as the sun, and his raiment was white as the light."[3] Some say,

[2] 2 Pet. i. 16—18. [3] Matt. xvii. 2.

again, that he took upon himself an authority to which he had no claim. We heard the voice which came from heaven, confirming his authority: *This is my beloved Son, in whom I am well pleased.*[4] Ye therefore, and those who come after you, may know the certainty of the things which ye have believed.

The Gospel rests on facts. And if a fact is properly authenticated at first, it is as certain at the end of a long chain of witnesses as at the beginning. Nothing ought to weaken belief, except a break in the chain. We may compare it to electric power conveyed along a wire. The wire may be of indefinite length: the extremity far out of our sight: but if the shock is felt, we are sure that at the extremity there is a battery which causes it. So we may be certain of the facts of all well-authenticated history: and no history is so well authenticated as the history recorded in the Scriptures. What Peter saw and heard, he related to others who did not see or hear: those others repeated the same to their own generation; and every successive generation since has handed down the truth, so that it is as sure to us as it was to the scattered disciples to whom Peter wrote. The chain of testimony is unbroken: no link is wanting: and we may be as convinced as they were that we have not followed cunningly devised fables when we have believed in the power and coming of our Lord Jesus Christ. To encourage his apostles, and enable them to encourage others, the Lord assumed the glory of that majesty, and received that testimony from God which Peter saw and heard *in the holy mount.* And after more than thirty years, Peter made use of

[4] Matt. xvii. 5.

the testimony for the purpose which it was given to serve. He recorded the impression fixed upon his own mind, that he might fix it on the minds of others. It was the testimony of one who knew that he must shortly put off his earthly tabernacle;[5] and we are accustomed to give especial credit to such testimony. But it is more; it is the declaration of a man who was not merely soon to die, but to die in attestation of the faith which he was affirming. And this witness declares, that he beheld the glory of the Lord Jesus, the glory as of "the only begotten of the Father, full of grace and truth."

On such testimony we believe in him. We who could not witness the miracles, believe through the word of these disciples. And our prayer should be, that our lives and our belief may agree; so that we too may hereafter behold his glory, "that glory which he had with the Father before the world was;" not, like the apostles on the holy mount, for a short and transient glimpse, but for ever and ever. His promise is no less; and to as many as receive it, and believe in his name, his promise will be fulfilled.

[5] 2 Pet. i. 14.

IX.

THE UNBELIEF OF THE JEWS.

JOHN i. 11.

He came unto his own, and his own received him not.

OF the Hebrew nation God had said, "This people have I formed for myself, that they might show forth my praise." And the Father and the Son are one. So that, when Jesus was born in Bethlehem, the city of David, and when he ministered throughout the towns and villages of Judæa, it is truly said, that he *came unto his own*, to his chosen nation, his peculiar people. *But his own received him not.* The Jewish nation in general, as we know, did not receive him as their Messiah: and even the people who had listened willingly to his discourses, or had been relieved by the merciful exercise of his power, suffered him to be led to execution, while not a single voice was raised in his favour. "The Son of man goeth as was determined of him!"

If we inquire on what ground they received him not, was it that he did not answer the predictions which had gone forth respecting him? We know that his lineage, his birth, his life, and his death, did fulfil the prophecies and correspond with the types concerning him, in the most minute and remarkable particulars. Was it that he did not show such signs and wonders and mighty deeds, as were reasonably to be expected from the Messiah! It was acknowledged,—"This man doeth many miracles;"—"No man can do the miracles which thou doest, except God be with him;"—"He saved others," though himself he did not save. Was it that his discourses and his doctrines were not in agreement with the character which he claimed? It was acknowledged, that "never man spake like this man:"—that "all men were astonished at the gracious words which proceeded out of his mouth:"—that "he taught as one having authority, and not as the scribes." And yet *they received him not.*

The reason was not in him, but in themselves. He came in a particular character. He came as a Saviour. He was announced as such by the angels. "Unto you is born this day a Saviour, which is Christ the Lord." For this he was promised, predicted, sent; for this he took our nature, ministered, and died; that he might redeem a lost world, and deliver a race which sin had ruined. Now, to receive one who comes in this character, and purports to be such a Saviour, requires a certain state of mind in those who so receive him. To receive one who offers deliverance, implies a sense of danger, a sense of destitution and helplessness. To receive redemption through Christ Jesus, was to acknowledge a state of bondage and condemnation. To receive eternal life as the gift of God for his sake, was to cast themselves on his mercy, to abandon all personal claim, to renounce all merit in themselves.

The Jewish people perceived this: against this their pride and their self-complacency revolted; and for this cause they *received him not.* So St. Paul expressly shows, arguing with his countrymen in his epistle to the Romans. They lost, he says, the blessing offered them: they did not *become the sons of God,* because they persisted in trusting to themselves, and refused to rely on Jesus as a Saviour. "They being ignorant of God's righteousness, and going about to establish their own righteousness, have not submitted themselves to the righteousness of God."[1] The fifth chapter of this Gospel supplies an example, where we find our Lord reasoning with the Jews around him. "Search the Scriptures; for in them ye think ye have eternal life: and they are they which testify of me." Here he addresses them as expecting eternal life, and thinking that they had it in their Scriptures; but not rightly interpreting the Scriptures, and therefore not having salvation, because they refused to seek it through him who is the author of it. "Ye will not come unto ME, that ye might have life." Ye will not come to the fountain, or ye might be cleansed. Ye withdraw yourselves from the physician, or ye might be healed. Ye will not seek the appointed door, or ye might enter in. Thus they maintained their self-dependence. They would not receive salvation "of grace." They *did not receive him,* because of their proud, unhumbled, self-confident, self-justifying heart. They would not humble themselves, that they might be exalted; but they would exalt themselves, and therefore they remained abased before God.

But more than this:—Jesus came as a Saviour, not only from the guilt, but from the power of sin. It was

[1] Rom. x. 3.

ordained concerning him, "Thou shalt call his name Jesus; for he shall save his people from their sins." While he invited them to receive eternal life, he also required them to repent; for "the wages of sin is death;"—to "bring forth fruits meet for repentance."

And here again they stumbled. A deliverer from a foreign yoke, a deliverer from Herod and the Romans, they would gladly have followed. But a deliverer from sin had no attraction for them. That yoke they had not felt heavy. They did not grudge the tribute which they paid to Satan.

We meet with an example in the eighth chapter of this Gospel. There our Lord, discoursing in the presence of a large company, said to some who believed on him, "If ye continue in my word, then are ye my disciples indeed; and ye shall know the truth, and the truth shall make you free." This saying offended his hearers. They answer,—"We be Abraham's seed, and were never in bondage to any man: how sayest thou, Ye shall be made free?" They would not understand,—it did not suit them to understand,—that "whosoever committeth sin, is the servant of sin." They did not understand—nor care to understand—that he alone who could renew the heart in righteousness and true holiness, could make them "free indeed."

To receive him who required them to be, and who would make them, "poor in spirit," and "pure in heart," and lovers of righteousness, and merciful, and meek,—was to lay aside their pride, and their sensuality, and their love of this present world, and their covetousness. And therefore *they received him not*. And "this was their condemnation: that light was come into the world; but they loved darkness rather than light, because their deeds were evil." This was their condemnation, that when *He came unto his own, his own received him not.* They rejected him, because of their proud, unhumbled, unsubdued, self-confident, self-justifying, heart. They depended on themselves that they were righteous, and "had need of nothing;" and have left a perpetual warning, lest there be in any "an evil heart of unbelief, so as to receive the grace of God in vain."

X.

PRIVILEGES OF CHILDREN OF GOD.

JOHN i. 12, 13.

12. *But as many as received him, to them gave he power to become the sons of God, even to those that believe on his name.*
13. *Which were born, not of blood, nor of the will of the flesh, nor of the will of man, but of God.*

ST. JOHN had before stated, that when the Son of God appeared, he did not meet with acceptance. "He came unto his own, and his own received him not." It was necessary in the divine counsels, that the word of God should be first spoken to the Jews: but they "put it from them, and counted themselves unworthy of eternal life." Yet not all. There were those who said, "Thou art the Christ, the Son of the living God." These opened their eyes to the evidence which proved him to be the Messiah. These neither opposed his doctrines, nor revolted from the redemption which he offered them. They closed with the mercy of God: they *received* Jesus, and *believed in his name;* and together with him, they received the privilege which he alone can give, the "adoption of children," and *became the sons of God.*

Became the sons, the children, of God. Were they not so before?

In one sense, all mankind are the sons of God. So Adam is called by St. Luke,[1] when he is tracing the line from which Joseph was descended. But the whole of the Jewish people were children of God in a higher sense. God sent a message to Pharaoh:[2] "Thus saith the Lord, Israel is my son, even my first-born." Accordingly Moses addresses that people in Deuteronomy,[3] "Ye are the children of the Lord your God." Jesus recognizes them as such, distinguishing them from the Gentiles:[4] "It is not meet to take the children's bread, and to cast it to dogs." And St. Paul speaks of the privilege enjoyed by his brethren:[5] "who are Israelites; to whom pertaineth the adoption, and the glory, and the covenants, and the promises."

Yet still we find, that they required, and were capable of, a further and more special adoption. There is a higher privilege, which they could only possess as disciples of Christ Jesus: a privilege which those Jews forfeited, who, when he came, received him not; and to

[1] Luke iii. 38. [2] Ex. iv. 22. [3] Deut. xiv. 1.
[4] Matt. xv. 26. [5] Rom. ix. 4.

which those were raised, who did receive him, and believed in his name. *To as many as received him,*—to those who acknowledged the character in which he came, and accepted the redemption which he offered,—to those he assigned the blessings which in no other way they could enjoy. *To as many as received him, to them gave he power to become the sons of God.* God's children. "Ye shall be my sons and daughters, saith the Lord Almighty." And justly are they so entitled. It is not a vain and empty term. For, by the adoption given them, they have the provision, and the education, and the inheritance of children.

They have the provision of children. As the Father of all, God has provided for the whole race of man. He sends them rain and fruitful seasons; he causes his sun to shine, and his rain to fall, "on the just and on the unjust." But a very different provision is made for those who belong to the covenant which is in Christ Jesus. They have the assurance that their God shall supply all their wants; that all needful things shall be added to them; for their heavenly Father knoweth that they have need of all these things. "For even the hairs of their head are all numbered."[6] The circumstances of their lives are so ordered, that all things work together for their good. If they are poor, it shall preserve them from temptation, and keep them humble; if they are rich, it is that they may be "rich in good works." If they are in adversity, it is that they may enjoy a peace which this world cannot give. If they are in prosperity, it is that they may take comfort from the sunshine of God's favour. Rich or poor, afflicted or prosperous, in

[6] See Matt. x. 30; Phil. iv. 19.

health or in sickness, in life or in death, "they are the Lord's."

Together with the provision, they have also the education of children. If they are the sons of God, they are "led by the Spirit of God,"[7] and prepared by his grace for the glory which is to follow. He purifies them from the corruption of their natural descent, and renews them after his own image: he withdraws their hearts from things below, and raises them to things above: he uses exactly that discipline which their character most needs, whether gentle or severe: sometimes he chastens them, that they "may bring forth more fruit;" but still he "dealeth with them as sons;" "yea, spareth them as a man spareth his own son that serveth him."[8]

And in the end they have the inheritance of children. "If they are children, then are they heirs; heirs of God, and joint-heirs with Christ."[9] If they are children, they are the "blessed of the Father," whose "good pleasure it is to give them the kingdom," "the kingdom prepared for them from the foundation of the world."[1] We need not know, or desire to know, more of this inheritance, than that it is worthy of the purchase of the blood of Christ; worthy of the promise of God's everlasting covenant. It is an "inheritance incorruptible, and undefiled, and that fadeth not away."[2]

Such are the privileges of those who are made the sons of God by faith which is in Christ Jesus. But who shall declare their generation? They *are born, not*

[7] See Rom. viii. 14. [8] See John xv. 2; Heb. xii. 7; Mal. iii. 17.
[9] Rom. viii. 17. [1] Matt. xxv. 34; Luke xii. 32. [2] 1 Pet. i. 4.

of blood, nor of the will of the flesh, nor of the will of man, but of God. It is not with their spiritual as with their natural birth: that comes of the will of the flesh, and of the will of man; but the spiritual being cannot be so handed down: God keeps it in his own power. The corruption of Adam descended in natural course to his posterity; but not so the grace of Adam, or of any since born his children: no man can produce it in another by his own means, or secure it for another by his will and desire. It is the gift of God. And though we are sure that it is bestowed according to just and equal laws, we are often foiled and baffled, if we attempt to trace their operation.

Therefore, when Peter, in the name of the Apostles, made his famous confession, "Thou art the Christ, the Son of the living God," the Lord replied: "Blessed art thou, Simon Bar-jona: for flesh and blood hath not revealed it unto thee, but my Father which is in heaven."[3] No special revelation had been made to Peter, or the other apostles, in whose name he spoke: the truth had not been declared to them in any other way than it had been manifested to the rest of the people who had witnessed the miracles of Christ, and heard his word. But these had received the truth with readiness of heart and will, whilst the chief rulers had disputed it, and cavilled at it, and blinded their own eyes and the eyes of the people against the light which shone before them. And this humble and willing heart is the gift of God. "The natural man receiveth not the things of the Spirit of God: for they are foolishness unto him: neither can he know them, because they are spiritually discerned."[4]

[3] Matt. xvi. 17.
[4] 1 Cor. ii. 14.

But although this birth, of which God is the Author, is of a secret and spiritual nature in its origin, its existence is not secret, but evidenced by proofs which are manifest. The apostles could not doubt that a change had taken place in them, when, instead of following the example of those who abandoned the Lord's company, they exclaimed, "Lord, to whom should we go? Thou hast the words of eternal life."[5] Neither could any who knew them doubt the spirit they were of, when they "left all," and went through the world, "preaching the Gospel to every creature:" and avowing, in defiance of threatenings and ill usage, that they "could not but speak the things which they had seen and heard."[6] This was proof that they had *received* Jesus: received him as what he came to be, and what God had exalted him to be, "a Prince and a Saviour:"[7] a Prince to rule and govern, and a Saviour to "deliver from this present evil world," and to "give eternal life to all them that obey him."

In every age and country, the same signs will follow all them that believe; the same principle of obedience, the same consciousness of dependence, through which "the Spirit itself bears witness with their spirit," that they are "children of God"[8] "through faith that is in Christ Jesus."

[5] John vi. 68.
[6] Acts iv. 20.
[7] Acts v. 31.
[8] Rom. viii. 16.

XI.

REGENERATION.

JOHN iii. 1, 2, 5.

1. *There was a man of the Pharisees, named Nicodemus, a ruler of the Jews.*
2. *The same came to Jesus by night, and said unto him, Rabbi, we know that thou art a teacher come from God: for no man can do these miracles that thou doest, except God be with him.*
5. *Jesus answered, Verily, verily, I say unto thee, Except a man be born of water and of the Spirit, he cannot enter into the kingdom of God.*

WE may feel assured that these words, though they convey a general truth applicable to all mankind, were especially suited to the frame of mind in which Nicodemus came to Jesus. "He needed not that any should testify of man; for he knew what was in man:" and therefore he addressed his language to the case of the individual inquirer. What, then, may we suppose to have been the character of Nicodemus? He was *a man of the Pharisees, a ruler of the Jews:* accustomed, therefore, to think highly of himself in comparison of others; accustomed to believe himself safe in God's favour; confident, perhaps, that he was, "according to the righteousness which is of the law, blameless." And how surprised would a person of such disposition be, when he heard from the lips of one whom he knew to be *a teacher sent from God, Except a man be born again, born of water and of the Spirit, he cannot see the kingdom of God.* A change must take place in him, which can only be compared to his being born anew, before he can be a member of that kingdom of God which is now come nigh unto you.

No doubt they are remarkable expressions:—to be *born again, born of water and of the Spirit.* But they exactly describe the thing intended. A man is first born "of blood, of the will of the flesh, of the will of man." But he is born corrupt; the offspring of a corrupt parent. An effect must be produced upon his heart, like that which water produces upon the body. As our Lord adds afterwards, "That which is born of the flesh, is flesh." He must be *born again of water and of the Spirit:*—born anew of water, inasmuch as he was born impure, and must now be cleansed:—of the Spirit, inasmuch as he must be "renewed in the spirit of his mind." The water cleanses; "the Spirit giveth life." The water represents that purification which he needs, and which is bestowed through the blood of Christ. The Spirit enables him to walk as one who is "purged from his old sins," his corrupt nature, and is mortifying the flesh, with its affections and lusts, and living not to this world, but unto God.

For this reason, our Lord appointed, as the entrance into his religion, a rite which should be an emblem of this change. He sent his disciples into all the world, BAPTIZING.

Baptism was no new ordinance, otherwise we should have more account of its introduction. We learn from Hebrew writers, that baptism had been practised among the Jews, when one who had been bred up in heathen darkness came to acknowledge the living and true God, and renounced the idols which he had been used to serve. Before he was admitted to their religion, he was baptized with water. He had been polluted by idolatry, and all its attendant wickedness; from this he must be purified. And his baptism with water was an emblem of the purification which he required and received. It did not purify, but it prefigured and betokened purification. It was an emblematical action, signifying, that as the water cleanses the defilement of the body, so must the corruption which has defiled the soul be purged and cleansed. And such is the declaration to Nicodemus, *Except a man be born of water and of the Spirit, he cannot enter into the kingdom of God.* Except a man be as thoroughly purified by the effusion of the Spirit on his soul, as his body would be purified by pouring on it a stream of water, he cannot enter into the kingdom of God, that kingdom which Nicodemus was inquiring of. He may esteem himself—perhaps Nicodemus did—clean in the sight of God; but he needs a cleansing which he can only receive from the Spirit, through faith in the Son of God, before he can belong to God's heavenly kingdom.

This may be best illustrated by considering the case of some who were thus *born again.*

The Jewish assembly, addressed by St. Peter on the day of Pentecost,[1] became convinced of the wickedness in which they had been led to concur; and "being

[1] Acts ii. 14, &c.

pricked in their hearts, said unto Peter and to the rest of the apostles, Men and brethren, what shall we do? Then Peter said unto them, Repent, and *be baptized* every one of you in the name of Jesus Christ for the remission of sins, and ye shall receive the gift of the Holy Ghost."

The idea of *baptism* was not strange or new to this assembly. They had known that proselytes from the heathen were baptized, when they had learnt to acknowledge the Creator of heaven and earth, revealed to the Jewish nation. The heathen washed away the corruption of their idolatrous traditions. And these must wash away the corruption of prejudice and unbelief and hardness of heart, which had led them to "crucify the Prince of life." They must make this acknowledgment, that they required to be cleansed by the water of regeneration; and were to rise out of it as "new creatures," from whom "old things had passed away."

"Then they that gladly received his word were baptized." Was it too much to say, they were *born again?* They had crucified Jesus: now they worshipped him. They had prided themselves in God's favour: now they humbled themselves, and entreated remission of their sins. They were enabled, for the sake of that future life now set before them, to fix their affections, not on the things that are seen, but on the inheritance which is above. They were indeed new creatures: before they had lived for earth, now for heaven. "All that believed were together, and had all things common; and sold their possessions and goods, and parted them to all men, as every man had need."

Another example occurs in the case of the Ethiopian who was returning from his worship at Jerusalem.[2] He had learnt through the Jewish Scriptures to serve God. But as yet he knew nothing of the Redeemer. A particular commission was given to Philip, as a Christian teacher, to explain to him the doctrine of the Gospel. "And as they went on their way, they came unto a certain water; and the eunuch said, See, here is water; what doth hinder me to be baptized?" Why may I not receive the benefit which Jesus, whom thou preachest unto me, came to bestow? Why may I not *enter into the kingdom of God,* being *born again of water and of the Spirit:* "putting off the old man, which is corrupt according to the deceitful lusts; and putting on the new man, which after God is created in righteousness and true holiness?"[3] Philip said, "If thou believest with all thine heart, thou mayest. And he commanded the chariot to stand still; and they went down both into the water, both Philip and the eunuch; and he baptized him." "And he went on his way rejoicing." Having thus given an evidence of his faith, having been admitted into the covenant of grace, having received the pledge of the Holy Spirit, he went on his way rejoicing.

These are practical illustrations of our Lord's meaning: *Except a man be born of water and of the Spirit, he cannot enter into the kingdom of God.* The kingdom of

[2] Acts viii. [3] See Eph. iv. 22—24.

God is a kingdom of holiness: and man by nature is not holy, but corrupt. The Saviour of the world has provided a way for his purification. Therefore the entrance into his religion is by an emblematical action, which indicates that man needs to be renewed and purified: that as water removes the defilement of the flesh, so the Spirit of God must remove the corruption of the heart. If a man comes like the Ethiopian, or like the Jews, of his own accord, and from personal conviction, and says, "See, here is water; what doth hinder me to be baptized?" he makes this acknowledgment for himself. If an infant is brought to baptism, the same acknowledgment is made by those who bring him. The parents, or whoever take the parents' place, come with this avowal. They feel that they have bestowed upon their offspring an earthly corrupt nature, which would lead, not to life, but to death; and therefore they present their child to him who can change that nature, and make it like his own. For "as in Adam all die, even so in Christ shall all be made alive." And we doubt not, but earnestly believe, that he who whilst on earth took up in his arms the little children, and blessed them, will likewise favourably receive the infants now brought to him, and baptized in his name. "For the word of faith is of so great power in the church of God, that by means of him who believes and offers an infant for baptism, or by means of him who baptizes the infant, the infant is cleansed, though as yet not capable of believing with repentance, or of making confession unto salvation."[4]

It behoves all, however, who are no longer children,

[4] Augustin, quoted by Wordsworth *in loco*.

to examine, how it is with themselves. Can it be said of them, that they have been *born again?* It *must* be true of them, if they belong to the kingdom of God. For "if any man be in Christ, he is a new creature."[5] He is entirely different from what he would be, if he were not in Christ Jesus. His trust is different: his views are different: his life is different. For he lives and thinks as one who knows, "that as many as are baptized into Jesus Christ, are baptized into his death." And "therefore they are buried with him by baptism into death; that like as Christ was raised up from the dead by the glory of the Father, even so they also should walk in newness of life. For if we have been planted together in the likeness of his death, we shall be also in the likeness of his resurrection."[6]

XII.

JESUS FORETELLS HIS SUFFERINGS AND DEATH.

MARK x. 32—34.

32. *And they were in the way going up to Jerusalem; and Jesus went before them: and they were amazed; and as they followed, they were afraid.*

THUS "the Lamb of God" was proceeding to the appointed place of sacrifice. For the time of the Pass-

[5] 2 Cor. v. 17. [6] See Rom. vi. 3—5.

over was at hand. And the feast of the Passover, whilst it was a memorial of the deliverance of the Israelites from Egyptian bondage, was also a type of that greater deliverance which Jesus should accomplish at Jerusalem. And as all things concerning him had been determined in the Divine counsels, he foretells *what things should happen to him,* that when they came to pass, it might be remembered that he had foretold them, and there might be a lasting proof that "when Herod, and Pontius Pilate, with the Gentiles and people of Israel, were gathered together" against the Lord's anointed, they could only do what "his hand and counsel determined before to be done."[1]

32. *And he took again the twelve, and began to tell them what things should happen unto him,*
33. *Saying, Behold, we go up to Jerusalem; and the Son of man shall be delivered unto the chief priests, and unto the scribes; and they shall deliver him to the Gentiles:*
34. *And they shall mock him, and shall scourge him, and shall spit upon him, and shall kill him: and the third day he shall rise again.*

The Son of man shall be delivered *unto the chief priests and the scribes.* And so it proved. The "great multitude" which met him as he left the garden of Gethsemane, came "from the chief priests and elders of the people."[2] And these *condemned him to death.* For Pilate had declared that he "could find no fault in him;" and was "determined to let him go." But they cried out, "We have a law; and by our law he ought to die, because he made himself the Son of

[1] Acts iv. 26—28. [2] Matt. xxvi. 47; xxvii. 1.

God." Thus they *condemned him.* But as the Roman government under which they were held, did not make it "lawful for them to put any man to death,"[3] they *delivered him to the Gentiles,* "to mock, to scourge, and to crucify him."[4] The history of his trial and death relates how literally this prophecy was fulfilled: how they taunted him, that when he had saved others, he could not save himself, or show himself to be the Son of God by coming down from the cross: how they insulted him with the emblems of power, the sceptre and the crown:—how they "spit in his face, and buffeted him; others smote him with the palms of their hands, saying, Prophesy unto us, thou Christ, who is he that smote thee?"[5] Thus he became "a reproach of men, and despised of the people. All they that saw him laughed him to scorn; they shot out the lip, they shook the head, saying, He trusted in the Lord that he would deliver him: let him deliver him, seeing he delighted in him."[6]

Meanwhile, they were explaining his own words, and words also which had been written long before. As Isaiah had foretold, "he was despised and rejected of men; a man of sorrows and acquainted with grief:" men "hid as it were their faces from him: he was despised, and they esteemed him not." "He was taken from prison and from judgment; he was cut off out of the land of the living; and was numbered with the transgressors."[7]

But it is added—*he shall rise again the third day.*

[3] John xviii. 31.
[4] Matt. xx. 19; xxvii. 2.
[5] Matt. xxvi. 68.
[6] Ps. xxii. 6—8.
[7] Isa. liii. 3, 8, 12.

And so, having been crucified on the day preceding the Sabbath which followed the Passover, it was very early on the morning after the Sabbath that the women hastening to the sepulchre, discovered that he was "not there, but was risen;" and that it was in vain for them to "seek for the living among the dead."[8]

All these things were present to his mind. They made part of that bitter cup, concerning which he afterwards prayed the Father, that "if it were possible, it might pass from him."[9] Notwithstanding, he set his face steadfastly towards Jerusalem. He went before his disciples, who were *amazed and afraid*, and remonstrated, saying, "Master, the Jews of late sought to stone thee; and goest thou thither again?"[1] For how else could the Scriptures be fulfilled, that thus it must be? How else could the purpose of his incarnation be answered, and atonement made for the sin of the world?

In all this, there is much in which our blessed Lord must stand alone, and no man can imitate his example. But there is a sense in which his example must be a pattern to all his followers. They must foresee, as he did, that the will of God may require of them many things distasteful to flesh and blood; many things repugnant to their natural disposition: may call them to self-denial and self-sacrifice, or even to mortification and suffering. But they must determine, as Jesus did, that not their own will, but the will of God be done: that whether the road be smooth or rugged, whether the consequence be "evil report or good report," he must be obeyed: even as Jesus, when

[8] Luke xxiv. 1—5. [9] Matt. xxvi. 39. [1] John xi. 8.

"it pleased the Lord to bruise him," to "put him to grief," to "make his soul an offering for sin,"[2] was "obedient even unto death," and "endured the cross, despising the shame." But there was "joy set before him;"[3] as there is also joy set before all who follow him: all who "suffer with him, that they may also reign with him." "He ever liveth at the right hand of God," noticing those who "confess him before men," that he may confess them before his Father and the holy angels; and may accomplish the promise which he has left for our comfort and encouragement: "Be thou faithful unto death, and I will give thee a crown of life."[4]

XIII.

AGONY OF GETHSEMANE.

MATT. xxvi. 36—39.

36. *Then cometh Jesus with them unto a place called Gethsemane, and saith unto the disciples, Sit ye here, while I go and pray yonder.*

37. *And he took with him Peter and the two sons of Zebedee, and began to be sorrowful and very heavy.*

38. *Then saith he unto them, My soul is exceeding sorrowful, even unto death; tarry ye here, and watch with me.*

[2] Isa. liii. 10. [3] Heb. xii. 2. [4] Rev. ii. 10.

39. *And he went a little farther, and fell on his face, and prayed, saying, O my Father, if it be possible, let this cup pass from me: nevertheless, not as I will, but as thou wilt.*

The Redeemer of the world, on this remarkable occasion, looks forward to the suffering which he had engaged to undergo. He looks forward to it with those feelings to which he had voluntarily subjected himself, in order that in our nature he might bear our penalty. And these feelings were, at the present moment, allowed to oppress him with aggravated force, that the purpose of his mysterious sacrifice might be better understood and valued. The Spirit, which supports his disciples, for a while deserted him, that his disciples might learn more perfectly the lesson taught them by his death. *Therefore, he prayed, saying, O my Father, if it be possible, let this cup pass from me.* If it be possible. If, consistently with the salvation of "those whom thou hast given me," this cross may not actually be undergone, let the bitter draught be spared me. Certainly it was *possible* that the sacrifice should not be offered for the sins of men. "But how then should the Scriptures be fulfilled?" "Ought not Christ to have suffered these things, and to enter into his glory?" We must also suppose it to have been *possible,* that sin should be pardoned, though this sacrifice was not actually made. If God had seen fit, he might have proclaimed an amnesty without this condition: but he did not. It was right in his view, that the penalty for sin should be really paid.

And shall not the Judge of all the earth do right?

For here, in this agony, we behold the nature of sin; here we behold the Lord Jesus bearing its weight: bearing the curse of the law. For as St. Paul shows,[1] "Cursed is every one that continueth not in all things which are written in the book of the law to do them." "The transgression of the law is sin:" and "the wages of sin is death." This concludes all mankind under a curse, for that "all have sinned, and come short of the glory of God." Christ interposes, and "redeems us from the curse of the law, being made a curse for us;" for again it is written, "Cursed is every one that hangeth on a tree." So that the indignation of God against sin is openly manifested, and yet the penitent believer in Christ is pardoned: "the promise by faith of Jesus Christ is given to them that believe."

In one sense, therefore, though not in the sense of those who thought to taunt the suffering Redeemer, that was true which the chief priests afterwards said in mockery, "He saved others, himself he cannot save." He could not *come down from the cross,* and deliver himself from the punishment which he had undertaken to bear, without frustrating the plan prepared for man's redemption. No sooner had he said, according to the dictates of his human nature, "Father, save me from this hour;" than he added in his divine wisdom, "yet for this cause came I to this hour." Throughout his life he had shown himself to be in possession of means which would have enabled him with ease to crush whatever dared oppose him. To the end, he gave proof that he laid down his life of himself, and that no man took it from him. But the same goodness which led

[1] Gal. iii. 10—13.

him to offer the ransom, determined him to endure unto the end, and forbad his using his divine power to save himself, until having submitted to the full weight of Divine wrath, he was enabled to say, "It is finished: and bowed the head, and gave up the ghost."

The practical lesson to be learnt here is very plain, and ought never to be absent from our minds: though it is the lesson which in all ages mankind have been most unwilling to learn, and slowest to acknowledge. It is not consistent with the Father's attributes that no evil consequence should follow the sins of men. Will He, it might be asked, will He so heavily condemn sin in his creatures, as Scripture affirms? "God is love." But God loved his Son: and his Son here offers the prayer, *If it be possible, let this cup pass from me.* And the prayer was not granted: the cup of suffering was drunk. Such must be our reflection when we are disposed to extenuate the evil of sin; when that which ought to be most shocking, its awful frequency, prevents us from dreading or lamenting it as it ought to be dreaded and lamented both in ourselves and others.

Another practical inference follows, which ought no less to affect our hearts. The suffering which is here recorded, shows the extent of Christ's love. Had he suffered less, we should not have rightly known the greatness of that mercy which he exercised towards mankind. It was much, indeed, that "when he was rich" in the fulness of heavenly joy, he should "become poor," for man's sake, and descend to a world like ours. But that he should place himself under the fierceness of that Divine wrath, from which his disciples are delivered, is a degree of love which "passes all understanding."

One return he requires of us; one return we can attempt to make,—our gratitude: gratitude which is to be shown by obedience to his will. "Because we thus judge, that if one died for all, then were all dead: and that he died for all, that they which live, should not henceforth live unto themselves, but unto him which died for them."[2] This is the principle of the Christian's practice; and this principle ought to receive fresh strength from every fresh contemplation of that "precious death," from which our life, our real and spiritual life, is derived.

XIV

THE RESURRECTION OF JESUS.

LUKE xxiv. 1—11.

1. *Now upon the first day of the week, very early in the morning, they came unto the sepulchre, bringing the spices which they had prepared, and certain others with them.*

THE death of Jesus had so completely dismayed his followers, that the assurance which he had given them of his resurrection seems to have vanished from their minds. He had often, and in many different ways, repeated to them the truth, that he "must be killed, and the third day rise again." He had spoken of it in the

[2] 2 Cor. v. 14, 15.

way of figure, saying to the Jews, "Destroy this temple, and in three days I will raise it up;" when "he spake of the temple of his body."[1] He had affirmed it plainly; for, going up to Jerusalem, he "took the twelve disciples apart in the way, and said unto them, Behold, we go up to Jerusalem; and the Son of man shall be betrayed unto the chief priests and unto the scribes, and they shall condemn him to death, and shall deliver him to the Gentiles to mock, and to scourge, and to crucify him: and the third day he shall rise again."[2] He had appealed to this event as the great proof of his truth; saying, "An evil and adulterous generation seeketh after a sign; and there shall no sign be given to it, but the sign of the prophet Jonas: for as Jonas was three days and three nights in the whale's belly, so shall the Son of man be three days and three nights in the heart of the earth."[3] And his enemies had been less forgetful than his friends. For after the body had been laid in the tomb, "the chief priests and Pharisees went to Pilate, saying, Sir, we remember that that deceiver said, while he was yet alive, After three days I will rise again. Command therefore that the sepulchre be made sure until the third day, lest his disciples come by night, and steal him away, and say unto the people, He is risen from the dead."[4]

His disciples, however, thought of nothing less. They resigned themselves to disappointment and sorrow, and had no other desire than that of paying the last tribute to his lifeless body. *The women which came with him from Galilee followed, and beheld the sepulchre, and*

[1] John ii. 19.
[2] Matt. xx. 17—19.
[3] Matt. xii. 39, 40.
[4] Matt. xxvii. 62, 63.

how his body was laid. And they returned, and prepared spices and ointments; and rested the sabbath day, according to the commandment: and now, very early in the morning of the third day, *they came unto the sepulchre, bringing the spices which they had prepared.* We even know the subject on which they were communing as they approached the place. They were not saying one to another, "Now we shall see the fulfilment of prophecy, and the truth of our Master's words:" but they were doubting together, "Who shall roll us away the stone from the door of the sepulchre? For it was very great."[5] This difficulty was soon removed: but it only opened the way to fresh astonishment.

2. *And they found the stone rolled away from the sepulchre.*
3. *And they entered in, and found not the body of the Lord Jesus.*
4. *And it came to pass, as they were much perplexed thereabout, behold, two men stood by them in shining garments:*
5. *And as they were afraid, and bowed down their faces to the earth, they said unto them, Why seek ye the living among the dead?*
6. *He is not here, but is risen; remember how he spake unto you when he was yet in Galilee,*
7. *Saying, The Son of man must be delivered into the hands of sinful men, and be crucified, and the third day rise again.*
8. *And they remembered his words,*
9. *And returned from the sepulchre, and told all these things unto the eleven, and to all the rest.*
10. *It was Mary Magdalene, and Joanna, and Mary the*

[5] Mark xvi. 3, 4.

mother of James, and other women that were with them, which told these things unto the apostles.

11. *And their words seemed to them as idle tales, and they believed them not.*

So slowly is the mind reconciled to truths which oppose our preconceived ideas. To Peter and the rest, the death of Jesus was a new and unexpected thing: they could not receive it, or reason upon it. So likewise his resurrection. The resurrection of the body had not been realised to their minds. An actual example, it seems, like this, was needed, to conquer incredulity, and establish the assurance that all men shall rise again with their bodies.

To dispel the doubts of his disciples, God saw fit to send his angels, *who said unto them, Why seek ye the living among the dead? He is not here, but is risen: remember how he spake unto you.*

It was indeed great ignorance of all that Jesus was, and of all that had been foretold concerning him, to seek among the dead for him, the living God. He could not lie imprisoned in the tomb, who "was in the beginning with God, and was God:" "who has life in himself, and quickeneth whom he will." The prophecy concerning him must be fulfilled,—"Thou wilt not leave my soul in hell, neither wilt thou suffer thine Holy One to see corruption."

Therefore the angels might justly rebuke these disconsolate mourners, and say, *Why seek ye the living among the dead?* Have ye been so slow to discover the character, so slow to perceive the power of your Divine Master, so dull to comprehend his words, as to think that he who is the giver of life, can be holden by the bands of death? *He is not here, but is risen:* your own eyes shall have the proof of it, before he ascends above to that place where ye must hereafter seek him, on the right hand of the Majesty on high. "He goeth before you into Galilee: there shall ye see him, as he said unto you."[5]

Two remarks arise from this. One has been expressed by St. Paul in writing to the Thessalonians, and offers a blessed consolation to those whose friends have been removed from this world, "dying in the Lord." "I would not have you to be ignorant, brethren, concerning them which are asleep, that ye sorrow not, even as others which have no hope. For if we believe that Jesus died and rose again, even so them also which sleep in Jesus will God bring with him."[6] Number not the living among the dead. Those for whom we weep are still living: they have entered upon an immortal and a blessed existence: they are not lying in the grave; they are risen to their Saviour and their God. Grieve not that they should "depart, and be with Christ."

2. But there is a spiritual, as well as a bodily resurrection: and in that sense the words, *Why seek ye the living among the dead?* ought to apply to the Christian in this present world. The apostle so applies them; and speaks of Christians as already "risen;"—"risen with Christ." Christ was not like the children of men. Their bodies perish; his could not perish in the grave. So, too, the Christian is not like other men, whose thoughts are fixed upon the earth; who are dead to God, dead to the concerns of the soul. The Christian

[5] Mark xvi. 7. [6] 1 Thess. iv. 13, 14.

is "alive unto God, through Jesus Christ." He must not be sought among the dead; he must not be found in the ways and haunts of sinners; he must not be sought among those who have none of the life of God within them; who are lovers of pleasure, more than lovers of God. If Christ had not risen, it had been evidence that he were not the Son of God. And so, he who is a Christian indeed gives evidence of his sincerity, when he is able to rise above the inordinate cares and desires and pleasures belonging to the present world, and to have his "conversation in heaven."

That therefore which the angels affirmed of Christ, is also, in its measure, true of those who believe in Christ. *They are not here, but are risen.* Their body, indeed, is still in this world: but their better part, the soul, is risen above it, and is dwelling in heaven with their Lord and Saviour. There are their affections set; there their treasure is; and where their treasure is, there will their hearts be also. Such is the apostle's inference;[2] saying to the Colossians, "If ye then be risen with Christ, seek those things which are above, where Christ sitteth on the right hand of God. Set your affections on things above, not on things on the earth." So, "when Christ, who is your life, shall appear, then shall ye also appear with him in glory."

[2] Col. iii. 1—4.

XV.

ATTRACTION OF THE CROSS.

JOHN xii. 23, 24.

23. *Jesus answered them, saying, The hour is come, that the Son of man should be glorified.*
24. *Verily, verily, I say unto you, Except a corn of wheat fall into the ground and die, it abideth alone; but if it die, it bringeth forth much fruit.*

JESUS uttered these prophetic words, on an occasion which would not at first seem likely to have drawn them from him. As the Feast of the Passover approached, and with it the sacrifice of the true "Paschal Lamb," certain Greeks had come to worship at Jerusalem, and desired to see Jesus, of whose fame, no doubt, they had heard.

These were Gentiles by birth and residence. But from some favourable circumstances they had become acquainted with the Jewish Scriptures and the Hebrew faith; and had turned so far from their national vanities, as to worship the living and true God, the Creator of the world. There were many such, like the centurion, whose servant was healed at Capernaum;[1] like Cornelius, whose "prayers and alms had come up as a memorial before God."[2] But as they did not profess the religion of the Jews, the apostles hesitated, when they came to Philip, *desiring to see Jesus*. The apostles did

[1] Matt. viii. 5. [2] Acts x. 4.

not yet understand that his light should "lighten the Gentiles." But Jesus saw through the mist by which they were surrounded, and knew that the accomplishment of the prophecy was approaching, when "kings should come to his light, and the Gentiles to the brightness of his rising."[3] He replied in mysterious words, saying, "*The hour is come, that the Son of man should be glorified. Verily, verily, I say unto you, Except a corn of wheat fall into the ground and die, it abideth alone: but if it die, it bringeth forth much fruit.*"

The Son of man, coming to his own world, and his own people, had not been received with glory. The only triumph which he knew, was that accomplishment of prophecy, when a colt, "an ass's colt," bore him into Jerusalem, and the multitude spread their garments before him. But now *the hour was come that the Son of man should be glorified.* He should burst the gates of the grave, and ascend to "the glory which he had with the Father before the world was."

But it is not his own glory which affects the mind of Jesus. That glory, in its proper sense, admitted of no increase. His glory is man's happiness, man's salvation; the bringing immortal souls "from darkness to light," from death to life, from "the power of Satan unto God."

And how should this be accomplished? In real truth, the words, Now shall the Son of man *be glorified,* were to be thus interpreted, Now shall the Son of man be crucified. The foundation of that glory must be laid on the cross, and in the grave. As the *corn of wheat must fall into the ground and die,* in order that it

[3] Isa. lxii. 2.

may *bring forth fruit*, and by dying send up an abundant produce, nourished by itself, partaking of a nature like its own; so should it be in the kingdom of God. The seeds of an abundant harvest, "bringing many sons to glory," must be sown in the grave.

The time, indeed, was then near, when it would appear as if the power of darkness had prevailed, and all the hopes were extinguished of those who had followed Jesus as "Lord and Christ." But he himself extends his view to the consequences of his death, by which "the prince of this world should be cast out," the dominion of Satan broken, and he, the "despised and rejected of men," should draw[4] towards himself a great multitude of all people and nations and tongues, who should look up to him as their Saviour, and acknowledge him as their Lord.

If this be so, there must be something in the nature of his Cross and Passion which has the power of affecting and attracting the heart: something through which the Spirit of God performs the office assigned to him, and "reproves the world of sin, of righteousness, and of judgment."[5]

And it is so. For, in the first place, the cross of Christ displays, by the most convincing proof, the nature of sin in the sight of God. The "lifting up" of Christ upon the cross was the inflicting upon him the worst punishment of the vilest sinners. But he was himself, confessedly, "without spot of sin." Even the Judge who delivered him to death, could "find no fault in him." They were the sins of men that he bore in his own body. And so bearing them, he displayed the

[4] John xii. 32. [5] John xvi. 8.

nature and the consequences of sin by a proof which nothing can refute, and with a clearness which nothing can conceal. Words may be disputed; but facts cannot be denied. And the fact of Christ's death, when he consented to be "numbered with the transgressors," proves the sinfulness and the danger of transgression. But it shows this, not to condemn, but to save; it opens a way of escape from the perilous state which it discloses. And so his words are made good. Dying, he *brings forth much fruit:* being "lifted up from the earth, he draweth men unto him," as their deliverer "from the wrath to come;" as the "mediator between God and man."

But there is another attraction of the Cross, not less powerful than the relief which it offers from the "terrors of the Lord." It removes that estrangement by which the affections of mankind are naturally alienated from God; alienated for this cause, that they are conscious of having transgressed against him. It gives a perpetual evidence of the love of God towards men: of his willingness, nay, his desire, to receive them to his favour. It enforces that gracious remonstrance of the Prophet, "Turn ye, turn ye unto me; for why will ye die, O house of Israel?" These are what Scripture calls, "the cords of a man;"[6] the cords by which man ought to be drawn—ties of love in return for love. Let us suppose a son, having incurred the heavy displeasure of his father by acts of disobedience, to have betaken himself to a foreign land, and to be living there without any of the thoughts which a son ought to feel towards a father. It is the true representation of man, in his

[6] See Hosea xi. 4.

natural state; "without God in the world;" "without the knowledge of God," because "not liking to retain him in their knowledge."

On a sudden, tidings are brought him of a message from his father. Perhaps he sees one approaching whom he fears as a messenger of vengeance, who has overtaken him in a far country. Such has always been the first impression of the guilty heart, when surprised by a sense of the Divine presence. Even the shepherds were "sore afraid," when "the angel of the Lord came upon them, and the glory of the Lord shone round about them." But the angel said unto them, "Be not afraid; for lo, I bring you good tidings of great joy." [7] And so the banished son is told not of anger, but of mercy; the messenger is come not to destroy life, but to save it. The father has not neglected his son, though he has been himself forgotten: he has sent for his restoration the one who was dearest to him on earth: one who had consented to leave the blessings of his home, and expose himself to hardship, peril, even death itself, that he might reclaim the wanderer. Surely this proof of the father's affection still existing, and showing itself by such signs, would move the hardest heart. It would prove, at the same time, the father's love, and the son's danger whilst alienated from him. Surely it would recall him to the father.

This, then, is the explanation of our Lord's words, in which he compares his death to the *corn of wheat,* which, falling into the ground and dying, *brings forth much fruit.* That death "draws men to him," by two of the most powerful affections which influence man's nature;

[7] Luke ii. 9—11.

by showing what we have cause to dread, by showing what we are bound to love. These are the thoughts and motives which the Holy Spirit employs, and so leads the heart to a lively faith, a thankful acquiescence in the revealed word. In every age, in every country, and in every class, the love of God towards mankind as displayed in the Gospel of Christ, is the argument which "effectually works in them that believe," to "bring forth fruit unto holiness, and the end everlasting life." And the Son of man, when crucified, effected that which he did not effect whilst present to the eyes of men, "full of grace and truth;" whilst astonishing the people by his words and by his miracles, and striking his adversaries to the ground by the majesty of his countenance. And so likewise the apostles, going forth as they were commissioned to go, and "preaching the Gospel to every creature," weak as they were, and without influence in themselves, had an argument to urge which the Lord himself could not have employed. He came "to give his life a ransom." But the ransom had not been actually paid. He had not yet "suffered, the just for the unjust, that he might bring unto God"[8] those who were alienated from him by ignorance and sin.

And therefore he looks onward to the time, not far distant, when "he shall see of the travail of his soul, and be satisfied:" when many should come from the east and from the west, from the north and the south, and sit down in the kingdom of God. He looks onward to the time, when "the promise of the Father"[9] should be fulfilled, and he should send the Holy Ghost to

[8] 1 Pet. iii. 18. [9] Luke xxiv. 49.

open the hearts which would otherwise be closed: when, as the Israelites looked up to the brazen serpent raised by Moses in the wilderness, and as many as looked on it were healed of their wounds,[1] so multitudes of all nations and kindreds and tongues should look towards the Son of man lifted up upon the cross, and his prophetic words should be explained by their accomplishment, "I, if I be lifted up from the earth, will draw all men unto me."[2]

XVI.

THE APOSTLES COMMISSIONED.

MATT. xxviii. 16—20.

16. *Then the eleven disciples went away into Galilee, into a mountain where Jesus had appointed them.*
17. *And when they saw him, they worshipped him; but some doubted.*

THE apostles, who at first doubted, had been now convinced. Even Thomas acknowledged the truth which he was slow to receive, and "because he had seen, he believed."[3] Those therefore who now *doubted*, were probably some of the five hundred brethren to whom, as St. Paul relates, Jesus appeared before his ascension, on some occasion not mentioned by any of

[1] John iii. 14. [2] John xii. 32. [3] John xx. 24—29.

the Evangelists.[4] Their doubts are our certainty. We have the satisfaction of knowing that they were not so transported with joy at the glorious event which they had not dared to expect, as to believe because they wished to believe. And though many things happened after the resurrection which have not been related, many things which we should gladly know if it had seemed good to the Holy Spirit to preserve them to us—this has been recorded, that *some doubted*, and could hardly be persuaded that Jesus himself stood before them.

18. *And Jesus came and spake unto them, saying, All power is given unto me in heaven and in earth.*
19. *Go ye therefore, and teach all nations, baptizing them in the name of the Father, and of the Son, and of the Holy Ghost;*
20. *Teaching them to observe all things whatsoever I have commanded you: and, lo, I am with you alway, even unto the end of the world. Amen.*

All things had been accomplished, which were to prepare for the establishment of the kingdom of Christ: his ministry, his death, his resurrection. Now the fruits were to appear; and he commissions his apostles that they go out and gather them. He had laboured, and he sends them to enter into his labours. *All power*, he says, *is given unto me in heaven and in earth:* power to send the Holy Spirit; power to convert the hearts of those who hear the word; power to assign to every man his place throughout eternity; power to bestow "the crown of righteousness" on those who, "by patient

[4] 1 Cor. xv. 6.

continuance in well doing, seek for glory, and honour, and immortality." *Go ye, therefore, and teach all nations;* (make disciples of them:) *baptizing them in the name of the Father, and of the Son, and of the Holy Ghost.* Instruct them, that there is one God and Father of all; and that "he is a rewarder of them that diligently seek him." Instruct them, that there is "one Mediator between God and man:" He is "the way, the truth, and the life:" "no man cometh unto the Father but by him." Instruct them, that the Holy Spirit, proceeding from the Father and the Son, will purify the hearts of all who come to God through Christ Jesus, and will enable them to "live righteously, soberly, and godly," as becometh those who are looking for a heavenly kingdom. In the name of this TRIUNE GOD baptize them: that they may be born again of water and of the Holy Ghost, and being cleansed from their sins, may be renewed in the spirit of their minds. For such is the appointed entrance into the covenant which God is pleased to make with man through Jesus Christ, that as many as believe in him shall not perish, but have everlasting life.

A gracious encouragement attends this command. *Lo, I am with you alway, even unto the end of the world.* This was a needful promise. Without it, the apostles might naturally have felt within themselves, Who are we, that we should *go and teach all nations?* Who are we, that we should oppose the authority of the chief priests and magistrates, should encounter the bigotry of the Pharisees and the enmity of the Sadducees? Who are we, that, leaving our own country, we should venture into the idolatrous world, and call upon men to give up "the vain traditions received from their fathers?" Who are we, that "the strong man armed" should yield up to us his palace and his goods, which he has so long held in undisturbed possession?

The promise which accompanied that command would alone answer those just and natural feelings. *Lo, I am with you alway, even to the end of the world.* I came upon this earth, to give my "life a ransom," to redeem to myself a people. And now I send forth you, and others after you, to bear the glad tidings of this salvation, to be the heralds of divine mercy, the messengers of peace; to overcome the power of Satan, not with a strong hand or a mighty arm, but with the still small voice of pardon. And certainly I will be with you, and "give you a mouth and wisdom, which none of your adversaries shall be able to gainsay or to resist." The wise shall be confounded; "the scribe, the disputer, of this world shall be silent before you; they that are weak and despised shall bring to nought the things which men esteem and honour. Because "the foolishness of God is wiser than men, and the weakness of God is stronger than men."[5]

Such was the promise to which the apostles trusted: and trusting to which, they went forth to contend against prejudice and malice, and authority and power. Trusting to this promise, a few weeks after it had been given Peter and John stood up in an assembly of their countrymen, and accused them of their wickedness in crucifying and slaying Him whom God "had sent to be a Prince and a Saviour." And what followed?

[5] See 1 Cor. i. 23—25.

Anger, violence, revenge? So we might expect; and so it must have proved, if He had not been with his servants, who had engaged to be *with them alway.* Surely it was seen, by the conversion of three thousand souls, that Jesus *was with them.* Trusting to this same promise, the apostles replied to the council, when forbidden to "speak at all or teach in the name of Jesus," "We cannot but speak the things which we have seen and heard."[6] It appeared from their boldness, and by the discomfiture of their enemies, that Jesus *was with them.* Trusting to this promise, Stephen rebuked the high priests and elders in the public council, because they, like their fathers, were resisting the Holy Ghost. The promise was visibly fulfilled: for when assailed by their violence and hurried to death, "he looked stedfastly up to heaven, and saw the glory of God, and Jesus standing on the right hand of God."[7] And so Paul at Rome, when brought before the emperor, at a crisis so fearful that "all men forsook him," none of his friends dared to support him: nevertheless, he affirms, "The Lord stood by me, and strengthened me; and I was delivered out of the mouth of the lion."[8]

The visible presence and the miraculous support, which the apostles received and the early church required, was gradually withdrawn. But the promise extends *to the end of the world.* And in full confidence that it will never fail, the ministers of Christ are daily going forth to oppose the power of this present world over the heart of man, strengthened as it is by the power of Satan: and success is granted them, according

[6] Acts iv. 13—20. [7] Acts vii. 51—55. [8] 2 Tim. iv. 16, 17.

to the good pleasure of Him "whose they are, and whom they serve." The word "does not return unto him void; but accomplishes that for which he sends it." Otherwise he would have died in vain; none would die with him unto sin. Otherwise he would have risen in vain: none would rise with him to the spiritual life of righteousness and holiness. Whereas from the apostles' days until now, in every age, and in every land, and among all the classes of mankind, Greek and Barbarian, bond and free, multitudes through the power of the Gospel have been turned from darkness to light, from the power of Satan unto God; have cast away the idols of their ignorance, and the idols of their hearts, "to serve the living and true God, and to wait for his Son from heaven," "building up themselves in their most holy faith, and looking for the mercy of the Lord Jesus Christ unto eternal life."

Because He, the Author of this salvation, is always with his faithful servants as they minister in his name, and renders the word of God which they proclaim effectual, that it may be "quick and powerful, discovering the thoughts and intents of the heart;" may convince the sinner, determine the wavering, encourage the fearful, and console the penitent.

XVII.

APPEAL OF PETER TO THE JEWISH ASSEMBLY. A.D. 33.

ACTS ii. 22—42.

22. *Ye men of Israel, hear these words: Jesus of Nazareth, a man approved of God among you, by miracles and wonders and signs, which God did by him in the midst of you, as ye yourselves also know:*
23. *Him, being delivered by the determinate counsel and foreknowledge of God, ye have taken, and by wicked hands have crucified and slain:*
24. *Whom God hath raised up, having loosed the pains of death: because it was not possible that he should be holden of it.*

THESE words were addressed by St. Peter to the assembly of his countrymen, brought together at the Feast of Pentecost, and astonished by the fact that the apostles were able to speak to every man in his own language, "as the Spirit gave them utterance:" so that the strangers from many different countries, "heard in their own tongues the wonderful works of God." Whilst "they were all amazed, and marvelled," Peter first reminds them, that one of their own prophets had foretold an event of this kind, when God "should pour out his Spirit, and show signs and wonders in heaven above, and in the earth beneath."[1] And he proceeds to declare its purpose. They had neglected, despised, rejected, nay, had crucified and slain him whom God had sent to be "a Prince and a Saviour." But not without *the determinate counsel and foreknowledge of God:* who had now fulfilled another prophecy, and "had not left his soul in hell, nor suffered his holy One to see corruption." Partly, indeed, this is the hope of all the people of God, that "though worms destroy this body, yet in their flesh they shall see God." They shall "come forth," shall "rise again at the last day." But not until they have *seen corruption.* "It is appointed unto all men to suffer the original sentence, "Dust thou art, and unto dust thou shalt return." But this did not Jesus. *His soul was not left in hell, neither his flesh did see corruption.*[2] In him, and in him alone, are the words of David verified, which, *being a prophet, he before spake of the resurrection of Christ.*

On this prophecy, hitherto lying in a dark place, the light had now shone. And this might prepare their minds for the fact which was to follow.

32. *This Jesus hath God raised up, whereof we all are witnesses.*
33. *Therefore being by the right hand of God exalted, and having received of the Father the promise of the Holy Ghost, he hath shed forth this, which ye now see and hear.*
36. *Therefore let all the house of Israel know assuredly, that God hath made that same Jesus, whom ye have crucified, both Lord and Christ.*

[1] Joel ii. 28—30. [2] Ps. xvi. 10.

37. *Now when they heard this, they were pricked in their heart, and said unto Peter and to the rest of the apostles, Men and brethren, what shall we do?*

So powerful was the effect of Peter's words upon the consciences of his hearers. In the phrase of Isaiah, they were "like the hammer which breaks the rock in pieces." In the phrase of St. Paul, they were like a double-edged sword, "piercing even to the dividing asunder the soul and spirit." Because the Spirit of God accompanied the apostle's words, adding weight to the hammer, and softening the rock; carrying the sword home, and making the soul sensible. *They were pricked in their hearts:* evidently because of that particular sin which the apostle had closely pressed upon them, that they had crucified and slain him, whom God had *made both Lord and Christ.*

There were some, indeed, among the number present, who had not been actively concerned in the death of Jesus. But even these, the foreign Jews *from every country,* would be conscious that whenever they had heard of Jesus in their visits to Jerusalem, they had neglected or derided him. The whole company acknowledge themselves to be in the same condition, and anxiously inquire, *Men and brethren, what shall we do?*

As a patient, whose physician might unexpectedly assure him that he had swallowed poison, and his life was in imminent danger—as the astonished patient would inquire, What hope or remedy remains? you are a man, and a brother, and can feel for such a state: only prescribe, and I am ready to comply;—such is the anxiety and the eagerness here expressed. *Men and brethren, what shall we do?*

Such a question, however, might be asked of a physician, and he might have no hope to give. He might be forced to acknowledge that the case was one for which he could offer nothing.

It is not so with the apostle. He has a ready answer, and a certain promise.

38. *Then Peter said unto them, Repent, and be baptized every one of you in the name of Jesus Christ for the remission of sins, and ye shall receive the gift of the Holy Ghost.*
39. *For the promise is unto you, and to your children, and to all that are afar off, even as many as the Lord our God shall call.*

With such confidence does Peter answer, and speak "as one having authority." He describes the issue as sure and certain. *Repent, and be baptized: and ye shall receive the gift of the Holy Ghost.* Ye shall receive both pardon for the past, and grace for the future. Your transgressions shall be forgiven, which at present exclude you from the favour of God: and your nature shall be renewed, which has hitherto been averse from his will. Ye shall be baptized "in the name of the Father, and of the Son, and of the Holy Ghost." The Father will receive you: the Son has made atonement for you: the Holy Ghost will sanctify you. Thus shall ye become members of Christ, children of God, and inheritors of the kingdom of heaven.

Such should be the blessing upon their repentance and their faith; the blessing which should be made over to them in baptism.

41. *Then they that gladly received his word were baptized: and the same day there were added unto them about three thousand souls.*

42. *And they continued stedfastly in the apostles' doctrine and fellowship, and in breaking of bread, and in prayers.*

So mighty was the effect produced upon that assembly. What was required of them was great indeed. It was required that they who had joined with the rest of their countrymen in rejecting Christ, should now acknowledge that he was the promised Messiah: nay more, that in him alone they could obtain "remission of sin." Others might not have been partakers of the same guilt: but their general spirit had been, no doubt, the spirit of men self-satisfied; approving themselves as righteous; "resting in their knowledge of God" and of his law, and believing that "they had need of nothing."[1] Now their views must be wholly changed. They must confess themselves sinners in the sight of God, who had no hope but in his mercy: they must accept the terms of pardon offered by him, and *be baptized in the name of the Lord Jesus Christ, for the remission of sin.*

Such, and no less, was the *repentance*, the change required. And yet so strong was the emotion produced upon their hearts, that three thousand persons *received the word gladly, were baptized,* and became the first fruits of the death of Christ, the first members of that company which no man can number.

The Lord had made an express promise, that although they had been few who followed him whilst on earth,

[1] Rom. ii. 17.

and became his avowed disciples, it should not be always so. "When He, the Comforter, is come, he will reprove the world of sin, and of righteousness, and of judgment. Of sin, because they believe not on me: of righteousness, because I go to the Father, and ye see me no more: of judgment, because the prince of this world is judged."[2]

We see, now, the explanation and the fulfilment of that promise. That so many, even *three thousand souls,* should so suddenly and so gladly receive the word, and be baptized as believers in Christ, can be ascribed to nothing but the Spirit of God taking away the veil from their hearts, and enabling them to see that all the promises to which their nation had been looking, all that "Moses in the law and the prophets had written," was now fulfilled in Him whom God had made "both Lord and Christ," but whom they "with wicked hands had crucified and slain."

It was no slight change, and required no small resolution. They would soon experience the truth of the Lord's warnings, when he said, "Whosoever will come after me, let him deny himself, and take up his cross, and follow me." They would have much to encounter from their friends; and many who had been their friends, would become their enemies. Brother would rise against brother, and a son would be at variance with his father. Nevertheless, they *continued stedfast in the apostles' doctrine, and in breaking of bread, and in prayers.* The Pharisees are no longer regarded as their examples of sanctity, nor the priests or scribes resorted to for knowledge and instruction.

[2] John xvi. 8—11.

The apostles had become their teachers, for they "had the words of eternal life." *In their doctrine and worship they continued stedfast.* Sacrifice and burnt offerings they no longer trusted to, as their mode of access to God. Those had been superseded by the one great sacrifice once offered for sin, of which the worship of the Law was but the type and shadow. This sacrifice they commemorated, and appropriated to themselves by *the breaking of bread,* as the Lord's body had been "broken for them," and as he had commanded them to do "in remembrance of him." And a new encouragement was given to their *prayers;* for he who was now their Teacher and Lord, had assured his disciples, that "whatever they should ask the Father in his name, he would grant it."[3] "For the Father himself loved them, because they had loved the Son, and believed that he came forth from God."[4]

Here, then, was at once the interpretation and the accomplishment of the Lord's mysterious words: "I, when I be lifted up from the earth, will draw all men unto me."[5] Three thousand souls, to which numbers were daily added, became the first fruits of the truth, now authoritatively declared and divinely enforced, that Jesus had been lifted up upon the cross, had died the death of sinners, that he might deliver from death as many as should repent and believe in his name. On "this rock," on the basis of this truth, he had declared that his Church should be built,[6] of which the first stones were now laid at Jerusalem, and of which the superscription is, "Glory to God in the highest, and on earth peace, good will towards men."

[3] 1 Cor. xi. 24.
[4] John xv. 16; xvi. 27.
[5] John xii. 32.
[6] Matt. xvi. 18.

XVIII.

APPOINTMENT OF DEACONS.

Acts i. 1.

1. *And in those days, when the number of the disciples was multiplied, there arose a murmuring of the Grecians against the Hebrews, because their widows were neglected in the daily ministration.*
2. *Then the twelve called the multitude of the disciples unto them, and said, It is not reason that we should leave the word of God, and serve tables.*
3. *Wherefore, brethren, look ye out among you seven men of honest report, full of the Holy Ghost, and wisdom, whom we may appoint over this business.*
4. *But we will give ourselves continually to prayer, and to the ministry of the word.*

The body of Christians which had been formed during the short period succeeding the Lord's ascension, presented a singular case. There was a community which, together with their families, must have consisted of thirty or forty thousand persons, of whom a large proportion were without the regular support arising from ordinary business or labour. Some, we must suppose, had been deprived of this, directly or indirectly, in consequence of their conversion. The enmity with which they would be treated, as departing from the common faith, and acknowledging Jesus to be the Christ, would pursue them in their vocations, and ruin their worldly business.[1] Others, like the apostles themselves, had abandoned their means of livelihood: their minds being wholly occupied with the interests of their new faith, or with the actual duties of extending it. For the support of these, a common fund was created by the liberality of others who had possessions. "All that believed were together, and had all things common: and sold their possessions and goods, and parted them to all men, as every man had need." "As many as were possessors of lands or houses sold them, and brought the prices of the things that were sold, and laid them down at the apostles' feet; and distribution was made unto every man according as he had need."

There is nothing extraordinary in this surrender. It was merely a proof that they were sincere. It was the natural effect of believing what these Christians believed.[2] Treasure was laid up for them in heaven: and where their treasure was, there was their heart also. Thenceforward the things of this world were only valuable to them, as they might be used to promote their own salvation, and that of others.

The creation of such a fund, by the negotiations attending the sale of property; and, still more, the management of it afterwards, would be matter of no small difficulty. If out of all the baptized converts, only a thousand families applied for relief, there would be employment for more time than the apostles could spare. They must become *servers of tables*, keepers of accounts, instead of dispensers of *the word of God*.

Moreover, there arose a murmuring of the foreign

[1] See Hebrews x. 33, 34. [2] Acts ii. 44; iv. 35.

Jews against the natives of Judea, as if their destitute families, and especially their *widows* or women, *were neglected in the daily ministration.* It is not probable that there was just ground for this complaint. It is far more likely that it arose out of those feelings of jealousy, which in nature are grievously predominant, and are hardly kept down by divine grace. We know by experience that such feelings were sure to exist, when numbers were to be supplied out of a common fund, to which all had an equal claim.

There is at first sight something very pleasing in the thoughts of a community supplied as these first Christians were. How delightful, we are inclined to say; there were none "among them that lacked:" none who had more than their necessities required. What was superfluous to one family supplied what was deficient to another.

This, however, is a state of things which cannot last long in this world. He who ordained that man should "eat bread by the sweat of his brow," also ordained that every man should eat the bread of his own labour: should support not his neighbour, but himself: should depend upon his own exertions, and enjoy his own possessions. It was only at Jerusalem, only at the first creation of the christian church, that this general rule was interrupted. No such practice prevailed, when new churches were gradually formed at Antioch, and Ephesus, and Philippi, and throughout the whole world. St. Paul speaks very vehemently on this point: saying, "If any provide not for his own, especially for those of his own house, he has denied the faith, and is worse than an infidel."[4]

[3] 1 Tim. v. 8.

There would, no doubt, be times, when a man could not provide for his own. And then another ordinance comes in, and supplies a remedy, "Look not every man on his own things, but every man also on the things (the wants, the interests) of others." "Charge them that are rich in this world, that they be rich in good works, ready to distribute, willing to communicate." Whoso hath this world's good, and seeth his brother hath need, and shutteth up his bowels of compassion from him, how dwelleth the love of God in him?"[4] To seek out, and to assist, the proper objects, is the business of christian charity. And of such assistance on the one side, and dependence on the other, the result is mutual good will. The one party gives that which is his own; that which he might retain as his own; that which he denies himself to part with. The other receives that to which he has no claim, except through the christian principles of his neighbour.

Here, however, at Jerusalem, was a common fund, to which all had an equal claim. And this event shows us the wisdom of the general ordinance, and the danger of annulling it. The multitude, who were so lately "of one heart and one soul," are now likely to be divided. Even their common faith and peculiar circumstances could not prevent *a murmuring*. Some thought that others obtained too much, and that they and their families *were neglected*.

For the present emergency, it was needful to maintain the system which had been begun. The apostles, however, provided, that as far as in them lay, there

[4] Philip. ii. 4; 1 Tim. vi. 17; 1 John iii. 17.

should be no reasonable cause of discontent. *Look ye out,* they say to the disciples assembled together, choose for yourselves *seven men,* (that number might suffice for the present,) seven men *of honest report,* (of known and approved character,) *full of the Holy Ghost and wisdom,* (men seen to be living under the influence of the Spirit of God,) *whom we may appoint over this business.*

5. *And the saying pleased the whole multitude: and they chose Stephen, a man full of faith, and of the Holy Ghost, and Philip, and Prochorus, and Nicanor, and Timon, and Parmenas, and Nicolas, a proselyte of Antioch:* [5]
6. *Whom they set before the apostles: and when they had prayed, they laid their hands on them.*

Laid their hands upon them. So Moses (Num. xxvii. 22) by divine command took Joshua, and set him before Eleazar the priest, and before all the congregation: and he *laid his hands upon him,* and gave him a charge, as the Lord commanded.

It was the solemn mode of invoking the grace of God, and commending the individual to his blessing. When young children were brought to Jesus, "he laid his hands upon them, and blessed them." [6] And one of the signs which were to accompany the apostles was, that "they should lay their hands upon the sick, and they should recover." [7]

[5] The *Grecians* were the complaining party. And it is remarkable that the names of those chosen to set the matter right are *Grecian* names. So careful were they to avoid the appearance of favour and partiality.

[6] Matt. xix. 15. [7] Mark xvi. 18.

Thus solemnly devoted to their office, the deacons entered upon their charge. It was not temporary. We find from the epistle to Timothy, that deacons were stated, ministers of the church. Neither was it merely secular; Stephen continued to preach the gospel: Philip did not hesitate to baptize. They were still engaged, therefore, in whatever might promote the progress of the Gospel. But especially, at present, they were to attend to the temporal affairs of the church, and were not devoted so entirely as the apostles *to prayer and the ministry of the word.*

Only a few months had elapsed since the death of Jesus. And already was a community united together, acknowledging him as their Lord and their God; and so numerous, as to require seven persons to administer their property. Surely the words of Gamaliel were verified; and "this counsel and this work" was not of men, but of God.[8]

[8] See Acts iv. 38.

XIX.

PROPAGATION OF THE GOSPEL.

ACTS viii. 1, 4.

1. *And at that time there was a great persecution against the church which was at Jerusalem; and they were all scattered abroad throughout the regions of Judea and Samaria, except the apostles.*
4. *Therefore they that were scattered abroad went every where preaching the word.*

IT was not to be expected that they should spare the flock, who had already in many cases attacked the shepherds. The first object of the chief priests and rulers must be to restrain the apostles. This had been tried. But now the persecution extended to those who followed them.

Looking onwards to these difficulties, the Lord had given a general direction, "When they persecute you in this city, flee into another."[1] The apostles themselves could not at present do so; it was needful for them, at all hazards, to remain at Jerusalem, and conduct the affairs of the church. But others were at liberty to seek safety in flight; and *were scattered abroad throughout all the regions of Judea and Samaria.* But the persecution, instead of crushing the infant church, tended

[1] Matt. x. 23.

to strengthen and enlarge it; and added another to the numerous instances in which "the wrath of man" is made, under providential direction, to minister to the praise of God. *They that were scattered abroad went every where preaching the word.*

Thus God's gracious purpose was promoted even by the enmity which persecuted these first believers. To whatever place or country they fled, where their connexions might be settled, or they might find a refuge among friends—wherever protection was offered them, they made a return of infinite value: they told the glad tidings of redemption; they spoke of what God had done; how he had remembered his people Israel, and fulfilled the promises which had kept them so long in expectation. And they would explain the evidence on which they had themselves received this truth; the facts which confirmed it; and how, rather than renounce the faith which they had embraced, and forfeit the peace which it had brought them, they had left their country and their homes; left all that was dearest to them in the world, looking for a better country, an "inheritance eternal in the heavens." *They that were scattered abroad went every where preaching the word.*

And this, not by a direct commission.[2] The apostles did not, as in other cases, set them apart from the work, and lay their hands upon them, and send them forth with fasting and prayer. Such a formal commission would not be given to the general body of believers.

[2] This evidently appears from the circumstances of the case, and is implied by the phrase used both here and in Acts xi. 20, *εὐαγγελιζόμενοι τὸν λόγον*, carrying the word of glad tidings. Hammond has an elaborate note to this effect.

The influencing motive was in themselves; in their own hearts. They had received the truth, the great truth, that "God was in Christ, reconciling the world unto himself:" that as there is, on the one hand, "no condemnation to them that are in Christ Jesus," so likewise there is salvation in no other: "for there is none other name under heaven given amongst men, whereby we must be saved."

This truth they had themselves received; and because they had received it, they were now scattered abroad, driven from their homes.

Though, therefore, they had no express commission, like the apostles, they had feelings like the apostles; like them, they "could not but speak the things which they had seen and heard." For they would find their friends, to whom they had come, in the very state from which they had been themselves so recently delivered: that state described by St. Paul, "resting in the law, and making their boast of God, but through breaking the law dishonouring God:"[3] "going about to establish their own righteousness, and ignorant of God's righteousness:"[4] depending upon ordinances and ceremonies, which were merely a lifeless form; with none of the temper and disposition which belongs to the kingdom of heaven: not poor in spirit: not pure in heart: not meek: not merciful: but proud, unholy, sensual, uncharitable. This was the general character of the Jewish people, as it appears disclosed in the New Testament. Such, then, would be the character of those friends and connexions among whom the Christians had taken refuge, who were now *scattered abroad.* And

[3] Rom. ii. 17, &c. [4] Rom. x. 3.

surely there was great reason why they should *preach the word* among these, and tell them of that blood by which "all that believe are justified from all things, from which they could not be justified by the law of Moses:" should tell them of that Spirit which is able to "turn the hearts of the disobedient to the wisdom of the just;" and to renew them in righteousness and true holiness, "after the image of him that created them."

Doubtless, they might have failed to do this. It is easier to go with the stream, and to suffer others to be carried down it, than to encounter and resist its force. And these might have followed the smoother path, and have allowed others to remain undisturbed in their errors, if the Spirit of God had not been strong within them, if the love of Christ had not powerfully constrained them. But they were thus constrained; and, therefore, they *went every where preaching the word*; declaring, that God had visited his people; had remembered his mercy; had fulfilled the promise made to Abraham; that their eyes had seen his salvation.

It is, in fact, one of the divine properties of the christian faith, that it contains within itself a provision by which it is diffused and extended. Its seed is in itself. The Christian loves his Saviour, and therefore is zealous for his glory. That glory is promoted when his religion is extended; therefore the Christian is zealous in extending it. The Christian also has an interest in all his fellow-creatures. These are benefited, inestimably benefited, when they are brought to the faith of Christ; and, therefore, the Christian is anxious to bring them over to that faith. He will both desire and endeavour to lead others into ways, which he knows to be ways of "joy and peace;" and still further, which he knows to be the only ways of safety to the soul.

This appeared not long afterwards, when we find the same principle operating still further, and urging the scattered disciples to a bolder measure. Hitherto they had *preached the word to none, but unto the Jews only.*

20. ***And some of them were men of Cyprus and Cyrene, which, when they were come to Antioch, spake unto the Grecians,*[5] *preaching the Lord Jesus.***
21. ***And the hand of the Lord was with them, and a great number believed, and turned unto the Lord.***

At first these messengers of the gospel, having been brought up in all the Jewish prejudices, must have felt some doubt whether they were acting in conformity with the will of God, in preaching the Lord Jesus to any *but unto the Jews only.* But when a *great number of the Grecians believed, and turned unto the Lord,* an end would be put to their doubts; however marvellous in their eyes, it was the Lord's doing. They turned to Him, towards whom no man can turn, "except the Father draw him." And if the Father so drew these Grecians that they should turn unto the Lord, there was no further doubt as to the Father's will, whether they themselves should *speak unto the Grecians.* It became

[5] A difficulty arises in the original from the word Ελληνισται, Grecians, commonly used to signify those of Hebrew parentage, but speaking the Greek language. This, however, must have been the language of the Jews, who are before mentioned, and mentioned in contrast with these Grecians. So that we are forced to understand here, by Grecians, persons who were by birth Gentiles. In some approved manuscripts the word is Ελληνες, and is received into the text by many modern Editors.

plain, that "God had granted unto the Gentiles also repentance unto life."

22. *Then tidings of these things came unto the ears of the church which was in Jerusalem: and they sent forth Barnabas, that he should go as far as Antioch.*
23. *Who, when he came, and had seen the grace of God, was glad, and exhorted them all, that with purpose of heart they would cleave unto the Lord.*
24. *For he was a good man, and full of the Holy Ghost and of faith: and much people was added unto the Lord.*

As was before stated, the apostles remained at Jerusalem. Having their residence there, from thence they directed measures which seemed desirable; and when needful, sent out some of their body, to make inquiry and advise. Such a messenger was Barnabas. He was now considered as an apostle; and he came in the name of his brethren to Antioch, in consequence of the tidings which had reached their ears. Had it been laudable zeal, or had it been unwarranted rashness, which preached the word to the Grecians? This question was easily answered, the doubt speedily removed, when *he came and saw the grace of God:* saw undoubted signs of a work which belongs to the Spirit of God alone. He finds *a great number* who had gladly heard the word of those who spoke to them, *preaching the Lord Jesus;* and who, having "received him and believing in his name," had been made heirs of the everlasting covenant, and *added unto the Lord.*

We may easily conceive that great effects would follow the arrival of a man like Barnabas among such a company of believers. The persons who had hitherto preached Jesus unto them, had spoken in the fulness of their hearts:—what they had believed, they had declared; what they had heard and known, they told; and what they felt, they had communicated. But here was a man, instructed in knowledge; mighty in the scriptures; able to bring out of his store "things new and old." One, too, *full of the Holy Ghost, and of faith*: who had for many years seen the progress of the word, and had experience of its effects upon the heart. He was also, we are informed, *a good man*:—some might have felt a lurking jealousy, when they saw the Gentiles admitted to the same privileges as the Jews, without respect of persons; but it was not so with Barnabas: he, *when he saw the grace of God, was glad, and exhorted them all, that with purpose of heart they would cleave unto the Lord.*

And very important was the main subject of his instruction, as here recorded. Our Lord, in his wonderful parable of the Sower, has told us what in such cases to fear and guard against. He has told of those who, when they have heard the word, immediately receive it with gladness; but have no root in themselves, and so endure but for a time; afterward, when persecution or affliction ariseth for the word's sake, immediately they are offended.[6] We have too much reason to dread this. We see the blossoms of the spring: the trees are white with them: it would seem as if the husbandman must "pull down his barns, and build greater," so large will be the store. But how few at last are gathered in! Some are rudely plucked off by violence; and some are gradually withered by untimely blasts; and some are

[6] Mark iv. 7.

unable to withstand the daily influence of the summer sun: and so one and another and another drops and fails, and small is the number which remains to reward the planter's labour.

Alas! it is but too exact a picture of the effect of example, opposition, and temptation upon the frail and corrupt heart which has once received the truth with joy.

This, then, was the danger against which Barnabas warned the infant church at Antioch. *They had turned to the Lord* with sudden impulse: they must *cleave to him with full purpose of heart.* For so the Lord himself had "said to those Jews which believed on him: If ye continue in my word, then are ye my disciples indeed; and ye shall know the truth, and the truth shall make you free."[7] The value of the plant is neither in the blade nor in the blossom; but in the ripened fruit. And the "honest and good heart" is that which, having "heard the word, keeps it, and brings forth fruit with patience." "We are made partakers of Christ, if we hold the beginning of our confidence stedfast unto the end."[8] "Blessed is the man that endureth temptation: for when he is tried, he shall receive the crown of life, which the Lord hath promised to them that love him."[9]

[7] John viii. 31. [8] Luke viii. 15; Heb. iii. 14. [9] James i. 12.

XX.

BAPTISM OF A PROSELYTE FROM ETHIOPIA.—A.D. 34.

ACTS viii. 26—39.

26. *And the angel of the Lord spake unto Philip, saying, Arise, and go toward the south unto the way that goeth down from Jerusalem unto Gaza, which is desert.*

27. *And he arose and went: and, behold, a man of Ethiopia, an eunuch of great authority under Candace queen of the Ethiopians, who had the charge of all her treasure, and had come to Jerusalem for to worship,*

28. *Was returning, and sitting in his chariot, read Esaias the prophet.*

29. *Then the Spirit said unto Philip, Go near, and join thyself to this chariot.*

WE see here a beautiful example of the watchful providence of God, waiting to be gracious: waiting to bestow fresh gifts at the proper season. It explains the text which says, "To him that hath shall be given." For here is set before us a person who, though living in a distant and heathen country, though charged with authority and duty there, still left all at the appointed time, and came up to Jerusalem, to worship the God whom he had learnt to serve. The state of his heart may be perceived from his employment: as he travelled, he was engaged in reading the prophet Isaiah.

Perhaps at Jerusalem he had heard the things which had come to pass; perhaps he had been directed, through some of those who were preaching the Gospel there, and proclaiming Jesus as the Messiah, to the prophecies which especially related to him. And he did not disregard what he heard. His heart had been already turned to God: he had not closed his eyes against the light which had shone upon him, and he was now seeking fresh light from prophecy, and waiting till "the day star should arise,"[1] and enable him to perceive its full meaning.

To accomplish this end, Philip is first sent by an angel of the Lord to the desert which lay between Jerusalem and Gaza: and now *the Spirit said, Go near, and join thyself to this chariot.*

30. *And Philip ran thither to him, and heard him read the prophet Esaias, and said, Understandest thou what thou readest.*
31. *And he said, How can I, except some man should guide me? And he desired Philip that he would come up and sit with him.*
32. *The place of the scripture which he read was this, He was led as a sheep to the slaughter; and like a lamb dumb before his shearer, so opened he not his mouth:*[2]
33. *In his humiliation his judgment was taken away: and who shall declare his generation? for his life is taken from the earth.*
34. *And the eunuch answered Philip, and said, I pray thee, of whom speaketh the prophet this? of himself, or of some other man?*

[1] 2 Peter i. 19. [2] Isaiah liii.

35. *Then Philip opened his mouth, and began at the same scripture, and preached unto him Jesus.*
36. *And as they went on their way, they came unto a certain water: and the eunuch said, See, here is water; what doth hinder me to be baptized?*
37. *Then Philip said, If thou believest with all thine heart, thou mayest. And he answered and said, I believe that Jesus Christ is the Son of God.*

It was an easy task for Philip to show how the prophecy to which the Ethiopian had been directed was accurately fulfilled in the life and death of Jesus, and of no *other man.*

The "good ground," so softened and prepared, the "honest and good heart," received the seed of truth. He said, *See, here is water; what doth hinder me to be baptized?*

Not long before, Philip had seen a like eagerness in a man of a very different stamp, Simon the soothsayer, who, thinking that he perceived an opportunity of gain, was quick to seize it; and offered money for what he thought would prove money's worth to him. So it is with all who are keen after any earthly good; they lose no opportunity, they suffer no delay. This quickness and eagerness is not extinguished, but transferred to a better object, when spiritual things take possession of the mind. There must be no delay. "The kingdom of heaven is like unto a treasure hid in a field; the which when a man hath found, he hideth, and for joy thereof goeth and selleth all that he hath, and buyeth that field." [3] So it was with this stranger. He felt within himself, If we know not what a day may bring

[3] Matt. xiii. 44.

forth, and if "there is but one name under heaven given among men whereby we may be saved," I must be inscribed with that name. I must receive that blessing whilst I can; and secure for myself the treasure which is laid up in Christ. *What doth hinder me to be baptized,* since that is the gate of his mercy, the entrance into the everlasting covenant? Let me at once put off the old man, which is "corrupt according to the deceitful lusts; and put on the new man, which after God is created in righteousness and true holiness."[4]

Such would be his thoughts. Philip encourages them, throws no obstacle in the way of his desire.

Simon, whose case had been before related, had not believed with all his heart, and had "no part nor lot in the matter," though the rite of baptism had been solemnised. If the Ethiopian did believe,—so believe that *Jesus Christ is the Son of God,* as to trust in him for all that the soul can need, or God sees fit to bestow,—then he had part in this salvation. The blood of Christ should "wash away his sins," as water cleanseth the defilement of the body: nay, there should be in him "a well of water, springing up into everlasting life:"[5] he should "receive the gift of the Holy Ghost,"[6] to comfort, and strengthen, and purify his mind.

38. *And he commanded the chariot to stand still: and they went down both into the water, both Philip and the eunuch; and he baptized him.*

39. *And when they were come up out of the water, the Spirit of the Lord caught away Philip, that the eunuch saw him no more: and he went on his way rejoicing.*

[4] See Eph. iv. 22—24. [5] John iv. 14. [6] Acts ii. 38.

We can easily conceive that this man would *go on his way rejoicing*. We can understand his feelings, and enter into the state of his mind. We know that he was acquainted with the Scriptures; which had brought him to perceive his condition in the world, as the creature of a pure and holy God. He must often have felt within himself a doubtful and anxious apprehension, as to his state in the sight of that God. The Scripture told him what God required: but he knew likewise his own heart and practice; and he could not but see in how many things he had offended, and "come short of the glory of God." Like a mariner on a stormy sea, in a sinking vessel, he would be full of doubts and fears. Now came certainty instead of doubt, and hope instead of fear. He had found an anchor for his soul, and fixed it upon Christ, the rock of ages. He had received a proof, proof not to be disputed, of God's "good-will towards men;" his love and pity for the creatures he had made. Nay, he had received for himself a token of that love, and was enrolled as one of his adopted children. So *he went on his way rejoicing*. A wanderer on the earth, he had been led into a safe and certain path. A creature of God, he had found assurance of his favour. A sinful being, he had found a remedy for his sin: a dying creature, he had found "life and immortality."

It would not be all joy with him, as he passed onward in his course. He would have, like other men, his troubles; like other Christians, he would have his trials; but for the future there was hope, and for the present there was joy: "joy and peace in believing."

XXI.

THE DISCIPLES CALLED CHRISTIANS.

Acts xi. 26.

The disciples were called Christians first in Antioch.

In the first progress of the Gospel, those converted to the faith were spoken of, and described, as brethren, as disciples, as believers. The time was now come, when they should be distinguished by the name of Him in whom they believed, whose disciples they were, and who had made them brethren. They were united together in a body under the title of Christians. And this honour was first given to the church of Antioch, where the grace of God had so remarkably prevailed.

Here, then, a new and peculiar class of men appears, an order of men unknown till within the last few years—unknown at Antioch till within the last few months. What has created them, and distinguished them from others?

One had come into the world offering deliverance from sin, and from the consequences of sin: offering peace with an offended God: offering pardon and acceptance now, and in the end eternal life. The words of Jesus were, "He that heareth my word, and believeth in him that sent me, hath everlasting life, and shall not come into condemnation; but is passed from death unto life."[1]

This was either believed, or disbelieved; received, or refused. Some mocked; some neglected; others actively opposed themselves. These remained what they had been before; they were still followers of the law of Moses, or they were still Gentile idolaters. Those who were now for the first time called Christians, were those who believed the message; received the offer: were baptized in the name of Christ, and professed themselves his disciples, his followers. And their faith was briefly this. The world is lost by sin: ruined through Adam's fall: "in Adam all died." But as many as commit themselves to Christ, sent of God for their deliverance, are recovered from that ruin; their sin is expiated: God treats them as righteous; and his Spirit makes them such; renews their nature, and prepares them for his heavenly kingdom.

The Jewish assembly, for example, are told, that there is "salvation in no other; for there is none other name under heaven given among men, whereby we must be saved."[2] Those, then, who received this word gladly, and were baptized, "the multitude of them that believed," acknowledged the fact, that in themselves they were ruined, and that in Christ they had deliverance from ruin. They that are safe need not a deliverer; but they that are lost.

Such was the confession of these Christians concerning their own state. But what was He who had appeared as their deliverer? He was the Son of God,

[1] John v. 24. [2] Acts iv. 12.

"who was in the beginning with God, and was God;" proved to be so, in that he had risen from the grave, and ascended up to the glory which he had with the Father "before the world was." When the Ethiopian[3] desired to be baptized, Philip said, "If thou believest with all thine heart thou mayest. And he answered and said, I believe that Jesus Christ is the Son of God." Then "he baptized him."

It was natural, therefore, that Christians should have been styled *believers.* But this term alone did not completely describe them. They were also *disciples.* They looked up to Christ as a teacher as well as a redeemer. Had they been asked a reason of the way of life, the new and peculiar practice which they followed, the reply would have been: He "whose we are," and to whom we have devoted ourselves, has left us an example, and laid down for us a law. We forgive our enemies, we avenge no injuries, because he, "when he was reviled, reviled not again; when he suffered he threatened not,"[4] but committed his cause to God. We are ready to distribute, glad to communicate of this world's good, according as God hath prospered every man, because we are followers of him, who, "when he was rich, yet for our sakes became poor, that we through his poverty might be made rich."[5] We "keep under our body, and bring it into subjection," because he has assured us that "such is the will of God, even our sanctification:" that they must be "pure in heart," who are to possess "the inheritance of the saints in light:" that "without holiness no man shall see the Lord." We "set our affections

[3] Acts viii. 37. [4] 1 Peter ii. 23. [5] 2 Cor. viii. 9.

on things above, not on things of the earth," because we are taught of him to "lay up treasure in heaven." "For what shall it profit a man, to gain the whole world, and lose his own soul?"

The inquirer, who had gone thus far in acquainting himself with the faith of these Christians, must ask one question more, if he had any experience of his own heart. He must naturally proceed to say, How is this change produced in you? How are ye enabled to moderate your affections; to subdue "the desires of the flesh and of the mind;" to live in the world, and not be of the world?

To this, too, there was an answer. We were "baptized in the name of the Father, and of the Son, and of the Holy Ghost."[6] It was promised, that as the children of God, through faith in his beloved Son, we should "receive the gift of the Holy Ghost," who should change our original nature, and "put a new heart and a right spirit within us," and bring us "to will and to do" that which is approved of God.[7] And so we experience it to be. Old things are passed away: all things are become new. "We have put off the old man, which is corrupt after the deceitful lusts; and are renewed in the spirit of our mind; and have put on the new man, which after God is created in righteousness and true holiness."[8] So that now "the lust of the flesh, and the lust of the eye, and the pride of life," are not objects of desire to be courted by us, but objects of suspicion to be dreaded. "They are

[6] Matt. xxviii. 19.

[7] Acts ii. 38; 2 Cor. i. 22; Eph. iv. 30.

[8] Eph. iv. 22.

not of the Father, but of the world."[9] And "the time is short." "The Lord is at hand." "Our conversation is in heaven." "We look not at the things which are seen, and are temporal; but at the things which are unseen, and eternal."

Such were those, who were *called Christians first in Antioch.* Their faith and their practice were one. They received the doctrine, not merely as a truth to be acknowledged, but to be acted on, that when all were dead, Christ died for all, that they which live, might live to him.[1]

And such must be those, at all times, who expect to inherit the promise, trusting to which these Gentiles "turned from idols to serve the living and true God, and to wait for his Son from heaven." They must maintain the same faith; be actuated by the same motives; obey the same commands. Then are they Christians "indeed," and "altogether;" and will be known as such, not only in this present world, but in the sight of men and angels at "the great day."

[9] 1 John ii. 16. [1] 2 Cor. v. 15.

XXII.

CONVERSION OF SAUL.

ACTS ix. 1—9.

1. *And Saul, yet breathing out threatenings and slaughter against the disciples of the Lord, went unto the high priest,*
2. *And desired of him letters to Damascus to the synagogues, that if he found any of this way, whether they were men or women, he might bring them bound unto Jerusalem.*

SAUL had been before mentioned as "consenting unto the death" of Stephen. He speaks of this afterwards himself, when describing his former state of mind. "I verily thought within myself, that I ought to do many things contrary to the name of Jesus of Nazareth. Which things I also did in Jerusalem: and many of the saints did I shut up in prison, having received authority from the chief priests: and when they were put to death, I gave my voice against them."[1] For he had been "brought up at the feet of Gamaliel:" "taught according to the most perfect manner of the law of the fathers," and, "according to the most straitest sect of their religion, had lived a Pharisee."[2] Therefore, being "zealous towards God," he "punished in every synagogue" those who professed their faith in Christ, and "compelled them to blaspheme."[3]

In all this, as our Lord had foretold, he supposed

[1] Acts xxvi. 9, 10. [2] Ib. xxii. 3; xxvi. 5. [3] Ib. xxvi. 11.

that he was doing God service:[4] was doing what his religion required of him. Without much inquiry, he judged that whatever opposed the opinion and practice of his forefathers, must be wrong: and being of an ardent, zealous mind, he hotly persecuted those whom he looked upon as enemies of what he himself was following.

That he did this in ignorance and unbelief,[5] he afterwards acquaints us. But did he excuse himself, because he was zealous, though ignorant, and sincere, though unbelieving? Far from it. He frequently abases himself as "the chief of sinners," because he "persecuted the church of God." He felt that his ignorance and his unbelief, were his sins: the sins of which he had need to repent, and did repent: because he was ignorant for want of inquiry, and unbelieving through prejudice and obstinacy.

He has left us an instructive example, to examine before we condemn: to be jealous of our own hearts: not to take for granted that nothing can be wrong which we imagine to be right; nothing right which we imagine to be wrong. Many have been fatally deceived, while pursuing what they held to be the good old way.

Doubtless, the heart, the conscience, the understanding, must determine our conduct. They are given us for that purpose. But the heart must be guided, for it is "deceitful above all things:" the conscience must be instructed according to God's law; the understanding directed by his grace: lest "ignorantly and in unbelief," but still to our eternal ruin, we "put darkness for light, and light for darkness."

[4] See John xvi. 2. [5] 1 Tim. i. 13.

Saul did this, whilst *breathing out threatenings and slaughter against the disciples of the Lord,* he set out for Damascus, a city where great numbers of Jews were resident, and many had been converted to the faith. These were now threatened with a heavy storm; when it pleased God in a most unexpected manner to disperse the cloud, and give them joy for heaviness.

3. *And as he journeyed, he came near Damascus: and suddenly there shined round about him a light from heaven:*
4. *And he fell to the earth, and heard a voice saying unto him, Saul, Saul, why persecutest thou me?*
5. *And he said, Who art thou, Lord? And the Lord said, I am Jesus whom thou persecutest: it is hard for thee to kick against the pricks.*[6]
6. *And he, trembling and astonished, said, Lord, what wilt thou have me to do? And the Lord said unto him, Arise, and go into the city, and it shall be told thee what thou must do.*
7. *And the men which journeyed with him stood speechless, hearing a voice, but seeing no man.*

Saul had been as an animal unsubdued to the yoke, and contending against his master: *kicking against the pricks,* or goad, which urged him. This was a conflict in which he must fail at last. Yet the voice which warned him to desist, was rather a gentle than an angry voice; not so much of just indignation, as of kind remonstrance. *Saul, Saul, why persecutest thou me?* Why persecutest thou Him, who came to bless thee: came that thou "mightest have life, and have it more abun-

[6] A proverbial expression. The unbroken bullock kicks against the driver's goad.

dantly?" Instead of contending against that which thou canst never overcome, "take my yoke upon thee, and learn of me: for I am meek and lowly of heart; and thou shalt find rest unto thy soul."

8. *And Saul arose from the earth; and when his eyes were opened, he saw no man: but they led him by the hand, and brought him into Damascus.*
9. *And he was three days without sight, and neither did eat nor drink.*

Such was the effect of what had taken place, both upon his body and his mind. His outward sight was closed. But his inward sight had received new strength and vigour. We are told, afterwards, how he was employed. "Behold, he prayeth."[7] He was engaged, then, these three days, in turning the eyes of his mind towards himself, with "mourning, and fasting, and prayer." The Spirit was "reproving him of sin, and of righteousness, and of judgment;" and laying the foundation of a life to be hereafter spent in faith, and not in unbelief; in the true service of God, and in zeal "according to knowledge."

The event shows, that what had happened to him was nothing in the common course of nature. A storm, or a stroke of lightning, might take away the senses for a time: might benumb the vital powers. But when the man recovered, he would be the same man: think, and judge, and act, as he had acted and judged before. Saul, when his bodily strength was restored, was no longer the same man. A change was effected in his heart, which can be effected by God

[7] Acts ix. 11.

alone. He was still zealous; but his zeal was not to destroy men's lives, but to save them. He was still sincere and active, but not presumptuous or rash: he humbly asks, *Lord, what wouldest thou have me to do?* What is thy will, in the employment of my talents, means, and opportunities?

Thus it is, according to the parable:[8] "When a strong man armed keepeth his palace, his goods are in peace." Satan, unknown to Saul, was in fact the master whom he was serving: was, as a strong man, forcing him to use his powers to destroy the Christian faith. And his goods were in peace. Saul, then, had no compunctious feelings: never perceived that he was the slave of Satan, and the adversary of God. But now it had happened, according to the conclusion of the parable:—"When a stronger than he shall come upon him, and overcome him, he taketh from him all the armour wherein he trusted, and divideth his spoils." Saul had been wrested out of the power of Satan; and the conqueror would turn to his own use "the spoils:" would engage in his service the faculties which Saul so eminently possessed; and employ the vigorous understanding, the acquired knowledge, the active zeal, and the unwearied energy of this new disciple, to "bear his name before the Gentiles, and kings, and the children of Israel."

It is not our business to inquire why the Lord saw fit to make Saul a *chosen vessel* for his service, and to bring him into his service by extraordinary means. "His ways are far above out of our sight." But though we cannot always perceive his reasons, we are

[8] Luke xi. 21.

quite sure that he has reasons. Ignorant or perverse men may act without reason; but it is impossible that God should do so. "Shall not the Judge of all the earth do right?"

In the usual course of God's dealings with man, his grace does not enlighten those who are acting as Saul was acting: giving way to perverseness, obstinacy, and malicious passions. His ordinary and sure mode of dealing is: "They that seek me, shall find me." "The meek will he guide in judgment."

But in every age he has been known to snatch some from the midst of sin, as "brands from the burning;" thus showing, that none need despair; that repentance is open to the worst; that "the blood of Christ cleanseth from all sin;" and that the power of the Holy Spirit is such as to soften the most stony heart. Paul himself was of opinion that this was the purpose of God's mercy to him, saying to Timothy, "Howbeit, for this cause I obtained mercy, that in me first Jesus Christ might show forth all long-suffering, for a pattern to them which should hereafter believe in him to life everlasting."[9]

And wherever the gospel has been preached, this example of the favour of God shown to one who had before been "a blasphemer, a persecutor, and injurious," has proved a comfort to the repentant sinner. It is calculated to give encouragement to any one who may remember former wickedness with anguish of soul. He has here an instance of one like himself, to whom "Christ Jesus did show forth his long-suffering:" that is, whom he received and pardoned. The

[9] 1 Tim. i. 16.

same merciful Lord has still the same will and the same power to save all who come to him in the spirit of Saul, humbly inquiring, "Lord, what wouldest thou have me to do?" He "will in no wise cast them out." He "will show them of his covenant." He "will guide them with his counsel;" he will hereafter "receive them in glory."

XXIII.

CONSTITUTION OF THE CHURCHES.

Acts xiv. 23.

23. *When they had ordained them elders in every church, and had prayed with fasting, they commended them to the Lord, on whom they believed.*

They who were performing this office were Paul and Barnabas, who had made a circuit through the different towns where congregations of Christians had been established, confirming the souls of the disciples, exhorting and instructing them. At the same time, they ordained certain members of the Church who were most fitted to become overseers of the flock, and take account of the souls of their brethren.

When nation rises against nation, and a country is overrun and conquered by a successful enemy, the victorious commander passes through it, inspects the fortresses, instructs and encourages those who garrison them, and puts those officers in charge who are most able to maintain discipline and secure fidelity. Of a like nature was the journey in which Paul and Barnabas were engaged, though they brought peace and not war, and though the kingdom which they were establishing was "not of this world." They had disturbed the reign of Satan, and weakened his power in all this district of Asia, and had set up, instead, the gospel of Christ. And now they visit the principal places where christian companies had been formed, acquaint them with the will of their Sovereign more perfectly, and *ordain in every church* those best suited for the purpose, who might instruct, rebuke, exhort with all authority.

These were called *elders*. It was a term familiar to the Jews, who had been accustomed to rulers and elders of the congregation.[1] In every company of believers, some would be more fit than others for such an office: would have more talent, more knowledge, more zeal, more opportunity of applying themselves to the work. And these being selected by those who knew them best, were approved by the apostles, and solemnly appointed to their office with fasting and prayer.[2] They were, in fact, pastors of their respective flocks. They were those whom fourteen years afterwards Paul summoned from Ephesus and other neighbouring churches to Miletus, and exhorted with so

[1] Exod. xvi. 22: xvii. 5. Numb. xi. 16. Deut. xxxi. 28.

[2] So Clement, 1st Ep., states, that the apostles, as they carried the gospel through regions or cities, established their first fruits (earliest and best converts) as bishops (*i. e.* elders), and deacons of those who should afterwards believe. Sometimes one, sometimes more than one, was appointed to each congregation.

much earnestness and warmth, that they would "take heed to the flock, over the which the Holy Ghost had made them overseers, to feed the church of God, which he purchased with his own blood." They were those, concerning whom Paul afterwards gave directions to Timothy and Titus;[3] that they should commit to other "faithful men" the truths which they had themselves received: being at the same time careful to "lay hands suddenly on no man," but to select those who were blameless, apt to teach, patient, lovers of good men, sober, just, holy, temperate, holding fast the faithful word, as they had been taught, that they might be able by sound doctrine both to exhort the believers and to convince the "gainsayers."[4]

Then, further, they are those concerning whom the apostle gives injunction to the different churches, that "the elders which rule well should be counted worthy of double honour, especially they who labour in the word and doctrine."[5] So he exhorts the Hebrews, "Obey them that have the rule over you, and submit yourselves: for they watch for your souls, as they that must give account, that they may do it with joy, and not with grief."[6]

Such was the first establishment of the Christian church, as it exists, in substance, to this day, in all countries where the faith of Christ is professed as the religion of the land. The charge of a collected company, whose abodes conveniently adjoined each other,[7] was assigned to elders or presbyters, one or more, who

[3] Acts xx. 28. See also 1 Pet. v. 1—7.

[4] Tit. i. 5—9; 1 Tim. iii. 2—4.

[5] 1 Tim. v. 17.

[6] 1 Heb. xiii. 17.

[7] παροικοι, as in our parishes.

were overseers of that particular flock or fold. These, as here appears, were *ordained*, appointed, by the apostles; and they had deacons to assist them in their charge.[8] When the increase of the church throughout the world, and the decrease in the number of the apostles, as they gradually were called to their rest, made it impracticable that they should superintend the whole, they commissioned others, who might first relieve, and then succeed them. Such was Titus in Crete, and Timothy at Ephesus.[9] "For this cause," says Paul to Titus, "left I thee in Crete, that thou shouldest set in order the things that are wanting, and ordain elders in every city, as I had appointed thee." And so he writes to Timothy, "I besought thee to abide still at Ephesus, when I went into Macedonia, that thou mightest charge some that they teach no other doctrine, neither give heed to fables."

Such was the form which the church assumed, as it prevailed and grew. In this form we find it throughout its history, as superintended by bishops, and instructed by presbyters or elders, with deacons to assist them.

[8] 1 Tim. iii. 12, &c.

[9] After a while, the title of *overseer*, or bishop, was confined to these. Originally, there was no distinction. A bishop was a presbyter, and a presbyter was a bishop. This appears in the passage cited in the text. St. Paul instructs Titus to *ordain elders in every city*, and then proceeds, in the next line, to describe these *elders* under the name of *bishop*. As likewise in 1 Timothy iii. 1. Again, in Acts xx., those elders summoned to Miletus are termed indifferently πρεσβυτεροι or ἐπισκοποι. Compare v. 17 and 28. This confusion would have been inconvenient, when one of the elders was made superintendent, and had pre-eminence. Then he became *the* overseer; that is, the bishop. Accordingly, the history of every church contains a catalogue of its bishops. In this Antioch, for example, Evodius is reckoned first, Ignatius second.

How wonderful the change! "The world had not known God."[1] The few who sought after him, "if haply they might find him,"[2] had no certain clue, still less any authorized guide. Now provision is made, that none should be "strangers to the covenant of promise, without hope, and without God in the world."[3] A light was raised, and conspicuously set up, and transmitted from hand to hand, and from age to age, which "should light every man that cometh into the world." The young, on first entering it, might be dedicated to their Creator. Christ had ordered that they should be brought unto him. Every age, every condition of life, might "walk with God;" "set him always before them." The rich might become rich indeed; no longer "having their portion in this world" alone. And with the rich "the poor met together;" equal in the sight of "the Saviour of all men." It was the characteristic of his religion, that "the poor had the gospel preached unto them." An order of persons was set apart, who should instruct the young, inform the ignorant, warn the thoughtless, reclaim the wandering, comfort the distressed, edify the whole, dispensing to each his portion in due season. Thus a people might be trained on earth, who should hereafter be raised to an everlasting kingdom in heaven. And the motto of the church, of the whole church, and of every division of it, was this: "God was in Christ, reconciling the world unto himself." He will have "all men to be saved, and come to the knowledge of the truth." "Let him that is athirst, come. And whosoever will, let him take of the water of life freely."[4]

[1] 1 Cor. i. 21. [2] Acts xvii. 27. [3] Eph. ii. 12.
[4] 2 Cor. v. 19; 1 Tim. ii. 4; Rev. xxii. 17.

XXIV.

PAUL AND BARNABAS AT ANTIOCH.

ACTS xiv. 24—27.

24. *After they had passed throughout Pisidia, they came to Pamphylia.*

25. *And when they had preached the word in Perga, they went down into Attalia:*[1]

26. *And thence sailed to Antioch, from whence they had been recommended to the grace of God for the work which they fulfilled.*

27. *And when they were come, and had gathered the church together, they rehearsed all that God had done with them, and how he had opened the door of faith unto the Gentiles.*

SETTING out on their mission more than a year before from this place, Paul and Barnabas had been solemnly *recommended to the grace of God.* The prophets and teachers who were of the church of Antioch, after fasting and prayer, had "laid their hands upon them and sent them away."[2] And *the grace of God* had been granted to their prayer, and had blessed their journey to an extent to which their hopes could scarcely have been raised. They could hardly have expected that in Cyprus, where their work began, the first fruits of their ministry should be the Roman governor, the chief person of the island. They could hardly have expected that in Pisidia, when the name of Jesus was proclaimed

[1] Both towns of Pamphylia: Attalia, a sea port, now called Sattalia. Hence back to the *Syrian* Antioch, A.D. 46.

[2] Acts xiii. 3.

to a mixed assembly of Jews and Gentiles, the Gentiles should be the first to entreat that they might hear more of the word of this salvation: that these especially should "be glad, and glorify the word of the Lord."[3] They had set out, trusting in God, and not counting their lives dear unto themselves. But now their trust had become confidence, and their hope experience. The Lord had not only supported them when opposed by Elymas, or delivered them from death at Lystra; but he had brought strength out of their weakness, and allowed them to be the first who should illustrate his parable, "So is the kingdom of God, as if a man should cast seed into the ground; and should sleep, and rise, night and day, and the seed should spring and grow up, he knoweth not how."[4]

These were the glad tidings with which they now returned. They had to tell of the accomplishment of the prophecy: how "the people that walked in darkness had seen a great light; they that dwelt in the land of the shadow of death, upon them had the light shined."[5] They had to tell of idolaters by birth and habit, who had cast aside their "vanities, and turned to the true and living God." They had to tell of those who having been long "dead in trespasses and sins, were now quickened to a new life," "renewed in the spirit of their minds," walking before God in righteousness and holiness, and waiting for his Son from heaven.

Such were *the things which God had done with them*: had brought to pass through their agency. And now the brethren from Antioch were assembled, to "thank the Lord for his goodness," and to say, "This hath

[3] Acts xiii. 48. [4] Mark iv. 26. [5] Isa. ix. 2.

God wrought," and "it is marvellous in our eyes." He had fulfilled all that had been foretold. He had "given knowledge of salvation to his people, the Jews, by the remission of their sins." "He had opened the blind eyes" of the Gentiles, "to bring out the prisoners from the prison."[6] The prophet had once asked, "Hath a nation changed their gods, which are yet no gods?"[7] Now, nations *had* done this: had cast away their "idols of silver and their idols of gold, which their own hands had made unto them for sin."[8] Now, they who had lived "without God in the world," "unto every good work reprobate," had been quickened into spiritual life; had been "sanctified, had been justified, in the name of the Lord Jesus, and by the Spirit of our God."

We may well conceive with what interest the Christians at Antioch would listen to this report of the apostles. Still they spoke only of themselves, as instruments in God's hands: it is not what *they had done*—how successful they had been—but what *God had done with them*:[9] how he had *opened a door of faith* to those against whom before the door was shut: he had held up a light to the Gentiles, and had opened their eyes to see it, and their hearts to be guided by it into the way everlasting."

It was indeed a mystery, "that the Gentiles should be fellow-heirs, and of the same body, and partakers of the promise in Christ by the gospel: a mystery which in other ages was not made known unto the sons of men, as it was now revealed unto the holy apostles and

[6] Luke i. 77; Isa. xlii. 7. [7] Jer. ii. 11.
[8] Isa. xxxi. 7. [9] Μετ' αὐτων, as also Ch. xv. 4.

prophets by the Spirit."[1] But though their eyes had been holden, that they should not perceive this, it was the will of God from the beginning, "according to his good pleasure which he had purposed in himself," "that in the dispensation of the fulness of times he should gather together in one all things in Christ:"[2] "according to the eternal purpose which he purposed in Christ Jesus our Lord."[3] He had clearly foretold this: saying, by the mouth of Isaiah,[4] "It shall come, that I will gather all nations and tongues, and they shall come and see my glory. And I will set a sign among them, and I will send those that escape of them unto the nations;" those that escape "from the untoward generation"[5] to which they belong, shall be my messengers to all quarters of the earth; "to Tarshish, Pul, and Lud, that draw the bow" —(to Africa and Lydia)—"to Tubal, and Java, and the isles afar off"—(to Italy and Greece)—"that have not heard my fame, nor seen my glory; and they shall declare my glory among the Gentiles. And they shall bring all your brethren"—(your brethren, then, inasmuch as they are made partakers of the covenant, children of God by adoption)—"for an offering unto the Lord out of all nations. And I will also take of them for priests and Levites, saith the Lord."

Not a word of this, might the apostles say, has fallen to the ground. We set out from you; and we have been to distant isles, and distant lands, where the true God was no more known than among yourselves three years ago; where, instead of Him, they were ready to

[1] Eph. iii. 5, 6. See also Col. i. 26. [2] Eph. i. 9, 10.
[3] Eph. iii. 11. [4] Isa. lxvi. 18—21. [5] See Acts ii. 40.

worship us his messengers, "men of like passions with themselves." To these we have *declared his glory*. And many of them have become *an offering unto the Lord:* they have presented themselves "a living sacrifice, holy, acceptable to the Lord:" and are paying him "a reasonable service," instead of following senseless vanities. And of these, some have been *taken as priests and Levites;* we have ordained them elders in every church, God having put grace into their hearts first to learn, and then to teach: so to receive in their own souls the "water of life," that they are able to lead others to the same "wells of salvation." Thus is multiplied, as was written, "the seed of David, and the Levites that minister unto God."[6]

Thus they would delight to compare prophecy with the things which they had seen and heard, and so to bring "the light upon a dark place," and hold it up for the consolation and instruction of the brethren. It would encourage them to look onward towards the fulfilment of that further prophecy, when "all the family in heaven and earth," which is named after the name of Christ, shall meet in heavenly places, and unite in "giving glory to the God of heaven;" "saying, Amen: Blessing, and glory, and wisdom, and thanksgiving, and honour, and power, and might, be unto our God for ever and ever."

[6] Jer. xxxiii. 22.

XXV.

DISPUTE CONCERNING THE LAW OF MOSES.

Acts xv. 1—11.

1. *Certain men which came down from Judea, taught the brethren, and said, Except ye be circumcised after the manner of Moses, ye cannot be saved.*

All was going on favourably at Antioch, where *Paul and Barnabas abode long time with the* disciples. Meanwhile a question had arisen which threatened much trouble to the christian cause.

The doctrine of the gospel is, "Being justified by faith, we have peace with God through Jesus Christ." The Gentiles, therefore, who received the gospel, and confessed that Jesus was the Christ, were baptized in the name of the Father, and of the Son, and of the Holy Ghost, and were brought into covenant with God. They were thus placed on a level with the Jews. And now some of the converted Jews began to feel what is described in the Lord's parable. "These last have wrought but one hour, and thou hast made them equal unto us, which have borne the burthen and heat of the day."[1] They murmured against this equality, and this neglect of the ordinances of the law; and they asserted that it was necessary for the Gentiles "to be circumcised, and to keep the law of Moses."

[1] Matt. xx. 12.

Paul and Barnabas resisted to the utmost this new precept. It was a burthen which these Gentiles might refuse to bear: it was a yoke not lightly to be laid upon them. But still further, it was a contradiction of the gospel; directly opposed to "the truth as it is in Jesus."

The christian doctrine is, that "God was in Christ, reconciling the world unto himself;" so that "he that hath the Son hath life, and he that hath not the Son hath not life." This was the message entrusted to the apostles: and the promise was clear. "He that believeth and is baptized shall be saved."

But now certain men from Judea interfere, and *teach the brethren, saying, Except ye be circumcised after the manner of Moses, ye cannot be saved.*

This would nullify the whole purpose of the gospel. They that were under the old covenant must stand or fall by the law of Moses: but they that were under the new, must stand or fall, according as they believed in Him who was "the end of the law for righteousness." [2]

With these, we are told, *Paul and Barnabas had no small disputation.* You assert, (they may have argued,) that except a man keep the law, and comply with the rite of circumcision, he cannot be saved. How then, if that be so, can Christ have done all that is necessary to reconcile man to God? How is the sacrifice of Christ complete, if the rite of circumcision must be added to it? Our doctrine is, "that a man is not justified by the works of the law, but by the faith of Jesus Christ; for by the works of the law shall no flesh be justified." [3] This is our doctrine. But your doctrine is, that a man

[2] Rom. x. 4.

[3] Gal. ii. 16.

is not justified except he obey the ordinances of the law. This is "another gospel;"[4] this is not the gospel which has been committed to us; nor is it any gospel, any glad tidings at all: for it is to shake the foundations of our trust: to remove us from the rock on which the anchor of our hope is fixed, and to build our house upon the sand. "Behold, I Paul say unto you, that if ye be circumcised, Christ shall profit you nothing."[5] Christ is become of no effect unto you, "whosoever of you are justified by the law: ye are fallen from grace." Ye no longer receive salvation as the free "gift of God, through Jesus Christ." Ye join the works of the law with his work, in the business of justification. And ye bring yourselves under that system by which no man can stand.[6] "For as many as are of the works of the law are under the curse: for it is written, Cursed is every one that continueth not in all the things which are written in the book of the law to do them." "Christ has redeemed us from the curse of the law, being made a curse for us: that the blessing of Abraham might come on the Gentiles through Jesus Christ: that we might receive the promise of the Spirit through faith."

To this effect, as we learn from the Epistles, would be the disputation of Paul and Barnabas. Still the christian congregations desired to know what was thought upon this question at Jerusalem, where resided James, and Peter, and other pillars of the church. It was agreed that inquiry should be made.

2. *When therefore Paul and Barnabas had no small dissension and disputation with them, they determined that*

[4] Gal. i. 6. [5] Ib. v. 2. [6] Ib. iii. 10—14.

Paul and Barnabas, and certain other of them, should go up to Jerusalem unto the apostles and elders about this question.

6. *And the apostles and elders came together to consider this matter.*
7. *And when there had been much disputing, Peter rose up and said unto them, Men and brethren, ye know how that a good while ago God made choice among us, that the Gentiles by my mouth should hear the word of the gospel, and believe.*
8. *And God, which knoweth the hearts, bare them witness, giving them the Holy Ghost, even as he did unto us;*
9. *And put no difference between us and them, purifying their hearts by faith.*
10. *Now therefore why tempt ye God, to put a yoke upon the neck of the disciples, which neither our fathers nor we were able to bear?*
11. *But we believe that through the grace of the Lord Jesus Christ we shall be saved, even as they.*

Such is the course of reasoning by which Peter meets the question raised here by the Judaisers. There were no words of the Lord Jesus, by which he had positively set aside the law of Moses. He had indeed uttered words which might be turned to a contrary purpose. He had said, "I am not come to destroy the law, but to fulfil." He had said, "One jot or one tittle shall in no wise pass from the law, till all be fulfilled." *We* know what these assertions mean; but the Judaisers might naturally employ them to support their own opinion. Peter therefore meets the question upon more general grounds. The Judaisers affirmed, "Except ye be circumcised after the manner of Moses, ye cannot be saved." He answered: Ye argue that conformity to the law of Moses is needful, in order that a man be saved; be accepted of God. But a man who is not accepted of God, cannot have the special and best gifts of God. These men have the special and best gifts of God. *God, who knoweth the heart, bare them witness:* has testified that he received the Gentiles who repented and were baptized in the name of the Lord Jesus Christ. *He bare them witness, and put no difference between us and them, giving them the Holy Ghost, and purifying their hearts by faith.* If they could *not be saved,* if he had not "appointed them to obtain salvation through the Lord Jesus Christ,"[7] they could not have enjoyed that which was the special purchase of his death: could not have received that Holy Ghost, whom, when he ascended, he promised to send down upon his disciples, that He might "abide with them for ever," to comfort, to strengthen, to direct them. If they had not been justified, they would not have been sanctified. But he who *purified their hearts by faith,* showed that they were justified in his sight: had in herited that promised of the Lord, "He that believeth and is baptized shall be saved."

Plainly, therefore, might it be seen that nothing more was needful to them, though they were not circumcised, and did not observe the law of Moses. There was clear proof that the kingdom of heaven was open to them, because God had admitted them to a preparation for that kingdom. And if this was evident, let them beware how they disturbed a work which God had wrought, or closed a door which he had opened. The law was burthensome even to the Jews, who had

[7] 1 Thess. v. 9.

been brought up in it. Placed on the neck of the Gentile converts, it would prove an intolerable yoke. Why should they be forced to comply with that which, after all, could do nothing towards their salvation; which was but a course of discipline to bring men to the real grounds of acceptance with God? For even we who have kept the law, so Peter continues, do not any longer look to that for salvation; but to the grace of our Lord Jesus Christ, who is "the end of the law for righteousness to every one that believeth."[8] *We believe that through the grace of the Lord Jesus Christ, we shall be saved even as they.*

So the apostle Peter dealt with this question; and his mode of treating it has rendered the subject profitable to every age.

No one would now contend, that "*except a man keep the law of Moses, he cannot be saved.*" But it is a question which personally concerns every one, whether he shall be himself saved: whether he has an interest in the covenant of grace; is within the number of the chosen. Peter here instructs us where to look for the answer; viz., to the heart, whether it is *purified by faith;* to the practice, whether it is governed by the Holy Spirit. *God has given to the Gentiles the Holy Ghost*—so the apostle argues—*even as he did unto us.* He will not cast off those, whom he has made a holy temple to himself. He has *purified their hearts by faith.* They need no further qualification. He who is *saved by the grace of the Lord Jesus Christ,* is purified through the faith which he holds.

For there is that in faith, which purifies; which leads

[8] Rom. x. 4.

to sanctification. It shows the consequence of sin—eternal death. It shows the vastness of the inheritance—eternal life. And thus it makes sin hateful; a thing to be dreaded and resisted; and raises the affections from things below to things above. If it does not this, it is not the faith which saves. It is not justifying faith, if it is not sanctifying faith. And to this inherent test we must look, far more than to any outward distinction or ordinance, when the question is asked, Who shall be saved?

Oh, for higher measures of that faith! That faith which sets Christ crucified before us; crucified that he might make atonement for transgression! That faith that sets him before us as Mediator interceding for our sins, negligences, and ignorances! That faith which shows that any trials, any sacrifices, any mortifications which we must submit to here, are "not worthy to be compared with the glory which shall be revealed." Such is the faith which cleanses the heart from corrupt works "to serve the living and true God, and to wait for his Son from heaven." And living and dying in this faith, *we believe that through the grace of the Lord Jesus Christ we shall be saved, even as they* who met in the assembly at Jerusalem, and were the first-fruits of the gospel of Christ.

XXVI.

PAUL AT PHILIPPI.—A. D. 53.

ACTS XVI. 11—14.

11. *Loosing from Troas, we came with a straight course to Samothracia, and the next day to Neapolis;*
12. *And from thence to Philippi, which is the chief city of that part of Macedonia, and a colony: and we were in that city abiding certain days.*

TEN or twelve years after this his first visit, St. Paul writes to a body of Christians at Philippi, speaking of their persons with great affection, and of their faith with great confidence. The commencement of their renewed and holy state is related here. How precious a harvest, from how small a seed! So rapid is the growth, when God gives the increase.

Philippi was a town of some importance. Many Romans were mixed up with the native inhabitants. For it *was a colony:* it had been made part of the Roman empire. These, of course, were idolaters. Nothing relieved the darkness, the gross darkness which covered the people, except the few gleams of light which occasionally shone in from the Jews, who, here, as elsewhere, had formed a settlement, and through their worship and their scriptures brought some of those around them to the knowledge of the true and living God.

Arrived there, Paul must be "about his Master's business." He must deliver the message with which he was charged.

13. *And on the sabbath we went out of the city by a river side, where prayer was wont to be made; and we sat down, and spake unto the women which resorted thither.*

There was not here a magnificent place of worship; no temple like that of Jerusalem, which our Lord's disciples could not pass without remarking in admiration, "Master, what manner of stones, and what buildings are here?"[1]

Still, however, in a strange land, and in a heathen city, these foreigners could not omit the worship of God; and we see, by what follows, that God was with them, and that their "prayers had gone up as a memorial before him."

Here, then, the apostles spake unto the Jewish women, and to those who were their fellow-worshippers. We know what would be the character of their discourse. We may take it from the words of Zacharias,[2] "Blessed be the Lord God of Israel; for he hath visited and redeemed his people, and hath raised up a horn of salvation for us in the house of his servant David: As he spake by the mouth of his holy prophets, which have been since the world began: That we should be saved from our enemies, and from the hand of all that hate us: To perform the mercy promised to our fathers, and to remember his holy covenant; the oath which he sware to our father

[1] Mark xiii. 1. [2] Luke i. 68.

Abraham, that he would grant unto us, that we, being delivered out of the hand of our enemies, might serve him without fear, in holiness and righteousness before him all the days of our life."

Thus would the apostles preach unto their Jewish hearers. That the prophecies were now all fulfilled: that the sacrifices of the law had been explained: they had been types and shadows of what was now come; of that one full, perfect, and sufficient sacrifice, which God had received for the sins of the whole world. Then they would appeal to the proof of this which he had given, in that he had raised up Jesus from the dead: who was now for ever at God's right hand, where "he must reign, till he hath put all enemies under his feet;" and till he hath received into his kingdom all such as shall believe in his name, and confess him as their Saviour and their Lord.

The sower sowed the seed. What would come of it? Would the birds of the air devour it, before it could sink within the heart? Would Satan be able to prevent its entering in, and taking root?

This we may ask, wherever the word of God is spoken: Shall it be heard, as if it were not heard? Thought of no more? Shall it be at first admitted, and begin to spring; and afterwards be cut off by difficulties and temptations, or so choked with cares and worldly things, as to produce no fruit? Or shall it make a firm lodgement within, take root downward, abiding root, and bear fruit upward to the glory of him who planted it?

This must depend upon the heavenly husbandman. In this case, certainly, he was present to bless the work of the sower. There was at least one "honest and good heart," which so received the word that it did take root and grow, and brought forth fruit many fold. The historian says,

14. *And a certain woman named Lydia, a seller of purple, of the city of Thyatira, which worshipped God, heard us: whose heart the Lord opened, that she attended unto the things which were spoken of Paul.*

Thyatira was a city adjoining that region of Asia, where Paul had intended to preach the gospel, but was "forbidden of the Holy Ghost." In her course of worldly business this woman is brought across the sea to Philippi; and there, by the mercy of Providence, she hears and receives the word of life, which she could not have heard at home. She *attended to the words spoken:* heard them in a different manner from others of the same assembly. This is clearly implied here: and it is no less distinctly stated, that this was the Lord's doing: the effect of his influence. *Her heart the Lord opened:* opened what is not open naturally: opened what without his grace would have been closed.

So it is everywhere, and at all times. "Some believe the words spoken, and some believe not." And those who have been led to receive the scriptures, "as they are in truth, the word of God," will not be slow to give God the glory: to acknowledge that if he had not moved their hearts, they would have remained for ever shut against his word.

At the same time, we are not surprised that God did distinguish this woman by his blessing. It is in agreement with his usual ordinance, that they who seek shall find. For observe her conduct. She was but a sojourner in Philippi, come thither as a seller of purple cloth, for which her part of Asia was famous. But she had not, when she left her home, left also her religion behind her. She had sought out those who worshipped God, and had gone with them to the place of prayer.

Neither was she so engrossed with worldly affairs as to neglect all other things. She was not in Jerusalem, or in Judea, where the sabbath would be observed by all; but she was in a heathen city, where it would be observed by none except the Jewish residents. She might therefore have carried on her trade, and sold her purple cloth; but she had been brought to the knowledge of that God, who, when he made the world, "blessed the Sabbath day and hallowed it:" and therefore we find her, not in the market, not offering her purple to the passers by; but joining the party which had gone *out of the city by a river side, where prayer was wont to be made.*

Perhaps there are many whose advantages have been much greater than this woman's, who might learn a lesson from her.

Such was the person *whose heart the Lord opened that she attended unto the things spoken of Paul.* She attended to them. We know by experience what it is to attend, or not attend, to a thing spoken, an offer made. If we think it concerns us, may convey to us some good, or relieve us from some evil, we attend to it: we give our mind to it; we lay hold of it. Otherwise it passes by us like the wind. The words of Paul did not pass by this woman. It was matter of consequence to her, that "God had so loved the world, as to send his only Son, that all that believe in him might not perish, but have everlasting life." She thought within herself, This is the very comfort which I need. If I have a soul which must return unto him who gave it: if there is an account held of "the things done in the body:" then, "blessed is the man whose transgression is forgiven, whose sin is covered." And blessed be God, who has laid on One,—One infinite and omnipotent to bear it—that iniquity which must otherwise have overwhelmed us at the Judgment day. "Yea, blessed be God for his unspeakable gift!"

Thus she attended to the things spoken. It might be expected, perhaps, that she would lay them up in her mind, to be thought more upon hereafter, and acted on at "a more convenient season." No such delay could satisfy her. If he that believeth and is baptized is saved: if he is saved who receiveth Jesus as the Christ, and the sign of receiving him is the being baptized in his name; what hinders my being baptized? So she would reason. And we read that *she was baptized and her household.* All persons are justly fearful of delay when they find an offer suit them. There often is, indeed, delay in things relating to the soul. The Lord's Supper, for example, becomes now often, practically, the seal of faith, as the sacrament of Baptism was the seal of faith to Lydia: and this is delayed by many, for want of fitness, they urge; but really for want of faith, for want of will, for want of a heart entirely surrendered up to God. But when we truly feel the value of what is offered us, we do not wait till to-morrow for what we may secure to-day. And so it was with Lydia, and with her household, moved no doubt by her advice, and influence, and example. *She was baptized and her household.* They entered into the fold of which Jesus was the shepherd. They were grafted upon the vine of which Jesus is the stem. They were made part of that family in heaven and earth, which is named after Him whose "name is above every name." They were made members of Christ, children of God, and inheritors of the kingdom of heaven.

St. John has left a test of a sincere profession, saying, "By this we know that we have passed from death unto life, because we love the brethren. He that loveth not his brother, abideth in death."[1] Now Lydia, if truly converted, and "led by the Spirit" of God, had passed from death unto life. And she at once gives this sign of the indwelling Spirit, this proof of true conversion, that her heart overflows with love to those who had now become her brethren. We find her saying, *If ye have judged me to be faithful to the Lord, come into my house, and abide there. And she constrained us.* She would not allow the apostle and his party to remain any longer at their own charges, or to lodge among the heathen in the city; they must abide at her house. But why is it added, *she constrained us?* No doubt, because they were as scrupulous in receiving, as she was free and hospitable in offering. They might urge, We shall be chargeable to you: we shall interfere with your interests; for we are the objects of suspicion and enmity; and as you esteem us, because we are the apostles of Christ, others, because we preach in his name, revile and persecute us. So they might truly say. Lydia, however, had made up her mind.

[1] 1 Ep. iii. 14.

If Christ was hers, the friends of Christ must be hers too. They had been the instruments by which she received a treasure which she valued above earthly friendship, or earthly fortune, or life itself. And she must show them the poor return which was in her power: she must give them the refuge of her home. For her own sake, with the courtesy and the delicacy which is one of the surest signs of heavenly grace, and as a favour to herself, she entreats them, *If ye have judged me to be faithful to the Lord, come into my house and abide there. And she constrained us.*

It was a happy company. Surely we may pronounce them so. "The kingdom of heaven is like unto a merchantman, seeking goodly pearls; who when he hath found one pearl of great price, goeth and selleth all that he hath, and buyeth that pearl." Lydia had found this pearl of great price, and had secured it for her own. And, doubtless, the Lord who opened her heart that she should attend to the things spoken of Paul, would not desert her now, but enable her to experience the "joy and peace of believing."

And Paul, too, would be happy. God had given him these firstfruits of his visit to Philippi. He had that proof that God was with him of a truth; and a fresh jewel was added to the "crown of rejoicing,"[1] which he was providing against the great day, when both he that soweth and he that reapeth may rejoice together.

[1] 1 Thess. ii. 19.

XXVII.

PAUL AND SILAS IN PRISON.

ACTS xvi. 25.

22. *And the multitude rose up together against them; and the magistrates rent off their clothes, and commanded to beat them.*
23. *And when they had laid many stripes upon them, they cast them into prison, charging the gaoler to keep them safely:*
24. *Who having received such a charge, thrust them into the inner prison, and made their feet fast in the stocks.*

THE apostles at Philippi had relieved from an evil spirit a young woman, whose masters had used her peculiar properties to assist them in their trade of soothsaying or divination. The cure which they effected had no influence upon the men who had profited by her malady, except to excite their indignation. When they saw that the hope of their gains was gone, they stirred up the people against those troublers of the city, those innovators in religion, who were "teaching customs contrary to the laws of Rome," Philippi being a Roman colony.

It is grievous to reflect, in every state of society, how many have a sort of vested interest in sin and error. And when the word of God is brought forward which refutes such error, and condemns such sin, then these bestir themselves: the "strong man armed" will not surrender "his palace" without a struggle; they instigate their party and inflame their neighbours, saying, *These men, being Jews,* (or whatever else they see fit to call them,) *do exceedingly trouble our city, teaching customs which* we have never been used to observe. And too quickly is the flame excited, and finds fuel to feed it in too many hearts. So it proved in the present instance, as soon as the rumour was spread, and the accusation heard.

25. *At midnight Paul and Silas prayed, and sang praises unto God; and the prisoners heard them.*

One who heard two prisoners thus engaged, would be led to suppose that they had been declared innocent, and were on the morrow to receive a full discharge. The case of Paul and Silas was very different. On the morrow they were to be brought before an angry populace, and tried by magistrates who had already treated them cruelly and unjustly: and now, while still suffering from the many stripes which had been laid upon them, they had been thrust into the inner prison, and their feet set fast in the stocks. Still they were tranquil and calm, "committing themselves to him that judgeth righteously:" nay, more than calm—joyful—and with hearts unfettered and spirits unrestrained, they *sang praises unto God,* so that their fellow *prisoners heard them.*

It was the fulfilment of their Lord's promise: "Peace I leave with you; my peace I give unto you. In the world ye shall have tribulation; but be of good cheer; I have overcome the world."[1]

It is interesting to inquire, how this promise is fulfilled: through what medium could men, who had the feelings and nature of men, be in this state of mind at such a time? Cruelly beaten, with the smart of many stripes upon them: placed in an inner prison, and in a painful posture: and with every reason to expect still further suffering on the morrow. Now we are truly told, by him who had himself undergone this, that "no chastening for the present seemeth to be joyous, but grievous."[2] How then is nature overcome? How was it overcome in this case? How were Paul and Silas enabled not to pray only;—that we might expect—many will pray at such a time who pray at no other—but to show signs of cheerfulness and thankfulness: to *sing praises unto God.*

Two things joined to produce this.

First, the Spirit of God, shed abroad upon their hearts. And next, the expectation of a great reward in heaven.

First, the Spirit of God produced that in them which Paul desired that it might produce in others: it "filled them with joy and peace in believing." It testified within them that they were children of God, for whose good all things should work together; and that he "of very faithfulness had caused them to be troubled." This thought was sufficient to outweigh all their present pain and trial: just as one unhappy thought, one pang of fear, one sting of conscience, one cloud of horror disturbing the mind, is able to over-

[1] John xiv. 27; xvi. 33. [2] Heb. xii. 11.

shadow every outward means of comfort, and to cover the richest or gayest scene with the spirit of heaviness.

"Why is thy spirit so sad, that thou eatest no bread?"[3] Such were the words of a queen to a king: of Jezebel to Ahab, when he had "come into his house, and laid him down upon his bed, and turned away his face, and could eat no bread." He had not been struck with illness: no calamity had come upon him: whatever could minister to his pleasure, his luxury, was within his reach. Yet there he lies, and might envy the poorest of his subjects, whose mind was at ease. He was under the influence of an evil passion, and therefore was he sad. He coveted the vineyard of Naboth; and disappointment in this desire made all that he possessed seem worthless in his eyes. He had none of the Spirit of God within him; therefore nothing could give him peace and joy. The apostles had that Spirit: and therefore they could feel joy, not only when comfort shone around them, as in the house of Lydia, but even now, when all outward comfort was withdrawn. They had a light which nothing could extinguish: a sense of peace which no injury could remove; and therefore they could "joy in tribulation also." They had that comfort with which all God's people are comforted; which he alone can give, and he alone can take away.

At the same time, the large measure of spiritual joy vouchsafed to Paul and Silas on this occasion, is not often the lot of Christians in ordinary life. It is a cordial, and reserved for great necessities. God suits his gifts to the circumstances of his people. He be-

[3] 1 Kings xxi. 5.

stows that in their seasons of affliction, of persecution, of earthly trial and privation, which he withholds at other times. He gives to every individual of his people according to their several necessity, according as he sees to be expedient for them. Comfort was now expedient for Paul and Silas: all without was dreary, they must be cheered within: and they were cheered; and *the prisoners heard them,* not murmuring over their misfortunes or their injuries, but *praying and singing praises unto God.*

But, doubtless, there was a thought through which this comfort was conveyed and impressed upon the heart. They "had respect unto the recompense of reward." They looked unto the end. It is the end which sweetens the present toil. A man "rises up early, and late takes rest, and eats the bread of carefulness:" not because such labour is in itself delightful to him, but because it leads to something he desires: he may so acquire honour, or obtain wealth: his family may be better provided for. And for this he bears the present toil. Such too is the principle of the Christian. He denies himself, he "keeps under his body, and brings it into subjection." He submits to reproach. He suffers, if need be. Because he looks beyond the present trial to the future reward. He is assured that his "light affliction, which is but for a moment, shall work for him a far more exceeding and eternal weight of glory."

This, then, was the immediate spring of comfort which the disciples were now tasting, and through which they were supplied with peace and joy. We know it was, for they have told us so. Paul tells us his habitual state: "To me, to live is Christ, and to die is gain." As the servant of Christ, and in obedience to his will, he was always labouring, and now he was suffering. Had his life been taken, as he had every reason to expect, it would have been his gain; it would have carried him earlier to that rest which awaited him: that rest, of which some years after he speaks with so much transport: "I am now ready to be offered, and the time of my departure is at hand. Henceforth there is laid up for me a crown of righteousness, which the Lord, the righteous Judge, shall give to me at that day: and not to me only, but to all them that love his appearing."[4]

Not to me only. These last words show that the comfort possessed by Paul and Silas, even under their sharpest trials, was not conferred on them peculiarly; belonged to them, not as apostles of Christ, but as believers in Christ. Those who can apply to themselves the same description, "To me, to live is Christ," may also enjoy the same reflection as the support of every day of trial, the encouragement of every day of labour, the comfort of every day of care:—Death must come: and "to die is gain."

[4] 2 Tim. iv. 6—8.

XXVIII.

THE PHILIPPIAN GAOLER.

ACTS xvi. 26—32.

26. *Suddenly there was a great earthquake, so that the foundations of the prison were shaken: and immediately all the doors were opened, and every one's bands were loosed.*
27. *And the keeper of the prison awaking out of his sleep, and seeing the prison doors open, he drew out his sword, and would have killed himself, supposing that the prisoners had been fled.*
28. *But Paul cried with a loud voice, saying, Do thyself no harm: for we are all here.*
29. *Then he called for a light, and sprang in, and came trembling, and fell down before Paul and Silas,*
30. *And brought them out, and said, Sirs, what must I do to be saved?*

THUS it appears, why this earthquake had been ordered by Him, who has all the elements under his command. Not so much on account of the apostles. They might have been set free as quietly as in the case of Peter, when he awoke from his sleep and found himself at liberty. But God had mercy in store for the keeper of this prison. The earthquake which shook the foundation of the prison, shook also that which is often more hard to move—the stony heart. The bands were loosed which had held the prisoners' limbs; those stronger bands were also loosed, in which Satan had held this keeper of the prison. He perceived by the earthquake, and by the conduct of the apostles which ensued, that some mighty power attended them, and that to persecute them was to oppose that power; to ill-treat them was to fight against God. So *he came trembling, and fell down before Paul and Silas, saying, Sirs, what must I do to be saved?* How can I escape the vengeance of this power which protects you, and which, by severely handling you, I have provoked?

We cannot but observe, here, the different dealings of God with men's hearts. Sometimes the voice which calls them is the still small voice, which no one hears except he to whom it is addressed. So it was in the case which had recently been related, the case of Lydia; of whom we merely read, that "the Lord opened her heart, so that she attended unto the things which were spoken by Paul."

It happens thus with many now, who are brought up in a christian land. As there are many, who, possessing the same privileges, see as if they saw not, and hear as if they heard not, and never understand, or come to the real knowledge of the truth, so there are others who do attend to the things spoken, and receive them into their hearts, softened and prepared by the dew of Divine grace. The "seed is cast into the ground, and springs, and grows up," silently and unobservedly.[1] They hear the voice of God, whilst it is yet the still small voice. And blessed are they who do

[1] See Mark iv. 27.

so; lest he either pass by them altogether, or come to them in the whirlwind or the storm.

Sometimes he does thus reveal himself. It needs not the thunder which rends the heavens; it needs not the earthquake which shakes the foundations of the prison; perhaps illness, in a few hours showing a man the precipice on which he stands, and disclosing the gulf below; perhaps affliction—"the desire of the eyes," the treasure of the heart, taken away "at a stroke;" perhaps reverse of fortune, depriving a man at once of all that he most loved, and reducing him to that which he most dreaded—these are voices in which God sometimes speaks, and forces them who have been too long deaf to his mercy, to listen to his anger.

One thing, however, we must constantly bear in mind. Whether it be the gentle voice, or whether it be the voice of thunder, it is not the voice, but the Lord who sends the voice, that produces any effect upon the heart. There may be the earthquake, but the Lord is not in the earthquake; not a soul is shaken. There may be the cloud, but the Lord is not in the cloud. Not a drop falls—not one tear of penitence is shed. The dispensation effects nothing; the Lord must direct the dispensation, that it may not return unto him void, but accomplish the thing for which he sends it. Many hearts are as little penetrated by the judgments of God, as by his mercies. And the earthquake would have been no more to this gaoler, than the gracious tidings proclaimed by Paul had been to the magistrates who imprisoned him, if the grace of God had not attended the sign of his omnipotence, and moved the heart to ask, *Sirs, what must I do to be saved?*

When the heart was moved to this inquiry, the answer was at hand. No need of hesitation or delay.

31. *And they said, Believe on the Lord Jesus Christ, and thou shalt be saved, and thy house.*

32. *And they spake unto him the word of the Lord, and to all that were in his house.*

Here was no time for a laboured discourse, or a long system of instruction. Neither was it necessary. For a few sentences may convey the whole "mystery of godliness." Mystery though it be, such as never can be exhausted; though there are wonders connected with the gospel such as "angels desire to look into;" yet the whole of saving truth may be spoken in few words. The apostles may be supposed to have replied in terms like these to the anxious inquiry made of them.

You desire to know whether there can be mercy for you, and you may be saved from the wrath to come,—delivered from the just vengeance of that God whom you have been offending all your life, and whose power has been now displayed before your eyes. There *is* mercy for you. That God delighteth in mercy. Judgment is his "strange work." He willeth not the death of a sinner, but rather that he should come to repentance. This is the very truth which we are commissioned to proclaim, and for proclaiming which we are thus treated. We declare, that "God so loved the world, that he sent his only begotten Son, that all that believe in him might not perish, but have everlasting life." He was appointed, and he consented, "to bear our sins in his own body" on the cross, "that he might bring us to God." Join thyself to the company of those who "receive him." Be baptized and admitted among his flock, and *thou shalt be saved, and thy house.* Thy family, which may follow thy example, all shall become part of the Lord's family. For "this day is salvation come into this house." And "whosoever shall call upon the name of the Lord, shall be saved."

In language such as this, we may suppose, the apostles *spake the word of the Lord* to the keeper of the prison and his household. They were ambassadors for Christ; the word of reconciliation was committed to them, that they might declare to the penitent rebel the terms of his forgiveness.

It was not all that was needful for him to know: he would still have much to learn both of doctrine and of precept. But this, and no other, must be the basis of his change of state; he must "arise, and wash away his sins" in the fountain of Christ's blood, and so enter upon a new life, following the commands of God, and walking from henceforth in his holy ways.

The case was urgent, and we cannot wonder if the work was sudden. The gaoler had seen that which feelingly convinced him that in a few hours he might be lost for ever. Therefore, *he took them the same hour of the night, and washed their stripes, and was baptized, he and all his, straightway.* The same grace which had reached his heart, extended to his household also; and they too received the message of the apostles, and were "baptized in the name of Jesus Christ for remission of sins."

In what follows, we perceive the manifest signs and proofs of that "new creature," which whoever is in

Christ Jesus will become, and must become. For he *brought them into his house, and set meat before them: and rejoiced, believing in God, with all his house.* So entirely his former thoughts had "passed away," and had been succeeded by others of a new and different complexion. Yesterday, he had no feeling for the apostles: bleeding from the stripes which they had received, unheeded, untended, he "thrust them into the inner prison, and made their feet fast in the stocks." He acted under command, and we need not accuse him of any extraordinary cruelty, but certainly he showed them no kindness, cared nothing for their miserable condition; for he had not yet learned to "put on, as the elect of God, bowels of mercy, kindness, meekness."[2] "Behold, all things are become new." Now he does care for them; now he has compassion on them; *took them the same hour of the night, and washed their stripes;* made amends, as far as might be, for former neglect and severity. Yesterday, it was their heinous offence that they were ministers of a God unknown to him; that they taught new customs, which it was not lawful for the people to receive. Now, it is their greatest honour, that they bear the message of the most high God. These men, who show us the way of salvation, must want no comfort or attention. *He brought them into his house, and set meat before them.* He thought nothing of the risk and danger which might follow such conduct towards the prisoners committed to his charge. Other considerations were now uppermost in his mind, and present inconvenience did not affright him.

[2] Col. iii. 12.

We are further told, that *he rejoiced, believing in God, with all his house.* He did not consider the faith which he had embraced as a thing to be submitted to, but to be rejoiced in. And with good reason. Is it no misfortune to be at enmity with God? to have nothing to hope from his mercy, everything to fear from his anger? Such had been the case with this man. Then, is it no blessing to be at peace with God?—to have nothing to fear from his anger, everything to hope from his mercy? Such now was the case with this man. "Being justified by faith, he had peace with God through Jesus Christ." He who before was "without God in the world," and who when taken from the world, could look only for "indignation and wrath, tribulation and anguish," was now reconciled to God by "the blood of the everlasting covenant;" his sins were blotted out, and he was "accepted in the Beloved." The "child of wrath" was become the child of God: the heir of the kingdom of darkness was become heir of the "kingdom prepared for the righteous." The sense of this, shed abroad in his heart by the Holy Ghost, would cause him to "rejoice in the Lord." "The God of hope filled him with all joy and peace in believing."

At the same time, the christian life is not always "joy and peace." We do not pretend that it is. The gaoler and his household, who now rejoiced, would doubtless find occasion hereafter for different feelings, while working out their salvation in the world. The very next day they might expect persecution from the magistrates, on account of the kindness shown to Paul and Silas. And not only would their outward comfort, but their inward peace, be disturbed; they would find resistance within, when their evil passions, now for a while subdued, began by degrees to rise against the new "law of the mind" which restrained them: when Satan, now dispossessed of his subjects, began to stir himself, and try to recover his dominion. The christian life is a race, and "he that striveth for the mastery" has much to do which is not always agreeable to flesh and blood. The christian life is a warfare, and "he that warreth" must endure hardships and trials, and be humbled sometimes, as well as sometimes triumph. In short, these, like others, must submit to the general rule, that "we must through much tribulation enter into the kingdom of God."

But still there was reason for rejoicing now. If there is "joy in heaven over one sinner that repenteth," there may well be joy on earth, when he who "was dead is alive again, he who was lost is found." There might hereafter be cause of sorrow for these very persons. But if we were never to rejoice on earth, because we might hereafter be called to weep, this world would be indeed a vale of tears. This man had secured to himself One who "is able to save unto the uttermost." Let not the foundations of their prison alone, but of the universe, be shaken; he need not fear, though "the heaven and the earth should pass away with a great noise, and the elements melt with fervent heat." He, "according to the promise, would look for new heavens and a new earth, wherein dwelleth righteousness." And meanwhile, he had One to rely on, who can be "touched with human infirmities," and "knows how to succour them that are tempted." Cheered by these thoughts, and hopes, and promises, we cannot wonder that he *rejoiced in God, with all his house.*

XXIX.

PAUL AT ATHENS.—A.D. 54.

ACTS xvii. 18—34.

18. *Then certain philosophers of the Epicureans, and of the Stoics, encountered him. And some said, What will this babbler say? other some, He seemeth to be a setter forth of strange gods: because he preached unto them Jesus and the resurrection.*

19. *And they took him, and brought him unto Areopagus, saying, May we know what this new doctrine, whereof thou speakest, is?*

20. *For thou bringest certain strange things to our ears: we would know therefore what these things mean.*

21. *(For all the Athenians and strangers which were there spent their time in nothing else, but either to tell, or to hear some new thing.)*

THE character of the people at Athens struck the sacred writer as unlike that to which he was accustomed in his own country. There was not the same activity in commerce and ordinary business. Still less was there the same certainty as to the great questions in which mankind are most concerned. The origin, or beginning of the world—the Divine nature—the duties of man—the real welfare of man,—all these things were settled for the Jewish people by their scriptures; but all these things were matter of doubt and dispute among the Athenians; and their philosophers, and the strangers who resorted thither for instruction, *spent their time in nothing else, but either to hear or to tell some new thing.*

It pleased God that one from a distant and obscure country should be now sent to declare to them truths which, with all their wisdom and searching, they never had discovered.

22. *Then Paul stood in the midst of Mars Hill, and said, Ye men of Athens, I perceive that in all things ye are too superstitious.*[1]
23. *For as I passed by, and beheld your devotions, I saw an altar with this inscription: To the unknown God. Whom, therefore, ye ignorantly worship, him declare I unto you.*
24. *God that made the world and all things therein, seeing that he is Lord of heaven and earth, dwelleth not in temples made with hands:*
25. *Neither is worshipped with men's hands, as though he needed any thing, seeing he giveth to all life, and breath, and all things:*
26. *And hath made of one blood all nations of men, for to dwell on all the face of the earth, and hath determined the times before appointed, and the bounds of their habitation:*
27. *That they should seek the Lord, if haply they might feel after him, and find him, though he is not far from every one of us:*
28. *For in him we live and move, and have our being: as certain also of your own poets have said, For we are also his offspring.*

[1] Or, as the phrase might be translated, *ye are disposed to venerate the powers above.*

29. *Forasmuch then as we are the offspring of God, we ought not to think that the Godhead is like unto gold or silver, or stone, graven by art and man's device.*

In these few words does Paul instruct the ignorance and refute the errors of these heathens.

Was the world made, or has it existed for ever? This was one of their questions. *God made the world, and all things therein.*

How is he to be worshipped? Will he inhabit the temples built in his honour? Will his favour be conciliated by the precious gifts which are offered at his altar?

He dwelleth not in temples made with hands; neither is worshipped with men's hands, as though he needed anything, seeing that he is Lord of heaven and earth, and giveth to all life, and breath, and all things. "They who worship him, must worship him in spirit and in truth."

Does it concern mankind that there is a God? Are they bound to reverence him, to consult his will? This the Epicureans denied.

He has made men for this very purpose, and *determined the bounds of their habitation, that they should seek the Lord, if haply they might feel after him, and find him.*

Does he notice men's conduct? Are their ways seen by him, and regarded by him?

He is not far from every one of us. Your own writers acknowledge this; for they say, *We are his offspring.* If then we are his offspring, *he is not like unto gold or stone;* he is a living God: *and in him we live, and move, and have our being.*

Thus does the apostle lay the foundation. He sweeps away the errors, that he may establish the truth. And then he proceeds to the more immediate subject of his ministry.

30. *And the times of this ignorance God winked at: but now commandeth all men every where to repent:*
31. *Because he hath appointed a day, in the which he will judge the world in righteousness, by that man whom he hath ordained: whereof he hath given assurance unto all men, in that he hath raised him from the dead.*

Till now, God had not seen fit to interpose, and make himself manifest to those who "did not like to retain him in their knowledge;" who gave no sign that they were really seeking after him, and desiring to find him. Now, however, the time of ignorance was past. God *now commandeth all men every where to repent.* They are no longer to walk after their own desires: they are no longer to make to themselves gods which are no gods: or think by an outward formal worship to pay that reverence which the Divine Majesty requires. *He hath appointed a day, in the which he will judge the world in righteousness:* he "will render to every man according to his deeds: to those who by patient continuance in well-doing seek for glory and honour and immortality, eternal life; but unto them that are contentious, and do not obey the truth, but obey unrighteousness, indignation and wrath, tribulation and anguish, upon every soul of man that doeth evil."[2]

[2] Rom. ii. 6—9.

But this judgment is to follow death. And they would ask, What can follow death? "Man giveth up the ghost, and where is he?"

God, who reveals this purpose, has given also evidence of his purpose. He has *given assurance* of it: in that *he hath raised from the dead that man whom he hath ordained;* and who shall come again to *judge the world in righteousness.* If Christ be not raised, then are our words vain. But Christ is risen; and by his rising has left a testimony of God's intention, and a proof of his power.

Thus does Paul, like the Baptist John, prepare the way for the Redeemer. The Baptist said, "Repent ye; for the kingdom of heaven is at hand." Be warned to "flee from the wrath to come." And so Paul acquaints the Athenians, that *God has appointed a day in which he will judge the world in righteousness.*

Are we surprised that here is yet no *gospel,* properly so called? No mention of the "Lamb of God, which taketh away the sin of the world?"

These hearers, as yet, were conscious of no sinfulness; needed no tidings of salvation, because they felt no sense of danger. We must first enact the law; we must first erect the tribunal; we must first give authority to the judge; we must first show that the result is, life or death; before the criminal will seek an advocate, or desire a mediator. And so far Paul has gone: he has made known to them the Governor of the world: he has declared the law: he has revealed the Judgment-day. Let them be awakened to their real state; let them be "pricked in their hearts," and say, "Men and brethren, what shall we do?" Let them ask, "Who shall stand when he appeareth?" Let them inquire, "Wherewith shall I appear before the Lord?" Then, how gladly would he proceed to preach unto them "a Saviour which is Christ the Lord:" how gladly declare the truth with which he was intrusted, "Whosoever shall call on the name of the Lord shall be saved."

But when they heard of the resurrection of the dead, some mocked. The idea of existence beyond this present world was not altogether strange to the heathens. Vague notions floated amongst them that the soul might survive, and continue to live in some new and different state. But what Paul meant by *the resurrection of the dead;* the resurrection of the whole man; with a body restored to him, with a consciousness of the same being which had lived, and thought, and felt, and acted, in this present world: this was entirely new to them; and when they heard of it, *some mocked,* and thought, no doubt, that it was enough to ask, "How are the dead raised up, and with what body do they come?"

And yet, had they inquired, instead of mocking, they might have found reason to see that it was not incredible that God should raise the dead. If man has been once formed—formed by the hand of a Creator—he may be formed again. God, who gave the first body, can restore "to every man his own body."[3]

But the seed fell by the wayside, and "the fowls of the air devoured it."

In other cases, when the seed is sown, the surface is

[3] See 1 Cor. xv.

less hard, but the event is still the same. So it proved with another class of these Athenian hearers. *Others said, We will hear thee again of this matter.* It was not so with the Ethiopian, who exclaimed, "Sir, here is water, what doth hinder me to be baptized?" It was not so with the gaoler at Philippi, who saw death on the one side and life on the other, and "at the same hour of the night was baptized, he and all his household, straightway." These Athenians put off the subject to a distance. *We will hear thee again of this matter.* Thou hast told an interesting tale. "When we have a convenient season, we will send for thee," and attend to it again. Nay, "now is the accepted time, now is the day of salvation." "To-day, if ye will hear his voice, harden not your hearts." The voice which, if ye had listened to it, might have been life from the dead, if now ye prove deaf to its summons, ye may hear no more for ever.

33. *So Paul departed from among them.*
34. *Howbeit, certain men clave unto him, and believed: among the which was Dionysius, the Areopagite, and a woman named Damaris, and others with them.*

The word, then, did not return altogether void. It had a purpose to perform, and it performed its purpose. *Some clave unto him.* The expression is strong. It implies that close adherence which we might expect when the soul is concerned. We may conclude that they followed Paul to his abode, and inquired more particularly into "the strange things which he had brought to their ears." Perhaps Dionysius, like Lydia at Philippi, constrained him that during the remainder of his stay at Athens he should abide at his house. The Spirit had so awakened his heart and conscience, that they responded to the things which he heard. He did not resist that feeling, and lightly dismiss the apostle till another time; but he, and *Damaris, and others with them,* pursued their inquiry till the seed took deep and firm root, and they *believed*—they became converts to the gospel of Christ.

Dionysius, we are told, was an *Areopagite:* a member of that council which was called after its place of meeting, *Mars Hill.* To be a member of that council, was to be a person of first importance. A person of such rank and station makes a greater sacrifice, if he leaves the party and the connexions to which he has belonged, than one who has fewer worldly interests to abandon. This, no doubt, was the ground of the Lord's remark, "How hardly shall they that are rich enter into the kingdom of God!" But there was no want of such persons among those who first embraced the gospel. There were enough to show that those whose education had enabled them to form a judgment upon a matter placed before them, when they were brought to attend to the apostles, found that which they could not resist: nay, which they could not be satisfied without securing it as their own. Some mocked, others postponed; but not for want of proof, but for want of will—will to inquire, or yield to conviction.

So Paul departed from among them: left the learned Athenians. Their learning would soon be of no avail. "Man returneth to his earth, and all his thoughts perish." But he left behind him a small but a faithful company, whose learning would not perish. They had been "made wise unto salvation through faith that is in Christ Jesus." And these through endless ages shall find fresh mysteries to look into, fresh wisdom to adore.

XXX.

PAUL AT CORINTH.

ACTS xviii. 9—17.

9. *Then spake the Lord to Paul in the night by a vision, Be not afraid, but speak, and hold not thy peace:*
10. *For I am with thee, and no man shall set on thee to hurt thee: for I have much people in this city.*
11. *And he continued there a year and six months, teaching the word of God among them.*

THERE are seasons when the servants of God need especial comfort and encouragement. And there are seasons when he sees fit to communicate such consolation. It was given to Paul at Corinth. He was assured of protection. *Be not afraid, but speak, and hold not thy peace: for I am with thee, and no man shall set on thee to hurt thee.* He was assured, too, of what still more concerned him, that his "labour should not be in vain in the Lord." *I have much people in this city.* And here we observe the all-seeing eye, which is ever watchful over the interests of the soul. The Lord knows his own; knows them while they are yet "a great way off," and provides that they shall be brought nigh. Many had already believed and were baptized; and he foresaw that many more would be "added to the church daily," and it would become that large body, to which Paul afterwards addressed his letters, and from which the light of divine truth was reflected throughout a wide adjacent region.

Another remark arises from these words. They point to a bright example of the power of divine grace. Even in that luxurious and dissolute city (for this, to a proverb, was the character of Corinth) the Lord *had much people.* Paul might have replied, Lord, we know that "the unrighteous shall not inherit the kingdom of God." We know that the sins of adultery, and uncleanness, and idolatry, and covetousness, are abominable in the sight of "the High and Holy One which inhabiteth eternity." And such sinners were these. To these very persons he writes, after a few years,[1] "Such were some of you: but ye are washed, but ye are sanctified, but ye are justified in the name of the Lord Jesus, and by the Spirit of our God."

Here, then, were these, the *much people* whom the Lord foresaw, and for whose sake he favoured Paul with a special vision, so that *he continued there a year and six months, preaching the kingdom of God among them.* But still greater is the consolation handed down to all future ages by the fact which this example sets before us. The Lord knows every heart, and no individual escapes his notice who is disposed "towards the attainment of everlasting salvation." He beholds them

[1] 1 Cor. vi. 11.

from afar, while they are yet "enemies of God through wicked works:" he calls them by his word: he justifies them by his merits: he sanctifies them by his Spirit: they are those of whom he speaks, saying, "All that the Father giveth me are mine. And they shall never perish, neither shall any pluck them out of my hand."

12. *And when Gallio was the deputy of Achaia,*[1] *the Jews made insurrection with one accord against Paul, and brought him to the judgment-seat,*
13. *Saying, This fellow persuadeth men to worship God contrary to the law.*
14. *And when Paul was now about to open his mouth, Gallio said unto the Jews, If it were a matter of wrong or wicked lewdness, O ye Jews, reason would that I should bear with you:*
15. *But if it be a question of words and names, and of your law, look ye to it; for I will be no judge of such matters.*
16. *And he drave them from the judgment-seat.*
17. *Then all the Greeks took Sosthenes, the chief ruler of the synagogue, and beat him before the judgment-seat. And Gallio cared for none of those things.*

On former occasions, as before at Philippi and at Thessalonica, the magistrates had readily listened to the accusations made by the Jews against Paul, and had been accomplices in the ill-treatment which he received. Here the case is different. Gallio disregards

[1] *i. e.* When Gallio was proconsul. He was the younger brother of the philosopher Seneca. It is singular that Seneca speaks of him as remarkable for courtesy; or rather, perhaps, that easiness of temper which makes men popular. "Nemo mortalium uni tam dulcis est, quam hic omnibus."

them. He perceives that there was no transgression of the public law, which it was his office to maintain; no danger of tumult, except what the enemies of Paul might excite; and therefore he would not enter into the matter, and drove them from the court. God had so willed it. He had said to "the noise of the waves, and the madness of the people," Peace, be still. He had promised Paul, *No man shall set on thee to hurt thee.* Therefore Gallio is an exception to the other magistrates, and that which had been done elsewhere could not be done at Corinth.

There is no such promise made generally. No such promise was made to the apostle, except on particular occasions. The general promise is, that "all things shall work together for good to them that love God;" that whatever is suffered, shall be repaid, repaid abundantly: but certainly it is not promised that no opposition shall be encountered, or injury received. All we know is, that nothing can happen which is not overruled. "Even the hairs of your head are all numbered."

We are glad that Paul should escape without injury. But we cannot approve the character of the magistrate Gallio, who *cared for none of these things.* Things were brought under his notice which might have interested him. The earnestness of Paul, regardless of the danger to which he was exposed: even the earnestness of the Jews in maintaining their ancient law: the warm and anxious feelings excited in each party, might have roused him from careless indifference. But he was alike regardless of truth and error. His concern was, to carry on his government with as much ease as possible. His conduct is a specimen of the manner in which persons occupied in worldly affairs, and wholly intent upon them, suffer the most important subjects to pass as it were before their eyes, and pay no heed to them. That might be said of him, which will hereafter be so awful a recollection: "Nevertheless, know this, that the kingdom of God hath come nigh thee."

"In the day of the revelation of the Lord Jesus," how different will be the light in which all things shall appear! The veil shall be removed which overspreads the carnal eye; and those things will prove to be realities which were as shadows, and those to be shadows which had been treated as the only realities. Then all who had formerly *cared for none of these things*, will acknowledge them to have been alone wise, who have sought the Lord while he might be found, and "fled for refuge to lay hold of the hope set before them."

XXXI.

PAUL AT MILETUS.

ACTS xx. 13—24.

13. *We went before to ship, and sailed unto Assos, there intending to take in Paul: for so had he appointed, minding himself to go afoot.*
14. *And when he met with us at Assos, we took him in, and came to Mitylene.*
15. *And we sailed thence, and came the next day over against Chios; and the next day we arrived at Samos, and tarried at Trogyllium; and the next day we came to Miletus.*
16. *For Paul had determined to sail by Ephesus, because he would not spend the time in Asia: for he hasted, if it were possible for him, to be at Jerusalem the day of Pentecost.*
17. *And from Miletus he sent to Ephesus, and called the elders of the church.*
18. *And when they were come to him, he said unto them, Ye know, from the first day that I came into Asia, after what manner I have been with you at all seasons,*
19. *Serving the Lord with all humility of mind, and with many tears, and temptations, which befel me by the lying in wait of the Jews:*
20. *And how I kept back nothing that was profitable unto you, but have shewed you, and have taught you publicly, and from house to house,*
21. *Testifying both to the Jews and also to the Greeks, repentance toward God, and faith toward our Lord Jesus Christ.*

It is affecting to find St. Paul thus calling upon the elders of the church, the elders of his own appointment over churches of his own planting, to bear witness to his faithfulness. He speaks, indeed, as one *serving the Lord with all humility of mind.* He appeals to them as knowing the character of his teaching. He had *kept back nothing that was profitable unto them.* He might have spoken, not as pleasing God, but men. But he did not; he spoke, "not as pleasing men, but God, who trieth the heart."[1]

The human mind, it seems, was the same then as now. The hearer might wish some truth to be kept back: the preacher might be tempted to indulge the hearer's wish. The prophet might prophesy falsely, because the people loved to have it so.[2]

Paul, however, *kept back nothing that was profitable, but showed and taught them both publicly and from house to house.*

The history shows his manner of *teaching publicly.* Wherever there were Jewish synagogues, these he entered, and expounding the law and the prophets, "showed from the Scriptures that Jesus was Christ." When, as at Ephesus, he could no longer attend the synagogue without danger, or when, as appears to have been the case at Athens, there was no Jewish synagogue, he used the most convenient place of meeting, as the school of Tyrannus; or even disputed in places of public concourse "with them that met with him."[3] Thus he acted as what he was, a herald, one who has something to announce; and the subject of his announcement was,

[1] 1 Thess. ii. 4. [2] See Jer. v. 31. [3] See xix. 9; xvii. 17.

Man a sinner, and Christ a Saviour: *repentance toward God, and faith toward our Lord Jesus Christ.*

But public preaching must not supersede private instruction. It opens the way for it; but does not supply it. The one draws the bow at a venture; the other carries the arrow home, and lodges it in the heart—not to wound, but to heal; not to destroy, but to save. Therefore he taught *both publicly and from house to house.* He had thus opportunity of pressing his doctrine more closely upon the conscience, and also of explaining it more accurately. He could resolve doubts, as well as declare truths. He could reach the individual case; and prove to every heart, which "knew its own bitterness," the nature of that "grace of God which had appeared unto all men."

Thus he fulfilled his mission, *to the Jews, and also to the Greeks.* Both, it seems, required the same. Both required *repentance toward God.* The Jews had offended against the law which God had revealed to them: the Greeks had offended against "the law written in their hearts." So that "there was no difference; for that all had sinned, and come short of the glory of God."[4] All, though in various degrees of guilt, were to come before God in one common attitude as sinners. But as repentant sinners, intending "to lead a new life, following the commandments of God, and walking henceforth in his holy ways." And, also, as sinners who sought acceptance with God, through *faith in the Lord Jesus Christ.* Repentance towards God was to lead to faith towards Christ Jesus. Sorrow for sin was to produce love of the Saviour. The law.

[4] See the argument in the Epistle to the Romans, ii. and iii.

convincing them of sin, was to bring them to Him who takes away sin. They were shown their condemnation in the sight of God, that they might embrace his offer of salvation. And if they were thus taught *repentance toward God, and faith toward our Lord Jesus Christ, nothing was kept back which was profitable for them.*

For the future, they must be deprived of his instruction: duty called him elsewhere.

22. *And now behold, I go bound in the spirit unto Jerusalem, not knowing the things that shall befall me there:*
23. *Save that the Holy Ghost witnesseth in every city, saying, that bonds and afflictions abide me.*
24. *But none of these things move me, neither count I my life dear unto myself, so that I might finish my course with joy, and the ministry which I have received of the Lord Jesus, to testify the gospel of the grace of God.*

The exact nature of his trials was not revealed to Paul. All that *the Holy Ghost witnessed,* was what from the first he had been taught to expect. From the first he had been shown "how great things he must suffer for Christ's sake."[5]

It is mercy to man that a map of his wanderings is not laid before him. "Sufficient unto the day is the evil thereof." Sufficient also is the provision against evil, if He is with us whom Paul was proclaiming: if we are able to say, through whatever unknown ways we may be called, "Thou art with me; thy rod and thy staff they comfort me."[6] This was Paul's support: he had a certain duty to fulfil, a certain course to follow; and he set out to meet the trials of every day in sure

[5] Acts ix. 16. [6] Psa. xxiii. 4.

confidence of "doing all things through Christ who strengthened him." And this alone was his desire, *that he might finish his course with joy.* As he more fully describes his state of mind, when writing to the Philippian disciples, "This one thing I do; forgetting those things that are behind, and reaching forth unto those things that are before, I press toward the mark for the prize of the high calling of God in Christ Jesus."[7]

His was a peculiar course. But so is every man's. Every man's condition is a course to himself, requiring to be run, like Paul's, with patience unto the end. Every situation, every relation of life, has its own duties, and its own difficulties. Every individual heart has its own temptations. We proceed, *not knowing the things that shall befall us; save this, that the Holy Ghost witnesseth,* that "strait is the gate and narrow is the way that leadeth unto life;" but that "God is faithful, who will not suffer us to be tempted above that we are able, but will with the temptation also make a way to escape, that we may be able to bear it."[8]

Whatever the course may be which the providence of God assigns to us, one object must be kept constantly in view, that we *finish our course with joy,* and *testify the gospel of the grace of God,* if not by words, as the apostle, by a christian life and character. Then shall *none of those things move us,* which might otherwise disturb or harass. They cannot hinder our *finishing our course with*

[7] Phil. iii. 13, 14. [8] 1 Cor. x. 13.

joy, if they do not divert us from it. Nay, they may even further our progress. Temptations, when resisted and overcome, add strength to the soul; leave it more settled than before. Tribulations past are an earnest of future support. Every turn in the course, when passed successfully, leaves the way shorter, and brings the prize nearer; till at last the Christian may say, "I have finished my course; I have kept the faith; henceforth there is laid up for me a crown of life, which the Lord, the righteous Judge, will give me at that day."[9]

XXXII.

PAUL'S FAREWELL TO THE ELDERS.

ACTS xx. 32—38.

32. *And now, brethren, I commend you to God, and to the word of his grace, which is able to build you up, and to give you an inheritance among all them which are sanctified.*

33. *I have coveted no man's silver, or gold, or apparel.*

34. *Yea, ye yourselves know, that these hands have ministered unto my necessities, and to them that were with me.*

[9] 2 Tim. iv. 11.

35. *I have shewed you all things, how that so labouring, ye ought to support the weak; and to remember the words of the Lord Jesus, how he said, It is more blessed to give than to receive.*[1]

THE father taken prematurely from his family commits the guardianship of his children to his wisest and dearest friend. Other duties now separated St. Paul from his christian family in this part of Asia; his children in the faith. But there is a guardianship under which he can confidently leave them. He *commends them to God, and to the word of his grace, which is able to build them up* as holy temples to the Lord. He says, *to build them up,* because the foundation was already laid. It was laid in "repentance toward God, and faith toward our Lord Jesus Christ."[2] Those whom he was addressing had been once "dead in trespasses and sins, fulfilling the desires of the flesh and of the mind." From these they had now turned, "to serve the living and true God." This was *repentance.* They were expecting a heavenly inheritance, through him who had purchased it with his own blood; "even Jesus, who had delivered them from the wrath to come." This was *faith in the Lord Jesus Christ.* And the elders who were now hearing Paul, and the churches over which they were overseers, had been placed upon this foundation.

A foundation is not laid without a purpose. It is useless, unless something be raised upon it. And the

[1] One of our Lord's remarks, not recorded by the Evangelist, but remembered by his disciples.

[2] Ephes. ix. 1, 2.

foundation of repentance and faith is laid, that on it a holy life may be built up. The will of God was, their sanctification.[3] They were called to holiness. They were called to disinterestedness, after the example which Paul himself had set them. They were called to brotherly kindness and charity, and not to self-indulgence or covetousness. And this sanctification is produced by the Spirit acting on the heart through the word. *The word of God's grace* alone can build the Christian up as a spiritual temple, living to his service and glory. Surrounded as we are by temptation; contending as we do, not only against flesh and blood, but against spiritual enemies ever watchful to destroy; with so many examples, on every side, of those who live only to this world and to themselves;—amid dangers like these, what but the Word of God constantly studied as a rule, constantly referred to as a standard, can keep us from "drawing back unto perdition?"

It comforted the apostle, that he left this with them: that he could *commend them to God and to the word of his grace,* through which they might endure unto the end, and receive *an inheritance among all them that are sanctified.*

This, he says, *the word is able to give.* THE WORD of God is, as it were, the title-deed by which the Christian knows what he is heir to. Why does he dare to look towards heaven? Because THE WORD assures him, that there are those for whom God has prepared a kingdom. And how dares he hope that he is among that number? THE WORD supplies him with the

[3] See 1 Thess. iv. 3.

evidence of his title. First, his *Faith;* and next, his sanctification; the sign of his *repentance;* the proof that "a new heart and a right spirit" have been wrought in him by the Spirit of God. The evidence of his title is not merely that he is baptized: though baptism is an essential mean of sanctification. The evidence is not that he eats and drinks at the Lord's table: though it is an essential part of sanctification "to show forth the Lord's death till he come." Still the mark of heirship is no outward rite. The inheritance is for *them that are sanctified.* And sanctification has its seat within, governing and directing the thoughts and words and works. Sanctification is no single act or quality, but it pervades the whole heart, and influences the whole man; regulates his desires, rules his designs, inspires his secret affections, and guides his outward actions. To be "poor in spirit;" to be "pure in heart;" to be "meek;" to be "merciful:" to "hunger and thirst after righteousness;"—this is to be sanctified. And blessed are they who are thus sanctified, for theirs is the *inheritance*— "theirs is the kingdom of heaven."

Leaving upon their minds this last assurance, the apostle departs; but first sets the seal to his exhortation.

36. *And when he had thus spoken, he kneeled down, and prayed with them all.*
37. *And they all wept sore, and fell on Paul's neck, and kissed him.*
38. *Sorrowing most of all for the words which he spake, that they should see his face no more. And they accompanied him unto the ship.*

Paul was dear to these persons beyond common and ordinary friendship, because the benefits they had received from him were more than ordinary benefits. And they knew not what his departure might cost them; how much of that spiritual blessing which they now enjoyed might be impaired, when they had no longer his instructions, his advice, his exhortations. Unwilling to lose a moment, *they accompanied him to the ship*. There they *must* part. The time will come on earth when dearest friends must be torn from one another. Blessed be God, there is a state where nothing shall separate them: nothing give occasion for the words which Paul had spoken, and which were above all grievous—*that they should see his face no more.*

Still there is One who, even in this world, cannot be separated from us; who will be with us in all circumstances, and in every country: who will not be parted from us even when that gulf is to be crossed which is our passage to eternity. To Him Paul commends those whom he loved,—saying, *Now, brethren, I commend you to God*. And the words of God to his people are, "I will never leave thee nor forsake thee."

XXXIII.

PAUL BEFORE AGRIPPA.

ACTS XXV. 24—31.

24. *As he thus spake for himself, Festus said with a loud voice, Paul, thou art beside thyself; much learning hath made thee mad.*

THIS was the impression on the mind of the Roman governor, Festus, when, together with his superior, Agrippa, he heard Paul declare the grounds of his faith in Jesus, confirmed as it was by those things which Moses and the prophets had said should come: "that Christ should suffer, and that he should be the first that should rise from the dead, and should show light unto the people, and to the Gentiles."

All these things, belonging to the history and writings of the Jewish people, were new and strange to Festus. As a heathen, he knew nothing of Moses, or the Prophets, or of an expected Saviour; and he supposed that Paul was a mere visionary, deceived by his imagination, and acting upon a dream as if it had been reality.

And so Festus might have thought, if there had been nothing connected with the dream. If Moses and others of old time had not written, and left "the sure word of prophecy:" if there had been no evidence that Christ had come in the flesh: if no account could be given, why he should suffer: if no expectation had been held out that he should rise from the dead, and no proof could be alleged that he had risen:—if none of these things had been connected with the vision; then he might be reckoned as the dupe of imagination, and his words treated as madness. But Paul confidently appeals to Agrippa as knowing what Festus was ignorant of; as knowing how prophecy and event, history and doctrine, confirmed each other.

25. *And he said, I am not mad, most noble Festus: but speak forth the words of truth and soberness.*
26. *For the king knoweth of these things, before whom also I speak freely: for I am persuaded that none of these things are hidden from him; for this thing was not done in a corner.*
27. *King Agrippa, believest thou the prophets? I know that thou believest.*
28. *Then Agrippa said unto Paul, Almost thou persuadest me to be a Christian.*

Paul had an advantage with Agrippa, which he had not on a former occasion when reasoning with Felix. He had now to deal with one who recognised the Scriptures: acknowledged that God had revealed himself to mankind. *King Agrippa, believest thou the prophets? I know that thou believest.* Agrippa had that general belief in the Divine word, which such men commonly have when brought up in a country where it is professedly received, and God is avowedly worshipped.

They are by no means prepared to deny the truth of revelation, any more than they are disposed to act as if it were true. Still, as Agrippa, when pressed closely by the apostle, could not deny that he believed the prophets; so in our own land, and in our own day, a belief rests upon the mind of many, though it does not influence the heart. And in time of trouble, of danger, of distress, they are ready to say, *Almost thou persuadest me to be a Christian.* They commence, perhaps, some plans of reformation; they abstain from practices which conscience condemns, and enter upon a course of life more consistent with christian faith. They illustrate that momentary feeling upon Agrippa's mind, when he said, *Almost thou persuadest me to be a Christian.*

29. *And Paul said, I would to God that not only thou, but also all that hear me this day, were both almost, and altogether such as I am, except these bonds.*

The words of Agrippa excited an affectionate emotion in the heart of Paul, while the thought arose within him—*Almost a Christian!* That profiteth little! Oh, that king Agrippa were indeed a Christian!

To be *almost* a Christian, only shows that truth has been neglected or resisted. "This is the condemnation, that light hath come into the world, and men love darkness rather than light, because their deeds are evil." Agrippa is himself an example. Before what passed at this examination of Paul, he probably knew little of the Christians, except that they were a sect called Nazarenes, and "everywhere spoken against." Now he knew what they believed, and on what their belief was grounded. Now he knew that they rested their faith on the very law and prophets which he himself confessed to be from God. But instead of yielding to conscience, and appointing a time when he might hear Paul again of this important matter; he rises up, and dissolves the assembly. Because on the instant it would cross his mind, that to become a Christian would be the destruction of his worldly prospects, and involve the new-modelling of his whole life. Therefore the movement of his conscience was but the turn of a thought, the feeling of a moment; like the spark which blazes up, and on which at the same instant a drop of water falls, and it is extinguished. But it has shown that there is something within, something which we should not have been aware of if the spark had not betrayed it; something which might have grown up into a continuing and steady flame, if means had been used to foster and not to quench it. When account is given "of the things done in the body," account must be given of the perverseness, the sinfulness, the hardness of heart, which checked that rising flame.

This would furnish just cause for Paul's passionate exclamation, and his prayer that Agrippa might be *altogether* a Christian. *Not only almost, but altogether.* He could be nothing else, if he were a Christian at all in any proper or available sense. There is no mid-way. To be a Christian, is to have sought acceptance with God through Christ, and to be looking for salvatior through faith in him. This admits of no middl course. If one is accused before men, there is r middle course; he must be either innocent or guilt and must plead either one or the other. So it is at the bar of God. Either we are trusting in ourselves that we are righteous; or because we are not righteous, we are trusting in Christ, who has made propitiation for our sins. Therefore there can be no mid-way as to FAITH; no meaning in being *almost a Christian.* Neither as to PRACTICE, can there be a middle course. Because either we are seeking "first the kingdom of God and his righteousness," or we are seeking this world first; that is, preferring it, wherever the interests of the one clash with the interests of the other. We cannot at the same time love God most, and mammon most. Either we are yielding to some desires, and habits, and temptations contrary to the gospel; or we are rejecting and opposing these, as they must who are *altogether Christians,* and bringing every thought, and word, and deed into obedience to Christ. Such must be their purpose and endeavour. Not because, to be altogether a Christian, a man must be altogether perfect. But because he must be altogether sincere in aiming at perfection, and allowing himself in nothing short of it.

This was the state of Paul's own heart; and knowing the comfort which he derived from the consciousness of this, and the blessed consequence which should follow, he earnestly desired that both Agrippa, and all before whom he was pleading, might be nothing less: might be *not only almost but altogether Christians.*

Agrippa, however, had now heard enough to satisfy his curiosity, and too much, perhaps, to maintain his ease of mind; and he would hear no more.

30. *And when he had thus spoken, the king rose up, and the governor, and Bernice, and they that sat with them:*
31. *And when they were gone aside, they talked between themselves, saying, This man doeth nothing worthy of death or of bonds.*

XXXIV.

PAUL AT ROME.

ACTS xxviii. 30, 31.

30. *Paul dwelt two whole years in his own hired house, and received all that came in unto him.*
31. *Preaching the kingdom of God, and teaching those things which concern the Lord Jesus Christ, with all confidence, no man forbidding him.*

PAUL had been told in a vision, that he must "bear witness" to his Lord at Rome. And it had been long his own earnest desire to visit that great city, and to enforce in his own person the doctrines which his Epistle had contained.[1] His wish was fulfilled, but not as he had designed. He was carried thither as a prisoner, who had appealed to Cæsar from the unjust tribunal of his countrymen. And thus it had been wonderfully ordered that he should have the opportunity, during *two whole years, of preaching the kingdom*

[1] Acts xxiii. 11; Rom. i. 13.

of God, and teaching those things which concern the Lord Jesus Christ, in the great city of the world: and that without hindrance. The very imprisonment in which he was held favoured him. Had he been able to enter into the Jewish synagogues, or to dispute, as at Athens, in the public places with them that met with him, the magistrates would have interfered, and the law would have put him down. But being confined to *his own hired house* "with the soldier who kept him," *he received all who came to him, no man forbidding him:* and though he was bound, "the word of God was not bound." Many, we may suppose, of his visitors were his own countrymen, whose lingering prejudices he would endeavour, and often successfully, to remove. But the greater number, probably, were Gentiles: providentially led, through acquaintance or connexion, to seek that light which God had set up, ready to enlighten every man.

During this sojourn at Rome, Paul did not forget the churches which he had planted elsewhere. His epistles to the Ephesians, Philippians, and Colossians, written at this time, show his anxiety concerning them. They also enable us to gather some particulars of his residence, which history has not elsewhere recorded.

We learn, for instance, something of the support and comfort which he received while dwelling in the midst of this idolatrous and luxurious city.

He was not left alone. There was collected round him a faithful band ready to live or die with him. "Marcus, Demas, Lucas, his fellow-labourers, and Jesus, which is called Justus: who are of the circumcision." These were his "fellow-workers unto the kingdom of God, who were a comfort to him."[2] So was Aristarchus, the companion of his voyage, whom, with Epaphras, he styles his "fellow-prisoner;" and Tychicus, who conveyed his letter to the churches.[3] Afterwards Timotheus came to him, "his own son in the faith:" and Epaphroditus, "a brother and companion in labour and fellow-soldier," who brought from Macedonia a token of affection from the Philippian brethren.[4] In this manner "his God supplied all his need:" he "had all, and abounded," through the kindness and gratitude of those to whom he had ministered blessings which no price could repay.

But though he wanted not comfort from without, his chief comfort was within. All was safe and peaceful there. He had made up his mind to "count all things but loss for the excellency of the knowledge of Christ Jesus:"[5] to seek as his sole dependance "the righteousness which is by faith of Jesus Christ." And in this confidence he could rest secure. "To live was Christ, to die was gain."[6] "Not as though he had already attained, either were already perfect:" he knew that as long as he continued in the flesh, he must be still "reaching forth unto those things that are before, pressing on towards the mark for the prize of the high calling of God in Christ Jesus."[7] Still this was no labour or sorrow to him: it left him in full enjoyment of the assurance which belonged to his faith. "He knew in whom he had believed: and that he was able

[2] Col. iv. 7, &c

[3] Col. iv. 10; Philem. 23; Col. iv. 7; Eph. vi. 21.

[4] Philip. ii. 19; iv. 18. [5] Ib. iii. 8. [6] Ib. i. 21.

[7] Ib. iii. 12 14.

to keep what he had committed to him unto the great day."[8]

A further comfort was derived to him through the success which was granted to that cause on which his heart was fixed. "Many of the brethren waxing confident by his bonds," gaining courage from his example, "became much more bold to speak the word without fear."[9] So that the truths of the gospel pervaded both the highest and the lowest stations. They reached the fugitive Onesimus, who had been slave to Philemon at Colosse, and had fled from his service to Rome. He, being converted to the faith, returned again to Philemon, "not now as a servant, but above a servant, a brother beloved."[1] Then the same truth which stooped to the fugitive slave, climbed also to the imperial palace. So God ordered it. The apostle comforts the Philippians under the thoughts of the durance in which he was held, by giving them to "understand that the things which had happened to him had fallen out rather to the furtherance of the gospel: so that his bonds in Christ were manifest in all the palace, and in all other places."[2] The cause for which he suffered had become known, the Saviour whom he proclaimed had been received: and when he sends his salutation to the distant brethren from those at Rome, he especially mentions "the saints of Cæsar's household."[3]

"So mightily grew the word of God and prevailed," during *the two whole years when Paul dwelt in his own hired house, and received all that came unto him, preaching the kingdom of God.*

[8] 2 Tim. i. 12. [9] Philip. i. 14. [1] Philem. 16.
[2] Philip. i. 12, 13. [3] Philip. iv. 22.

All along he had entertained a confidence that he should be preserved through the present danger to further service. "I trust in the Lord," he had written to the Philippians, "that I myself also shall come shortly." And again to Philemon: "I trust that through your prayers I shall be given unto you."[4] So it proved; no one seems to have appeared against him: and after two years' confinement he found himself at liberty: able to enjoy what he had so earnestly longed for, the sight of his beloved churches once more, and to carry on again the ministry which he had received.

At length he returned to Rome,[5] "always abounding in the work of the Lord." And then the time arrived when he should cease from his labours, and his works should follow him. He was called to give account before the Emperor Nero of the new and strange doctrine which he was teaching: and so evident was the danger, that no one dared to "stand with him. All men forsook him." Only He remained, "who is closer than a brother."[6] "The Lord stood by him, and strengthened him." For the moment, "he was delivered out of the mouth of the lion."[7] But, as he foresaw, whilst writing the account to Timothy, the delay was not for long; the season was near when he must seal with his blood the testimony which he had so long given. For this he was fully prepared. Many

[4] Philem. 21.

[5] After an interval of uncertain duration, of which "we know scarcely anything." (See Burton, Lect. ix.) The fact of the book of Acts closing its history with these two years, seems conclusive proof that Luke composed, or rather finished it, at this period of time. (Id. p. 275.)

[6] Prov. xviii. 24.

[7] 2 Tim. iv. 17.

years before he had said, "I am ready, not to be bound only, but also to die at Jerusalem, for the sake of the Lord Jesus." Longer experience had not made him less ready to do or to suffer for the Master whom he served. We possess his parting words: "I am now ready to be offered, and the time of my departure is at hand. I have fought a good fight, I have finished my course, I have kept the faith: henceforth there is laid up for me a crown of righteousness, which the Lord, the righteous Judge, shall give me at that day: and not to me only, but unto all them also that love his appearing."[8]

Thus, like the prophet before him,[9] who, taken himself from his earthly trials, cast down his mantle to encourage his successor: so has Paul, in his last recorded sentiments, left for others the comfort wherewith he himself was comforted of God. A crown of glory was prepared for him. But not for him only, the apostle in labours most abundant, in grace above measure: but for all them also that "love the Lord's appearing:" for all the faithful brethren in every age and country, whose hearts have been directed by the Spirit "to the love of God, and the patient waiting for Christ."[1]

[8] 2 Tim. iv. 6—8.

[9] See 2 Kings ii. 12, 13.

[1] 2 Thess. iii. 5.

XXXV.

ELECTION OF THE THESSALONIAN CHURCH.

1 Thess. i. 2—5.

2. *We give thanks to God always for you all, making mention of you in our prayers;*
3. *Remembering without ceasing your work of faith, and labour of love, and patience of hope in our Lord Jesus Christ, in the sight of God and our Father;*
4. *Knowing, brethren beloved, your election of God.*

When in answer to our Lord's inquiry, "Whom say ye that I am?" Simon Peter made his famous confession, "Thou art the Christ, the Son of the living God;" Jesus answered, "Blessed art thou, Simon, for flesh and blood hath not revealed it unto thee; but my Father which is in heaven."[1] The truth and confidence of the reply, discovered the source from which it came. St. Paul's assurance here is founded on the like grounds, when he says, *Knowing, brethren beloved, your election of God.* He had witnessed the readiness with which they had listened to him and Silas: he remembered the *work of faith* which he had seen, the energy with which they strove to fulfil the will of God: he remembered the *labour of love* which

[1] Matt. xvi. 16, 17.

they had exercised, the *patience of hope* of future recompense, which had enabled them to encounter persecution and to surmount all opposition. And as these effects of his doctrine upon their hearts could only be produced by the Spirit of God, he had manifest proof that God had chosen them, and given them a place in his favour. The Jews, indeed, would deny this, and claim to themselves the privilege promised of old to the children of Abraham, and refuse a share of it to others, being jealous and indignant, that "God had granted unto the Gentiles also repentance unto life." The answer to their exclusive spirit, was the character of the Thessalonian Christians. There is a state of heart and life by which we are taught to "know that we are of the truth," and may "have confidence towards God." [2] And this state of heart and life was so exhibited in the Thessalonians, as to make it plain that God had "predestinated them unto the adoption of children by Jesus Christ unto himself, according to the good pleasure of his will."

How came this, it may be asked,—that some were thus predestinated unto the adoption of children, and others were passed by? That apostles should visit Thessalonica or Philippi, and should not visit Tyre or Sidon? That some who had been "dead in trespasses and sins were quickened," whilst others remained in darkness, and brought the children of light into much affliction?

These are among "the secret things which belong to the Lord our God."

Thus much, however, we can perceive and under-

[2] 1 John iii. 19—21.

stand. God purposed in himself to collect a people "out of every kindred and nation under heaven," who should be blessed with all spiritual blessings in Christ Jesus, and in the dispensation of the fulness of times should inherit an everlasting kingdom. So an earthly benefactor might, if he chose, take the children of certain inhabitants of his place or neighbourhood, adopt them as his own, educate them, make them heirs of his wealth. God, who worketh all things after the counsel of his own will, did this originally by the Jewish nation: adopted them as his "peculiar people." Now he was doing the same by others: he sent his apostles to one city, and passed by another, according to his good pleasure. We know not the grounds of his selection: but we are assured that "the Judge of all the earth will do right," though "his ways are far above out of our sight." And as the provision made by Him that the gospel should be preached at Thessalonica or Philippi, was proof that he had chosen those cities to be recipients of his mercy, so was there a like proof in regard to the individuals who had embraced the faith, and been baptized in the name of the Lord Jesus. That they had been aroused by the word preached to them, had cast off the works of darkness, and were now following after holiness; this was proof that God had chosen them to salvation, through sanctification of the Spirit and belief of the truth. Unless he had a favour unto them, he would not have put it into their hearts to receive the gospel. Thus was made manifest their election of God.

Another proof was the manner in which God had wrought with the apostle, "confirming his word with signs following."

5. *For our gospel came not unto you in word only, but also in power, and in the Holy Ghost, and in much assurance; as ye know what manner of men we were among you for your sakes.*

In the present day, the gospel may be said to *come in word,*—in word, unaccompanied by outward signs. Its ministers declare the truth as revealed in Scripture, and enforce it by such arguments as they are able to employ. It was otherwise with the early messengers of the gospel. Writing to the Romans, St. Paul says, "I will not dare to speak of any of those things which Christ hath not wrought by me, to make the Gentiles obedient by word and deed; through mighty signs and wonders, by the power of the Spirit of God; so that from Jerusalem, and round about unto Illyricum, I have fully preached the gospel of Christ."[3] In writing to the Corinthians, he speaks to the same purpose; and says concerning his enemies in that city, "I will come to you shortly, and will know, not the speech of them that are puffed up, but the power. For the kingdom of God is not in word, but in power."[4] It is maintained by the power of the Holy Spirit, showing that God is present with those servants whom he approves. And so here, at Thessalonica, the gospel had *come not in word only,* depending on the faithfulness or talents of him who spoke the word, but also *in power, and in the Holy Ghost, and in much assurance.* Paul had shown signs amongst them, which proved that he came attested by the Spirit of God, manifesting itself in the power imparted to him: a power which he exercised

[3] Rom. xv. 18, 19. [4] 1 Cor. iv. 19, 20.

among them for their sakes; not to obtain glory to himself, but to convince them that if they resisted him, they would "resist the Holy Ghost."

To whatever place the gospel is brought, or by whatever heart it is received, it must *come not in word only, but in power.* Not indeed now in that power which was displayed at Thessalonica, where, as elsewhere, we may suppose the "gifts of healing" were exercised, and "the working of miracles," and "divers kinds of tongues," and "the interpretation of tongues;"[5] but in that *work of faith, and labour of love, and patience of hope,* which are no less supernatural, no less the operation of the Holy Ghost, than his outward manifestations. These must never fail: for these alone can show that the Christian is "delivered from this present evil world," and is setting his affections on things above, not on things below; and whilst he is performing the duties of the station to which he is called on earth, he is still seeking "first the kingdom of God and his righteousness," and having "his conversation in heaven."

[5] See 1 Cor. xii. 9, 10.

XXXVI.

THE COMING OF THE KINGDOM OF GOD WITH POWER.

MARK ix. 1.

1. *And he said unto them, Verily, I say unto you, that there be some of them that stand here, which shall not taste of death, till they have seen the kingdom of God come with power.*

WHEN these words were spoken, the *kingdom of God* had already *come*. It came, its foundation was laid, when "the Word was made flesh, and dwelt among us." But it did not *come with power*, when Mary "brought forth her first-born son, and laid him in a manger;" and when they to whom his birth was made known, and who welcomed him, were not the rulers, and the rich, and the mighty of the land, but "shepherds abiding in the fields, and keeping watch over their flocks by night."

The kingdom of God had come, and proceeded further, when Jesus chose his twelve apostles, who should be with him, and hear his doctrines, and convey them throughout the land, calling upon all men to "repent and believe the gospel." But it was not a kingdom coming *with power*, when they who proclaimed it were fishermen of Galilee, unlearned men, of an obscure district, whose very speech betrayed their humble origin.[1]

The kingdom of God was established, when Jesus was lifted up upon the cross, and paid the price of reconciliation, taking away the sin which separated mankind from their heavenly Father. But it did not *come with power*, whilst he was thus "despised and rejected of men;" smitten, reviled, and mocked by those whom he came to save: so weak in human eyes, that even his disciples "all forsook him and fled."

Here, however, the Lord foretells a time, a time not so distant as the death of some then standing near him, when *the kingdom of God should come with power*.[2]

A like prophecy might have been uttered concerning David, when his subjects revolted from him under the instigation of Absalom, and in a state of weakness and humiliation scarcely less than that of Jesus, he was forced to leave the royal city with a few followers, and "tarry in the plain of the wilderness."[3] It might have been then foretold, The inhabitants of Jerusalem shall shortly see David returning to his throne with power.

[1] Acts ii. 7.

[2] Instead of the phrase used by Mark and Luke, "the coming of *the kingdom of God*," we read in the parallel passage in St. Matthew, "the Son of man coming in his kingdom." Therefore the two phrases must allude to the same thing. And it appears from Matt. xxiv. 7—30, Mark xiii. 26, Luke xxi. 27, that the coming of the Son of man, and the destruction of Jerusalem, are identical. This seems necessarily to refute the explanation of Chrysostom and others of the ancients, who imagined that our Lord's words referred to the Transfiguration, and were fulfilled by it. Not to mention that the phrase, *There be some standing here who shall not taste of death*, would never be used concerning an event which was to happen within eight days.

[3] 2 Sam. xv. 13—23.

And this prophecy would have been verified, when David was escorted back to Jerusalem victorious, his enemies slain or scattered, the people contending together for the honour of first restoring him, and those who had deserted or opposed him, praying for his forgiveness and imploring his favour.[4]

In like manner the prophecy of our Lord was fulfilled, when the guilty nation which had rejected their heavenly King, suffered the penalty of their iniquities: when desolation was brought upon the city which had not admitted him to the throne of David; and his authority was confirmed by this accomplishment of all that he had foretold. The hinderance was then removed which had hitherto withstood the progress of the Gospel. The law given by Moses yielded to the "grace and truth which came by Jesus Christ." The chief priests and elders had opposed to the teaching of Christ the teaching of Moses. "We are Moses' disciples," they said; "we know that God spake unto Moses: as for this man, we know not whence he is."[5] Stephen, ministering in the name of Jesus, was accused of "speaking blasphemous words against Moses, and against the law."[6] And the charge laid against Paul was, that he taught the Jews "to forsake Moses," and spoke against the law and the temple.[7] When, then, the Roman forces overran the country, and laid it waste; desolated Jerusalem by a siege, which has scarcely a parallel in history for horror; and scattered abroad the surviving remnant of the people; then the enemies of the kingdom of God were vanquished; the

[4] 2 Sam. xix. 10—12, &c.
[5] John ix. 28.
[6] Acts vi.
[7] Ib. xxi. 21—28.

Jewish polity, the religion of Moses, was overthrown: of the temple "not one stone was left upon another:" and, as Hosea had foretold, the Jews remained "without a king, and without a prince, and without a sacrifice, and without an image, and without an ephod, and without teraphim."[8] It was "the sign of the Son of man in heaven."[9] It was the fulfilment of the prophecy, "Hereafter ye shall see the Son of man sitting on the right hand of power, and coming in a cloud with power and great glory."[1] The Christians, warned by their Lord, "fled into the mountains:"[2] and saw from their places of refuge the triumph of the Son of God, in the destruction of his enemies, and the overthrow of the nation which would not "have him to reign over them." They saw the prophecy accomplished, in *the coming of the kingdom of God with power*. And some were at that time standing by our Lord, who *did not taste of death* till this was done.

In another sense, and that an important sense, they all *saw the kingdom of God come with power*. They saw the fulfilment of the promise, which assured the disciples, that the Comforter, when he should come, should reprove (or convince) "the world of sin, and of righteousness, and of judgment."[3] They saw the effect of that Spirit, when on the day of Pentecost three thousand persons "gladly received the word" of truth, as preached by Peter, and were baptized in the name of Him, whom shortly before they had joined in crucifying. They saw "the Lord adding to the church daily

[8] Hos. iii. 4. [9] Matt. xxiv. 30.
[1] Matt. xxvi. 64; Mark xiii. 26; Luke xxi. 27. [2] Matt. xxiv. 16.
[3] John xvi. 8.

such as should be saved:"[4] they saw "a great company of the priests" abandon the prejudices in which they had grown up, and the law which they had administered, and "become obedient to the faith."[5] They saw the Gentiles beseeching that the word might be preached to them, and "turning to God from idols to serve the living and true God, and to wait for his Son from heaven."[6]

Had there been no other victory gained against the most vehement opposers of the gospel, this would sufficiently have explained and justified the words, *There be some of them that stand here, which shall not taste of death, till they have seen the kingdom of God come with power.*

XXXVII.

THE GROWTH OF THE KINGDOM OF GOD.

MARK iv. 26—29.

26. *So is the kingdom of God, as if a man should cast seed into the ground;*
27. *And should sleep, and rise night and day, and the seed should spring and grow up, he knoweth not how.*

[4] Acts ii. 47 [5] Acts vi. 7. [6] 1 Thess. i. 10.

28. *For the earth bringeth forth fruit of herself: first the blade, then the ear, after that the full corn in the ear.*
29. *But when the fruit is brought forth, immediately he putteth in the sickle, because the harvest is come.*

This parable describes the manner in which the gospel should grow secretly, and make its gradual way, both in the world at large, and in the hearts of individuals. *So is the kingdom of God as if a man should cast seed into the ground.* At the time when he uttered the parable, the Lord was himself the sower: he was eradicating the errors of the Jewish people, and sowing eternal truth in their stead: he was declaring the real nature of God's heavenly kingdom, and revealing the way which leads to it: he was opening to mankind the secrets of their own corrupt hearts, and the renewing change which they required; he was explaining what is, and what is not, "true and undefiled religion." Thus he *cast seed into the ground,* which should long remain. It was to remain in the memories of those who received it, till called forth by the influence of the Holy Spirit; and disclosed by a gradual development, "to the Jew first, and afterward to the Gentile." It was to be transmitted slowly, and by degrees, from city to town, and from town to village: from province to province, from country to country. And thus would spring up *first the blade, then the ear, after that the full corn in the ear.* First, the number of the names together would be about an hundred and twenty. Not long after would be added unto them about three thousand souls. By degrees the word of the Lord would increase, and the number of the disciples multiply in Jerusalem greatly, both of men and women, and "a great company of the priests would be obedient to the faith." Then the gift of the Holy Ghost would be poured out upon the Gentiles also: multitudes would so "learn Christ," as to turn from their idolatrous "vanities to serve the living God;" to "be renewed in the spirit of their minds:" and to "put on the new man, which, after God, is created in righteousness and true holiness." The complaint of the unbelieving Jews at Thessalonica acknowledges the growth of the plant; for they said, "Those that have turned the world upside down have come hither also."[1] And Demetrius at Ephesus stirred up his fellow craftsmen, saying, "Ye see how not alone at Ephesus, but almost throughout all Asia, this Paul hath persuaded and turned away much people."[2]

So "mightily grew the word of God and prevailed," till at last what had been sown a little seed became greater than all herbs, and shot out great branches. Those false gods which the ancient countries of Europe and Asia had "ignorantly worshipped," gave way before the God of all the earth: and the temples which had been raised to Satan paid honour to Him who came to destroy the works of Satan. The gospel grew up no longer a tender herb, but a forest tree; which for a while is overshadowed by those around it, and remains unobserved amongst the rest: till at length it rises above them, and spreads its branches on every side, and attains the lofty height which belongs to its nature, while the small shrubs and plants below

[1] Acts xvii. 6. [2] Ib. xix. 26.

gradually disappear, and cannot continue to exist under its shade.

All this, and much more, was foreseen by our Lord when he uttered this parable. He knew that the seed which he came to sow should spring and grow up, men knew not how.

And what Christ, the chief husbandman, and his apostles after him, then did in person, has been carried on since, and is constantly carrying on, by those who believe his word. The sowers who *cast the seed* are of various orders. They are the ministers, to whom a field is intrusted that they should dress and keep it; they are the parents, whose duty is to imbue the infant mind with the Scriptures from its youth; they are the masters of families, who, like faithful Abraham, "command their household that they keep the way of the Lord;" they are the missionaries, who cause the heathen to hear, "every man in his own tongue, the wonderful works of God;" they are the zealous Christians, who in whatever station or circumstances, use their means and opportunities to drop the fructifying word into the ground of the human heart.

And these act like the husbandman, who casts his seed into the furrow. He knows that it will lie there, through a long and dreary period, before it springs up and repays his labour. Still, in the appointment of Providence, he may expect *first the blade, then the ear, after that the full corn in the ear.*

So is it with the Christian, who, in whatever circumstances, may cast the gospel seed. To the fears of the minister, it may often seem to be thrown away upon hopeless ignorance. The parent may discover no depth of earth to receive it. With the master, it may appear choked among the cares of the world, and the desire of other things. In other cases, it is trampled underfoot, or devoured by the fowls of the air.

Yet it may happen, under the most unpromising circumstances, that while we *sleep and rise, night and day,* the seed shall spring up, and *the earth bring forth fruit.* The early season may be unfavourable, and there shall be no sign of vegetation. But seasons vary: and in the course of God's providence a more hopeful time may come. "In the morning sow thy seed, and in the evening withhold not thine hand: for thou knowest not whether shall prosper, either this or that, or whether they both shall be alike good."[3] The changes which occur in life, from health to sickness, from prosperity to adversity, may be like the change of the seasons from cold to heat, or from drought to moisture; and the long-dormant seed may at last show signs of growth. First appears a seriousness unknown before, a sense of the value of the soul, an apprehension of eternity. Then a movement of the heart towards Him, who invites all who have ears to hear: and at last, a true scriptural faith, attended by "works meet for repentance;" proving, that though man *knows not how* the growth takes place, the Spirit has wrought it. For repentance, "and works meet for repentance," are fruits of the Spirit. As we know that there has fallen the genial rain, and the ripening sun has shone, when we see a golden harvest repaying the husbandman for his toil and patience: so when we see

[3] Eccles. xi. 6.

love, and peace, and gentleness, and piety abounding, we know the work of the Spirit of God. "It is the Lord's doing, and it is marvellous in our eyes."

This late reward of labour is seen in the conversion of nations, as well as of individuals. The missionary who carries into a heathen country "the knowledge of God, and of Jesus Christ whom he hath sent," is often obliged to sit down for years, and see no springing blade. Nothing can support him but the spirit of faith: of faith in Him who has pronounced that his word "shall not return unto him void, but shall accomplish the thing whereto he sends it."[4] But after patient waiting he is commonly permitted to see symptoms of spiritual life; the blade of christian faith and hope and charity springs up among the rank weeds of heathenism, and rewards his persevering toil.

So it proved in the islands of the Pacific, where in late years the power of the gospel has been remarkably displayed. "For sixteen years, notwithstanding the untiring zeal, the incessant journeys, the faithful exhortations of several devoted men, no spirit of interest or inquiry appeared: no solitary instance of conversion took place: the wars of the natives continued frequent and desolating, and their idolatries abominable and cruel. The heavens above seemed to be as brass, and the earth as iron. At length the set time came, and God was pleased to commence the work of conversion in such a manner as to secure all the glory to himself. This is worthy of special notice: for the missionaries, at the time the work commenced, were driven away from the island of Tahiti by war, and cut off from all

[4] Isa. lv. 11.

communication with it. Two native servants, formerly in the families of the missionaries, had received, unknown to them, some favourable impressions, and had united together for prayer. To these a number of persons had attached themselves, so that on the return of the missionaries to Tahiti at the termination of the war, they found a number of praying people; and they had little else to do, but to help forward the work which God had so wonderfully and unexpectedly begun."[5]

What is this, but the *seed springing up and growing*, the husbandman *knows not how!*

And then, *when the fruit is brought forth, immediately he putteth in the sickle, because the harvest is come.* There is a fit time, when He who caused the seed to be sown, and the blade to grow up and flourish, gathers in the ripened grain. If we speak of an individual Christian, at the season when he sees fit, the heavenly husbandman will take him to his rest. And also, when the fulness of time arrives, he will *put in his sickle*, and reap the great harvest of the world. "The Son of man shall come in his glory, and all the holy angels with him," and "gather the wheat into his garner."

One remark remains. In order that there may be the *full corn in the ear*, there must be *first the blade*. There must be spiritual life. The seed must not be lying idle and inactive, so that no one could perceive whether any had been sown. The Lord must not have cause to say, what he said of the Israelites of old, "What could have been done more to my field, that I

[5] Williams's Enterprises in the South Sea, Vol. i. p. 16.

have not done in it? Wherefore, when I looked that it should bring forth fruit," is there no *blade,* no *ear,* no *full corn in the ear?*[6]

XXXVIII.

PURPOSE AND EFFECT OF THE GOSPEL.

1 John i. 5—10.

5. *This then is the message which we have heard of him, and declared unto you, that God is light, and in him is no darkness at all.*
6. *If we say that we have fellowship with him, and walk in darkness, we lie, and do not the truth:*
7. *But if we walk in the light, as he is in the light, we have fellowship one with another, and the blood of Jesus Christ his Son cleanseth us from all sin.*

The general purpose of the Gospel is declared in these few words. It is termed a *message,* which the apostles were taught to communicate. And it relates, first, to the nature of God. The Gospel discloses the way in which God deals with man: and in order to comprehend this, we must first have a right knowledge of Him with whom we have to do. *God,* then, *is light.* God is essentially all that on earth the idea *of light* suggests to us: purity; knowledge; glory; with no-

[6] See Isa. v. 4.

thing of an opposite tendency; unpolluted, unfading light; *in him is no darkness at all.*

And the purpose of his *message* is, to draw mankind towards this light, that it may be reflected in themselves. As the darkest body, when brought to approach a shining flame, derives a brightness from it: so must it be with those who profess to have been brought nigh to God through the Gospel of his Son. *If we say that we have fellowship with him, and walk in darkness, we lie, and do not the truth.* As he is light, so all who are united to him must be light. He calls them to be partakers of his own holy nature: "and every man that hath this hope in him, purifieth himself even as he is pure." This is the proof that our hearts are drawn to him, and united with him, that we "cast off the works of darkness," and *walk in the light,* as "children of the day," whose deeds will bear to be exposed;[7] nay, which "shine before men," and attract others to the light to which they owe their brightness. Then are we indeed part of that family, which God has created for himself through Jesus Christ. *We have fellowship one with another:* we are joined together as brethren who have "one Lord, one faith, one baptism:" *and the blood of Jesus Christ cleanseth us from all sin.* Naturally, we are under the guilt of sin, and the power of sin. *But the blood of Jesus Christ cleanseth us* from both. It cleanseth us from the guilt of sin, because "he suffered for sin, the just for the unjust," and God has consented to receive that propitiation. And it cleanseth us from the power of sin, because he imparts to us a new nature, and "delivers us from the corruption

[7] See a similar passage, Eph. v. 8.

which is in the world," through the following of those inclinations and desires which oppose the will of God, and lead to the transgression of his laws.

This train of thought leads the apostle to add reasons why such *cleansing* is needful.

8. *If we say that we have no sin, we deceive ourselves, and the truth is not in us.*
9. *If we confess our sins, he is faithful and just to forgive us our sins, and to cleanse us from all unrighteousness.*

The Christian is not freed from sin, but is cleansed from its guilt by the constant sprinkling of the blood of Christ — like the vessels of the sanctuary in the Jewish temple, which did not remain uniformly pure, but were continually contracting stain. But they were as constantly purified, when sprinkled with the blood of the sanctuary.[2] The case with the Christian is the same. *If we say that we have no sin, we deceive ourselves.* The nature of the soul is not so changed as to become perfect. Perfection it never reaches in this world, though still going on unto perfection. The heart is still "deceitful," though no longer "desperately wicked:" the spirit is still pressed down by the law of sin which is in the members, and cannot do the things it would.[3] So that *if we say that we have no sin, we deceive ourselves, and the truth is not in us.*

Neither, indeed, so saying, or so thinking, could we have any right understanding of the Gospel. The Gospel is proposed to us, not as those who *have no sin*, but as those who "have sinned," and must answer for their sins. It comes as a remedy for the state of man

[2] Heb. xi. 21. [3] See Rom. vii. 23.

as he is: for fallen man. It addresses us as offenders against God, and condemned as offenders. Scripture does not say, Blessed is the man who is without sin: though, doubtless, such a man, if he could be found, would be of all men the most blessed. But its language is, "Blessed is he whose transgression is forgiven, whose sin is covered."[4]

St. John, therefore, teaches us to keep on our minds a constant sense of this. *If we confess our sins, He is faithful and just to forgive us our sins.* If we confess that we come before him as suppliants for his mercy, and not as those who claim a right: then *He is just and faithful to forgive us our sins, and to cleanse us from that unrighteousness* by which we should otherwise appear defiled before him. The very attributes which would condemn us, are then enlisted on our side. His faithfulness is pledged in our behalf; for his prophet has declared, "To this man will I look, saith the Lord, even to him that is poor and of a contrite spirit, and trembleth at my word."[5] So also is his justice. Looking to ourselves, indeed, we dare not claim justice at his hands. We dare not draw as it were a balance with Him, our deserts on one side, and our demerits on the other. If we had no other hope than that which might be thus afforded us, our prospects would be dark indeed. But yet God's justice is pledged, not to our condemnation, but to our pardon. It pleased him "to put to grief" his beloved Son, that he might bear the sins of many. "The Lord laid on him the iniquity of us all." And having thus laid the iniquity upon him, having received at his hands the full and sufficient satisfaction, the only

[4] Psa. xxxii. 1; Rom. iv. 7. [5] Isa. lxvi. 2.

satisfaction which could be paid to the Divine holiness, he will not charge the burden on those who trust in him: who, in obedience to his word, have committed their souls to him, that he may "present them pure and faultless before the presence of his glory."[6]

Such is the state of mind which from first to last befits the Christian. There is an opposite state of mind.

10. *If we say that we have not sinned, we make him a liar, and his word is not in us.*

The word of God is all founded on the principle, that man is a sinner. Therefore to deny that *we have sinned* is to deny the truth of his word: to make him false who has spoken it.

We may disclaim the idea of *saying that we have no sin.* There are but few who would plainly state it. But without asserting so in plain terms, there are many ways of practically saying it.

To excuse our offences against the Divine law, on the plea of a corrupt or weak nature, and to pretend that we are as free from blame as that nature would allow:—this is one way of *saying that we have no sin.* And whoever does so say, *deceives himself.* Has he studied to amend that nature by all the means which God has put into his power? To "purify his heart through the Spirit?" To "keep his body in subjection?"

Others form to themselves a law, and profess to be governed by it, and *say that they have no sin,* if they keep within the boundaries of this law of their own.

[6] Jude 24.

They set up an imaginary charity, and an imaginary sincerity, some standard of duty fixed by themselves, and with this they are satisfied. St. Paul tells us that he had once lived under an error of this kind. "I had not known sin," he declares, "unless the law had said, Thou shalt not covet."[7] He had kept to the letter of the law, but he overlooked its spirit. Like the Pharisees, who devoted to some other purpose the money which might have assisted their needy parents, and then thought themselves free from the obligation of the commandment, "Honour thy father and thy mother."[8]

If we would understand ourselves and our condition, we must represent to our minds the law which God has prescribed to us, the love of God and of our neighbour, in all its fulness, and in all its various bearings upon our lives. Then let a man try his thoughts and his actions by this rule, and say whether he *has no sin;* nay, whether he has lived according to this rule, even in the degree in which he might have approached it, with more constant watchfulness and prayer.

Certainly, *if we say we have no sin, the word of God is not in us.*

And yet, *to confess our sins,* would be of no value, if it led to nothing more. To confess our sins, without lamenting them, or to lament them without striving to correct them, would be an abuse of God's mercy. To argue, God is merciful: if we confess our sins, he will forgive our sins:—therefore we need use no diligence to keep ourselves pure from sin:—this would be to turn the grace of God into a reason for offending him.

[7] Rom. vii. 7—10. [8] Mark vii. 10—13

The Christian confesses his sin, not because he is satisfied with it, but because he is striving against it; because he sets before him a standard which he has not reached, yet can never be contented without reaching. He does not make a trade of sinning and repenting: except as far as a person who is climbing up a steep and slippery rock may be said to be always rising and falling. Still he mounts higher and higher, though at the expense of many a fall: whilst another, who refuses to climb, remains upon the plain below, and never reaches the prize which is proposed to him.

And the state of mind which is thus produced, is the Christian state of mind. It unites us closely with our God and Saviour in two ways; both as showing us the need of his blood, to *cleanse us from all unrighteousness;* and of his grace, by which we may be strengthened more and more, and enabled to "run with patience the race which is set before us." We are then comforted with the assurance, that *if we confess our sins, God is just and faithful to forgive us our sins;* for that "not according to works of righteousness which we have done, but according to his mercy he saved us, through Jesus Christ our Lord."

XXXIX.

SEED SOWN ON GOOD GROUND.

MARK iv. 20.

And these are they which are sown on good ground; such as hear the word, and receive it, and bring forth fruit, some thirty fold, some sixty, and some an hundred.

THE former part of the parable to which these words belong, had spoken of hearts which are hard, like *the way side,* and give no admission to the seed, or word of God. Other hearts are light and shallow, so that the seed will not take root in them; and some are overgrown with cares, so that they bear no produce. The ears are like the years of famine in Pharoah's dream, "withered, thin, and blasted with the east wind."[1] Still the promise is fulfilled; the word of the Lord does "not return unto him void, but accomplishes that whereunto he sends it."[2] There are hearts which the grace of God opens, that the word enters them, and lodges in them, and makes head against tares and briars, and so becomes fruitful. There are "honest and good hearts,"[3] *such as hear the word, and receive it, and bring forth fruit, some thirty fold, some sixty, and some an hundred.*

[1] Gen. xli. 23. [2] Isa. vi. 11. [3] Luke viii. 15.

These, *when they hear the word, receive it.* St. Matthew says, "understand it." St. Luke, "keep it."[4] The receiving, the understanding, the keeping it, all represent the same thing: all describe the same sort of character, the same state of mind, a simple, teachable state: such as our Lord intends, when he says, "Verily, I say unto you, Whosoever shall not receive the kingdom of heaven as a little child, shall in no wise enter therein."[5] The scribes and Pharisees, and the Jewish people in general, when they heard the word, did not "understand it:" refused to "receive or keep it." When Jesus declared to them, "If a man keep my saying, he shall never see death; the Jews said unto him, Art thou greater than our father Abraham, which is dead, and the prophets are dead: whom makest thou thyself?"[6] When he said to some who followed him, "If ye continue in my word, then are ye my disciples indeed; and ye shall know the truth, and the truth shall make you free:" others retorted and said, "We be Abraham's children, and were never in bondage to any man: how sayest thou, Ye shall be made free?"[7] When he said, "For judgment I am come into this world, that they which see not might see, and that they which see might be made blind: some of the Pharisees which were with him heard these words, and said unto him, Are we blind also?"[8] They refused to understand that "all have sinned, and come short of the glory of God;" and that "eternal life" is to be sought, not as the reward of man's deservings, but as "the gift of God through Jesus Christ." They did not

[4] Matt. xiii. 23; Luke viii. 15. [5] Luke xviii. 17.
[6] John viii. 51—53. [7] Ib. viii. 31—33. [8] John ix. 39, 40.

so receive the word, as to confess that "in ourselves," i. e., in our flesh, "dwelleth no good thing:" that, tried by the holiness and purity of the Divine law, "no man living shall be justified." This was the great stumbling-block of the Jews; who, "being ignorant of God's righteousness, and going about to establish their own righteousness, did not submit themselves to the righteousness of God."[9] The same doctrine gives offence to many still, who plead a weak and frail nature; who plead the strength of temptation, and the example of an evil world;—who in some way or other elude the acknowledgment, that all are alike "concluded under sin," "being justified freely by the grace of God through the redemption that is in Christ Jesus."[1]

Others dispute the nature of the ransom; in the same spirit as the Jews, when they "strove amongst themselves, saying, How can this man give us his flesh to eat?" For Jesus had declared, "I am the living bread which came down from heaven; if any man eat of this bread, he shall live for ever; and the bread that I will give is my flesh, which I will give for the life of the world." "Many of his disciples, when they heard this, said, This is a hard saying, who can hear it? And from that time many of his disciples went back, and walked no more with him."[2]

Meanwhile there was "the honest and good heart," in one who had been cured of blindness, and affirmed of him who opened his eyes, "He is a prophet."[3] When the Pharisees reviled him, and said, "Give

[9] Rom. x. 3.
[1] Gal. iii. 22; Rom. iii. 24.
[2] John vi. 51—60.
[3] John ix. 17.

God the praise; we know that this man is a sinner;" he boldly replied, "We know that God heareth not sinners; but if any man be a worshipper of God, and doeth his will, him he heareth. If this man were not of God, he could do nothing."[4]

There was much in the appearance of Jesus which prejudiced the Jews, and indisposed them to *receive his word.* They looked for greatness: he came in weakness. They looked for majesty: he was meek in character, and lowly in condition. They expected a royal throne, to which all nations should come and bow the knee: he went through the villages teaching, and had not always "where to lay his head." So likewise in the gospel, wherever it is made known, there is much which men may dispute and cavil at. The gospel addresses them as what they are naturally unwilling to own themselves; it addresses them as sinners requiring pardon; nay, not pardon only, but atonement; the satisfaction furnished by another, which they could not offer from themselves. Those are happy who receive this truth, "the eyes of their understandings being opened." But all do not receive it. Like the Pharisees[5] of old they are offended at it; and complain, Are we to be condemned, who are not publicans and sinners; not extortioners, unjust, adulterers; who "fast twice in the week, and give tithes of all we possess?"[6] So still the cross of Christ, the propitiation for the sins of the world, is to some "a stumbling-block," and to others "foolishness;" whilst they ask, How can the obedience of one make up for the disobedience of another? How by

[4] John ix. 24—33. [5] John ix. 40; Luke xi. 45. [6] Luke xviii. 12.

the transgression of one can many be made sinners, or by the obedience of one can many be made righteous?[7] Yet still, to as many as receive it, this doctrine "is the power of God unto salvation."[8] It shows them at once the holiness of God, and the sinfulness of sin: and it gives them a foundation to rest on, which they could never find in themselves; never find in their own repentance or obedience. And so being justified by the blood of Christ, shed for the remission of their sins, they "have peace with God;" and going forth "in his fear, and in the comfort of the Holy Ghost," they *bring forth fruit, some thirty fold, some sixty, and some an hundred.*

And this was the purpose of the husbandman who sowed the seed; that the result should be FRUIT: "the fruit of the Spirit, which is love, joy, peace, long-suffering, gentleness, goodness, faith, meekness, temperance."[9] *The word* is, that Christ "gave himself for us, that he might redeem us from all iniquity, and purify unto himself a peculiar people, zealous of good works."[1] And when this word is *sown in good ground,* it brings forth fruit: all who receive it *bring forth fruit,* though not all in equal proportion or abundance.

This agrees with our experience in life. As there is a great difference in the natural powers of different men, so is there also in their spiritual attainments. Unto one five talents are given, to another two, to another one; "to every man according to his several ability."[2] The apostles themselves varied in the degree of their fruitfulness. St. Paul says concerning

[7] See Rom. v. 12—21. [8] 1 Cor. i. 18. [9] Gal. v. 22, 23.
[1] Tit. ii. 14. [2] Matt. xxv. 15.

himself, what is proved by his history, that he "laboured more abundantly than they all:"[3] his trials were severer, his efforts in the cause of the gospel more widely extended. So amongst the early Christians, when they "who had lands or houses, sold them, and brought the prices of the things that were sold, and laid them down at the apostles' feet:" those who had such possessions, and made this sacrifice, gave clearer proofs of zeal and earnestness, than they who received the produce of the same, when "distribution was made to every man according as he had need."[4] Again, some who *received the word*, and kept it, and were "added to the church," retained their comforts, their families, and homes. But others gave themselves up to aid the progress of the gospel: like Aquila and Priscilla, of whom St. Paul says, that "for his life they laid down their own necks:"[5] to whom not only he "gave thanks, but all the churches of Christ." Onesiphorus was another, who stood by the apostle at a time of special danger, for he "oft refreshed him, and was not ashamed of his chain," when he was imprisoned at Rome.[6] So he speaks of Tychicus, that he was "a beloved brother, and a faithful minister and fellow-servant in the Lord."[7] And so it is written of Dorcas, that she was "full of good works and alms-deeds which she did," insomuch that her death was the cause of general lamentation.[8]

It is the same in every age. As in the heavens above us there appear stars innumerable, and no two stars have the same precise size, or the same brightness:

[3] 1 Cor. xv. 10. [4] Acts iv. 34—37. [5] Rom. xvi. 11.
[6] 2 Tim. i. 16. [7] Col. iv. 7. [8] Acts ix. 36—39.

so amongst the disciples of Christ, there are different natural capacities, and different degrees of grace; there is in some much, in others little zeal; in some much, in others little self-denial; in some a perfect command over the evil passions, in others, a daily conflict, and sometimes hardly an effectual conflict, against the remainder of sin. Some are scarcely able to rise above the temporal things which draw them downwards. Others soar upward as on eagles' wings, and though still encompassed with the flesh, and dwelling here below, have "their conversation in heaven." But as the stars, though differing from one another in glory, have all some brightness: and as they all agree in this, that they are governed by the same laws, and obey the will of their Creator: so it is, and must be, with all those who *receive the word:* they set before them, as the rule of life, the precepts of their heavenly Father; they endeavour to bear "fruit unto holiness;" they all have the "testimony of their conscience, that in simplicity and godly sincerity," according to the will of God, and not according to the course of this world, they are desiring to walk before God in righteousness. For this they know;—there can be no other proof that they have understood, and received, and kept the word, except that they *bring forth fruit, whether it be thirty, or sixty, or an hundred fold.*

XL.

NATURE OF CHRISTIAN FAITH.

MATT. viii. 5—13.

13. *And Jesus said unto the centurion, Go thy way, and as thou hast believed, so be it done unto thee. And his servant was healed in the selfsame hour.*

THESE words were spoken to a Roman officer, by birth a heathen, but brought by the providence of God to serve in Judea.

This person was in distress, because a servant, and one dear and useful to him, was lying at home *sick of the palsy, grievously tormented.* He had heard the fame of Jesus; indeed, we must suppose, from the confidence which he expressed, that he had seen proofs of his power. So he laid aside the prejudices which as a Roman he would feel towards one who was a Jew; and came, and opened his grief. Jesus at once replied, "*I will come and heal*" thy servant. The man by his answer displayed both his own humility, and his sense of our Lord's majesty: saying, "Lord, I am not worthy that thou shouldest come under my roof: but speak the word only, and my servant shall be healed. For I am a man under authority, having soldiers under me; and I say to this man, Go, and he goeth; and to another, Come, and he cometh; and to my servant, Do this, and he doeth it." *Then Jesus said unto the cen-*

turion, Go thy way: and as thou hast believed, so be it done unto thee."

These last words especially deserve attention, as illustrating the nature of that FAITH to which the promises of the gospel are annexed. For this is not always rightly comprehended. Faith is sometimes spoken of as if it were supposed to be a peculiar faculty, connected with religion alone, and differing from any feelings or principles by which mankind are actuated in dealing with the things of this present world. Whereas, in fact, it is the principle which runs through the whole of human life, the principle which is called into exercise in the events and transactions of every day. The *object*, indeed, of faith is peculiar, when it is directed towards the Saviour of the world: but the *nature* of faith is the same in respect to the gospel, as when we give credit to the words, or put our trust in the power, of the fellow creatures with whom we are concerned in the ordinary course of human affairs.

One reason, perhaps, why the nature of faith is sometimes misunderstood, may be found in the fact that the word is used in two different senses in the New Testament. Both senses are equally important, but they are not identically the same. The word faith, in our version, sometimes signifies belief in the word of God, as delivered in Scripture, and sometimes signifies reliance on Jesus Christ, as our Mediator and Redeemer.

St. Paul, in writing to the Hebrews, describes faith as "the substance of things hoped for, the evidence of things not seen."[1] Here he manifestly refers to that belief in the word of God which makes things revealed

[1] Heb. xi. 1.

no less plain to us, than if they were evident to our senses, and we could see or handle them. As when the Christian is said to "walk by faith," and not "by sight:" to be governed by what he believes, and not by what he actually sees; believing in that heavenly kingdom which the Scriptures disclose to us, no less firmly than if he saw its King seated upon his throne, and the "faithful servants" entering in.

But the same apostle writes, in his letter to the Romans, "Being justified by faith, we have peace with God through Jesus Christ." And again, "By grace are ye saved, through faith; not of works, lest any man should boast." And elsewhere, he speaks of "the righteousness which is by faith of Jesus Christ, unto all, and upon all them that believe."

It is clear that in these later passages, the word *faith* means something very different from a mere belief in the Scriptures, that they proceed from God: something more than a belief in the promises which they hold out to all who obey his word. The faith which St. Paul intends, when he "desires to be found not having his own righteousness, but that which is through the faith of Christ:"[2] is not faith of the same kind as that which Noah showed, when "moved with fear" of the threatened deluge, "he prepared an ark for the saving of his house;" or the same as Abraham showed, when he believed the Divine promise, that a son should be born to him in his old age. In the case of Noah and Abraham, there was belief in the *word spoken*, that it would prove true. Whereas St. Paul speaks of faith in a *person*, that he could save from

[2] Phil. iii. 9.

death. In the original language, both kinds of faith are expressed by the same word. The same word is used to signify the crediting what is spoken, and the trusting in a person. And being the same word in the original, the same word is employed in our translation of the original; but must be understood according to the scope of the passage in which it occurs. Because, though we cannot rely on a person in whose existence we do not believe, we may very possibly believe in the existence of a person on whom we do not profess to rely.

It is the more needful to make this distinction, because there is reason to fear that many rest satisfied with the general confession of our Creed, that Jesus Christ is the Son of God, "who for us men, and for our salvation, came down from heaven." This is the foundation, the necessary foundation of Christian faith: but it is no more than the foundation, on which must be built the individual reliance upon Christ which is felt, when we appropriate his atonement to ourselves. The case is so important, that it cannot be too strongly insisted on; and may justify an illustration from an example of what is daily occurring in the world. Suppose, then, that I am told by one whom I have every reason to credit, that there is within my reach an excellent physician, whose skill is indisputable, whose advice may safely be depended on. And I believe it. I feel no doubt of it: the fact remains upon my memory.

This is one sense of the word faith, namely, belief in the report of those whose testimony is credible. Just as our belief in the incarnation of the Son of God is founded on the undeniable records of history.

It may happen in the course of time, that an attack of illness leads me to apply to my own use the information which I have received. I send for the physician; put my life in his hands, ready to do all that he requires, to submit to whatever he prescribes.

This is not only to believe in the existence and the skill of the physician, but to rely upon it, to put all my trust in it. And it affords an example of that faith, by which, being justified, we are "accounted righteous before God." In the first place, we believe the assurance of Scripture, that God, in pity for the state of the rebellious world, sent his well-beloved Son for our redemption: so that "he who hath the Son hath life, and he who hath not the Son hath not life." So far well. Still it is possible that we may believe this, as a fact of which we entertain no doubt; but it may lie upon the surface of our minds, not influencing us, not acted upon, any more than the knowledge that there is in our own neighbourhood an excellent physician.

The Centurion had a different faith from this, when he said, *Lord, speak the word only, and my servant shall be healed.* And we have his faith, when we apply the assurance of Scripture to ourselves, when we cast ourselves upon the Divine Physician, as those who have no health in them, and exhort him to make us whole; to cure our sinfulness by his propitiation, to heal our spiritual disease, by the inward renewing of our souls.

Faith, therefore, it appears, is no extraordinary faculty or property of the soul, which has nothing in common with ordinary life. Christian faith is peculiar only in its application. The usual business of life is conducted on the same principle, the same reliance on others, as the Centurion showed in applying to Jesus in his trouble. Return, for instance, to the illustration. Suppose, when struck with illness, we consult our physician; who says, Your case is one of imminent peril: this illness may be unto death. But there is a method of cure. And if you have sufficient sense of your danger, and sufficient confidence in me to follow what I prescribe, your life may be preserved.

Not a single day passes, when a transaction of this kind does not take place. A physician engages, as far as human foresight can venture to engage, to effect a cure. The sick man trusts him, and follows his advice; though it may demand a very different course of life from that which he would otherwise pursue; though it may even remove him from his own country, and require him to sojourn in a foreign land.

In what respect does this differ from the case of those to whom the Gospel is proposed? The Lord Jesus addresses them, as being in a state which, if remained in, must be fatal to the soul. When he affirms it to be the purpose of his Incarnation, that "as many as believe in him, may not perish;" he implies, that they must perish without him. When he promises that they who believe in him "shall not come into condemnation," but shall "pass from death unto life:" he implies, that without him they are in a state of death. But he shows at the same time, like the physician, that there is a way of escape; that the danger may be averted; that he came into the world for the purpose of taking off the condemnation. Though "no man cometh unto the Father, but by Him:" through Him "all may have access unto the Father."

Faith in Christ, therefore, reliance upon the promise of the Gospel, is no strange thing; but a state of mind which is familiar to us, with the nature of which we are daily conversant. Only let the same need be felt, as induces the dying man to send for his physician, as induced the Centurion to seek out Jesus, and entreat his aid.

There is indeed one difference, which must not be forgotten. In ordinary cases, we rely upon one of our fellow men. In the case which concerns the soul, we rely upon "our Lord and our God."

XLI.

THE BLESSEDNESS OF FAITH.

JOHN xx. 29.

Jesus saith unto him, Thomas, because thou hast seen me, thou hast believed: blessed are they that have not seen, and yet have believed.

A PROOF of Christ's resurrection, of his resurrection in the same body which had died, had been given to Thomas, which banished every doubt. But it is a proof which others can never possess. And he was allowed to require it, and it was granted him, to confirm the faith and increase the comfort of future Christians. *Jesus saith unto him, Thomas, because thou hast seen me, thou hast believed.*

It was needful that the Lord should be seen in the form of man by those who were to bear witness concerning him. It was needful that some should be able to say, like St. John, "The Word was made flesh, and we beheld his glory." We saw his miracles, and we heard his discourses.

So, again, after his resurrection he was seen not by the apostles only, but "by above five hundred brethren at once."[1] They saw, and "*because they saw believed.*"

But he could not possibly be seen by those who were hereafter to become his disciples, and have life through his name. These must believe in him "through their word:" that is, on the report of those who had lived with him in the flesh, and witnessed his death and his ascension.

Looking forward to these, the Lord declares to his incredulous apostle, *Blessed are they that have not seen, and yet have believed.* Like those to whom St. Peter wrote, and of whom he speaks, after mentioning the name of Christ: "whom not having seen, ye love; and in whom, though now ye see him not, yet believing, ye rejoice with joy unspeakable and full of glory."

Our Lord has left to these, and such as these, the comfort of knowing that they were in his mind, and graciously thought of, from the moment when the

[1] 1 Cor. xv. 6.

salvation wrought by him was about to be published to the world. He pronounces them BLESSED.

First, because they are at peace with God. "Being justified by faith, they have peace with God through Jesus Christ." And without this there is no peace. The desire of it first led them to the Redeemer. The desire of it first brought them to apply to him, and to ratify in their own persons the covenant of their baptism. And this they possess and enjoy: it is not a blessing for which they are to wait till some future time; of which they are to have no present sense or knowledge: they are not to linger in hope that the favour of God, his acceptance of their persons, his forgiveness of their sins, will be made over to them at some distant day: but it is already theirs; and their privilege is, in the language of the Liturgy, "being cleansed from their sins, to serve God with a quiet mind."

This is the foundation of their blessedness. They are blessed, also, because they are delivered from "the dominion of sin," delivered from this present evil world, "and enabled through the Spirit working in them to subdue the lusts of the flesh." They are blessed also, because they have secured to themselves, as they pass through this weary wilderness, a shepherd full of kindness, full of care, and full of power. They have the confidence expressed by St. Paul, "My God shall supply all your need." They have the assurance which was granted to him, "My grace is sufficient for thee."

In all this there is as much of blessedness as the present life is capable of receiving.

Still it is our present life: and it is life in a fallen world. The sinfulness which adheres to the heart, even after the power of sin is broken, still interrupts and disturbs its peace. And the many wants, the many afflictions which exist, and from which the children of God are not exempted, often make us confess and feel, that here is not our hope: that the blessedness promised to the Christian is something which cannot be found below: that he must set his affections on things above, and look there, at God's right hand, for "the fulness of joy, and pleasures for evermore."

And this is the real cause, why the Lord here so solemnly pronounces those blessed who believe: because theirs is the kingdom prepared of God for the righteous; because theirs are the good things which "eye hath not seen, nor ear heard, neither hath it entered into the heart of man to conceive." We grievously undervalue this: our spirits, tied and bound by this present world, are unable to think of it as it deserves. But our Lord knew, well and fully knew, the nature, and the reality, and the extent of that happiness. He had a complete acquaintance with the things laid up at God's right hand for them that love him: and therefore he says, *Blessed are they that have believed,* because they shall possess those joys. At the moment, they may not feel themselves blessed. But he to whom the future is present; he to whom what shall be is as if it were; he sees beyond their trials, their labours, and their sorrows, and anticipates the end. He knew, for example, that his apostles should suffer all that makes this life grievous; imprisonme the scourge, reproach, hunger, cold, and nakedne Yet he said, "Blessed are ye: for great is your rewa in heaven." He knew that his followers would oft groan heavily in spirit, being burdened with the sen of their inward corruptions and rebellious desir Yet he said, "Blessed are the poor in spirit." I knew that many of those whom God would hereaft give him, would languish in poverty, would be o pressed by sickness and by pain. Yet he said, "Bless are ye that weep now, for ye shall laugh." The ca may be compared to what took place at the death the first martyr, Stephen. Those who stood by, a saw him stretched along the ground, bleeding, a bruised, and maimed, and gasping for breath, mig pity him, as if brought to the lowest state of hum wretchedness. But what was his real feeling and co dition? "Behold," he exclaims, "I see the heave opened, and the Son of man standing at the right ha of God."[2] And so the Lord Jesus. He is well awa that grief and trial and tribulation are the lot of ma of his own people. But he sees also the heavens open and the earth receding:—earth receding, with all load of sin and misery; and the heavens opening wi all the glory which is to be revealed:—and therefc he says, *Blessed are they that have believed;* for the "shall be a performance of those things which we spoken of the Lord."

These are the thoughts which may animate t

[2] Acts vii. 56.

faithful disciple of Christ under all the trials and difficulties of his earthly warfare. His Lord, who knew them all, has pronounced him *blessed.* And he is blessed. Blessed now in the favour and support of Almighty God: and—what is alone important in the sight of Infinite Wisdom—blessed for eternity.

XLII.

THE NEW CREATURE.

2 Cor. v. 17.

If any man be in Christ, he is a new creature: old things are passed away; behold all things are become new.

It is interesting to trace the course of the apostle's mind, by which he is brought to this conclusion. He begins with himself: reflects upon his former state, and compares his present views and sentiments. Formerly, he had judged concerning Christ, the expected Messiah, after the manner of the Jews, as one who should redeem them from their worldly enemies, instead of dying for their sins. Now, he only knew Christ, as crucified on earth, and having his kingdom in heaven. Formerly, he had looked for acceptance with God through the law of Moses, and satisfied himself that he was, "touching the righteousness which is of the law, blameless."[1] Now, he had seen that *old things were passed away:* for that "if righteousness were of the law," and man could be justified by fulfilment of the law, then "Christ had died in vain:"[2] without intelligible reason. So that *all things were become new* in his opinions upon this point: "what things were gain to him, those he counted loss for Christ;" and desired only "to be found in him, not having his own righteousness, which is of the law, but that which is through the faith of Christ, the righteousness which is of God by faith."[3]

Now the man is what his principles make him: and Paul, sitting at the feet of Gamaliel, or living according to the strictest sect of the Jewish religion as a Pharisee, was a totally different person from Paul living as a preacher of that faith which once he destroyed. The change was like what he terms it: *a new creation:*[4] *old things were passed away; behold all things were become new.* He reflects on himself as he once was, and sees himself no longer the same: regards things and persons in as different a light, as if he was in a new world.

And this leads him to a more general remark. The terms he had used, do not only apply to his own case,—do not only describe the difference between Paul the persecutor and Paul the apostle,—but *if any man* be in Christ Jesus, he *is a new creature.*

Doubtless it is so. If a man has embraced the religion of Christ, and is living in the faith of the Son of God, *he is a new creature:* a change is wrought in him which cannot be otherwise adequately described: a change, if not from his former habits, certainly from

[1] Phil. iii. 6. [2] Gal. ii. 21. [3] Phil. iii. 7—9.
[4] *καινη κτισις.*

his original nature; when he has "put off the old man, which is corrupt according to the deceitful lusts, and is renewed in the spirit of his mind; and has put on the new man, which after God is created in righteousness and true holiness."[5]

Probably, however, in this sentence Paul chiefly alludes to that new principle of life of which he had been just speaking; how "he judged, that if one died for all, then were all dead; and that he died for all, that they which live, should not henceforth live unto themselves, but unto him who died for them."[6] *If any man be* truly *in Christ*, this will be his ruling principle; and whosoever does live on this principle, will be a totally different person from what he would be otherwise: a totally different person, perhaps, from what in former ignorance he has been. In that case, he can look into himself, and find a *new creation:* his acquaintance can see his change of sentiments and habits, and say, *old things are passed away; behold all things are become new.* The great truth of the gospel, Christ dying for man, and man without him dead, cannot be received into the heart without producing an effect which no slighter expression can suit, no weaker phrase describe. All the sentiments combined, which might be felt towards a physician, who had recalled us from the grave; towards a deliverer, who had rescued us from a cruel tyrant's power; towards a benefactor, who had ransomed us from bondage; towards a companion, who had laid down his life to preserve his friend; all these would fall far short of the feelings which the Christian

[5] Eph. iv. 22–24. [6] 2 Cor. v. 15.

ought to entertain, and desires to entertain, towards his Saviour.

And these are not barren feelings; they lead to action: they lead to vital religion, to practical Christianity; to that which alone deserves the name of Christianity. They lead to habits which are new to all who have not uniformly directed their lives according to the principles of their baptism.

Therefore, if any man be in Christ Jesus, he is a new creature: being made so, not by caprice or desire of singularity, but through the principles which govern him, and the sentiments which are dominant in his mind.

And it follows, that if any man be not a *new creature,* he is not *in Christ Jesus:* "Christ profiteth him nothing," unless he is changed from what he would be by nature, and has the signs of grace. The purpose of the gospel is not fulfilled in him, unless he is "delivered from this present evil world."[7] And whosoever is so far delivered from this present world, from its cares, its pursuits, its pleasures, as to seek first the kingdom of God and his righteousness, *he is a new creature: old things are passed away* with him, *behold, all things are become new.*

[7] Gal. i. 4.

XLIII.

THE CHRISTIAN THE TEMPLE OF GOD.

1 Cor. iii. 16, 17.

16. *Know ye not that ye are the temple of God, and that the Spirit of God dwelleth in you?*

As if St. Paul had said, I have had occasion, in the course of my preceding argument, to speak of a building, of an architect, of a foundation: and not without meaning. *Ye are the temple of God.* Ye, the Christians of Corinth, are raised up to the glory of God; just in the same manner as the many temples which adorn your city, are intended to honour the gods, (which are no Gods) to whom they are dedicated. St. Paul uses the example frequently in writing to the Corinthians,[1] probably because their city was famous for the grandeur and richness of its temples. And it is a striking example. The whole christian body dispersed throughout the world, constitutes one magnificent temple built of God to his own honour. Every community of christian worshippers, such as those who were united in the faith at Corinth, or Philippi, or Ephesus, is also a temple of the living God; "built upon the foundation of the apostles and prophets, Jesus Christ himself being the chief corner-stone; in whom all the building fitly framed together groweth unto an holy temple in the Lord."[2]

[1] See 1 Cor. vi. 19; 2 Cor. vi. 16. [2] Ephes. ii. 20, 21.

And not only so; but the same may be affirmed of every individual Christian; as Paul does say, both here, and afterwards;[3] "Know ye not, that your body is the temple of the Holy Ghost, which ye have of God, and ye are not your own?" For as the members of Christ's church in the world at large, form one vast building, in which God may be glorified; so each single Christian is a separate temple or shrine, raised for the same purpose, and called to a share of the like glory.

The example is very accurate. There is a close resemblance in the manner in which the temple built of stone, and the living temple which Christians form, are chosen and set apart to the service of God.

The first temple of which we read in sacred history, is that which David planned, and Solomon afterwards completed with extraordinary magnificence at Jerusalem. It was built upon a spot which Araunah the Jebusite had used as a threshing floor.[4] At that spot the pestilence ceased which was raging through the land. And God commanded David to rear an altar there, in token of the mercy which he had shown in staying the hand of the destroying angel.

From that time the spot was made sacred, which before had been occupied for a common though useful purpose. Before, its business had been of this world, ministering to men that bread which whoever eateth shall hunger again.[5] It afterwards became holy ground, and was to supply the food which nourishes the soul for ever.

The case was very similar, when, in obedience to

[3] 1 Cor. vi. 19. [4] See 2 Sam. xxiv. 18, &c. [5] See John vi. 36, &c.

the will of God, the Gospel was preached to these Corinthians. The command was given to David, "Go and rear an altar to the Lord in the threshing-floor of Araunah." And so the word was given to the apostles: "Go ye, and teach all nations, baptizing them in the name of the Father, and of the Son, and of the Holy Ghost."[6] They who received the word, were taken from a state in which they were bringing no honour to God: nay, worse, were dishonouring and denying him, worshipping instead the work of their own hands, the image of men like themselves, and following not his will, but the devices and desires of their own hearts. So that it was not with them, as with the threshing-floor where the temple of Jerusalem was built; which, though not a sacred place, had been used innocently; these, before they were called to be believers, had been actually profane: before they entered into the house of God, they had been engaged in the work and doing the will of Satan. From this state they were taken, that they might serve God: acknowledge his right to rule over them: and live no longer unto themselves, but unto Him who had called them to "glorify him in their body and their spirit, which are his."[7] So that as we should describe a christian church, as a holy place, a peculiar building: so St. Peter says of Christian men: "Ye are a chosen generation, a royal priesthood, a holy nation, a peculiar people; that ye should show forth the praises of him who hath called you out of darkness into his marvellous light."[8]

Thus it proved, for instance, at Ephesus. The people to whom the Gospel was preached there, had

[6] Matt. xxviii. 19. [7] 1 Cor. vi. 20. [8] 1 Pet. ii. 9.

been living in a way which more especially dishonours God; for they had pretended to power which only He can possess, and to knowledge, which belongs to Him alone.[9] But at the preaching of Paul, "power fell on them all, and the name of the Lord Jesus was magnified: and many that believed, came, and confessed, and showed their deeds. Many of them also which used curious arts brought their books together, and burned them before all men: and they counted the price of them, and found it fifty thousand pieces of silver."

Nay, we need not go beyond these very Corinthians for an example. In their former ignorance they had done those things which cannot be done by men who are holy to the Lord. St. Paul says of them,—after describing the practices which are abominable in the sight of God,—"Such were some of you. But ye are washed, but ye are sanctified, but ye are justified in the name of the Lord Jesus, and by the Spirit of our God."[1]

Thus it is when a man like Zaccheus,[2] or a body of men like the Ephesians or Corinthians, are taken from things common and worldly, or still more from things profane and wicked, and consecrated to God as believers in Christ Jesus. It is with them as with the spot on which a church is raised. "Old things are passed away; behold, all things are become new." What was common, is made sacred. What was this world's property, now belongs to God. What did belong to earth is now concerned with heaven.

But the dignity to which man is thus raised, like all

[9] Acts xix. 17—19. [1] 1 Cor. vi. 9—11. [2] Luke xix. 7—9.

dignity, has duties connected with it. That which is set apart to the glory of God, must not disgrace his name. So that the apostle reminds the Corinthians:

17. *If any man defile the temple of God, him shall God destroy: for the temple of God is holy, which temple ye are.*

False teachers *defile the temple of God.* Their errors, to which he had been before alluding, tend to make those who are misled by them unworthy of their high calling. Let all beware therefore, and take heed to the doctrine which they built upon the foundation of christian faith, lest it should be said of them, in the language of the Psalmist, "Thy holy temple they have profaned."[3]

And so likewise any wickedness *defiles the temple of God;* defiles the soul, which ought to be preserved pure and without spot, like God's own sanctuary. And if a person admitted into his bosom a wilful sin, and allowed it to keep possession there, he was like one who, without proper purification, dared to worship in the temple, or to take that which is holy, and cast it to dogs or swine.

Let them be warned, therefore, and remember, that *the temple of God is holy, which temple ye are.* The temple in which God is worshipped, is consecrated for the express purpose, that ever afterwards it may be separated from places profane or worldly. They were in like circumstances. They had been dedicated to God, and made his children "through the adoption that is in Christ Jesus." If they *defiled the temple of*

[3] Psa. lxxiv. 7.

God, they could only expect to be shut out "from his presence and the glory of his power." The "house of prayer" must remain holy, as befits a house of prayer, and not be turned into "a den of thieves."[4]

XLIV.

FAITH WORKING BY LOVE.

Matthew xxv. 34—40.

34. *Then shall the king say unto them on his right hand, Come, ye blessed of my Father, inherit the kingdom prepared for you from the foundation of the world.*
35. *For I was an hungered, and ye gave me meat: I was thirsty, and ye gave me drink: I was a stranger, and ye took me in.*
36. *Naked, and ye clothed me: I was sick, and ye visited me: I was in prison, and ye came unto me.*
37. *Then shall the righteous answer him, saying, Lord, when saw we thee an hungered, and fed thee; or thirsty and gave thee drink?*
38. *When saw we thee a stranger, and took thee in? or naked and clothed thee?*
39. *Or when saw we thee sick, or in prison, and came unto thee?*

[4] Matt. xxi. 13.

40. *The king shall answer and say unto them, Verily I say unto you, Inasmuch as ye have done it unto one of the least of these my brethren, ye have done it unto me.*

It may at first sight appear remarkable, that the test or proof of character brought forward in the description of the day of judgment here given us by our Lord, is taken entirely from works of mercy and charity. Ye have clothed the naked, and relieved the hungry, and visited the prisoner: what is done to the least of these my brethren, is done unto me: *Come, ye blessed of my Father, receive the kingdom prepared for you from the foundation of the world.*

This, at first sight, seems opposed to the whole tenor of the Gospel, which declares that "we are accounted righteous before God, only for the merit of our Lord and Saviour Jesus Christ, by faith, and not for our own works and deservings:"[1] that "by grace we are saved; not of works, lest any man should boast:" that, so far from relying upon our good deeds, our justice, our integrity, our zeal, or our charity, our language is to be, when we "have done all," "we are unprofitable servants," who can advance no claim.[2]

The account, however, here given of the day of judgment, does not contradict this truth. But it discloses the real nature of faith in Christ Jesus; which is not a mere assent to the history of his Advent and Incarnation;—which is not a presumptuous confidence in his merits: but is the "receiving him" with the whole heart, as "the way, the truth, and the life:" alike the Redeemer to atone, and the King or Lord to guide

[1] Art. xi. [2] Luke xvii. 10.

and rule. This is the faith which unites him to us, and us to him. This is the faith by which "he is made unto us wisdom, and righteousness, and sanctification, and redemption." This is the faith according to which "man believeth unto righteousness."

And this faith will naturally and necessarily lead to the works here described of active charity.

For, first, those who have this faith, obey their Lord's precepts. And his precepts tell us, that the characteristic of his disciples is to "have love one towards another;" and that the law and the prophets are all comprehended in this, that, "whatsoever we would that men should do unto us, we do also unto them."

Secondly, those who have genuine faith in Christ will imitate his example. And we well know that his example was the model of that benevolence which his precepts enjoin. If, then, he "went about doing good," so must his disciples. "If he so loved us," as our faith avows that he did, "we ought also to love one another."

Thirdly, those who truly believe in Christ, learn of him to view their fellow-creatures in a light peculiar to the Christian: for their fellow-creatures are those whom he so loved, as to descend from heaven for their redemption; those whom he so pitied as to lay down his life for their sakes. And therefore it is, that if hungry, they are to be fed; if naked, they are to be clothed; if strangers, they are to be cared for; if sick, or in prison, they are to be visited; if erring, they are to be reclaimed; if young, they are to be nurtured; if ignorant, they are to be instructed. Thus manifesting our "love not in word, neither in tongue, but in deed and in truth, we know that we are of the truth, and shall assure our hearts before him."[3] For he has said, *Inasmuch as ye have done it unto one of the least of these my brethren, ye have done it unto me.*

Those, then, who are here represented as the righteous, who "go into life eternal," are rewarded for their works. But the ground of their acceptance is still their faith. For faith is the cause why they have wrought these works. Faith is the principle; works, the effect. Holiness, purity, temperance, integrity, mercy, charity, are proofs of the existence and of the soundness of the principle from which they spring.

Whereas, on the other hand, the absence of brotherly kindness and charity is proof of the absence or the inefficacy of that on which all depends: is evidence, discernible by men, of the absence of that inward principle which men cannot discern, but which He discerns who knows what is in men; absence of that genuine faith, which, wherever it exists, must produce active love towards all our fellow-creatures. So that one way in which we are taught to "know that we have passed from death unto life," is "because we love the brethren." "He that loveth not his brother, abideth in death."[4]

It appears, therefore, that in the description here given us of the judgment-day, the one class is accepted, not because they had works independently of faith, but because their faith in the Redeemer "wrought

[3] 1 John iii. 19. [4] 1 John iii. 14.

with their works, and by works was their faith made perfect."[5] While the other class is rejected, not because they had no works to justify and save them (for what would be the hope of any man, if he trusted to be saved or justified by anything he had done or can do?); but because their conduct had shown, that they had no real faith in him whom they had been used to call by the name of Lord and Saviour. "For as the body without the spirit is dead, so faith without works is dead also."[6]

XLV.

RELIEF SENT FROM ANTIOCH TO JUDEA.

Acts xi. 29, 30.

29. *Then the disciples, every man according to his ability, determined to send relief unto the brethren which dwelt in Judea:*
30. *Which also they did, and sent it to the elders by the hands of Barnabas and Saul.*

The brethren in Judea were exposed to particular distress, in consequence of a wide-spreading famine,

[5] See James ii. 22. [6] Ib. ii. 26.

which affected the whole Roman empire in the time of the emperor Claudius, about forty-four years after the birth of Christ. And this calamity gave occasion to the charity here mentioned, which was, as far as we know, or have reason to believe, the first transaction of the kind in the history of the world. Certain inhabitants of Antioch meet together, and hearing of a calamity by which the inhabitants of another country, a distant and unconnected country, are brought into distress, make a common contribution, *every man according to his ability,* and send it for their relief.

If men enter upon a new course of conduct, we conclude that some new motive has been brought to bear upon them. In the present case, what was that motive? They *determine to send relief unto the brethren which dwelt in Judea.* But men had always been *brethren,* descended from the same Father. They had always been united under a common lot, made subject to common calamities, which may be much alleviated by being shared. Still they had not been brought to look on one another in this light, as objects of mutual interest and assistance. Every man had "looked on his own things," and no man on "the things of others." Their private interests absorbed and employed them.

Now, however, a new system begins. A new influence was coming into operation. Those who were united in the christian faith were bound together by ties which could not be unavailing. The love of God manifested in so extraordinary a manner towards themselves, had set them an example which they must imitate, had imposed on them a duty which they must needs perform. St. John has explained this: "Brethren, herein was love; not that we loved God, but that he loved us, and sent his Son to be the propitiation for our sins. If God so loved us, we ought also to love one another."[1] We ought to love one another, when he has given us this proof of the way in which he regards mankind. We ought to love one another, because such is the will and the command of him who so loved us. And "he that loveth not his brother whom he hath seen, how can he love God whom he hath not seen?"[2] If he love not the children who are before his eyes, how can he love the Father, who is far above out of his sight, but who has required this proof of his gratitude, this offering of a heart thankful for the benefits which it has received?

But there was another reason why these Christians were forward to assist their suffering brethren in a way which had not before been usual. They had learnt to look upon the things of this world in a new light. They had learnt to see their possessions as something beyond the means of private enjoyment, or personal gratification: to see them as given for a purpose, and to be employed for a purpose. The bent of the heart is shown by the manner in which these earthly things are used. And the heart is shown to be rightly bent, when they are used to honour and serve the Almighty giver.

"The children of this generation" see but one use of wealth: how they may most fully gratify the inclination which urges them most strongly: whether it be to hoard up stores which their family may afterwards enjoy, or whether it be to follow a course of vanity and self-indulgence. Too commonly, their language is that expressed in our

[1] Eph. iv. 10. [2] 1 John iv. 20.

Lord's parable; "Soul, thou hast much goods laid up for many years; take thine ease, eat, drink, and be merry."[3] Then, in the pursuit of the objects which gratify them, their fortune is engaged: and even if they had the inclination to be charitable, they have not left to themselves the means.

It is not so with one who has received the faith of Christ as the rule by which he is to live. He knows that this world's good is a talent placed in his hands, of which he is to make use in conformity with the will of him to whom he owes it. That will is laid down in terms too clear to be mistaken.[4] "Charge them that are rich in this world, that they be not high-minded, nor trust in uncertain riches, but in the living God, who giveth us richly all things to enjoy: that they do good, that they be rich in good works, ready to distribute, willing to communicate: laying up in store for themselves a good foundation against the time to come, that they may lay hold on eternal life."

Under this view, it was given as a rule to these early Christians, that "upon the first day of the week every one of them should lay by him in store according as God had prospered him."[5] This produced a common stock, for the use of "the household of faith:" for the christian family congregated together: partly to support the pastors and teachers, and partly to assist the destitute persons of the flock. Sometimes, as on this occasion, there was a further call, for the relief of more distant brethren. These were of the same family, though settled elsewhere: still they were disciples of the same Lord, and had the same faith and hope as the Chris-

[3] Luke xii. 19. [4] 1 Tim. vi. 17—19. [5] 1 Cor. xvi. 2.

tians of Antioch. So that *every man, according to his ability, determined to send relief unto the brethren which dwelt in Judea.*

Charity, however, like wisdom, "dwells with prudence."[6] The fund which might have been useless, perhaps injurious, unless placed under discreet management, was intrusted to the care of *the elders.* Elders had been ordained, as was indispensable, over the different churches throughout Judea, and the distribution of the relief fund was placed in their hands.

It is thus that God intends that Christians should minister to one another. He has placed them in different ranks, and with different opportunities, and has given them a bond of union. They are not connected by an uniform condition, which is contrary to the course of the world. But they are connected by a common interest, under which what is superfluous to some, makes up what is wanting to others. So "the rich and the poor meet together: the Lord is the maker of them all."[7]

[6] See Prov. viii. 12. [7] Prov. xxii. 2.

XLVI.

EXCELLENCE OF CHARITY.

1 Cor. xiii. 8—13.

8. *Charity never faileth: but whether there be prophecies, they shall fail; whether there be tongues, they shall cease; whether there be knowledge, it shall vanish away.*
9. *For we know in part, and we prophesy in part.*
10. *But when that which is perfect is come, then that which is in part shall be done away.*

St. Paul had before described the excellence of that spirit of love, which is here termed charity, and had shown that without it all mental qualifications, as the faculty of speaking with tongues, or prophesying, would be nothing worth in the sight of God. He now adds another and a stronger reason besides those which he had before mentioned, *why charity* is far above all outward gifts or qualifications. *It never faileth:* it is a quality engrafted on the soul by the Holy Spirit, and will abide with it for ever, no otherwise changed than in being "made perfect." Whereas, *whether there be prophecies, they shall fail: whether there be tongues, they shall cease: whether there be knowledge, it shall vanish away.* Tongues, or prophecies, may be compared to a language which is spoken in the country where a man now is, but will be no longer needed when he leaves it.

Charity is an universal language; not only spoken here on earth, but in heaven also; the possession of it is like the possessing that which all ages and all countries have agreed in reckoning valuable; so that he who has such a treasure, will every where be rich. Such is the difference between charity, and those outward gifts which the Corinthians too highly prized. *Prophecies*, and *tongues*, and *knowledge*, edify the church on earth; they instruct, they convince, they build up in the faith those who are here to be made "wise unto salvation." But, for that very reason, they are only needful for a time. They who "shall be accounted worthy to obtain that world, and the resurrection from the dead,"[1] and "are as the angels of God in heaven," they will no longer need the *prophecy* which is to explain God's counsels, or the *tongues* which are to make them known. *When that which is perfect is come, then that which is in part shall be done away.* The glimmering ray of knowledge which we can now attain will lose its value, being eclipsed by the full and unclouded light of heaven; just as the morning star vanishes away before the brightness of the sun when it is risen. It will not be so with that brotherly love which has sprung up in the soul together with prophecy and knowledge. *Prophecies shall fail, and tongues shall cease,* whilst the *charity* which they have aided to produce remains, and flourishes for ever in the genial climate which the soul is to inhabit hereafter.

In making this contrast between christian love and outward qualifications, St. Paul delicately warns the Corinthians of their errors and their danger. Much in

[1] Luke xx. 35.

their conduct had been very contrary to love and charity. Meanwhile they had prided themselves in their spiritual gifts, and thought highly of their knowledge. The apostle reminds them of the imperfection of that knowledge. The knowledge of the wisest man, as to the Almighty, his counsels or his attributes, is but the knowledge of a child; and will so appear, *when that which is perfect is come.*

11. *When I was a child, I spake as a child, I understood as a child, I thought as a child; but when I became a man, I put away childish things.*
12. *For now we see through a glass darkly; but then face to face: now I know in part; but then shall I know even as also I am known.*
13. *And now abideth faith, hope, charity, these three; but the greatest of these is charity.*

This brings us to a further proof of the excellence of *charity*. It had been before shown to be superior to tongues and prophecies. But it is also superior to *faith* and *hope*. Faith and hope are very different from tongues and prophecies. These were soon to fail and cease, and not to be revived; the need of them would be over in the church: whereas faith and hope can never fail on earth, or the church itself must fail with them. To the end of time, faith must not cease, or hope vanish away. *Now abideth faith, hope, charity. These three* unite together, and form the Christian character.

The faith of which Paul here speaks, is that which is described in the eleventh chapter to the Hebrews: that faith by which we lay hold of the promises of

God revealed in his word; that faith which is "the substance of things hoped for, the evidence of things not seen."[2] That faith is the Christian's breath: it gives him life, new life, as a child of God: it gives him vigour, to behave as one of God's family, and be active in his service; if that faith were to cease whilst he remains here below, his life as a Christian would expire, and he would "return again to his dust."

And if *faith* is needful that the Christian may live, *hope* is needful that he may be supported and animated in life; and thus enabled to meet his labours and his trials, as he "works out his salvation in the world." Paul even says, elsewhere, "We are saved by hope;"[3] we never should have perseverance to hold on our way, if we had not *hope* to sustain and encourage us. He also calls it "the anchor of the soul;"[4] the anchor fixed upon the eternal world, which keeps the soul at rest amidst the storms of temptation, and stedfast and secure through all the adverse winds which threaten to divert it from its onward course, and wreck it among the rocks and quicksands of this present world.

Therefore *now abideth faith and hope.* But the time will come when faith and hope will have performed their office. They will have brought the vessel into "the haven where it would be:" and the sails by which it has been borne along may be taken down, and the anchor by which it has been kept secure may be laid aside. The things believed in, will be things seen; the things hoped for, will

[2] Heb. xi. 1. [3] Rom. viii. 24. [4] Heb. vi. 19.

be things possessed and enjoyed. No need of faith, where there is no doubt or uncertainty; no need of hope, where all is "fulness of joy, and pleasures for evermore."

But it is not thus with CHARITY. *Charity never faileth.* It now abideth with faith and hope: but it *is greater than these,* because it will abide, when faith and hope are done away. It is, in truth, that quality which faith and hope are to contribute towards producing: that quality which proves the renewal of the soul through "sanctification of the Spirit and belief of the truth." And having been here, as in an elementary state, formed, and nourished, and exercised, it accompanies the soul to those regions where all is love; it is admitted into the presence of God; and "God is love; and he that dwelleth in love, dwelleth in God and God in him."[5]

Examples show these things most plainly: and the first martyr, Stephen, is well fitted to illustrate Paul's meaning. Stephen was full of faith, and full of hope: and, animated by faith and hope, he so keenly reproved the high-priest and his council, that they "cast him out of the city, and stoned him."[6] "But he, looking stedfastly up to heaven, saw the glory of God, and Jesus standing at the right hand of God; and said, Behold, I see the heavens opened, and the Son of man standing at the right hand of God."

Faith, then, and hope, were now ceasing: Stephen beheld the Saviour, in whom before he had believed; saw the glory of God, of which he was immediately to partake; and the hope which had thus far encouraged

[5] 1 John iv. 16. [6] Acts vii. 54—60.

him, was now realized. But his last words were words of CHARITY. "He kneeled down, and cried with a loud voice, Lord, lay not this sin to their charge. And when he had said this, he fell asleep." His body returned to the earth; and "his spirit returned to God who gave it:" and with the spirit, the charity by which it was filled and animated. Had his departing soul been inflamed with wrath and hatred, like that of his enemies, it would have ascended to God a malicious and angry soul. But it did ascend to God as a loving and forgiving soul: and that is the frame in which heaven must be entered, and heaven must be enjoyed. "Blessed are the merciful; for they shall obtain mercy." "Every one that loveth is born of God, and knoweth God." "If we love one another, God dwelleth in us, and his love is perfected in us."

And, therefore, though we "have all faith that we could remove mountains," and "full assurance of hope," that God hath chosen us for his own, if "we have not charity, we are nothing." We have not that spirit which marks the children of God. We have not that spirit which "accompanies salvation," and belongs to the kingdom of heaven.

Still, we may well rejoice that we are not to look upon this, or any other christian grace, as the ground of our pardon and acceptance with God. Who would venture his salvation on his freedom from all envy, selfishness, wrath, or other uncharitable temper, even for a single day? Alas! "in many things we all offend:"[7] fall very short of what perfect charity re-

[7] James iii. 2.

quires. Every work of self-examination must also be a work of repentance; and must send us, as it were, afresh, to claim our interest in Him, "whose blood cleanseth from all sin," and who "ever liveth to make intercession" for his faithful though unworthy followers.

XLVII.

THE PROPER USE OF THE LAW.

1 Tim. i. 5—11.

5. *Now the end of the commandment*[1] *is charity out of a pure heart, and of a good conscience, and of faith unfeigned:*
6. *From which some having swerved have turned aside unto vain jangling;*
7. *Desiring to be teachers of the law; understanding neither what they say, nor whereof they affirm.*

Christian teachers do not aim at the right object, unless their doctrine tends to enforce *the end of the commandment*, the great purpose of the revealed word.

[1] Properly, *the sum of what thou shouldest charge them.* The word rendered here commandment, is the noun derived from the verb παραγγελλω, rendered *charge* in verse 3.

That end is here declared to be *charity*, or love, proceeding *out of a pure heart, and a good conscience, and faith unfeigned.* Faith is the source; sincere love to God and man flow out of it; love to God, who has reconciled us to himself by the blood of the atonement, and so purified the heart and conscience; and love to mankind as creatures of God, objects of the same mercy, and partakers of the same redemption.

From these, the real purposes of the gospel commandment, *some had swerved: had turned aside* to what deserved no better name than *vain jangling* or babbling: and ignorantly undertaking to make the law, and not the Gospel, the ground or subject of their teaching; *desiring to be teachers of the law, understanding neither what they say, nor whereof they affirm.* Because so to teach the law, as they taught it; to make the letter of the commandments which Moses gave to the Israelites, the test of a man's spiritual state and eternal hope, was to be ignorant of the nature of the gospel: and not to understand that "as the law came by Moses, so grace and truth came by Jesus Christ."[2] Moses declared the will of God, and the duty of man: and, so far, there is no difference between the gospel and the law. God has uniformly the same will: man has universally the same duty. But Moses could not declare, except through the dark hints of type and prophecy, what provision God had made for man's defect of duty, and departure from God's will. Moses could show, that "the wages of sin is death:" as in fact he did show, when he issued the divine commands, and then added, "See, I have set before thee life, and death,

[2] John i. 17.

blessing and cursing."[3] But Moses was not empowered to say, "The gift of God is eternal life, through Jesus Christ our Lord."[4] He placed his people in a state of discipline, which was to lead them to the atonement of the Cross. But it was no Christian teaching to be a *teacher of the law,* unless it were so used as to bring the hearer to Christ, as "the end of the law for righteousness to every one that believeth."[5]

"Do we then make void the law through faith? Yea, we establish the law."[6]

8. *We know that the law is good, if a man use it lawfully:*
9. *Knowing this, that the law is not made for a righteous man, but for the lawless and disobedient, for the ungodly and for sinners, for unholy and profane, for murderers of fathers, and murderers of mothers, for manslayers,*
10. *For whoremongers, for them that defile themselves with mankind, for men-stealers, for liars, for perjured persons, and if there be any other thing that is contrary to sound doctrine:*
11. *According to the glorious gospel of the blessed God, which was committed to my trust.*

The law is not laid down *for a righteous man:* it is not the test by which he is to be judged: he neither looks to be absolved, as having exactly kept it: nor is he condemned, because in anything he has come short of it. The christian man is not dependent on the Mosaic sentence, "Cursed is every one that continueth not in all things that are written in the law, to do them."[7] In this respect, Christ has released

[3] Deut. xxx. 19. [4] Rom. vi. 23. [5] Ib. x. 4.
[6] Ib. iii. 31. [7] Gal. iii. 10.

us "from the curse of the law, being made a curse for us. If absolute obedience to the letter of the commandments were to be the ground of our justification in the sight of God, who could be saved? And, therefore, *the law is not made for a righteous man.* It is not to be urged against him, that he is not "without sin;" that "in many things he offends:" that "the flesh lusteth against the spirit:" that "he cannot do the things he would." This is not to be urged against him; because he does not plead innocence as the ground of his justification. When asked at the bar of God, Hast thou transgressed the law in thought, or word, or deed? Guilty, or not guilty? he does not pretend that in nothing has he transgressed. He does not plead his own righteousness, but the merits of Him who died for his unrighteousness.

But the law is made for the lawless and disobedient, for the ungodly and for sinners, for unholy and profane, for whatever is contrary to sound doctrine, according to the glorious gospel of the blessed God. For these *the law is used lawfully;* used to show to the wicked and impenitent the heinousness of their sin; to show them the holy nature of Him "with whom they have to do;" to prove the justice of their condemnation; that they may cast away the rebellious arms which they have wielded against the Most High, and lay them at the foot of the cross; and so may obtain mercy, and partake of the blessings of redemption. *The law was made for* Zaccheus, whilst practising the covetous and fraudulent habits of the class to which he belonged. For him the law was made, saying, "Thou shalt not steal;" "thou shalt not covet;" "and whatsoever ye would that men should do to you, do ye also unto them." Had he persisted in the habits of covetousness and extortion, that law would have condemned him "at the great day." But, on the other hand, the law was not made for Zaccheus, after he had repented of his covetousness, and showed his repentance by restitution, and his change of heart by active and ample charity. It would not be his condemnation, that for many years he had committed those offences against the law, of which he had now repented. Neither would it be his condemnation, that if God were to mark every deviation from the strict holiness of the law, he could not abide the test, even now that he was a converted man: because the "promise by faith of Jesus Christ is unto all them that believe,"[2] and they look to eternal life, not as merited by them, but as purchased for them.

Those, therefore, who desire to *be teachers of the law*, ought to *understand what they say*. Otherwise, they may make those hearts sad, which God does not purpose to afflict; or, on the other hand, thoy may leave those hearts secure and at ease, which ought to be humbling themselves in dust and ashes. *The law is good, if a man use it lawfully*. It is, as it were, the mark at which the Christian should aim, in all he says, and thinks, and does. And the more carefully he aims, the nearer to the mark will he come; and the nearer he comes to the mark, the more he will resemble what the gospel is designed to make him. So, to teach the law, is to *use it lawfully;* to use it in agreement with that word, which "is truth;"[1] and which tells us, that not according to

[2] Gal. iii 22.

works of righteousness which we have done, doth God save us, "but according to his mercy, through Jesus Christ our Lord."[3]

XLVIII.

THE OLD AND NEW COVENANT CONTRASTED.

JOHN i. 17.

The law was given by Moses, but grace and truth came by Jesus Christ.

A COMPARISON is here drawn between the first and second dispensation. And the difference is strongly marked by the circumstances attending them.

The law was given by Moses. Moses was a highly favoured servant of God, selected to communicate his will to the chosen nation. Yet he was a man: one of the fallen race of Adam. *But grace and truth came by Jesus Christ.* God, having a design of mercy, sent forth his Son—his well-beloved Son, in whom he was well pleased:—and he, "the mighty Lord," was proclaimed as "the Prince of Peace."

[3] Titus iii. 5.

Again, when Moses was summoned to receive the declaration of God's purposes, Mount Sinai burned with fire; blackness, and darkness, and tempest surrounded it, and there was heard "the sound of a trumpet, and the voice of words; which voice they that heard entreated that the word should not be spoken to them any more: and so terrible was the sight, that Moses said, I exceedingly fear and quake."[1] But the *grace and truth* which *came by Jesus Christ*, was characterised by its different announcement. All was condescension in God, and comfort to mankind. "Fear not; I bring you good tidings of great joy, which shall be to all people." "Glory to God in the highest; on earth peace, good will towards men."

Still it was an advantage which we must not undervalue, that *the law was given by Moses* to the Israelites. It was an "advantage, great every way, that unto them were committed the oracles of God." God did not pass them by; or give them up, like other nations, "to a reprobate mind," ignorant of him and of his will. They were taught his "statutes and his judgments, which if a man do, he shall continue in them." And they were many, more than we pretend to number, who were thus led to "do justice, and love mercy, and walk humbly with their God," and to direct their lives "according to the commandments and ordinances of the law."

What, however, would be the effect of this law of God, if we had no other revelation of his will? What, but to condemn all mankind? As the apostle says, to "conclude all under sin," that "every mouth may be

[1] Heb. xii. 18—21.

stopped, and all the world become guilty before God?" This law, whether given to the Israelites by Moses, or repeated by Jesus in his discourses, may all be summed up, as he has himself summed it up, under these two heads: "Thou shalt love the Lord thy God with all thy heart; and thy neighbour as thyself." And who can hold up his hand and affirm, I am guiltless of any transgression against these commands?

If, then, the terms of the law are such as to condemn those who transgress it—and such must be the terms of every law,—it is clear that "by the law is the knowledge of sin:" that "by the deeds of the law no flesh shall be justified:" and we have eternal reason to be thankful, that *grace and truth came by the Lord Jesus Christ*. The apostle has taught us how to feel and reason; saying, "The strength of sin is the law: but thanks be to God, which giveth us the victory through our Lord Jesus Christ."

It is right to be often reflecting upon this: to call to mind, how many things we have done which we ought not to have done: how many things we have left undone that we ought to have done: and that our only comfort must be, "By grace are ye saved;" "by Jesus Christ all that believe are justified from all things, from which we could not be justified by the law of Moses." Thus the law is used by the Spirit to "convince of sin, and of righteousness, and of judgment;" becomes "a schoolmaster, to bring us unto Christ:" to awe the transgressor into a thankful acceptance of his mercy. In earthly cases, we often find the criminal hardened in his denial of guilt, confident of escape, sullen, obstinate: but when an unexpected witness appears against him, and his guilt is clearly shown, his spirit fails, his conscience shrinks, and the terror of death subdues, if it does not soften him. The effect of the law upon our hearts should be of a like nature: should be to soften them, now, in time, that we may not at last fall into the hands of an unpropitiated God. It seems to say, Why contend and dispute against God? Ye cannot change him who is unchangeable: ye cannot alter his will, which is fixed from everlasting upon the pillars of eternal right: but ye may reject his counsel against yourselves, (it is but too possible,) ye may despise his mercy, and then, too late, experience his anger. Whether ye will hear, or whether ye will forbear, ye must submit to die, and to stand before God, to be judged by that law which he has ordained. "Woe to him that striveth with his Maker!" Repent, and return unto the Lord: there are still the means of peace and reconciliation: *grace and truth came by Jesus Christ:* cast upon him your burden, and find rest unto your souls.

Therefore, as the demand of the law is perfect obedience, so the offer of Christ is perfect forgiveness. Perfect obedience no man has paid, or can pay. Perfect forgiveness every one may enjoy who seeks to be accepted through the righteousness which is of God by faith. The two covenants have this great distinction. One is command, the other is mercy; mercy which assures us, that though man had transgressed the covenant of command, God had still in store a covenant of grace: that though man had fallen far short of the obedience which God required, God has not altogether cast off his unworthy servants. "Herein was love, not that we loved God, but that he loved us, and, while we were yet sinners, has reconciled us to himself by the death of his Son."

But here a question meets us, which occurred to St. Paul, when arguing in this same strain. "Wherefore then serveth the law?"[2] Are we at liberty to disparage it, to neglect it? God forbid. "Think not," said our Lord himself, foreseeing what might be alleged, "think not that I am come to destroy the law and the prophets; I am not come to destroy, but to fulfil."

And there are three uses which the law serves, all which tend to establish the Christian character: there are three considerations which it suggests to the mind, all which we must attentively cherish.

We read the commandments of the law, as Moses gave them to the Israelites. The Lord Jesus enforced them, explained them, extended them, showed that the spirit of them, and not the letter only, must be fulfilled. The apostles still further point out their bearing upon the heart and life.

The first thought should be, This is God's will respecting me. My Saviour kept all these laws perfectly. Not that I might not keep them, but that he might leave me an example as well as an injunction to follow his steps, and walk as he walked. These, then, are to be my rule; and by these I must exercise myself, that I may "keep a conscience void of offence towards God and towards man."

[2] Gal. iii. 19.

The second thought is of another nature. These are the commands of God. This law is his law—my Maker's law. What could be my hope, if he were to reward me according as I had kept it from my youth up? If that were to be my "righteousness, that I had continued in all the things that are written in the law to do them?" Thanks be to him who has "redeemed me from the curse of the law:" whom God has made to me "wisdom, and righteousness, and sanctification, and redemption."

A further inquiry must follow, Do I keep these commandments? Do I allow myself in the wilful neglect of any of them? Is it my aim, my desire, my prayer, to love the Lord my God with all my heart, and my neighbour as myself? to bring every thought, word, and wish, into captivity to the obedience of Christ? Do I direct my life by the law, and try myself and judge myself by the law, though I trust not to be "under the law before God?"

This use of the law remains under the Gospel: and those who most constantly use the law for those purposes, are those who understand the Gospel best.

Whatever, then, our state is, there is use in the law. If we are yet unreconciled to God, the law condemns us: warns us "to agree with our adversary quickly;" to apply unto Christ, who bore our sins in his own body, that we may find rest unto our souls.

If we have already sought shelter under his cross, still our eye must be kept upon the law. The longer we examine it, the better shall we learn to measure that which is beyond all measure, the goodness of Him who has blotted out the record of our transgressions.

We must still look to it, as the rule by which we are to be guided; as the standard by which we are to judge ourselves now, and hereafter to be judged: that we may see how far, how very far, we come short of that standard, and be humble.

XLIX.

THE MYSTERY OF MAN'S REDEMPTION.

1 Tim. iii. 16.

Without controversy great is the mystery of godliness: God was manifest in the flesh, justified in the Spirit, seen of angels, preached unto the Gentiles, believed on in the world, received up into glory.

St. Paul had just been speaking of *the truth* maintained and supported by the church of Christ. This leads him to break out into an expression of ardent admiration of that truth, on which rests the redemption and sanctification of man. *Without controversy, great is the mystery of godliness:* wonderful is that scheme, which brings man from Satan to God, from impiety and sin to piety and holiness.

And then he sets before us the principal features of that scheme: *God manifest in the flesh,* being the foundation of the whole: "the Word, which was in the beginning with God, and was God," becoming flesh, and appearing in the form and nature of man: assuming that nature which he came to save, for the purpose that through his death he might overcome death; that by "giving his life a ransom" for our sins, he might take away that which is "the sting of death;" take away the guilt of sin, and the consequent wrath of God.

On this double nature of Christ the whole scheme depends. If he were not man, he could not "taste of death," and "make propitiation for our sins." If he were not God, his propitiation would not avail. It was needful, therefore, that this twofold nature should be proved; that he should be *justified* when he affirmed it of himself. And he was *justified; justified by the Spirit* which was with him, and exhibited the power of God whilst all could see that he bore the form of man. They were bold assertions, "As the Father hath life in himself, so hath he given to the Son to have life in himself. As the Father raiseth up the dead, and quickeneth them; even so the Son quickeneth whom he will."[1] But these assertions were *justified* at the grave of Lazarus, when Jesus said, "Lazarus, come forth;—and he that was dead came forth."[2] It was a bold assertion, "He that hath seen me, hath seen the Father."[3] "I and the Father are one." But he who thus spoke, was *justified in the Spirit,* when he did what God alone can do; when he read the inmost thoughts, discovered the most secret actions, penetrated the recesses of conscience, and "knew what was in man."

[1] John v. 21, 26. [2] Ib. xi. 43. [3] Ib. xiv. 9; x, 30.

Then, further, he was *seen of angels:* seen and admired by that heavenly host, who, as we are assured, take an interest in the circumstances of mankind, and "desire to look into" the things contrived for their salvation.[4] We can even imagine how these inhabitants of heaven may have contemplated our fallen world, and with that sympathy which is always found in company with goodness, have desired its restoration. But in vain; for heaven, they knew, was holy, and its inhabitants must be holy: and how shall the impure and corrupt be fitted to dwell with holiness and purity? Therefore they would see, and delight in seeing, the counsels of God unfolded in the gospel; by which sin is condemned, whilst sinfulness is pardoned; holiness is vindicated, whilst mercy is exercised; and the Psalmist's prophecy is fulfilled, when mercy and justice meet together, righteousness and peace embrace each other. They would see, and rejoice in seeing, this revelation of God's will *preached to the Gentiles;* so that the nations which had hitherto been walking in darkness might partake of the light which Christ had set up, and all the nations of the earth might "look unto him and be saved." "For so the Lord commanded:"[5] "and when the Gentiles heard this, they were glad, and glorified the word of the Lord:" and thus he whom the Jews had crucified, *was believed on in the world. Great* too was this *mystery.* When the inhabitants of Nazareth heard Jesus teaching in the synagogue, they were astonished, saying, "From whence hath this man these things? Is not this the carpenter, the son of Mary, the brother of James and Joses, and of Jude and Simon? And are not his sisters

[4] 1 Pet. i. 12. [5] Acts xiii. 47, 48.

here with us?"[6] The Gentiles might have added, Is not this he whose birthplace was a stable; who had "no form or comeliness," "no beauty that we should desire him:" whose companions were unlearned and unknown, chosen from obscure vocations? Is not this he, whose countrymen refused to hearken to him, or receive him as their Deliverer? Whose teaching they despised and rejected, whom they covered with reproach, and put to death with shame?

Yet was he *believed on in the world.* Multitudes, when St. Paul wrote, were trusting in him, and had committed their souls to him, for time and for eternity: in Judea, and Samaria, and even to the uttermost parts of the earth. The little seed, which had been sown in Jerusalem, had taken root downward, and was bearing fruit upward: was spreading its branches far and wide, and the nations of the earth were seeking shelter under them. Surely there was reason to say, *Great is the mystery of godliness,* Christ *believed on in the world.*

And, lastly, *received up into glory.* The chief priests and elders had boasted, "He saved others, himself he cannot save;" and when they had compassed his death, when they had seen his body laid in the tomb, and there secured, they thought to have attained all their ends, and given the last blow to his pretensions.[7] But his own words proved true, "Except a corn of wheat fall into the ground and die, it abideth alone; but if it die, it bringeth forth much fruit."[8] As the dry and shrivelled grain to all appearance perishes, but soon

[6] Mark vi. 2, 3. [7] Matt. xxvii. 48. [8] John xii. 24.

springs up again a vigorous and fruitful blade; so the body of humiliation which had been buried in the grave, rose again in the form of God, and was received up into its own place; that which had borne "the image of the earthly" body, now bore "the image of the heavenly," and is "for ever set down on the right hand of the majesty on high:" thus perfecting the mystery which accomplished the redemption of mankind from sin and death, and opened the way of everlasting salvation.

This is that "mystery of Christ, which in other ages was not made known unto the sons of men,"[9] as it is now revealed unto them by the Spirit: "to the intent that unto the principalities and powers in heavenly places might be known by the church the manifold wisdom of God, according to the eternal purpose which he purposed in Christ Jesus our Lord."

[9] Eph. iii. 5—12.

L.

THE NATURE OF THE KINGDOM OF GOD.

ROMANS xiv. 17.

The kingdom of God is not meat and drink; but righteousness and peace, and joy in the Holy Ghost.

AMONG the many causes of dispute which existed between the Jews and the Gentiles when they became disciples of Christ, one was the difference of their practice in regard to those meats which were forbidden to the Hebrews as "unclean" by the law of Moses. The Gentiles, of course, had no scruple about them; neither need there have been any on the part of the Jewish brethren; for as St. Paul says, he "knew and was persuaded of the Lord Jesus, that there is nothing unclean of itself." The ceremonial law of Moses had been set aside. But it is hard to conquer early prejudices; and the Jews were offended by the liberty in which the Gentiles indulged. St. Paul exhorts his Gentile converts to avoid this occasion of controversy, and not to "destroy the work of God for meat." For himself, he had "rather eat no meat whilst the world standeth," than cause his "brother to offend:" to give offence to a brother Christian. It was well to see clearly the nature of the Gospel, as not dependant on outward things: not consisting in abstinence from meat, or in indulging in them. But let their minds be turned to other and better objects; to "things that make for peace, and things wherein one may edify another. *For the kingdom of God is not meat or drink; but righteousness, and peace, and joy in the Holy Ghost.* And thus a question, which was merely local and temporary, furnished occasion for issuing a general truth, which will be important to the end of time. For it assures us, first, that the kingdom of God is RIGHTEOUSNESS. What we seek, and must attain as Christians, is a holy, pure disposition: the conformity of the whole heart to the law of God. From the moment that a man is earnest in religion, this is what he aims at and desires. He does not so soon acquire it: but he strives and prays for it; and a promise is made, that he shall not strive and pray in vain. "A new heart will I give you, and a new spirit will I put within you:[1] and I will cause you to walk in my statutes, and ye shall keep my judgments, and do them." We find our Lord declaring from the first, that in this his religion consisted. The Jews had been used to look to other things: but he assures them, "Blessed are the meek, the pure in heart, the merciful, the humble:" those that "hunger and thirst after righteousness."[2] And so St. Paul: "In Christ Jesus, neither circumcision availeth anything, nor uncircumcision; but a new creature:"[3] a heart converted from its natural course of worldliness and sinful indulgence, and following, instead, the ways of godliness, and meekness, and patience, and holiness, and charity.

Men have invented for themselves many tests, by

[1] Ezek. xxxvi. 26. [2] Matt. v. 2—9. [3] Gal. vi. 15.

which to judge of their own or others' religion. This is one which cannot be mistaken. "Let no man deceive you; he which doeth righteousness, is righteous."[4] Whatever else we have, by whatever name we are called, if we have not *righteousness*, we have not the first needful evidence of any part or lot in the kingdom of God.

2. Next, the kingdom of God is PEACE. St. Paul had been speaking of disputes and jealousies. Instead of these, he tells us that they who belong to the kingdom of God are of a quiet, kind, peaceable disposition. The spirit of the Gospel is a spirit of peace. The Gospel was ushered in with a promise of "peace on earth."[5] God had sent to mankind a message of reconciliation through Jesus Christ; and required that they should show to one another the same kindness and long-suffering which he had shown to them. And certainly there is everything in the Gospel to promote a spirit of peace among men, and to repress a spirit of discord. Discord often arises out of the affronts which one man receives from another; such as those probably met with, who differed from their neighbours about the meats they might partake of, or the days they should keep holy. But one who has the Gospel in his heart cannot help feeling, that even if he is unjustly affronted or offended, he has himself much more offended God. If God has borne with him, ought he not to bear with his brethren?

Another cause of discord among men is their striving after the same object, each labouring to get beyond his neighbour. But this rivalry is moderated, with one

[4] 1 John iii. 7. [5] Luke ii. 14.

who is seeking first the kingdom of God. For he is constantly looking forward to the time when all this will avail him nothing. "The world passeth away, and the lust thereof: but he that doeth the will of God abideth for ever."[6]

Another cause of difference among men is their jealousy and envy of each other: of another's knowledge, or another's honours, or another's gains. But one who belongs to the kingdom of God loves his neighbour as himself; and does not therefore grudge him what he knows, or what he gains; does not envy him if he is praised and honoured.

The Gospel, therefore, promotes peace, by cutting off the root from which discord springs. And that peaceable spirit which a man feels towards others, comes back upon himself: he is freed from those angry and discontented passions which destroy the comfort of the soul. What more miserable to the person who feels them, than envy, hatred, malice, and uncharitableness? Such an one's heart is in a continual storm. But such passions have no place in the kingdom of God. Therefore *the kingdom of God is peace.*

3. The last sign which Paul here mentions of the kingdom of God, is JOY IN THE HOLY GHOST. The Holy Ghost takes up his abode with those who are trusting in Christ. And in the heart where he dwelleth, there is both peace and joy. For he is "the Comforter." He soothes the heart with a hope of pardon and acceptance with God. He "bears witness with our spirits," that we are received as children of God through Christ

[6] 1 John ii. 17.

Jesus; and fills us with comfort like that which the apostle himself experienced, when he said, "I know whom I have believed, and am persuaded that he is able to keep that which I have committed unto him against that day."[7] He also sheds joy over our hearts, by enabling us to make head against sin, our greatest enemy. Nothing except sin can be the cause of lasting sorrow to the Christian. But the aid of the Holy Spirit gives us victory over sin: and hence comes joy to the heart. Not that joy which is shown in loud and noisy mirth; not perhaps that joy which can be discoursed of to another, or expressed in words; but a pure and holy joy notwithstanding: a joy arising from just confidence that our souls are committed to God, and safe in his hands; and that as long as we continue faithful, whatever may befall us here is only part of a mysterious plan which is designed to lead to everlasting glory.

Thus plainly are we told what the kingdom of God does and does not consist in. Not in outward things or observances. These may be ours, and yet we may not be within the kingdom. The things really needful, are *righteousness, and peace, and joy in the Holy Ghost*. These, therefore, are the things to seek. *Righteousness*, by the word of God, by self-inquiry, by prayer, by watchfulness, by self-denial: and *peace*, by *following after the things that make for peace*, and avoiding all those evil affections and desires by which peace is disturbed. In proportion as we advance in this righteousness and peace, will be our *joy in the Holy Ghost*. For to advance

[7] 2 Tim. i. 12.

in them, is to be triumphing over the enemies of our salvation; and this is cause of joy. It is to be proceeding towards a state of eternal holiness and happiness; and this is cause of joy. And it is the Holy Spirit who gives this victory, and leads onward in the way: therefore such *joy* is in *the Holy Ghost:* a joy "with which the stranger intermeddleth not," and which nothing of the present world can either bestow or destroy.

LI.

THE WATER OF LIFE.

JOHN iv. 13, 14.

13. *Jesus answered and said unto her, Whosoever drinketh of this water shall thirst again:*
14. *But whosoever drinketh of the water that I shall give him shall never thirst; but the water that I shall give him shall be in him a well of water springing up into everlasting life.*

THE meeting of our Lord, at the Samaritan town of Sychar, with a woman who had come to draw water from the well, gave occasion for one of those interesting conversations, in which he was accustomed to deliver the great truths which he left for the instruction of future ages. He had spoken of himself as able to supply living water to those who needed it. The woman understood the literal words, but not the figurative meaning. And her question, Whence hast thou this living water?—leads him to describe the effect of the Spirit which he sheds abroad upon the heart. First he points out the difference between the spiritual and the temporal supply. *Whosoever drinketh of this water shall thirst again.* How truly does this characterise the things which are most valued in this world! *Whosoever drinketh shall thirst again.* The pleasures of the world, whenever they are made the chief object, are found to be truly unsatisfying: wearying when present, yet leaving the mind restless till it returns to them, and is again wearied. Riches, honours;—these, too, they who have tasted, *thirst again;* something is still wanting, and yet remains to be acquired, often even on the brink of the grave.

It is not thus with the living water, drawn from the well of salvation.

1. It never fails. It is a living spring, perpetually flowing; not a "broken cistern," which may be soon exhausted. The more grace is sought, the more is grace bestowed. If all the world would ask—for all have need to ask, and all must ask at the right source—but if all would ask and seek, not one should be refused. The invitation has no limits. It is wide as the prophet's words, "Ho, every one that thirsteth, come ye to the waters!"[1]

[1] Isa. lv. 1.

2. Next, it always satisfies. *Whosoever drinketh of the water which I shall give him, shall never thirst.* No craving void ensues, no restless desire is left to harass and disturb. It brings with it, and sheds over the soul, a calm, a satisfying comfort, which nothing else can give, and which only those who have enjoyed it can understand.

3. And, thirdly, it has an object and an end to which nothing earthly can be compared. *It springeth up into everlasting life.* It proceeds in a course which is to lead to that inestimable and inconceivable blessing.

And in this view, how justly may the Spirit which Jesus communicates be described as a spring of *living water.* Consider such a spring. It has its source in the rain and dews which God has provided to water the earth and make it fruitful. And the living water which Christ affords, proceeds from God. He so loved the world that he sent his only Son to be the author of salvation.

The spring, small commonly at its source, gains strength as it flows along. So the Spirit in the heart may at first be as a drop, to which other and fresh drops are continually added, till it becomes a clear and sparkling stream.

The spring, too, proceeding from its perennial source, and flowing onward, purifies its channel as it runs. It carries down before it whatever is muddy and impure and would impede its current, and what remains is clear and beautiful. Such likewise is the effect of the Spirit of Christ upon the soul. It meets at first with much that is of an uncongenial nature, much that would sully and corrupt it. But this it gradually clears away. The "lust of the flesh, the lust of the eye, and the pride of life, and whatsoever is not of the Father but of the world"—these it carries off, and suffers not to rest and choke the stream. Nothing remains but the purer properties of the renewed heart, temperance, and patience, and godliness, and meekness, and charity. These are seen to shine beneath the flowing water, and reflect that "Sun of righteousness," from which their beauty is derived.

As a last point of resemblance, I observe that the stream still runs. It does not stagnate. It seems to have an object, from which it will not be long diverted; it cannot be stopped or restrained. It seeks the wide river, or the still wider ocean, in which it is to be received at last. Such too is the living water of the Spirit. It is *in the heart a well of water springing up into everlasting life.* For this it was given: and for this it flows, and will flow on until the end come. When it first began, this was the object at which it aimed; and this it keeps constantly in view till that object is reached. It turns aside whatever would impede its course: and it gathers strength as it continues to flow. Christ, its author, gives fresh supplies from his fulness; gives "grace for grace;" till at last he receives the soul, renewed and purified, into a sea which knows no storms. There it shall glide on through all eternity, in undisturbed peace and in unsullied purity.

Just cause were there to say, *If thou knewest the gift of God—thou wouldest have asked of him, and he would have given thee living water.* As was proved, in the first instance, by the apostles. They had "known the gift of God;" had been led to Jesus; had drunk of his words; had received his doctrine; were in due time filled with his Spirit: and not only were their own hearts purified and cleansed from their natural corruption, but truths flowed from them which were as a living spring of water to mankind, as "floods upon a dry ground." Before his Holy Spirit was shed upon them, they were themselves as "a dry ground where no water is:" parched and barren in their own hearts, and affording little benefit to others. But when "they were filled with the Holy Ghost, they spake the word of God with boldness:"[2] The waters of salvation flowed freely from their mouths: and "daily in the temple and in every house they ceased not to teach and preach Jesus Christ."[3] And those again, who had learnt from them, when they were scattered abroad, and permitted to remain no longer at Jerusalem, "went everywhere preaching the word."[4] And that word which they preached, had the effect which water has upon the sinking frame or upon the barren ground. It comforted the drooping heart, and "revived the spirit of the contrite ones." It made "the wilderness blossom as a rose," and "be like a watered garden." The heathen, hitherto barren and unprofitable, became abundant in the fruits of righteousness. Instead of the works of the flesh, the fruits of the Spirit appeared: "love, joy, peace, long-suffering, gentleness, goodness, faith, meekness, temperance."[5]

[2] Acts iv. 31. [3] Acts v. 42.
[4] Acts viii. 4. [5] Gal. v. 22.

And such will always be the effect of the Spirit which they who believe in Jesus shall receive. It shall be in themselves a well of water, "springing up into everlasting life." And it shall not be confined within themselves; but run over and communicate its blessings. As the influence of evil is unhappily diffusive, so, no less, is the influence of good: and the running stream does not more surely indicate its progress by the fertility which adorns its banks, than the zealous Christian sheds around him the effects of that Spirit by which his heart is filled, and his practice animated. *Rivers of living water* flow to others, out of the abundance of his own heart, out of the fulness which the Lord gives: and which shows, that not to the apostles only, but to the men of every age, He is a fountain of life, from which refreshment, and strength, and health, and salvation, are continually supplied to every one that believeth.

LII.

PRACTICAL UNBELIEF.

HEBREWS iii. 12—14.

12. *Take heed, brethren, lest there be in any of you an evil heart of unbelief, in departing from the living God.*
13. *But exhort one another daily, while it is called To-day; lest any of you be hardened through the deceitfulness of sin.*
14. *For we are made partakers of Christ, if we hold the beginning of our confidence steadfast unto the end.*

IT is important to inquire into the state of those persons to whom St. Paul addresses his exhortation, and the whole argument which follows. We must see what he means by *unbelief*, and who they are whom he warns against it. He is not writing to those, who are called in the Acts of the Apostles, "the unbelieving Jews:" those who, like himself in his early career, denied that Jesus was the expected Messiah. His epistle is to the "Jews that believed;" i. e. who had been brought to acknowledge that "God had made that same Jesus whom they had crucified, both Lord and Christ."

The *unbelief*, therefore, which he fears, is the unbelief of practice, *in departing from the living God:* the denying him in works, though in profession acknowledging him. This is the danger against which he warns them to be watchful, and to *exhort one another daily. Take heed,* he says, *lest any of you be hardened through the deceitfulness of sin:* lest sin, "which so easily besets us," and watches for every opportunity to betray the heart, should lead you into acts of disobedience and departure from God, inconsistent with the faith which ye profess, the faith which ought to actuate and direct your lives.

For this had been the case with their forefathers, who perished in the wilderness. A *rest* had been promised to them; a goodly inheritance; a rich and fruitful land, fitted to be a type of the heavenly Canaan. But "they could not enter in, because of unbelief."

And yet these Israelites, who perished for want of faith, did not deny the existence or the power of God; did not deny that he had delivered them from Egypt; or that there was such a country as Canaan, or that it was "a goodly land." They had not been like Pharaoh, who profanely asked, "Who is the Lord, that I should obey his voice? I know not the Lord, neither will I let Israel go."[1] They had not thrown off their allegiance to God, or said, "What is the Almighty, that we should serve him; or what profit should we have, if we pray to him?"[2] No such unbelief as this could be charged against them; and yet they were cut off from the inheritance *because of unbelief.*

Looking back to their history, we find that six weeks after their departure from Egypt, their pro-

[1] Ex. v. 2. [2] Job xxi. 15.

vision began to fail. They had seen the wonders which God had already done for their deliverance, and might have trusted that he had still the same power and the same will to save. But instead of making their requests known to him by prayer and supplication, "the whole congregation of the children of Israel murmured against Moses and against Aaron, and said unto them, Would to God we had died by the hand of the Lord in the land of Egypt, when we sat by the flesh pots, and when we did eat bread to the full: for ye have brought us forth into this wilderness, to kill the whole assembly with hunger." [3]

The mercy of God relieved them from these unworthy fears, and "gave them bread from heaven." They proceeded on their journey, and another difficulty arose: the supply of water failed. "And the people murmured against Moses, and said, Wherefore is this, that thou hast brought us out of Egypt, to kill us and our children and our cattle with thirst?" [4]

At the command of God, Moses smote the rock, and the waters flowed. But he preserved the memorial of their sin, by calling the name of the place Massah (chiding), and Meribah (temptation), "because of the chiding of the children of Israel, and because they tempted the Lord, saying, Is the Lord among us or not?"

The long-suffering of God bore with his people through these and through other sins of unbelief; and now a year had passed, and they reached the borders of the land which had been promised "to Abraham and his seed for ever." But here a fresh trial of their

[3] Ex. xvi. 1—5. [4] Ex xvii. 1—3.

faith arose. A man from each tribe was sent forward into Canaan, to "see the land, what it is; and the people that dwelleth therein, whether they be strong or weak, few or many; and what the land is, whether it be fat or lean, whether there be wood therein or not; and to bring of the fruit of the land."[5]

The spies returned, and reported of the land that it was good; "surely it flowed with milk and honey." But they said, "We be not able to go up against the people, for they be stronger than we; all the people that we saw in it were of great stature, and we were in their sight as grasshoppers."

And all the children of Israel murmured against Moses and against Aaron, and said unto them, "Would God that we had died in the land of Egypt; or would God that we had died in the wilderness! And wherefore hath the Lord brought us into this land, to fall by the sword, that our wives and our children should be a prey? Were it not better for us to return into Egypt? And they said one to another, Let us make a captain, and let us return into Egypt."[6]

Then was the sentence passed, that this fickle, wavering, faithless people should not enter into the promised rest. "Because all those men which have seen my glory and my miracles which I did in Egypt and in the wilderness, have tempted me now these ten times, and have not hearkened unto my voice; surely they shall not see the land which I have sworn unto their fathers, neither shall any of them that provoked me see it: but my servants Caleb (and Joshua) because

[5] Numb. xiii. 17—33. [6] Numb. xiv. 2—4.

they had another spirit with them, and have followed me fully, them will I bring into the land, and their seed shall possess it."[7]

This history enables us to understand the sort of faith with which the word of God must be received and observed, in order that it may profit those that hear, and bring them to the salvation which it offers. By perceiving the nature of that unbelief which proved fatal to the Israelites, we learn the character of that faith which God approves and rewards. Had it been sufficient to believe that God had prepared for his people a rich inheritance, the Israelites believed. They acknowledged that the land of Canaan was "a good land." Had it been sufficient to believe that God had invited them to possess the land, this too they believed. But possession was to be obtained by labour, and resolution, and present self-denial; and their faith was not strong enough to endure the labour, to inspire the resolution, to risk the present sacrifice; their reliance on God gave way, under dread of the enemies they must encounter; and therefore because of unbelief they could not enter in.

This, therefore, was the unbelief against which St. Paul warns the descendants of these men: the unbelief which prevents a man from "denying himself, and taking up the cross," and following the demands of the gospel to the end: which satisfies him with being "almost a Christian;" which prevents his "using all diligence," that he may "bring every thought into captivity to the obedience of Christ." When all was smooth

[7] Numb. xiv. 22—24.

and easy with the Israelites, they were content to proceed along their way: when obstacles threatened them they provoked God by murmuring, they sinned against him by disobeying. And by this practical unbelief they lost the promised land.

As St. Paul proceeds to say, the word preached, the promises made, the glad tidings of a better country, "did not profit them, not being mixed with faith in those that heard it."

It is a constant, and a needful warning. In a country like ours, where the gospel is generally professed, where it is, as we style it, the national religion, a species of faith exists which may be called passive faith. Men grow up with a general knowledge of the Bible: in their youthful days they have learnt its principal truths, and they repeat them as their creed. They do not deny them, or even doubt them, any more than the Israelites denied the being or the power of the Most High. They believe the Scriptures, much in the same way as they believe other histories of former times; they have no doubt that the persons lived and the events took place which are related there.

In this way is the gospel preached to many. It reaches no further. They do not doubt that it came from God; that Christ Jesus was born into the world, and passed through his ministry, and died upon the cross, and rose again. So far their belief goes, but stops there; it remains upon their minds a passive principle, not an active, vital principle. The gospel is a mere history to them. Their belief does not lead them to commit their souls to Christ, by an actual, intelligent operation of faith; neither does it lead them to study his will that they may fulfil it, and live to his glory. It does not work in their minds, as leaven works when mixed with a mass of meal: or as some liquor poured into another produces a disturbance in it: and therefore "the word preached does not profit, not being mixed with faith in them that hear it." St. Paul, whilst using this phrase, seems to have been thinking of the remedy of some disease, which requires a certain state of the constitution to make it salutary; or which must be united with other substances, that it may produce the intended benefit. So, he says, the word of God must be mixed with faith in the hearers, or no effect will follow; there must be a corresponding quality in the heart, that the word may profit: may lead to such a course of thought, and feeling, and action, as we find from Scripture to "accompany salvation."

But the word does profit, and carry the soul in safety through time and to eternity, when received with that lively faith which, hearing the sayings of Christ, proceeds to do them: which apprehends the gospel as the remedy provided of God for the disease under which all are labouring, and which must, without that remedy, be fatal: which looks upon Jesus Christ as the physician who must be followed fully and altogether. Such faith is not dead, but living; not barren, but fruitful; not inert, but active: and when the *word preached is received* with this faith, *it profits:* it becomes the rule by which the heart is directed; it is made the test by which all things are judged and weighed; it regulates the thoughts, it inspires the words, it actuates the deeds.

It sets aside all other grounds of trust, and fixes the soul on a sure foundation. It admits of no other rule of life than that which the word prescribes.

If the Israelites had possessed such faith as this, they would have entered into the promised rest. But they could not enter in because of unbelief. They had no such lively sense of the blessings offered them as was sufficient to prevail against present trials: no such sure affiance in Him who had chosen them to be his people, as could induce them to cast themselves upon Him, to be guided by his counsel and protected by his power. They preferred present ease to future rewards, and therefore they were not counted worthy to enjoy them. "As surely as I live, saith the Lord, ye shall not come into the land which ye have despised."[8]

But if there is warning in this passage, there is also encouragement. If through unbelief the Israelites were lost, so by the exercise of faith were those saved whom the Scriptures record, who first believed in Jesus: those for whom the Lord prayed, because they had "continued with him in his temptations:" those who, because they adhered to him, were cast out of the synagogue; those who "gave up their possessions" to support the common cause; those who "took joyfully the spoiling of their goods," and "received the word in much affliction," — thinking that the jewel of eternal life which they had found, was worthy of any price that they might be called to pay. Upon them the "word preached" accomplished its merciful design. For St. Paul's phrase implies that it has a merciful design. God intends that it should *profit;* it only fails through the fault of

[8] See Numb. xiv. 28—31.

those who hear. Just as the husbandman scatters gooc seed. But that does not vegetate, which falls upon a stone.

LIII.

STEDFASTNESS IN THE FAITH.

1 Thess. iii. 1—5.

1. *Wherefore when we could no longer forbear, we thought i good to be left at Athens alone;*
2. *And sent Timotheus, our brother, and minister of Goc and our fellow labourer in the gospel of Christ, to esta blish you, and to comfort you concerning your faith.*
3. *That no man should be moved by these afflictions: fo yourselves know that we are appointed thereunto.*
4. *For verily, when we were with you, we told you befor that we should suffer tribulation: even as it came to pass and ye know.*
5. *For this cause, when I could no longer forbear, I sent t know your faith, lest by some means the tempter hav tempted you, and our labour be in vain.*

The Thessalonians who received the word, and pro fessed the faith of Christ, were exposed to much perse cution. The violence which forced the apostle to leav the city hastily, was not likely to spare his disciple who remained, and could not escape the enmity of their countrymen.[1] He had before spoken of this; saying, "Ye became followers of us, and of the Lord, having received the word in much affliction, with joy of the Holy Ghost."[2] And again: "Ye became followers of the churches of God in Judea which are in Christ Jesus; for ye also have suffered like things of your own countrymen, even as they have of the Jews." Paul, therefore, feared lest these persecutions should have the effect which Satan who stirred them up desired, and stifle the faith of these new-born Christians. He feared *lest by some means the Tempter should have tempted them*; taken advantage, as he is wont to do, of the circumstances in which they were placed, and turned them aside from the profession of a religion which cost them so dear. St. Peter had the same apprehensions, and writes in a like strain, entreating his disciples "not to think it strange concerning the fiery trial which was to try them; as though some strange thing had happened unto them:"[3] warns them that "their adversary, the devil, as a roaring lion, walketh about, seeking whom he may devour; whom resist (he adds) stedfast in the faith, knowing that the same afflictions are accomplished in your brethren that are in the world." For, at that time, persecution, in its strictest sense, was the lot of every Christian; a part of the faith which they had embraced.

We live in different times, and have little experience of such trials. Some may, indeed, even now, have to encounter a sneering look, or an ungracious frown; or a false accusation may be urged against them, of self-

[1] Acts xvii. 10. [2] 1 Thess. i. 6; ii. 14. [3] 1 Pet. iv. 12, &c.

interest, perhaps, as if they had some private ends to serve, when they show themselves earnest in religion. Some may, even now, be called to make a voluntary sacrifice; they may be forced to part from friends, who are not like-minded with themselves: or it may be their duty to abandon some way of life, which they cannot innocently pursue. These trials should not be underrated: they are hard to human nature. But the apostle says, *We told you before that ye should suffer tribulation:* the Scripture uniformly shows that the gate of life is a narrow gate, the way of religion an uphill way: and those who resolve to "follow the Lord fully," must be prepared to lose what may be valuable as "a right eye," to part with what may be dear as a "right hand." The faith of a Christian, in all ages and circumstances, must be tried, and must prove able to bear the test; we may be thankful that ours is not, like that of the Thessalonians, and of many in later days than theirs, a "fiery trial."

Paul knew the weakness of human nature, and the malice of that enemy who would pervert it. So he thought it worth while to deprive himself of the services of Timotheus, his *fellow-labourer in the gospel,* and to be *left at Athens alone,*[4] whilst he sent his brother minister *to establish the Thessalonians, and comfort them concerning their faith.* He felt for them, as a father for his children. And he acted as a father. He did what Jacob had done: who said to his son Joseph, "Do not thy brethren feed the flock in Shechem? Come, I will send thee unto them. Go, I pray thee, and see whether it be well with thy brethren, and with the flocks; and

[4] See Acts xvii. 13.

bring me word again."[5] And thus Paul to Timotheus, his "own son in the faith:" "Go, I pray thee, to Thessalonica, and see how it be with the poor afflicted believers there: and *establish them, and comfort them concerning their faith,* and warn them *that no man be moved by these afflictions; for they themselves know that we are appointed thereunto.*"

It may be thought, perhaps, that he might have satisfied himself in another way. God had made these Thessalonians to differ from others: he had first provided that they should hear the gospel: he had then opened their hearts to listen to the word; to "believe, and consort with Paul and Silas;"[6] so that the apostle had before spoken of their "election of God."[7] And afterwards, in his second epistle, we find him "thanking God, because he had from the beginning chosen them to salvation through sanctification of the Spirit and belief of the truth."[8] Might he not then have trusted, that "whom God predestinates, them he also calls; and whom he calls, them he also justifies; and whom he justifies, them he also sanctifies?"[9]

We know, indeed, that Paul did derive comfort from the thought of God's protecting care over his people; and did look up to the support by which he sustains them, as his best hope for their security. So he writes to the Philippians: "Being confident of this very thing, that he which hath begun a good work in you will perform it unto the day of Jesus Christ."[1] And again, to these same Thessalonians, afterwards, "The

[5] Gen. xxxvii. 12—14. [6] Acts xvii. 4. [7] 1 Thess. i. 4.
[8] 2 Thess. ii. 13. [9] Rom. viii. 30. [1] Phil. i. 6.

Lord is faithful, who shall stablish you, and keep you from evil."[2]

But he also felt that he could never be assured of God's purpose and will concerning them, unless he saw the proofs of it in their way of living. They could not have been effectually called, unless they were walking "worthy of their vocation." They could not be justified before God, and at peace with him, unless they were meeting the trials which assailed them by stedfast continuance in the faith. He was to read their "election of God," not in "the book of life," which was hidden from him, but in the book of their own conduct, which was open before him. Therefore he was anxious concerning them: he *could no longer forbear, and sent to know their faith, lest by some means the tempter had tempted them, and his labour be in vain.*

Plainly, in the apostle's mind, there is one proof of a safe state which may be trusted, and no other: namely, a life agreeable to the faith: a practice not moved aside by difficulties or unsettled by temptations. A dependance upon divine grace is needful to our comfort: there is no other defence against our own frailty, and "the corruption that is in the world." But it must be that dependance which makes the heart hopeful; not that which makes it careless. It must be that dependance which teaches us when and where to stretch out our hands for aid; not that which keeps the hands folded. There is (as it were) a double motto on the Christian's seal: on one side, "The Lord knoweth them that are his:" on the other, "Let every one that nameth the name of Christ depart from iniquity."[3]

[2] 2 Thess iii. 3. [3] 2 Tim. ii. 19.

This was the proof of justifying faith, which St. Paul was anxious to find in his Thessalonian converts; and this was the proof of which it rejoiced his heart to be assured. For Timotheus returned from his visit to Thessalonica, and brought back tidings such as Paul had scarcely dared to hope for. The christian company which he had formed remained a christian company: had not been moved by the afflictions which they suffered; but, though persecuted, were not forsaken; though cast down, were not destroyed. And it is important to observe the proofs which satisfied him. *Timotheus*, he says, *came from you unto us, and brought us good tidings of your faith and charity, and that ye have good remembrance of us always, desiring greatly to see us.* Thus he judged of their faith by its effects. He judged of the manner in which the seed of Divine truth had taken root in their hearts, by the produce which followed it. So when the Hebrew spies were sent by Moses to examine the country of Canaan, he enjoined them, "Bring back of the fruit of the land."[4] "And they cut down a branch with one cluster of grapes, and they bare it between two on a staff: and they brought of the pomegranates and of the figs: and as they returned they said, We came into the land whither thou sentest us, and surely it floweth with milk and honey; and this is the fruit of it." And so Timotheus. We came unto Thessalonica, and surely the Lord hath much people in that city: their faith is stedfast, though severely tried; the waves have beat against it, but it has not fallen, for it is founded upon a rock. And this is the fruit of it: *Charity* prevails among them:

[4] Numb. xiii. 17, &c.

they have love towards one another and towards all men: and they *have good remembrance of thee,* their father in the faith, as "owing to thee their own selves:" like the dutiful children of an absent parent, they *desire greatly to see thee,* as thou also to see them: that thou mightest establish them and comfort them concerning the faith, and "exhort them, with full purpose of heart, to cleave unto the Lord."

Such was the assurance which Timotheus gave of the faith and charity which he had witnessed. It gladdened the apostle's heart, and he says, *Therefore, brethren, we were comforted over you in all our affliction and distress by your faith; for now we live, if ye stand fast in the Lord.*

We live. The tidings of your faith is like a cordial poured into the system when nature fails: life revives. This strong expression arises out of strength of feeling. Paul had feared for this people. He knew what human nature is when exposed to temptation. Another people, of whom he had once much hope, were removed from the doctrine which he had taught them unto another gospel:[5] and though they had "once run well," afterwards "fell from grace." And might it not be so with the Thessalonians? Those were his fears; and hearing of the trials to which they were subjected, his heart languished through such apprehensions: he seemed as one whose spirit was gone. Like Jacob, who refused to be comforted when the news of his son Joseph's death was brought to him, and said, "I will go down into the grave unto my son mourning."[6] But afterwards, when the brethren returned from Egypt, and brought him good tidings of the life and prosperity

[5] Gal. i. 6, 7. [6] Gen. xxxvii. 35.

of this much-beloved son, the spirit of Jacob revived, and he said, "It is enough; Joseph my son is yet alive; I will go and see him before I die."[7] And so the spirit of Paul revived, when he learnt that faith and charity still flourished in the hearts of the Thessalonian converts; in all his affliction and distress such tidings were as a cordial to him; strengthened and refreshed his soul. *We live,* he says, *if ye stand fast in the Lord.*

These warm feelings, of anxiety on the one hand, or of joy on the other, must have an origin. There must be a cause to excite them. The cause, in the apostle's mind, was a lively conviction of the miserable state in which the Thessalonians had been whilst alienated from God, and a clear view of the blessedness to which they were brought when they received Christ Jesus as the Lord. On the one hand was "outer darkness," "the blackness of darkness for ever:" on the other, "glory, and honour, and immortality." With St. Paul, to depart from the gospel of Christ, whether by denying it with the lips, or in the practice, was to depart from everlasting happiness, and to sink into everlasting perdition. He would mourn over such a fall from grace, as we might grieve for one whom we had long watched hanging on the edge of a precipice, when at last he quitted his hold, lost his footing, and dropped into the gulf below.

And so it will always be. According to the clearness of our faith in God's word, revealing to us on the one hand a blessed immortality, and on the other an eternity

[7] Gen. xlv. 28.

of misery; —according to the way in which we receive the truth, whether merely as a fact to be confessed, or as it is indeed, a truth to be lived on,—according to this will be the feelings with which we regard our own religious state or that of others. We sometimes find a physician evidently anxious and watchful, where the patient himself, or his nearest friends, are in no apprehension or alarm. The physician is alarmed because he has better knowledge,—because he is aware of the consequences of certain symptoms of disease, in which one ignorant or thoughtless perceives no danger. So it is in religion. According to our knowledge,—according to our faith, which is to realize that knowledge, will be our anxiety when we see our fellow-creatures exposed to temptation, as the Thessalonians were exposed—will be our joy, when we see them rising, like the same Thessalonians, superior to their trial, and *standing fast in the Lord.*

LIV.

CHRIST THE SAVIOUR OF SINNERS.

1 TIM. i. 15, 16.

15. *This is a faithful saying, and worthy of all acceptation, that Christ Jesus came into the world to save sinners; of whom I am chief.*

ST. PAUL had been reflecting on the mercy shown him; mercy which he had so little ground to expect, he who had been before "a blasphemer, and a persecutor, and injurious" to the church. And now, as if looking round for some reason to account for this goodness, he seems to find it in this; that the great purpose of the gospel might be set forth in him, and made manifest to the world. *This is a faithful saying, and worthy of all acceptation, that Jesus Christ came into the world to save sinners.* The mercy which he was so thankfully acknowledging, was not a benefit bestowed on himself alone, while the like forgiveness was denied to others: but it was a fulfilment of the very object which brought the Redeemer into the world. "He came to seek and to save that which was lost." He came *to save sinners.*

To save sinners. At first, this seems extraordinary. Can sin deserve the favour of Almighty God, so that he should send his Son into the world, not to condemn the world, as we might expect, but to deliver it from condemnation?

On the contrary, we know that sin, so far from being beheld with favour, is hateful to God; can never be pleasing in the eyes of Him, who cannot look upon evil. But it received his pity. The consequences which it brings upon the sinner, moved his compassion. And, therefore, *Christ Jesus came into the world to save sinners.*

But how to save them? By allowing them to sin on, for he had borne the penalty? By encouraging them to continue a careless, ungodly, wicked life, and then look up to him, that he might relieve them from its punishment? We know that this cannot be. The sinners that he came to save, are repentant sinners.

"I came," he says, "to call sinners to repentance."[1] His precept was, "Go, and sin no more."[2] He came to save such sinners as Zaccheus, who entered upon a new life of integrity and charity:[3] such sinners as the Jewish assembly, who were "pricked in their hearts" at the wickedness which they had consented to, in "killing the Prince of life:"[4] such sinners as Paul himself, on whom "the grace bestowed was not in vain, but he laboured more abundantly than they all," in maintaining the religion which he once had laboured to destroy.[5]

When, therefore, in sermons or religious books, we find such a title applied to our Blessed Lord, as "the Friend of sinners:" we must always bear in mind, in what sense He is to be called their friend. He who was in the beginning with God, and was God; he who was "holy, harmless, undefiled, without blemish, and without spot;" he who "was in all points tempted like as we are, yet without sin:" he can never be the friend of sinners, as such, and remaining sinners. But he is justly so called; because he came "to save them from their sins." To save them, first, from the guilt of sin; for "God made Him, who knew no sin, to be sin for us, that we might be made the righteousness of God in Him."[6] To save them, further, from the wrath of God which threatens sin; that being justified by his blood, we might be "saved from the wrath of God."[7] And still more, which was the intent of all the rest, to save them from the power or dominion of sin. "God sent

[1] Luke v. 32. [2] John v. 14; viii. 11. [3] Luke xix. 8.
[4] Acts ii. 37. [5] 1 Cor. xv. 10. [6] 2 Cor. v. 21.
[7] Rom. v. 9.

him to bless us, in turning away every one from his iniquities."[8]

All this he had done for St. Paul; and the sense and feeling of this deliverance was uppermost in his mind. Of sinners thus rescued from eternal death, *I*, he says, *am chief*. And now, how different his life! He had been brought from the power of sin to holiness, from the practice of sin to all good works. Once he had been cruel to his fellow-creatures, "haling men and women, and committing them to prison," if they refused to blaspheme their Saviour's name. Now his whole life was spent in the service of his fellow-creatures, in warning, exhorting, teaching them, "as a father does his children." Formerly he had been disobedient to God; preferring his own judgment to the plain revelation of God's will. He was now submissive as a child, at the feet of his Saviour, desiring to "know nothing save Jesus Christ, and him crucified:" for thirty years continuing in the same attitude of mind as at his first conversion, when his words were, "Lord, what wilt thou have me to do?"[9] So devoted was he to the interests of his heavenly Master; thinking no sufferings too great, no labours too painful, no hardships too severe, no danger too threatening: though he knew that wherever he was called to go, afflictions would be his lot. But "none of these things moved him."[1] Still, whilst he wrought the works of the zealous and laborious apostle, in his heart within he remained the meek and humble Christian: never forgetting his former

[8] Acts iii. 26. [9] Acts ix. 6. [1] Ib. xx. 24.

sinfulness; but always, when he spoke of God's mercy, adducing himself as the proof of it; and never reproving sin, without acknowledging that he himself had been the chief of sinners. So circumspect withal, so careful and upright in his way of life, that he was able to declare in the face of his enemies, "Herein do I exercise myself, to keep always a conscience void of offence, toward God, and toward men."[2]

Such are the sinners whom the Lord Jesus came to save, such are those whom he does save; those who hear the call which summons them to repentance; those who, while they trust in Him for the remission of sins that are past, live in his faith and fear, and are governed by his laws; are guided by his counsel now, that hereafter he may receive them to his glory.

Two important truths result from this example of St. Paul's own case.

First, there are none who, through repentance and conversion of heart, may not receive pardon. St. Paul declares that he himself was made an instance of special and signal mercy for this very reason, that no penitent sinner might despair of the same acceptance.

16. *Howbeit for this cause I obtained mercy, that in me first Jesus Christ might show forth all long-suffering, for a pattern to them which should hereafter believe on him to life everlasting.*

[2] Acts xxiv. 16.

And we can understand this. For the first idea of many a penitent, especially if their sins have been of the more gross and heinous kind, is the thought that pardon cannot be extended to offences such as theirs. Here, then, is a perpetual proof that these fears are vain. In the case of the same apostle, who proclaims to us that *Jesus Christ came into the world to save sinners, he hath first shown forth all long-suffering, for a pattern to them who should hereafter believe in him to life everlasting.* A pattern, that if their repentance is sincere, their forgiveness is certain; that if their faith is genuine and true, their title to eternal happiness is surely sealed.

Further, we learn from this example, that there are none who may not be converted and renewed, through Him who has engaged to give a new heart and a right spirit to them that trust in him. No greater change can be required, than that which took place in St. Paul, when he, who had been a persecutor, became a preacher of the gospel; when he who had blasphemed the name of Christ, became his zealous servant; when he who had been violent and injurious against every Christian, became an example of that charity which "hopeth all things, beareth all things." Therefore, *for this cause* also *he obtained the mercy* which produced this change, that in him all future believers might have an example: *a pattern* of what they can be made, *a pattern* of what they must be made, before they can hope for an inheritance in the kingdom of God. They must be "followers of God, as dear children, and walk in love, as Christ hath loved us. All bitterness, and wrath, and clamour, and evil-speaking, must be put away from them, with all malice: and they must be kind one to another, tender-hearted, forgiving one another, even as God, for Christ's sake, hath forgiven them."[3]

LV.

FOOD SUPPLIED IN THE WILDERNESS.

MARK vi. 35—44.

35. *When the day was now far spent, his disciples came unto him, and said, This is a desert place, and now the time is far passed:*
36. *Send them away, that they may go into the country round about, and into the villages, and buy themselves bread: for they have nothing to eat.*
37. *He answered and said unto them, Give ye them to eat. And they say unto him, Shall we go and buy two hundred pennyworth of bread, and give them to eat?*
38. *He saith unto them, How many loaves have ye? go and see. And when they knew, they say, Five, and two fishes.*
39. *And he commanded them to make all sit down by companies upon the green grass.*
40. *And they sat down in ranks, by hundreds, and by fifties.*

[3] Eph. iv. 3; v. 1, 2.

We can hardly doubt that the person who described this scene, with all its exact particulars, must have been an eye-witness of what he relates, and have told or written what he remembered. There is no reason to suppose that Mark was an eye-witness. But he is believed to have written under the direction of St. Peter: and the whole circumstances appear to have remained fresh and vivid in his recollection. We seem to hear him relating what took place; and saying, It was late in the evening, and the place in which we were was desert and uninhabited: so we came to the Lord as he was teaching, and reminded him that it was time for the people to disperse, that they might *go into the villages, and buy themselves bread: for they had nothing to eat,* having left their homes with no intention of being so long absent. He told us to supply them. It would have cost far more than we could afford. *Two hundred pennyworth of bread* would not have satisfied the multitude: and all that we could find amongst our own company, was *five loaves and two fishes.* However, he directed us to *make them all sit down.* It happened that, though a desert, it was a green and grassy place. And he gave us a lesson of order. If the multitude had sat down in a crowd, as they were standing, there must have been confusion, and some would have been passed over: so he commanded us to arrange them *by companies upon the green grass:* fifty or a hundred together in a rank; *and so they did all eat, and were filled.*

It was exactly the sort of scene which was likely to remain impressed upon the mind. Many things which Jesus did, and far more which he said, could never have been remembered and repeated without that assistance which he promised, saying, "The Holy Ghost, whom the Father will send in my name, he shall teach you all things, and bring all things to your remembrance, whatsoever I have said unto you."[1] But the Spirit need not dictate what the natural man recollected: and this miracle so impressed those who witnessed it, that it, and it alone, is related by all the Evangelists.[2].

41. *And when he had taken the five loaves and the two fishes, he looked up to heaven, and blessed, and brake the loaves, and gave them to his disciples to set before them; and the two fishes divided he among them all.*
42. *And they did all eat and were filled.*
43. *And they took up twelve baskets full of fragments, and of the fishes.*
44. *And they that did eat of the loaves were about five thousand men.*

It must be designed that an important inference should be drawn from a narrative which is made so prominent in the gospel history. And it furnishes a beautiful example of the way in which the Lord, as a true shepherd, watches over the circumstances of his people, and makes provision for wants which would otherwise distress them. The multitude had followed Jesus to this desert, because they saw his mighty works, and many, perhaps, that they might receive benefit from him. He did not allow those to suffer hunger, who because they had seen his miracles believed in him. Far more surely will he comfort others,

[1] John xiv. 26.

[2] Matt. xiv. 15—21; Luke ix. 12—18; John vi. 5—14.

who "not having seen, have yet believed." And they who have opportunity to observe the course of his providential dealings with men, often become acquainted with cases of supply in need, no less unexpected than the increase here made in the loaves and fishes. The changes and reverses which happen in the world, bring many of the servants of Christ to the state of Elijah, when "he arose and went for his life," which was threatened by the revenge of Jezebel.[3] "He went a day's journey into the wilderness. And as he lay and slept under a juniper tree, behold, an angel touched him, and said unto him, Arise and eat. And he looked, and behold, there was a cake baken on the coals, and a cruse of water at his head; and he did eat and drink, and laid him down again." The Lord whom he served, saw that "the journey was too great for him," and sent him refreshment in the hour of need. And "these things are written for our example, on whom the ends of the world are come." There is indeed a difference in the way in which God's people are supplied. An angel came to Elijah's aid. And here in the wilderness five loaves and two fishes were made to feed five thousand persons. But He who could command material things to change their nature, that nature which he himself had given them, and which he who gave it, can alter as he sees good:—he can no less govern the hearts of men, and divert their charity into the channel which he desires. So to soften hearts, and overcome their natural selfishness, is as much his work, as to increase the supply of food till it satisfied five thousand men.

[3] 1 Kings xix. 2—8; 1 Cor. xi. 24.

Indeed he has ordained a regular provision, by which support more needful than bodily refreshment may be supplied. The communion of his body and blood affords that nourishment to his faithful disciples, which the increase of the loaves afforded to his followers in the desert. "Hungry and thirsty, their soul faints within them," as they carry on their conflict against the world without, and the flesh within. Perhaps Satan takes advantage of an hour of natural weakness, and harasses them with unusual trials.

This, then, is the season when that grace is most needful which is made perfect in weakness, and is sufficient for every trial. And this is the season for receiving fresh strength from those outward means which the Lord instituted for the express purpose of maintaining spiritual life in the believer. "He took bread, and blessed it, and brake it, and gave it to his disciples, and said, Take, eat; this is my body. And he took the cup, and gave thanks, and gave it to them, saying, Drink ye all of it; for this is my blood of the new testament, which is shed for many for the remission of sins." The bread, however, was not *his body*, nor the wine *his blood*, except in a figure. The one, then, was to remind them of the other. The figure was to recall the reality. The bread was to remind them that his body broken for them was the price of their redemption. "Take, eat; this is my body."[4] This is my body, which shall be broken for you, when I bear your sins upon the cross, even as this bread is broken in my hands. And as the bread which I bless and break, is nourishment to the eater; so this my

[4] Matt. xxvi. 26—28; 1 Cor. xi. 24.

body is the "bread of life;" "the living bread which came down from heaven:" "my flesh, which I will give for the life of the world:" "if any man eat of this bread, he shall live for ever."[5]

The blood, again, reminds Christians of the sacrifice which their salvation cost, because, although "without shedding of blood is no remission," "the blood of Christ cleanseth from all sin." As he said, "Drink ye all of this; this is my blood of the new testament, which is shed for you and for many for the remission of sins." This is "the blood of the everlasting covenant," which "whoever drinketh, hath eternal life: and I will raise him up at the last day."

Thus, in this memorial of his cross and passion, this symbol of the inexhaustible grace of the Redeemer, we find enough to revive our hopes and encourage our exertions. As bread is the most universal nourishment, and as wine is the most salutary cordial to the human frame, so in the virtue of Christ's propitiation we seek support and refreshment in all time of our tribulation, in all time of our wealth, in the hour of death, and the day of judgment. And as the inhabitants of Bethsaida were strengthened to return home by the miraculous nourishment supplied to them, so now the disciples of Christ proceed in their warfare against the enemies of their salvation, strengthened by the bread of life, and refreshed by the blood shed for them and "for many, for the remission of sins."

[5] See John vi. 50, &c.

LVI.

SECURITY OF THE PHILIPPIAN CHURCH.

PHIL. i. 3—7.

3. *I thank my God upon every remembrance of you,*
4. *Always in every prayer of mine for you all making request with joy,*
5. *For your fellowship in the gospel from the first day until now;*
6. *Being confident of this very thing, that he which hath begun a good work in you will perform it until the day of Jesus Christ.*

THE city of Philippi was remarkable as being the first on the continent of Europe which received the gospel. St. Paul was specially directed thither. Whilst he was engaged amongst the churches of Asia, a vision appeared to him in the night; "There stood a man of Macedonia, and prayed him, saying, Come over into Macedonia, and help us. And after he had seen the vision, immediately he endeavoured to go into Macedonia, assuredly gathering that the Lord had called him for to preach the gospel unto them." So they came unto Philippi, "which is the chief city of that part of Macedonia, and a colony; and were in that city abiding certain days."

Not many, but important days. The seed of the

gospel was sown, and not in vain. Paul was permitted to drop the seed into the ground, but not to witness its growth. For after a short residence in the house of his first convert, he was hurried to prison with Silas his fellow labourer, on a charge that "these men, being Jews, did greatly trouble the city, and teach customs which it was not lawful for them, being Romans, to observe." Mindful, therefore, of the saying of the Lord Jesus, "When they persecute you in one city, flee unto another,"[1] they departed from Philippi, and proceeded to Thessalonica.

The plant, however, which during this short sojourn they had introduced, was not allowed to wither. The earthly husbandman was removed to another scene. But the heavenly husbandman is always the same, and always watchful: and under the culture of his grace there sprang up "first the blade, and then the ear, and after that the full corn in the ear." So that now, twelve years after the apostle's visit, there were congregations with their elders and officers whom he could contemplate with unusual satisfaction, and address as the *saints in Christ Jesus which were at Philippi.* These had not rejected the gracious message of reconciliation, but had turned from their idols to worship the living and true God, and "to wait for the hope set before them."

These formed the Christian congregation to which this letter was addressed: and from that time *a good work was begun in them:* they commenced a new course of life, "the life of faith in the Son of God:" they became "a peculiar people, redeemed from all iniquity,

[1] Matt. x. 23.

and zealous of good works;" they lived not unto themselves but unto God; not for this world, but for eternity.

But there is a singularity in St. Paul's expression. He does not say that *they began* this good work; but that this good work *was begun in them:* begun by another; that other being God.

He has good reason for so speaking. The preaching of the gospel is compared to the sowing of seed. When the seed is cast upon the ground, it may, or may not, vegetate and grow. If the fowls of the air devour it; if the ground is strong or impenetrable; if no warmth or no moisture follows; the seed is thrown away; no blade springs up. Only where there is a soil properly prepared; only where the dews and rains and sun promote its vegetation, does the blade appear; and when it does appear, then we might say that a work was begun in the field. And so, too often, the seed of the word falls upon a heart barren as sand, or hard as stone; and no work follows; only when the Spirit of God conveys the word within, and hides, and keeps, and cherishes it in the heart, does the seed spring up and grow, and "bring fruit unto perfection." In this very place, Philippi, for instance,—we read of one among many to whom Paul was preaching, "whose heart the Lord opened, that she attended unto the things which were spoken of Paul. And she was baptized, and her household."[2] Thus was *the good work begun* in her. But we are expressly informed that God began it. He opened her heart, that she attended unto the things spoken. And in every one who is "working

[2] Acts xvi. 14.

out his salvation" through faith in Christ Jesus, it is "God who worketh in him both to will and to do of his good pleasure."[3]

Not, indeed, that he is passive in this. None can be merely passive, in whom the work of salvation is going on. They are acted upon; but they are active too. God performs the work; but the material which he fashions is not wood or stone, which has nothing to do with the impression made on it. God leads the man, first to perceive that he shall profit nothing if he "gain the whole world, and lose his soul." He inclines him to seek the kingdom of God and his righteousness: he shows him that Christ, who is "the Lord our righteousness," is the way to that kingdom; and thus drawing the soul through the conscience and understanding, and disposing the will to follow what the conscience and understanding approve;—he begins the work which without him would never be begun, and carries on the work which without him would never be carried on. And thus it was that God had begun a work in the Philippians, for which Paul *was thankful on every remembrance of them.*

No other cause of thankfulness could be so great as this. They might have been still worshipping they knew not what; the work of men's hands. They might have been still without hope, because "without God in the world." They might have been walking in those ways which man in his natural state pursues; of which "the end is destruction." And now, instead of this, "behold, what manner of love the Father had

[3] Phil. ii. 13.

bestowed on them, that they should be called the sons of God!" [4]

All this was occasion of joy. But joy and fear are often near to each other in this world. There is the joy of possessing; there is also the fear of losing. And St. Paul might have felt this fear, whilst thinking of his Philippian converts, still exposed as they were to enemies without, and to the evils of a corrupt heart within: "the law of their members warring against the law of their mind," and Satan striving to "draw them back unto perdition." Against this reasonable apprehension he finds comfort in the power by which they are sustained, and which was engaged on their side. There was One with them greater than themselves. It was not of themselves, that they had turned from "the vain tradition received from their fathers." It was not of themselves that they had "cast off the works of darkness," and entered upon a course of sober, righteous, and godly living. It was not of themselves, that when others wondered at them[5] for their change of habits and heavenly conversation, they had been enabled to give a reasonable answer of the "hope that was in them," [6] and to go on perseveringly. It was God whose Spirit had begun this good work in them, and strengthened them thus far to continue stedfast and faithful. There was ground, therefore, to hope that he would "keep them from falling," and *perform the work* of salvation *unto the day of Jesus Christ*, the final overthrow of Satan and his cause.

[4] 1 John iii. 1. [5] 1 Pet. iv. 4. [6] 1 Pet. iii. 15.

In God there is no variableness, no change. If any difference were made in their state, it could not be from Him. The danger was from themselves. And Paul finds a reason in themselves, as well as in God's mercy and faithfulness, why he felt thus confident respecting them.

7. *Even as it is meet for me to think this of you all, because I have you in my heart: inasmuch as both in my bonds, and in the defence and confirmation of the gospel, ye all are partakers of my grace.*

It had not proved with them, as with the weak and unstable, that "when tribulation or persecution arose because of the word," they turned aside from the faith which it cost so much to maintain. They *had been partakers of the same grace* with the apostle himself, not counting their possessions, not counting their freedom, not counting their life dear unto themselves, in *the defence* of their faith, and in *the confirmation* of their profession. To them, as to him, "it had been given"—grace had been bestowed upon them "to suffer" in the cause of Christ: to "have the same conflict" with enemies, to undergo the same losses and reproaches, which "they had seen" the apostle undergo in their own city, and which at that time he was contending against at Rome. This was proof that the truth had root in their hearts: when the heats of temptation and the storms of persecution beat against the plant of faith, and it did not fail or wither. And therefore *it was meet for him to think this of them all, that He who had begun a good work in them would perform it until the day of Jesus Christ,* and bring them to the end of their course with joy.

Faith must always be brought to some test, though not now, as formerly, to the test of bonds and persecution *in the defence and confirmation of the gospel.* If Satan does not now oppose us by torture and imprisonment, he has means of temptation in his power scarcely less dangerous. But when we can look back upon passions resisted, in obedience to the commands of God; upon appetites restrained, though clamorous for indulgence; upon evil tempers subdued, though striving for the mastery; upon unlawful gains rejected, which might have been obtained if the gospel had not condemned them:—then we have signs of a good work begun, and may humbly hope that the good work will be *performed until the day of Jesus Christ.* In the prospect of our stability, we depend not on our own weakness, but on God's faithfulness. Still we could not dare to presume on his strength for protection, unless there were some proof in our own ways and habits, that "the grace which had been bestowed on us, had not been bestowed in vain."[7]

[7] See 1 Cor. xv. 10.

LVII.

PRAYER AND WATCHFULNESS.

MARK xiv. 38.

Watch ye and pray, lest ye enter into temptation. The spirit truly is ready, but the flesh is weak.

IT is not said as an excuse for sin, that *the flesh is weak;* but as a reason for watchfulness: that the flesh may obey the law of the inner man, instead of the spirit yielding to the weakness of the flesh. Hence the command, *Watch ye, and pray, that ye enter not into temptation:* that temptation may not take hold of the mind, and so possess it, as to put its stedfastness in peril. A man may be exposed to temptation, without *entering into temptation.* The danger begins when temptation finds its way into the heart, and parleys with it, so as to enter in and allure the affections.[1] David was placed in outward circumstances of great temptation, when, in his campaign against Saul, he found his implacable enemy sleeping in a cave, and might at once have slain him, and brought his difficulties to an end.[2] But the temptation made no impression: he instantly restrained it, rebuked his men, and refused to admit into his mind the prospect of advantage or the feelings of revenge. Daniel also was exposed to temptation, when he was

[1] Owen on Temptation.

[2] 1 Sam. xxiv. 4—6.

designed for a place in the palace of the king of Babylon, and "a daily provision of the king's meat, and of the wine which he drank, was appointed him."[3] But he, too, and his companions, refused to *enter into temptation;* and "purposed in their hearts that they would not defile themselves" by partaking of things which their law forbade, and the weakness of the flesh might render dangerous. In actual temptation there is little opportunity for the exercise of those means by which men are enabled to overcome it. Habitual prayer and watchfulness are the discipline by which they are made capable of resistance; capable of using their arms, when the enemy actually advances and the combat begins. In order to be prepared for that trial, they must use earnest vigilance over the besetting sins of their state, habits, disposition: must foresee temptation, and constantly pray, that with it "a way be made to escape, that they may be able to bear it;" that in the hour of danger, such thoughts, such resolution, such inward strength may be supplied by the Spirit, as shall enable them to "withstand in the evil day."

Now we can readily believe, that both David and Daniel, being men who lived in the fear of God, had watched and prayed against the sins to which their circumstances particularly exposed them. David, for instance, had reason for vigilance, lest the habits of life which he was obliged to lead, might overcome his sense of duty, and hurry him into acts of cruelty and injustice, or of greater violence than self-defence required. And Daniel was in danger lest, being placed amongst persons who knew not the true and living God, and

[3] Dan. i. 4—6.

practised no restraint of appetite, he should "run with them into the same excess of riot," and become "partaker of their sins."

These teach us by their good example. Others warn us by the evils into which they fell. When the city of Ai was taken under the command of Joshua, strict orders had been issued that the spoil of the city should "come into the treasury of the Lord," and no part of it be reserved for private uses.[4] But one of the tribe of Judah, named Achan, disobeyed the order, and thus describes the working of his heart, and the way by which he *entered into temptation.* "When I saw among the spoils a goodly Babylonish garment, and two hundred shekels of silver, and a wedge of gold of fifty shekels' weight, then I coveted them, and took them; and behold, they are hid in the earth in the midst of my tent, and the silver under it."[5]

Now Achan was brought into this temptation in the way of duty. He did not seek it, by going heedlessly or rashly into the snare. And such "temptation is common to man." Human life is such, that occasions of sin must be encountered by every one. Therefore, the *entering into temptation* is not the being exposed to the opportunity of sin, but the allowing the heart to entertain the thoughts of it, and yield to its solicitations. And our endeavour must be, not so much that no evil shall ever be proposed to us, "for then we must needs go out of the world;" as that we may be "kept from the evil;"[6] kept from approaching it, kept from taking part in it, kept from touching the pitch

[4] Josh. vi. 19. [5] Josh. vii. 21. [6] John xvii. 15.

which surrounds us, and which we cannot touch without being defiled.

To this end the direction is given, *Watch and pray.* These cannot be separated. Watchfulness leads to prayer, and prayer to watchfulness. To *watch,* is to search into our hearts, and examine our temper of mind, and discover the evil to which we most incline: to recall the occasions when we have been betrayed through this corruption, and as far as in us lies to guard against the like occasions. To *watch,* is to reflect on the outward circumstances in which we are placed; the danger of offending God to which they chiefly expose us; and so to take heed lest the evil come upon us unawares. If the three disciples had considered the many warnings of their Lord, who had foretold the trials which were approaching, they would not have been *found sleeping,* but in the attitude of watchfulness and prayer. If Peter in particular had called to mind the time, when thinking himself too full of faith to be affected by fear, he ventured upon the waters to meet his Lord, and yet gave way when the waves became boisterous;[7]—he would have set himself to prayer and supplication, that the ready spirit might not again be betrayed by the weakness of the flesh. For there can hardly be watchfulness without prayer, any more than there will be fervent prayer where there is not habitual watchfulness. Whoever seriously considers either his spiritual weakness, or his spiritual danger, must of necessity apply for health and strength to the only source from which they can be derived.

[7] Matt. xiv. 30.

The love and practice of these duties are the surest proof of a renewed heart; the easiest test of our spiritual state. If the need of them is not felt and acted on, danger is at hand. If the seasons of them are few, easily omitted, and often neglected; danger is at hand: the same sort of danger to the soul, as that which threatens the body, when the usual appetite for food or exercise is found to fail. Where there is a true renewal of the heart, there is a taste for these duties: and a decline in the practice of them is evidence of the decline of grace, and therefore of the approach of danger. So that St. Paul, after arming the Ephesian Christians with "the breastplate of righteousness," and "the shield of faith," and "the helmet of salvation," and "the sword of the Spirit," adds at last this direction, that they may be able to use their armour to good purpose, "*Praying* always with all prayer and supplication in the Spirit, and *watching* thereunto with all perseverance."[8]

[8] Eph. vi. 14—18.

LVIII.

CONFIDENCE IN PRAYER.

JAMES i. 5, 6.

5. *If any of you lack wisdom, let him ask of God, that giveth to all men liberally and upbraideth not; and it shall be given him.*
6. *But let him ask in faith, nothing wavering. For he that wavereth is like a wave of the sea, driven with the wind and tossed.*

WAVERING, is doubting. When we ask a benefit of a fellow-creature, we may ask with a doubt upon our minds—though even this we should not disclose—a doubt whether he have the power, or whether he have the will, to grant what we are seeking at his hands. But when we ask of God, and ask for spiritual wisdom, there must be no such *wavering:* his power we know; to doubt that, would be to disparage his attributes; and his will we know, for he has declared it; to doubt that, would be to discredit his word. And therefore our Lord himself, in making the same promise, has added the same condition.[1] "All things whatsoever ye shall ask in prayer, believing, ye shall receive." Again,[2] "Have faith in God. For verily I say unto

[1] Matt. xxi. 22. [2] Mark xi. 23.

you, that whosoever shall not doubt in his heart, but shall believe that those things which he saith shall come to pass, he shall have whatsoever he saith." Again, "If thou canst believe, all things are possible to him that believeth."[3]

Are we surprised that so much stress is laid on *confidence?* Because it is thus seen, where the heart is really resting; whether on itself and its own resources, on any earthly means; or whether it can really cast its care upon God with an equal sense of helplessness and of hope, saying, "Lord, undertake for me." It was the absence of this faith in the Israelites which Isaiah severely rebukes. "Thus saith the Lord, the Holy One of Israel; In returning and rest shall ye be saved: in quietness and in confidence shall be your strength: and ye would not. But ye said, No, for we will flee upon horses; therefore shall ye flee: and we will ride upon the swift: therefore shall they that pursue you be swift."[4]

Thus were the Israelites *double-minded, unstable:* taking in their mouths the name of the Lord, but really in their hearts trusting to mortal strength and human means. Exactly as a *wave of the sea, driven by the wind and tossed:* one while rising towards God, and then sinking down to the feebleness of human power. This doubting, double, wavering mind receives no blessing. "Let not that man think that he shall receive anything of the Lord."

Still there must here be some reserve. It is possible that a meek and contrite heart may *waver,* conscious

[3] Mark ix. 23. [4] Isa. xxx. 15, 16.

of its own unworthiness. With what confidence, it might say, can I approach the great and holy God? How can I expect the strength or wisdom that is from above, the gift of the Spirit, to which I have so often "done despite?"

Now this is not the sentiment of a double mind, but of a humble mind. This is not the mind which shall receive no favourable return. Such a mind must not be depressed, but encouraged. Here is "the bruised reed." It is not the will of God that the heart which is bruised should be broken. Here is "the smoking flax." The mercy of God would not quench it, but kindle an abiding flame. There is no limitation to the promise, "Ye shall seek me, and ye shall find me, when ye shall search for me with all your heart."[5]

Doubt not, therefore, but earnestly believe, that if any man *lack wisdom,* he may *ask of God,* and find *that he giveth to all men liberally.* He deals with us as a father with his children. He secures our application to him, by letting us feel our daily need. Perhaps here is the secret cause of many of the trials, both inward and outward, which befall the Christian. They drive us to prayer. Thus God keeps us dependent on himself, and promotes that free and gracious intercourse which belongs to those whom he has adopted in Christ Jesus: who, as his children, have liberty to come boldly to the throne of grace; to "cry, Abba, Father." For if earthly parents, with all the evil that is in their hearts, still seldom fail in giving good gifts to their children; "shall not your Heavenly

[5] Jer. xxix. 13.

Father give his Holy Spirit to them that ask him?" *Only let them ask in faith, nothing wavering.*

Many things, no doubt, we might ask, and not obtain. God will grant the petitions of his servants as may be most expedient for them. The unlimited promise is given, not to every prayer, but to the prayer for spiritual aid; for *wisdom,* true and heavenly wisdom; wisdom we shall not seek in vain, if we *ask in faith, nothing wavering:* nothing wavering in our desire for it, nothing wavering in our conviction that it must come, and can come, from God alone. Seasons there will be when the Christian's path may seem to himself so dark and perplexing, so beset with difficulties, that nothing is before him but despair. And yet, in that darkest hour and day of gloom, there is light prepared and safety provided; the way we know not, for "we walk by faith, and not by sight;" but it is sure, for "He that keepeth Israel shall neither slumber nor sleep." In the history of Elisha it is related that the king of Syria had resolved to seize the prophet, and encompassed the city in which he was lodging "with a host of men, horses, and chariots."[6] The servant of the man of God rising early perceived this, and said, "Alas, master! how shall we do? And he answered, Fear not: they that be with us are more than they which be with them. And Elisha prayed and said, Lord, open his eyes, that he may see. And the Lord opened the eyes of the young man, and he saw; and behold, the mountain was full of horses and chariots of fire round about Elisha." There was a power encompassing him,

[6] 2 Kings vi. 15.

invisible to mortal eye, but seen by the prophet's faith, which restrained the enemies of Elisha.

And thus it is that God's children are preserved and strengthened, and guided in a way that they know not. The timid Christian faints at the thought of the difficulties which he must encounter, the enemy without and the enemy within, one assaulting and the other betraying, as he works out his salvation against the power of Satan in an evil world. We may use the words of Elisha, and say, "Open his eyes, Lord, that he may see." Could his eyes be thus opened, he would behold the preparation made for his security: no assault of Satan, for which a way of escape was not provided; no inward weakness which there was not grace to strengthen; no outward obstacle which there was not power to overcome. In fact, we have abundant proof of this, in what God has already done, and is daily effecting for those who take him at his word, and do *ask wisdom of Him, nothing wavering.* Do we not find the truth confirmed; *He giveth to all men liberally, and upbraideth not?* In all the temptations which poverty or wealth, which contempt or honour, which the feebleness of age or the frailty of youth present, do we not find wisdom given, by which the children of God are carried safely through all their trials? We see those who have this world's good, not "trusting in uncertain riches," but "rich towards God," rich in good works. We see others, whose lot is poverty, able, like Paul of old, "in whatsoever state they are, therewith to be content." We see one who is honoured of his fellowmen, "lowly in his own eyes," and "setting others before himself." We see the simple become wise; the meek become bold in the cause of God. We see the beauty and energy of youth preferring "the reproach of Christ to the pleasures of sin for a season," and devoting the first fruits of life to the service of their Saviour. We see the feeble and delicate braving pain with cheerfulness, and the heart that bleeds with sorrow smiling through tears. In short, we see *wisdom* supplied, the very wisdom which the case requires, to those that are the children of God through faith in Christ Jesus, and in the strength of that faith plead his gracious promise, and ask for "grace to help in every time of need." God does bestow wisdom upon his people; and so gives encouragement to all, that they turn to the same heavenly Father, to ask the like wisdom, and to experience the like almighty power.

LIX.

CHRIST A SURE REFUGE.

Hebrews vi. 17—20.

17. *God, willing more abundantly to show unto the heirs of promise the immutability of his counsel, confirmed it by an oath:*
18. *That by two immutable things, in which it was impossible for God to lie, we might have a strong consolation,*

who have fled for refuge to lay hold upon the hope set before us:

19. *Which hope we have as an anchor of the soul, both sure and stedfast, and which entereth into that within the veil;*

20. *Whither the forerunner is for us entered, even Jesus.*

WRITING to the Hebrews, St. Paul uses an expression which they would be at no loss to understand. He represents heaven as the place *within the veil:* such as was that holiest part of the temple, where especially God was supposed to dwell, and which only the High Priest was allowed to enter. This is the heavenly kingdom, which Jesus, "when he had overcome the sharpness of death, opened for all believers:" and *whither he has entered for us, the forerunner* of his redeemed people, being *made a high priest for ever:* whose appointment is not for a time, and whose atonement is not annual; but "once for all, a full, perfect, and sufficient satisfaction."

The *hope set before us entereth* into this kingdom: anticipates its future blessedness: as St. Paul says, "we walk by faith, and not by sight:" "our conversation is in heaven." And the effect of this is, *a strong consolation:* a firm, a sure consolation, in the *immutability of God's counsel,* the unchangeable covenant by which he has bound himself to cancel the sins of those who have *fled for refuge* to the cross of Christ. "Blotting out the handwriting of ordinances which was against us, which was contrary to us, he took it out of the way, nailing it to his cross."[1] St. Paul is the

[1] Col. ii. 14.

better able to speak of this consolation, because it had comforted his own heart. God had pardoned him; though he hardly forgave himself, "because he had persecuted the church of Christ:" and he often laments, that he had been before "a blasphemer, and a persecutor, and injurious." But he recalls to mind;—This is a faithful saying, that "Christ Jesus came into the world to save sinners; of whom I am chief."[2] And knowing, that this propitiation had been made; that God had *confirmed by an oath* his acceptance of this propitiation: and inwardly feeling that he had availed himself of the promise, and claimed it for himself by faith:—he says, in the conscious thankfulness of his heart, *we have a strong consolation.*

But the consolation is more than a deliverance from wrath; it is a promise of blessedness. "He that hath the Son hath life."[3] He that has fled to him for refuge, has "life for evermore." "The gift of God is eternal life, through Jesus Christ."[4] In all the changes and trials of this earthly scene;—and they are many;—in those afflictions and reverses from which the children of God are no more exempt than others;—they *have a strong consolation,* who are warranted in believing that their "light affliction, which is but for a moment, is working for them a far more exceeding and eternal weight of glory:"[5] who know, with the apostle, "that if their earthly tabernacle be dissolved, they have a building of God, not made with hands, eternal in the heavens."[6]

[2] See 1 Tim. i. 12—16. [3] 1 John v. 12.
[4] Rom. vi. 23. [5] 2 Cor. iv. 17. [6] Ib. v. 1.

St. Paul justly terms this hope, *an anchor of the soul, both sure and stedfast.* The anchor is fixed on one side to the ship, on the other to the rock on which it rests; and thus, although the winds blow and the waves roar, the vessel rides secure. *The hope set before us* is such an anchor. It "stablishes, strengthens, settles" the soul: which contemplates with the eye of faith those things which the natural eye has not seen, and which the heart of man cannot conceive; those "good things which God hath prepared for them that love him."

On this hope the Christian rests. Like the ship which, safely anchored in its haven, is able to outride the storm that shatters other vessels, which have sought no refuge. *Sought* no refuge. For this too must be remembered. The refuge must be *sought.* St. Paul speaks of it as a thing done, a precaution taken. His words imply an active personal appropriation of the means of deliverance. *We have a strong consolation, who have fled for refuge,* by an active exercise of mind and will. And there must be such an active exercise.

The gospel shows to man his natural state; a state of one ruined by sin, alienated from God. Our own reflection of what is in ourselves; our own observation of what is passing around us, must confirm, too surely to be disputed, the words of Scripture, which declares that "all have sinned, and come short of the glory of God." But, again, Scripture "concludes all under sin," not that all might perish, but that "the promise of God through Jesus Christ might be unto them that believe." Scripture offers a way of redemption from the natural state of sin and death. It holds up the Lord Jesus Christ as a Deliverer to all who commit themselves to him. And so to commit ourselves to Him, is our part: just as it is the part of the mariners to cast out the anchor that their ship may be securely moored in its place of refuge. Like them, from a sense of danger, we look out for security. We find it in the hope set before us, and make it our own by that inward movement of the heart which is expressed by the word faith, or believing: believing in the deliverance which he has wrought, and the safety which he offers, and therefore intrusting ourselves to him.

This is our *strong consolation*. And we may justly say, "Blessed are they which are in such a case; yea, blessed are the people that have the Lord for their God." [1]

[1] Psa. xxxiii. 12.

LX.

THE AFFECTIONS DUE TOWARDS JESUS CHRIST.

1 PETER i. 8.

Whom having not seen, ye love; in whom, though now you see him not, yet believing, ye rejoice with joy unspeakable, and full of glory.

THE apostle, in the preceding verse, having named the name of Christ, kindles as a man is wont to do at the mention of his dearest friend, or most valued benefactor. He breaks forth into the expression of those feelings which he knew the brethren entertained towards their Lord and Saviour. He speaks of their loving him, and of their rejoicing in him.

There must be a reason for these feelings. There must be a reason for this love. We cannot love God or man without a moving cause. And the cause why the Christian loves the Lord Jesus Christ is, that he is the author of all his hopes. He looks to himself, and sees that he has offended against God. And what has he to offer, that God may be gracious to him? "Wherewith shall he come before the Lord?" He has nothing wherewith to pay, when Christ steps in and satisfies the whole debt: "gives his life a ransom for many." Can he fail to love him to whom he owes a benefit like this?

But again, he looks towards himself, and finds corruption within. He "finds a law, that when he would do good, evil is present with him." "Who shall deliver him?" Once more he turns to the same Redeemer, from whose grace he may receive both the inclination and the power to obey; may be enabled "to do all things through Christ who strengtheneth him."

Can he fail to love that gracious Being, who has first prepared an eternal inheritance for him, and is now preparing him to enjoy it, and take possession?

This, however, is a feeling which can be only understood by those who have raised their thoughts beyond this present world, and set out in earnest to seek the kingdom of God. They who have never seriously considered the death which is before them, or the judgment which is to follow, can see no reason why the Saviour should be desired or loved. Having never felt the burthen of that debt which lies upon them, they feel no gratitude towards him who pays it. Having no inclination to be purified from a sinful nature, the author of a new nature has no value in their eyes. As the prophet said, "There is no beauty in him that they should desire him."

It is not till a man begins in earnest to provide for his everlasting salvation, that he can enter into the expression of the apostle concerning Jesus Christ, *whom, having not seen, ye love.* Till then, he hears his name as the name of a Master who demands his service, or a Ruler who commands him to change his way of life, and leave the things to which he is too much attached, the only things of which he has learnt the value. But when he has once determined within himself, that this life is nothing to him, if only he can "attain that world, and the resurrection from the dead," then he will love the gracious Lord, who has opened the gates of heaven to him: who has reconciled him to God, and given him an inheritance among the saints in light.

2. The other account given of Christians is, that they *rejoice* in Christ Jesus: rejoice in him *with joy unspeakable and full of glory*: joy which realises the prophet's words, "How beautiful upon the mountains are the feet of him that bringeth good tidings, that publisheth peace!"[1]

Our Lord, in one of his parables, represents a debtor, who, owing ten thousand talents to his lord, was "to be sold with his wife and children, and all that he had, that payment might be made." But the creditor had compassion on him, and forgave him all that he owed. That man would *rejoice* in his benefactor. And so a criminal, respited from punishment through the intercession of some powerful friend, *rejoices* in his preserver.

In the same manner, the Christian feels, that if he is "not appointed unto wrath," it is through the "one Mediator between God and man, the man Christ Jesus:" and that if his transgressions are blotted out, it is because the death of Christ has made satisfaction for them all; full, complete satisfaction. This he be-

[1] Isa. lii. 7.

lieves, and believing, *rejoices with joy unspeakable.* It exactly meets his wants, and calms his fears. "Holy, holy, holy, is the Lord Almighty." And what are we his creatures? Weak, erring, sinful. "We have sinned, and come short of the glory of God." O how short of that glory have we come! "Who can understand his errors?" Who can enumerate the times, in which by thought, word, and deed, he has offended the divine Majesty! Then how delightful the language of the Gospel, "Behold the Lamb of God, which taketh away the sin of the world!" Behold an "advocate with the Father, Jesus Christ the righteous, who is the propitiation for our sins," who is able to "present us pure and blameless before the throne of God." Able and willing. Able, because he can plead the full, perfect, and sufficient atonement which he has made; and willing, because having been "tempted in all points, like as we are," he "can be touched with our infirmities."[2] In Him, therefore, we have "all things which pertain to life and godliness:" we have "wisdom, and righteousness, and sanctification, and redemption;" and having this, *we rejoice in him with joy unspeakable and full of glory.* Our thoughts instinctively turn towards Him, in sorrow or in joy, in fear, or in hope: in the hours of our weakness or our energy. Christ mitigates the sorrow, allays the fear, strengthens the weakness. The joy is in his favour: the hope is through his mercy: the energy is in the power of his might. If the mind contemplates this earthly life, it takes, as it were, a new colour from the fact that Jesus dwelt here, in form and fashion as a

[2] Heb. iv. 15.

man. If the thoughts rise towards the world above, there again Christ meets us, "set down at the right hand of God," waiting for the overthrow of his enemies;[2] and no less watching over the interests of his people; dear to him, and to the Father also, "because they have loved the Son, and believed that he came out from God."[3] If the conscience reverts, as it often should revert, to sins repented of and forsaken, there is the blessed consolation that "the blood of Jesus Christ cleanseth from all sin."[4] Or if the man grieves, as he should grieve, over present infirmities and shortcomings, he still rejoices to think of Christ as knowing our frame, and "in that he himself hath suffered being tempted, as able to succour them that are tempted."[5] If he looks onward to the valley of the shadow of death, which some time or other must be passed through, Christ is there, with his "rod and staff to comfort."[6] Or if he looks beyond the grave to the judgment which is to follow, Christ will be seated there as Judge: and has pledged his sacred word that those who confess him before men, he also will confess before his Father and the holy angels.[7]

So full of encouragement, of comfort, of joy, are the thoughts of Christ which Scripture teaches us to entertain: when the prayer of St. Paul for his Ephesian disciples is accomplished in us, and "Christ dwells in the heart by faith; and being strengthened with might by his Spirit in the inner man, we are able to comprehend what is the breadth, and length, and depth, and

[2] Psa. cx. 2. [3] John xvi. 27. [4] 1 John i. 7.
[5] Heb. ii. 18. [6] Psa. xxiii. 4. [7] Matt. x. 32.

height, and to know the love of Christ, which passeth knowledge."

One great use of this passage is, to show us ourselves; it holds up a glass, by which we may learn how far we are Christians indeed. For the apostle describes such, as lovers of Christ: *whom having not seen, ye love:* —as trusters in Christ: *in whom, though now ye see him not, yet believing:*—as rejoicers in Christ: *ye rejoice in him with joy unspeakable, and full of glory;* in its nature like that of an angel's joy.

Our first impression is, that they who felt so deeply and so sensibly, had advantages which we have not, so that more might be expected from them than from ourselves. But it was not so. Had they lived with our Lord on earth, heard his discourses, witnessed his sufferings? St. Peter is particular in telling us that they had not. Many who had heard his discourses and seen his miracles, were amongst his bitter enemies: but these who are here represented as rejoicing in him and loving him, had no more looked upon him with their bodily eyes than we ourselves. *Whom not having seen, ye love.* They were among those of whom our Lord spoke, when he said, "Blessed are they who have not seen, and yet have believed." [8]

By faith, then, these were led to value the Redeemer: by considering his words, as related by those who heard them: by receiving his assurances, and pondering them in their hearts. Faith is capable of raising the affections, and bringing them to that love which is due to a Saviour, and to that joy which springs from the blessings of redemption.

[8] John xx. 29.

If, therefore, any are disposed to say, We believe: God help our unbelief! — We love, but it is a feeble spark :—We rejoice, but it is with trembling :—how can we learn to believe more firmly, to love more truly, to rejoice more heartily? The answer is, According to the degree of your faith, will be the degree of your love and joy. And we know how faith is increased. "Faith cometh by hearing." Faith cometh by prayer. Faith cometh by meditation. Faith cometh by a hearty desire, that the religious duties which we practise, and the word of God which we study, may enable us to "grow in grace, and in the knowledge of the Lord Jesus Christ:" and so lead us to the "end of our faith, even the salvation of our souls."

LXI.

THE RULING PRINCIPLE.

ROMANS vi. 16.

Know ye not, that to whom ye yield yourselves servants to obey, his servants ye are to whom ye obey: whether of sin unto death, or of obedience unto righteousness?

SIN is here called a master, and is said to rule. Yet some might ask, What is sin, which is here treated as a person? What is it but a name?

Sin is that principle within us, in which the corruption of our fallen nature consists: that principle which is opposed to what is right, and, being right, is required of God. It appears in various forms: and in all those forms it rules. Pride is sin: and the vain, haughty, self-conceited man is the servant of pride. Malice is sin: and the envious, slanderous, revengeful man is the servant of malice. Covetousness is sin: and the dishonest, hard-hearted, extortionate man is governed by covetousness. Intemperance is sin: and the man who indulges any of the bodily appetites beyond the rules which God prescribes, is the slave of intemperance.

And we may see, by a few examples, how just the term is: how properly sin may be termed a master whom men obey and serve.

Sin acted as a master over Joseph's brethren, at the time when they resolved, first, to kill him, and afterwards sold him as a slave to the travelling merchants who were providentially passing by.[1] Joseph was advancing towards them. "And they said one to another: Behold, this dreamer cometh. Come, let us slay him." What urged them to such a purpose? Envy, hatred, malice. Joseph was a better son than themselves, and therefore their father loved him better. God had intimated to him by a prophetic dream, that he should hereafter be lord over his brethren. Therefore "they hated him, and could not speak peaceably unto him." And these feelings mastered them, governed them. When opportunity was given, envy, hatred rise up in their hearts, and issue a command: "Now slay this dreamer." They obeyed the impulse, though God

[1] Gen. xxxvii. 18—20.

had given a contrary command, and declared, "Whoso sheddeth man's blood, by man shall his blood be shed." They despised the command of God, and followed the command of sin. *And his servants ye are, whom ye obey.*

Again, sin acted as a master over Gehazi, the servant of Elisha.[2] His sin was of another form; took the shape of covetousness. His master the prophet had been enabled to cure the Syrian officer Naaman of his leprosy. Naaman would have loaded him with valuable gifts in return. But Elisha was the *servant of righteousness*, and would receive none. Then it was that Gehazi's real master, the ruler of his heart, awoke as it were, and gave his orders. The prophet had spared Naaman, who would gladly have enriched him. Let Gehazi run after him, and take something from him. Gehazi willingly obeyed: and under false pretences carried back with him "two talents of silver, and two changes of garments:" took them up privately, and "bestowed them in the house." What was this, but to be the slave of covetousness? *His servants ye are, whom ye obey.*

The case of Pilate supplies another example. His ruling principle was ambition; love of popular favour and worldly advancement. He saw the innocence of the Lord Jesus, who was brought before him. He was anxious "to release him." His understanding showed him that the Jews were accusing Jesus out of envy: and his conscience warned him, that he ought to "have nothing to do with that just man:" not to be the instrument of Jewish malice.[3] Had he followed the dic-

[2] 2 Kings v. 20—27. [3] John xix. 1—16.

tates of his conscience, he would have set Jesus free. But just as he was on the point of discharging him, his master ambition came in, and said, by the mouth of the Jews, "If thou lettest this man go, thou art not Cæsar's friend." Thou wilt lose thy credit at court: perhaps forfeit thy present government: certainly not obtain a better. So when Pilate heard these words, he heard them as a servant hears his master's order: they were to him a command: and overcoming all sense of justice and duty, he "delivered up Jesus to them to be crucified."

Thus it is that sin acts as a master over those who yield to it: nay, as a master who will not give up his power. Some, perhaps, in a moment of penitence, in a season of conviction, may desire to escape from their bondage, and break their chains. But ever and anon the master returns: sets before them the temptation to which they have been used to yield, the pleasure, or the company, or the gain to which they have been long accustomed: and when he says, Enjoy this, and disregard the consequences,—they obey, for they are his servants, and his yoke is over them. How many of the victims of intemperance have resolved never again to taste the poison which is destroying them! How many a gamester has vowed that he will no more risk the ruin of his fortune, his family, and his peace! A few hours after, the master sin appears: bids him return to the place which he had determined to avoid, bids him rejoin the company which so lately he renounced; says, "as one having authority, Come, and he cometh; Go, and he goeth." Such is the tyranny of sin: such the dominion under which he holds his captives: they cannot do the things which their conscience tells them should be done; and the things they approve not in their inner mind, those they do: because their master fetters their will, and makes it agree with his own.

Such, then, says St. Paul here, had been the case with those to whom he wrote. They had been the servants of sin. Following the desires of the flesh and of the mind, they had yielded themselves to a dominion which is contrary to God and righteousness, and been "led captive by Satan at his will." But it was to men in this unhappy state; it was because this was the helpless condition of the world, that Jesus Christ had come, to impose a new and a very different yoke upon them. And these Roman brethren had listened to the voice of the Deliverer: had been made free from their former master, and had now become the *servants of God and of righteousness*. Paul thanks God that they had obeyed from the heart that form of doctrine which was delivered them. They had obeyed that doctrine which taught them how the Lord Jesus had laid down his life, that he might redeem to himself a people: might free them from the service of sin, and bring them to God. So that now sin had no more dominion over them. He might issue his command, and say, "Rejoice, O young man, in thy youth, and walk in the ways of thine heart and in the sight of thine eyes."[4] Sin might urge this; but urge in vain. They had chosen another master, who has said, "Mortify your members which are upon earth:" for "know thou, that for all these things God will bring thee into

[4] Eccles. xi. 9.

judgment."[5] Ambition might try its power with them, and say, Come, make to thyself a name. Seek wealth, seek honour, seek to be spoken well of. But they had another master, even God: and he warned them, "Whosoever will[6] be the friend of the world, is the enemy of God." Covetousness might put in its claim, and give some tempting reason why they should enrich themselves, and disregard the interests of others. But they were "made free" from the power of such temptations, and had become "servants to God:" and the maxim of his family is, "What shall it profit a man, if he should gain the whole world, and lose his own soul!"

This is the answer to that question which corrupt nature is too ready to ask: May we not continue in sin, since we are not under the law, but under grace? It would frustrate all God's purposes. He has "redeemed us from all iniquity," that we might yield ourselves unto God. But "whoso committeth sin, is the servant of sin," still under the yoke, for which the Son of God came to "make him free." *For his servants ye are, whom ye obey, whether of sin unto death, or of obedience unto righteousness.*

[5] Col. iii. 5; Eccles. xi. 9. [6] βουληθῃ. James iv. 4.

LXII.

THE SUFFICIENCY OF CHRIST TO SALVATION.

Col. ii. 8—15.

8. *Beware lest any man spoil you*[1] *through philosophy and vain deceit, after the tradition of men, after the rudiments of the world, and not after Christ.*
9. *For in him dwelleth all the fulness of the Godhead bodily.*
10. *And ye are complete in him, which is the head of all principality and power.*

It is part of Satan's malice to turn men aside from the plain truths which Christ has revealed, and *spoil them* of their blessings *by philosophy and vain deceit.* He had perverted the Jewish nation in this manner. God had prescribed them laws, which should "be their righteousness." But they had made the commands of God of none effect through their traditions;[2] and interpreted the divine law *after the rudiments of the world.* And now "the simplicity of the Gospel" was corrupted under the pretence of wisdom: as if something must be added to the work of Christ, and the redemption wrought by him were not in itself sufficient. St. Paul warns the Colossians against such

[1] μη τις ἐσται ὁ συλαγωγων—lest any rob or despoil you of what ye have gained.

[2] Mark vii. 13.

false teachers: assuring them, *Ye are complete in him:* "filled with his fulness:" all things are fulfilled in you, which are needful for your salvation. Ye have that which is required for your pardon and acceptance with God: for his satisfaction is "perfect and sufficient." Ye have that which is required for your sanctification; having the promise of his Spirit to lead you into all truth, and being enabled to "do all things through Christ which strengtheneth you." The branch which is united to its stem, has all that it needs to give it life and fruitfulness. And so have ye, whilst "rooted in the faith, and stablished." Ye have Him with you as your Lord and Saviour, who is "one with the Father," into whose hands "the Father hath committed all things;" *who is the head of all principality and power,* in whom *dwelleth all the fulness of the Godhead,* not merely as God was present in the Jewish tabernacle, or "above the mercy-seat in the temple," but in a bodily form.

There were some, perhaps, who would deny this completeness, and object, that they had not circumcision. It was by circumcision, said the Judaizing teachers, that the people of God were distinguished. So God himself ordained, and prescribed the ordinance to Abraham and his seed for ever.

St. Paul furnishes the reply: affirming that they had a circumcision superior to that of which the Jews were fond of boasting. That circumcision is made by the operation of men. They had the circumcision of the Spirit. They were consecrated to God as Abraham was, though not by outward but by inward means. That is the true circumcision, which *puts off the body of the sins of the flesh.* And this they possessed, who were "in Christ Jesus."

11. *In whom also ye are circumcised with the circumcision made without hands, in putting off the body of the sins of the flesh by the circumcision of Christ:*
12. *Buried with him in baptism, wherein also ye are risen with him through the faith of the operation of God, who hath raised him from the dead.*
13. *And you, being dead in your sins and the uncircumcision of your flesh, hath he quickened together with him, having forgiven you all trespasses;*
14. *Blotting out the handwriting of ordinances that was against us, which was contrary to us, and took it out of the way, nailing it to his cross;*
15. *And having spoiled principalities and powers, he made a shew of them openly, triumphing over them in it.*

Here, in few words, the apostle points out to the Colossians the blessings of their redemption through the sacrifice of the cross. Your natural state, he says, was a state of death: for sin is death; and ye were *in your sins.* Receiving the faith of Christ, and committing yourselves to him in baptism, your first nature is as it were *buried with him:* and *ye are risen with him* to a new and better nature *through the faith of the operation of God:* who first raised Him from actual death, and now raises his followers from spiritual death, quickening them to a new life of righteousness and holiness. So he hath dealt with you Gentiles, *having forgiven you all your trespasses.* But this is not all that has been done. There was a *handwriting of ordinances that was against us;*—equally against us Jews and you

Gentiles;—which must bring all under condemnation. The ordinance said, "Cursed is every one that continueth not in all the things that are written in the book of the law to do them."[3] This doom was *against us: contrary to us:* for it made all men guilty before God.[4] This *handwriting Christ hath blotted out: hath taken it out of the way, nailing it to his cross:* so that it can never be brought against us, any more than a bond can be brought against a debtor which has been cancelled, pierced through, and torn. So that *the principalities and powers* which had long held mankind under their dominion, are *spoiled* of their captives: Christ has led them captive in their turn, and *made a show of them openly,* like vanquished kings in the procession of their conqueror, *triumphing over them* by his Cross which he lifts up, as the warrior lifts up his banner and "draws all men after him."[5]

See, then, in review, the benefits of which St. Paul here speaks, when *the handwriting of ordinances* is cancelled.

The law was laid down before the Israelites; and they bound themselves by a promise, saying to Moses, "All that the Lord our God shall speak unto us, we will hear it and do it."[6] The law was not thus plainly revealed to the Gentiles; but still there was a law of nature and of conscience, distinguishing between good and evil: so that they who followed their conscience and reason, might do by nature the things contained in the law, "fearing God and working righteousness."[7]

[3] Gal. iii. 10. [4] See Rom. iii. 9—31. [5] John xii. 32.
[6] Deut. v. 27. [7] Rom. ii. 14; Acts x. 35.

Hold up this *writing of ordinances*, this law that is "holy, just, and good," before a man, and examine according to that law his thoughts, and words, and works; will it not be *contrary to him*, and condemn him? Could any man be able to say, I have continued in all things that are written in the law, and done them? Has not "the law in his members" overcome "the law in his mind," so that "when he would do good, evil was present with him?"[8]

Here, then, is a debt incurred, concerning which it must be confessed we have "not to pay:" and there is but one hope, that it may be *blotted out*.

It has been *blotted out*. Jesus Christ has cancelled it, *taking it out of the way, and nailing it to his cross*, that it may no more appear against us. On the one side may stand Satan, the accuser of mankind, first their betrayer, and then their accuser,[9] and show against them *the handwriting of ordinances:* the law prescribed by God, and transgressed by man. But the Christian rebuts the charge. Not by denying that the debt was justly due; but by alleging that it has been paid; paid in full: and as a proof, there is *the handwriting that was against* us, no longer in its perfect and obligatory state, but *nailed to the cross of Christ:* that the debt, and the payment of the debt—the bond, and the discharge—may appear together.

Thus then the case stands. There is a handwriting against us. There is a law written in the heart. Who has not disobeyed his conscience? There is a law written in the book of God. Who has not transgressed that law?

[8] Rom. vii. 14—23. [9] Rev. xii. 10.

And there is a day when we shall give account of such transgression. "We must all appear before the judgment-seat of God," when the dead shall be judged according to their works.[3]

Have we provided, each for ourselves, that this account, which is against us, shall be *taken out of the way*, so as not to prove our condemnation? Have we secured this, as a man would make sure the cancelling of a bond, which, if enforced against him, would ruin him for ever? Have we carried our debt of trespasses and sins that stood against us, to the cross of Christ, and by a personal exercise of faith have we nailed it there?

Then may we trust that the promise is ours, and will be made good to us "in that day:" "I will forgive their iniquity, saith the Lord, and I will remember their sins no more."[4]

[3] Rev. xx. 12, 13. [4] Jer. xxxi. 34; Heb. viii. 12.

LXIII.

THE MERCIFUL PURPOSE OF GOD TOWARDS HIS PEOPLE.

Romans viii. 28—30.

28. *We know that all things work together for good to them that love God, to them who are the called according to his purpose.*

Many things may befall the Christian, which seem very inconsistent with his welfare, very unlike what was to be expected by those who enjoy the Divine favour. Paul, for instance, was permitted to lie bound in prison two whole years at Cæsarea, and thus cut off from all opportunities of usefulness.[1] It required strong faith to bear up against such circumstances: strong conviction that He who orders all things, orders all things with a view to the good of his people.

Paul, therefore, meets any doubts that might occur, and prevents the despondency which trials and reverses might sometimes occasion. The Christians at Rome were exposed to these, and must often have required the encouraging assurance that all things, whether prosperous or adverse, *work together for good to them that love God, to them that are the called according to his*

[1] Acts xxiv. 26, 27.

purpose. According to his original purpose, he has determined that there shall be a people devoted to him; here on earth living in his faith and fear and love, and hereafter to be received to his glory. And they to whom Paul wrote, had been *called according to that purpose.* They were foreknown and predestined from the beginning:—for "known unto God are all his works from the foundation of the world." Therefore tribulations, or persecutions, instead of injuring them, should serve as means towards their final salvation. God had a *purpose,* a design respecting them which should not be frustrated. All the difficulties and trials which they might be appointed to undergo, should contribute to accomplish that design.

29. *For whom he did foreknow, he also did predestinate to be conformed to the image of his Son, that he might be the first-born among many brethren.*

It was no chance, no contingency, which had brought them to their present state. All the steps which led to it, were ordained. They who were now *the called,* were those whom God had from the first *foreknown.* He *foreknew* those, for instance, who became the disciples of Paul at Corinth, and formed the Christian church in that city. God had detained Paul there, when otherwise he might have removed to a place which seemed more promising: the Lord spake to him by a vision, "Be not afraid, but speak, and hold not thy peace: for I have much people in this city."[2] As he "knows them that are his," when their

[2] Acts xviii. 10.

hearts are turned towards him: so he foreknows them that will be his, when their hearts yet appear to be far from him. He foreknew the ready faith of Lydia and the rest of the Philippian church, when he directed Paul's course from Bithynia to Macedonia.[3] The end, and the means to accomplish that end, were alike providentially designed.

And a part of these means, of which salvation is the end, are the circumstances which the people of God pass through. They must be endued with a certain character; the character of Christ. They must be *conformed to his image.* And therefore they must be placed in the circumstances by which that character is produced and exercised. He had been "a man of sorrows and acquainted with grief." As the prophet said, "We did esteem him stricken, smitten of God, and afflicted."[4] It might be that such should be the appointed lot of some of those whom he was bringing to glory; that in this sense, as well as in others, he *might be the first-born among many brethren,* who should, like him, be "made perfect through sufferings."[5] These, therefore, must be prepared, if need be, "to suffer with him, that they might be also glorified together." God's purposes might be thus, and only thus, fulfilled. The same foreknowledge and wisdom would order and direct the whole.

But perhaps the afflicted Christian may want a proof of this. Like Hezekiah of old, he may doubt of God's merciful intentions towards him; and as that king said, "What shall be the sign that the

[3] Acts xvi. 7—12. [4] Isa. liii. 3, 4. [5] Heb. ii. 10.

Lord shall heal me?"[6] the sufferer may be disposed to ask, How shall I know that the Lord has a favour unto me, and out of very faithfulness causes me to linger in affliction? This proof is given, in his present state and condition: in what God has already done.[7]

30. *Moreover, whom he did predestinate, them he also called: and whom he called, them he also justified: and whom he justified, them he also glorified.*

God has already made him to differ from others, in "calling him to repentance and the knowledge of the truth." He has not been left in darkness, but the light of the gospel has been manifested to him. Neither has he been permitted to close his eyes against the light, and choose to abide in darkness. The Lord has opened his heart, to attond unto the things spoken by his messengers. He has been called, and he has obeyed the calling: and therefore has this proof that "God has predestinated him unto the adoption of children by Jesus Christ unto himself, according to the good pleasure of his will.[8] Why should he not trust that the mercy which has brought him thus far, will accompany him unto the end?

For all things are in due order. The ultimate glory which God designs for his people, is already theirs in his will and purpose: but it can only be

[6] 2 Kings xx. 8.

[7] Ειδες ποσα ἡμιν ἐχαρισεν· μη τοινυν ἀμφιβαλλε περι των μελλοντων. —Chrysos.

[8] Eph. i. 5.

granted them in his appointed way. It can only come to them through the Son; and that the Son may bestow it, he must be believed in: and that he may be believed in, he must be made known; set forth as "the author of eternal salvation to all them that obey him."

This due order had been observed, and all these things had met together in the case of those to whom Paul was writing, and whom he encourages under trials, and the prospect of trials, by assurance of future glory. The favour of God had taken its regular course. These had been already *called*, and having embraced the truth, were also *justified*. And they who have been thus called by the Spirit of God working in due season to "redemption through Christ Jesus," are those whom he has predestinated to everlasting salvation:[9] those who in his purpose and design are already *glorified*. Just as Joseph, when carried down to Egypt as a slave, or when lying for years in the prison to which he had been condemned, in the purpose and foreknowledge of God was "governor over all the land of Egypt."

It is a natural question arising from these words, Are we among that blessed company here spoken of, whom God has predestinated to everlasting glory? No special revelation is given to tell us this. The first token of divine favour belongs to us. God has already granted us an "advantage great every way:" we have been planted in a Christian land, and by baptism enrolled amongst his family. This indeed is

[9] Art. xvii.

not alone sufficient. We know that "many are called" to outward privileges, who are not finally "chosen" to inherit the heavenly kingdom. But though nothing can prove that we are predestinated to glory, except a faith and practice conformable to the gospel;—still our outward calling is an earnest of the goodwill of God towards us, which nothing but our own unbelief and hardness of heart can render vain. As the wife of Manoah argued,[1] "If the Lord were pleased to kill us, he would not have showed us all these things." We cannot expect that "the book of life" should be opened before our eyes. But if my heavenly Father has sent down a message to me, and the messenger is his beloved Son, inviting me to his service here, and his inheritance hereafter, what more can I ask, what further assurance of his favour shall I desire?

LXIV.

JOY AND PEACE IN BELIEVING.

ROMANS xv. 13.

Now the God of hope fill you with all joy and peace in believing, through the power of the Holy Ghost.

THIS prayer of the apostle in behalf of the brethren

[1] Judges xiii. 23.

at Rome, to whom he was writing, is, in effect, a prayer that a belief of the gospel, *i. e.*, that faith in Christ Jesus as a Prince and a Saviour—a Saviour to redeem, a Prince or Lord to rule—that this faith should be to them a cause of happiness, a ground of lasting tranquillity:—that in *believing* the word of God, as declared by his beloved Son, and now preached to the world by his disciples, they might find *joy and peace* in their hearts. Such is St. Paul's prayer; and it agrees with the manner in which the coming of the Son of God was first announced. The angels calmed the fears of the shepherds, saying, "Behold, I bring you good tidings of great joy, which shall be to all people." And their hymn was, "Glory to God in the highest, and on earth peace, good will towards men."

Yet this is not the light in which the religion of the gospel is always viewed. Neither is it always the first result, that *joy and peace* should be immediately produced by the truths which the Gospel reveals. That must depend on the education, and the practice. One who has happily been brought up in the nurture and admonition of the Lord, and maintained the covenant to which he was pledged in baptism—he will be able to "rejoice in the Lord always," and be "kept in perfect peace." But if, unhappily, the case has been otherwise, the mind may be disturbed, rather than quieted, when thoughts of God and of eternity are presented to its view in powerful demonstration. Peace, or what is called peace, may be interrupted rather than promoted, when the awful truths disclosed to us in the gospel of Jesus Christ are either for the first time heard, or for the first time attended to. Yet there must be something faulty in our views of religion, if they do not agree with St. Paul's view. If we judge of it as a thing needful indeed, but not delightful; as what must be submitted to as a resource in age or sickness, but which we should never think of courting as the ground of comfort and satisfaction, we still have much to learn, and much to unlearn. For our views of religion must be mistaken views, if they differ from those of the apostle: and we here perceive what he expected to be the result of what he emphatically terms, *believing*. He knew that the ministry intrusted to him, was the ministry of reconciliation: that his message was, "God in Christ reconciling the world unto himself:" he knew that this message was one of *joy* to sinful man: and therefore he prayed, that it might be received with joy; and through the *power of the Holy Ghost* the result might be "grace and peace from God our Father."

Now *joy and peace*, as is evident, are affections of the mind, arising out of the circumstances in which a man for the time may be placed.

Joy, is commonly a sudden, and comparatively a transient emotion, produced by some unusual or unexpected source of satisfaction. We have an instance in the case of the aged Simeon, who had long been looking for the Consolation of Israel, and to whom it was now revealed that the Child then presented by his parents in the temple was the Saviour for whose advent he had been habitually praying. "Lord," he exclaims, in a sudden transport of exultation, "now lettest thou thy servant depart in peace; for mine eyes have seen thy salvation." In more ordinary life we find an example in the patriarch Jacob, when the unlooked-for tidings reached him that his favourite and long-lost son was not only living, but governing the land of Egypt. When at length he was convinced of the fact, "It is enough," he exclaimed, "Joseph, my son, is yet alive, I will go and see him before I die."

This is a specimen of the feeling which we term *joy*; the emotion which St. Paul expected to be produced by the influence of their faith upon the minds of his brethren at Rome.

There must, therefore, be that in the Christian faith, which is calculated to excite this joy. An unexpected deliverance, for example, is cause of joy. Let any parent, who has been alarmed, like the Patriarch, by the rumour of a son's death, receive assurance of his safety: there is joy. Let two friends, who had been engaged in a murderous battle, meet each other in safety and in victory: there would be joy. Let there be deliverance from shipwreck, recovery from a dangerous sickness: these are occasions of joy.

And the gospel is cause of joy to believers, because it offers such deliverance: because it tells of danger removed, of calamity averted: because it gives tidings of blessings bestowed, and blessings promised, which the heart of man could never have imagined. It relieves from the wrath of God, and brings assurance of his favour: and the joy of having this assurance, is the joy of *believing:* of believing that there is no condemnation to them that are in Christ Jesus; who has endured the sentence which sin had incurred, and given his life a ransom, that he might "open the kingdom of heaven to all believers."

Well, then, might the apostle speak of *joy*, as an effect of the gospel upon the mind. For this was the truth which the Roman Christians had received, had credited, had acted on; and therefore he prays that they may experience that blessing, which is the promise of the gospel, and be *filled with joy in believing.*

The Philippian gaoler (as described in Acts xvi.) tasted, we may conceive, this joy: when, struck at once by a sudden danger, and sensibly convinced of the Majesty which he had offended, he heard the promise of unlooked-for mercy: "Believe in the Lord Jesus Christ, and thou shalt be saved." He had been brought to that knowledge of danger which made him feel the value of deliverance. He had understood the truth, that "It is a fearful thing to fall into the hands of the living God." He was told of One, who had preserved him from such ruin: who had borne in his own body the sins, of which he dreaded the eternal consequences. Therefore we read, that "he *rejoiced*, believing in God with all his house." And so the Ethiopian, baptized by Philip on his journey, "went on his way, *rejoicing*."

Happy indeed would it be, if all the joy which the world desired, or sought, were such joy as an apostle might pray for, a joy which has its origin and source in heaven! It is a joy which does not fade away: a joy "in the light of God's countenance!" a joy, "the fulness of which is at God's right hand for evermore."

The other state of feeling expected by the apostle,

peace of mind, is of a different character from *joy*. It is of a more gentle, calm, enduring nature. If we were to seek for a comparison, we might liken the mind in a state of joy, to a river suddenly swollen, flowing in a torrent which its banks can no longer contain. In a state of peace, the mind may be compared to the same river returned into its appointed channel, gliding quietly along, giving fertility to the plains and refreshment to the flocks as they graze beside the still waters. Scripture may also furnish us with an example of this state of mind. It was the state of king David's mind, when, after long expectation and many hardships, he found himself at length securely seated on the throne of Israel. "Then," as we read,—"then went king David in, and sat before the Lord, and said, Who am I, O Lord God, and what is my father's house, that thou hast brought me hitherto? And this was yet a small thing in thy sight, O Lord God; but thou hast spoken also of thy servant's house for a long while to come." Here is represented to us that inward satisfaction which a man enjoys, when, looking on what is past, and on what is yet before him, he sees ground of comfort, and reason for hope, and his mind is *in peace*. It is not so strong or vehement a feeling as that of joy, but it is a more calm and abiding feeling, more suited to the condition of our ruined nature, even when that ruin has been repaired. And, therefore, we find it placed, not first, but second in the apostle's sentence, as if implying, that into that state the mind should settle and subside. This is the order of nature, as will appear, if we suppose a case by way of illustration.

[1] 2 Sam. vii. 18, 19.

We may figure to ourselves a person seized by a party of enemies, and carried into captivity, with no expectation for the remainder of life but of misery and bondage. We may conceive, again, that his misfortune had reached the ears of his friends at home, and he should learn that a ransom had been prepared, which should restore him to his freedom. The sudden change would fill him with a joyous transport, which we could not picture in too glowing terms. That would be realized which we read of the Israelites of old: "When the Lord turned again the captivity of Sion, then were we like unto them that dream. Then was our mouth filled with laughter, and our tongue with singing."[2] But if we were to see the same man returned to his native country, seated in the bosom of his family, and pursuing the usual tenor of his life, we should see him in a state of peace, no longer excited by emotions which the bosom could scarcely hold, but enjoying the comfort which belongs to security and ease.

Such, then, is intended to be the permanent Christian state; a state in which the mind has peace; peace arising from the presence of comfort, and the absence of fear; the peace of knowing and believing "the love which God hath to us." It is the privilege of the Christian to abound in this consolation. He is conscious of a transaction, so to speak, between himself and God; conscious that he, on his part, has received the gracious offer of acceptance through his Son Christ Jesus: and from this consciousness, a trust arises that God, on his part, has admitted him to his favour,

[2] Ps. cxxvi. 1, 2.

adopted him into his family, and made him heir of life eternal. That such a transaction has taken place, is a cause of *joy*: that it is an enduring covenant, is a perpetual ground of *peace*, of *peace* which can be derived from no other source. There are thoughts which the Spirit suggests, thoughts maintained in the heart by the power of the Holy Ghost,—which soothe the cares which might otherwise perplex, compose the fears which might otherwise disturb, relieve the trials which belong to our fallen state, and spread a healing balm over the woes to which all the sons of Adam are alike subject, but against which the Christian alone has secured a remedy. He is reconciled to God: can look up to him as to a gracious Father, and can say, "The Lord is my Shepherd, I shall not want." All that is needful for his temporal good, is his. It is promised him, engaged to him. Far more, all that is needful for the salvation of his soul, is his. The enemy shall not prevail to hurt him. If he is in prosperity, God is blessing him. If prosperity be denied, God is still blessing him: all things are working together for his eventual good. If he looks back upon the past, he sees that he has been led "by a way that he knew not:" and this gives him confidence for the future, that he will be still led by the same gracious hand. And in prospect, is eternal life; the "rest which remaineth for the people of God," in that kingdom which "hath no need of the sun, neither of the moon, to shine in it; for the glory of God doth lighten it, and the Lamb is the light thereof."

And so that state of mind is realized, which the

apostle desires for the Christians at Rome: that gift of the Holy Spirit to the heart, when he "beareth witness with our spirit, that we are the children of God:" and we learn by experience, what can never be understood till the heart itself interprets it, the reality of that "peace of God which passeth all understanding."

LXV.

HARDNESS OF HEART.

MARK iv. 11, 12.

11. *And he said unto them, Unto you it is given to know the mysteries of the kingdom of God: but unto them that are without, all these things are done in parables:*
12. *That seeing they may see, and not perceive; and hearing they may hear, and not understand; lest at any time they should be converted, and their sins should be forgiven them.*

THERE must be a reason for this difference, which at first sight appears contrary to the usual dealings of God with man. There seems here to be "respect of persons." To those *who were about him with the twelve* apostles, our Lord says, *Unto you it is given to know the mysteries of the kingdom of God;* but to others, *to them that are without, all these things are done in parables:* they see, but they do not perceive the meaning of what they see: they hear, but they do not understand: so that the effect of hearing and understanding does not take place; they are not converted or healed.

St. Matthew, in his report of this same discourse, adds the reason. "In them is fulfilled the prophecy of Esaias, which saith, By hearing ye shall hear, and shall not understand; and seeing ye shall see, and shall not perceive. For this people's heart is waxed gross, and their ears are dull of hearing, and their eyes have they closed; lest at any time they should see with their eyes and hear with their ears, and should understand with their heart, and should be converted, and I should heal them."[1]

The different treatment, therefore, of *them that were without,* and of the apostles and others who were *about him,* corresponded with the difference of their conduct. Each party reaped as they had sown: were dealt with according to their spirit and behaviour. Of those *that were about him with the twelve,* that account was true, which Peter afterwards gave of himself and his brethren, "Behold, we have forsaken all, and followed thee."[2] They acknowledged Jesus as the "Christ, the Son of the living God."[3] They sat around him, and heard his words; believing that they were "the words of eternal life."[4] They repelled all proud imaginations, and high

[1] Matt. xiii. 14, 15; Isa. vi. 9, 10.
[2] Matt. xix. 27.
[3] Ib. xvi. 16.
[4] John vi. 68.

thoughts which exalt themselves against the knowledge of God, and became as "little children," who look to their teachers for instruction, without dispute or cavil. Very different was the case of *those without*, as related in the preceding chapters of this gospel. A man was brought to Jesus, sick of the palsy, "and he said unto him, Man, thy sins be forgiven thee. And immediately he arose and went forth before them all. But there were certain of the scribes sitting there, who said in their hearts, Why doth this man speak blasphemies?"[5]

Again, the Lord had called the publican Matthew from his occupation, and was entertained by him at his house, where many publicans and sinners were assembled. They seize the occasion of reviling him. "Behold a gluttonous man and a winebibber, a friend of publicans and sinners!"[6]

Again, in passing through the corn fields on the sabbath day, his disciples began, as they went, to pluck the ears of corn. Here too was found cause of accusation; "Why do they on the sabbath day that which is not lawful?"[7] Even his miracles of mercy were censured. "They watched him, whether he would heal on the sabbath, that they might accuse him."[8] Can we wonder, that to men of this temper, *all things were done in parables?*

But only done in parables, as long as this temper remained. No sooner did the heart show willingness to learn, and the ear become ready to hear, than *the mysteries of the kingdom* were disclosed. "He that hath

[5] Mark ii. 7, &c. [6] Mark ii. 15, 16.
[7] Mark ii. 24. [8] Mark iii. 2.

ears to hear, let him hear." Nicodemus, for instance, instead of following the example of his brethren, came to consult Jesus, and acknowledged that God was with him.[9] Immediately the Lord opened to him that important truth, the leading doctrine of the Gospel, "Except a man be born again, born of water and of the Spirit, he cannot see the kingdom of God." Another came to inquire of him, not as many, "tempting him," but with good intentions, and asked, "Master, what shall I do to inherit eternal life?"[1] "All things pertaining to life and godliness" were immediately placed at his command. "If thou wilt be perfect, come, follow me, and thou shalt have treasure in heaven." It was the constant complaint and grief of the Redeemer, "Ye will not come unto me, that ye might have life."[2] "If any man thirst, let him come unto me, and drink."[3] "Him that cometh unto me, I will in no wise cast out."[4] "O Jerusalem, Jerusalem, which killest the prophets, and stonest them that are sent unto thee; how often would I have gathered thy children together, as a hen doth gather her brood under her wings, and ye would not!"[5]

There is a time when the heart, which has hardened itself against the word, becomes as the rock which no power can penetrate. No man can ever tell, when that time has arrived. God has often been pleased to smite the hearts of those who seemed most obdurate, and the waters of humiliation and penitence have flowed forth, as when Moses struck the rock in the desert.[6] But we

[9] John iii. 1, 2. [1] Matt. xix. 20, &c. [2] John v. 40.
[3] John vii. 37. [4] John vi. 37. [5] Luke xiii. 34. [6] Numb. xx. 11.

are warned by the example of the Jewish nation, that advantages, "great every way," may be neglected, till they are no longer left us to be abused. As it is written, "To-day, if ye will hear his voice, harden not your hearts:"[7] lest the only power that can soften them, be never exerted in your cause.

This is the first, but not the only inference. As there were eyes too blind to see, and too firmly closed to be enlightened; so there were eyes which seeing did see, and hearing did understand. There were minds instructed to "know all parables." Many of the same people, concerning whom Isaiah wrote the prophecy which said, "hearing ye shall hear, and shall not understand, and seeing ye shall see, and shall not perceive:" many of these came to "know of the doctrine that it was of God:"[8] *understood* with their heart, and were *converted, and their sins were forgiven them.* They saw what concerned them, that God had opened to mankind a door of salvation, by which, "whoever would," might enter: as the Lord himself described it, might "go in and out, and find pasture:"[9] find that which would supply his spiritual wants, and lead him in the way everlasting. The apostles and the company around Jesus had chosen this good path; and of those, and of all who "through their word" are following the same road, it may be truly said, "Blessed are your eyes, for they see, and your ears, for they hear." "God, who commanded the light to shine out of darkness, hath shined in their hearts, to give the light of the knowledge of the glory of God in the face of Jesus Christ."[1]

[7] See Heb. iii. 12—19. [8] John vii. 17.
[9] John x. 9. [1] 2 Cor. iv. 6.

LXVI.

FUTURE GLORY.

ROMANS viii. 18—27.

18. *I reckon that the sufferings of this present time are not worthy to be compared with the glory which shall be revealed in us.*

St. Paul, in the preceding sentence, had spoken of *sufferings.* "If we suffer with Christ, we shall also reign with him." This leads him to add here; And it is worth while. So *I reckon:* I calculate. Such is my judgment, and on this judgment I act: my life is directed by it: *that the sufferings of this present time are not worthy to be compared with the glory that shall be revealed in us.*

And yet if we reflect upon the apostle's life, it was certainly a life of no light suffering. As he himself said concerning it: "If in this life only we have hope, we are of all men most miserable."[1] We are little able to conceive justly of this in days like ours, when godliness has so much apparent comfort and reward with it, as to recompense, even now, the sacrifices it demands. Very different was St. Paul's case, as he

[1] 1 Cor. xv. 19.

describes it: "Of the Jews five times received I forty stripes save one. Thrice was I beaten with rods; once was I stoned; thrice I suffered shipwreck; a night and a day I have been in the deep: in journeyings often, in perils of waters, in perils of robbers, in perils by mine own countrymen, in perils by the heathen, in perils in the city, in perils in the wilderness, in perils in the sea, in perils among false brethren: in weariness and painfulness, in watchings often, in hunger and thirst, in fastings often, in cold and nakedness."[2]

And yet he says, *I reckon that the sufferings of this present time are not worthy to be compared with the glory that shall be revealed in us.* It is that glory, which had long been vaguely expected, and ardently desired: which many prophets and righteous men had aspired after, but had not enjoyed: God having declared his promises and reserved his blessings, "that they without us should not be made perfect."[3]

19. *For the earnest expectation of the creature waiteth for the manifestation of the sons of God.*
20. *For the creature was made subject to vanity, not willingly, but by reason of him who hath subjected the same in hope.*
21. *Because the creature itself also shall be delivered from the bondage of corruption into the glorious liberty of the children of God.*
22. *For we know that the whole creation groaneth and travaileth in pain together until now.*
23. *And not only they, but ourselves also, which have the*

[2] 2 Cor. xi. 24. [3] Heb. xi. 40.

> *firstfruits of the Spirit, even we ourselves groan within ourselves, waiting for the adoption, to wit, the redemption of our body.*

Here *the whole creation* is described as restless, unsatisfied, disordered, looking for some better state of things; such as was represented to Isaiah; "Behold, I create new heavens and a new earth; and the former shall not be remembered, nor come into mind."[4] Such as St. Peter had in his thoughts, when he wrote: "Nevertheless, brethren, we look for new heavens and a new earth, wherein dwelleth righteousness."[5] We cannot but allow, that the world, both moral and natural, is in a state of disorder, and wants a "restitution of all things:"[6] *waiteth for the manifestation of the sons of God.* It *was made subject to vanity,* to frailty, *not willingly,* not of its own will or accord, *but by reason of him who hath subjected the same in hope:* by permission of its Ruler, who has thus *subjected it,* yet not without hope of regeneration; not without hope of deliverance from a state of bondage and corruption into a purer and nobler state of freedom. Who can deny, that at present *the whole creation,* in all its parts, *groaneth and laboureth together?* Such was the effect of the original sentence: "Cursed is the ground for thy sake: thorns and thistles shall it bring forth to thee; in sorrow shalt thou eat of it all the days of thy life."[7] The Christian is indeed raised above the natural state; taken out of the general

[4] Isa. lxv. 17. [5] 2 Pet. iii. 13.
[6] Acts iii. 2. [7] Gen. iii. 17.

bondage and corruption: he has *the firstfruits of the Spirit,* which gives him a foretaste of heavenly things, and enlivens his present gloom with the prospect of "glory, and honour, and immortality." Yet is he "not already perfect:" he still carries about him a body of death, and is anxiously waiting for his final *adoption* amongst God's children, "the saints in light:" for the complete *redemption of the body,* when there shall be no more sin, or pain, or death; for the "former things shall have passed away."[8]

Indeed, were it not for the *bondage of corruption,* to which so long as we remain in this feeble state we must be subjected, our whole circumstances would be changed: salvation would not be future, but present: not something to be expected or trusted to, but now possessed and enjoyed. We know that it is not so.

24. *For we are saved by hope: but hope that is seen is not hope: for what a man seeth, why doth he yet hope for?*
25. *But if we hope for that we see not, then do we with patience wait for it.*

We are saved *by hope.* It is not by immediate possession, but *in hope,* that we have been brought into this state of salvation.[9] "Now abideth faith, hope, charity:"[1] these are the wings on which the Christian is borne on his way to heaven. But if he already saw his future inheritance, he would not require faith to show it him: and if he already enjoyed his inheritance, he would not need to *wait for it in*

[8] Rev. xxi. 4. [9] ἐσωθημεν. [1] 1 Cor. xiii. 13.

patience. For what a man seeth, why doth he yet hope for? But we do with patience wait for it, on the assurance of hope unto the end: and sustain our present weakness with the promise of *the glory that shall be revealed.*

Nay, we have a support beyond ourselves, by which that which is weak in us is strengthened, and that which is wanting to us is supplied.

26. *Likewise the Spirit also helpeth our infirmities; for we know not what we should pray for as we ought: but the Spirit itself maketh intercession for us with groanings which cannot be uttered.*

27. *And he that searcheth the hearts knoweth what is the mind of the Spirit, because he maketh intercession for the saints according to the will of God.*

Thus the same Spirit, who, as had been before said,[2] witnesses with our own hearts, and assures us of our relationship to God, does *also help our infirmities:* supplies the imperfection of our prayers: *makes intercession for us with groanings which cannot be uttered,* but are accepted of God, *that searcheth the heart,* and sees that *the mind of the Spirit* is in unison with the desire of *the saints,* his faithful people, though they *know not what they should pray for as they ought,* and need an intercession more powerful than their own.

So vast is the interest engaged in the salvation of man, in bringing him to *the glory that shall be revealed.* We must judge of the nature of that glory, not from

[2] Rom. viii. 16.

what man thinks in his low and grovelling nature, which "cleaves unto the dust," but from the agency which Scripture represents as being employed in raising him above it. And so we may better understand the sentiment with which Paul began, *I reckon that the sufferings of this present time are not worthy to be compared with the glory that shall be revealed in us.* "For the things which are seen, are temporal: but the things which are not seen, are eternal."

LXVII.

SUPERSTITIOUS USAGES CONDEMNED.

COL. ii. 20—23.

20. *Wherefore if ye be dead with Christ from the rudiments of the world, why, as though living in the world, are ye subject to ordinances,*
21. *(Touch not; taste not; handle not;*
22. *Which all are to perish with the using;) after the commandments and doctrines of men?*

THE *rudiments of the world,* are the inventions of the mind when left to itself, and framing its own religion. The natural heart turns to outward forms of mortification, of purification, which are to it in the place of sanctity. And they, who undertake to teach others, *subject* their followers to these ordinances. The Pharisees did this. They indeed were not left to themselves; they "sat in Moses' seat," and ought to have expounded the law of Moses, "neither adding thereto, nor diminishing from it." But our Lord reproved them, saying, "Ye make the commandments of God of none effect through your traditions:"[1] and we learn from St. Mark, that "the Pharisees and all the Jews, except they wash their hands oft, eat not, holding the traditions of the elders. And many other things there be, which they have received to hold, as the washing of cups and pots, brasen vessels and tables." After a like principle of nature, but with more excuse, the Hindoos have their *rudiments of the world:* are governed by the maxims of their priests; instructing them to "abstain from meats:" to use ablutions at certain times and in certain rivers; not to eat with those who are not of the same sect as themselves. The Mahometans have their fixed hours of prayer; their appointed words to repeat, and posture to use; their seasons of fasting and abstinence.

Now all these are *rudiments of the world:* they proceed from man, and not from God: from a principle of carnal, and not of heavenly wisdom. Yet some rules of this kind had been pressed upon the Colossians, "after the tradition of men, and not after Christ:" not after Christ, because he had not taught them: not after Christ, because they had another salvation in view than that which he had wrought, and pretended

[1] See Matt. xv. 9; Mark vii. 3, 4.

to another way of pleasing God than that which he had revealed. And therefore St. Paul asks, *If ye be dead with Christ from the rudiments of the world,*—if Christ has freed you from the corruptions, the errors, the superstitions in which the world was held—if he is the light of the world by which every man should walk and be guided—*why as though living in the world,* instead of being "taken out of the world," *are ye subject to ordinances* of man's invention, commanding you to *touch not, taste not, handle not,*—to abstain from meats, to deny yourselves innocent gratifications, which God has not forbidden? Why not rather "stand fast in the liberty wherewith Christ hath made you free?"[2]

These things, like the matters which they concern, all *perish in the using*:[3] leave no lasting benefit on him who practises them. What follows, for instance, from the annual fast of the Mahometan, except an increased desire after self-indulgence? Is the Hindoo become more pure in heart, because after a weary pilgrimage he has bathed in the sacred river? Were the Pharisees cleansed from the defilement of a proud and carnal heart, because they refused to eat with "unwashen hands?" There is nothing in these practices to affect the heart: to wean its affections from things below, or raise them to things above.

23. *Which things have indeed a show of wisdom in will worship, and humility, and neglecting of the body: not in any honour to the satisfying of the flesh.*

These stated ordinances, these arbitrary mortifica

[2] Gal. v. 1.

[3] ἐστι εἰς φθοραν τῃ ἀποχρησει: tend to destruction in the using, φθοραν τοις χρωμενοις.—Chrys.

tions, have *a show of wisdom.* Those who practise them are wondered at and admired by the multitude: assume the pretence of superior sanctity, in *neglecting the body,* and denying themselves what others enjoy. So it was with the Pharisees of old. They "disfigured their faces, that they might appear unto men to fast."[4] They "loved to pray standing in the synagogue and in the corners of the streets, that they might be seen of men."[5] But there was nothing acceptable to God in such abstinence or such prayers. Rather were they made to serve instead of what he does approve. So the prophet remonstrates with the Jews: "Is it such a fast that I have chosen: a day for a man to afflict his soul? Is it to bow down his head as a bulrush, and to spread sackcloth and ashes under him? Wilt thou call this a fast, and an acceptable day to the Lord? Is not this the fast that I have chosen? to loose the bands of wickedness, to undo the heavy burdens, to let the imprisoned go free; and that ye break every yoke? Is it not to deal thy bread to the hungry, and that thou bring the poor that are cast out to thy house? when thou seest the naked, that thou cover him?"[6]

The outward form was to the Jews instead of the converted heart. And such is the danger of all *will-worship and voluntary humility,*—it is not made the means of righteousness, but practised in the stead of righteousness. The man has observed so many fasts, denied himself so much gratification, repeated so many prayers: and he is satisfied; he has atoned for his sins; or he has entitled himself to a reward; or he has done something towards earning his salvation. But his heart is not drawn towards the love of God, nor

[4] Matt. vi. 16. [5] Matt. vi. 5. [6] Isa. lviii. 5—7.

is he "led by the Spirit" to uprightness, or humility, or charity; he is as much a prey as ever to irregular "desires of the flesh and of the mind." Prescribed fastings, repetition of prayers, abstinence from things which God has prepared for the use of men, are *not in any honour to the satisfying of the flesh:* they may have a show of subduing the flesh, but the flesh is not so subdued. And therefore the gospel does not command us to *touch not, taste not, handle not,* but to "use the world, as not abusing it;" to "walk not after the flesh, but after the Spirit:" to "glorify God in our body and our spirit, which are his."

To *neglect*, i. e., to deny or mortify *the body*, with this view, that it may be more subservient to the inner man, more obedient to the motions of the Spirit of God,—has not only *the show of wisdom*, but the reality; and is a part of christian practice needful to all. It was no vain *subjection to ordinances*, no *will worship* in Daniel and his companions, when they refused to "defile themselves with the portion of the king's meat, or with the wine which he drank."[8] It was a pious precaution against the sins to which they might be exposed in the luxurious court at Babylon. St. Paul too, whilst he maintained his liberty, and affirmed that "all things were lawful for him," felt likewise, that "all things were not expedient:"[9] and would not "be brought under the power of any."[1] There might be reasons for abstaining from what he was at liberty to use. "It is good neither to eat flesh, nor to drink wine, nor any thing whereby thy brother stumbleth or is made weak."[2] Such abstinence and self-denial is *of honour*

[8] Dan. i. 8. [9] 1 Cor. x. 23. [1] 1 Cor. vi. 12. [2] Rom. xiv. 21.

to the satisfying of the flesh; has its value towards "keeping under the body, and bringing it into subjection:" tends to make it conform "to the obedience of Christ." The man *touches*, or refrains from touching, *tastes*, or refrains from tasting, as God permits, and as he finds expedient to his soul's health; being "not without law to God," nor "using his liberty as a cloke" of licentiousness, though not *subject to ordinances* of man. "For every creature of God is good, and not to be refused, if it be received with thanksgiving. For it is sanctified by the word of God and by prayer."[3] And "the kingdom of God" consists not in outward forms, whether observed or neglected; "is not meat or drink," whether abstained from or indulged in; "but righteousness, and peace, and joy in the Holy Ghost."[4]

LXVIII.

THE SALVATION OF THE RIGHTEOUS.

1 Peter iv. 18.

If the righteous scarcely be saved, where shall the ungodly and the sinner appear?

To one part of St. Peter's sentence here we readily agree: we assent to the danger awaiting *the ungodly and*

[3] 1 Tim. iv. 5. [4] Rom. xiv. 17.

the sinner. But what must we think of his first assertion, that *the righteous scarcely are saved?* The righteous, the consistent Christian; they who have believed the voice of God speaking in the Gospel, and they who have obeyed it, *scarcely are saved.*[1] Many have been at a loss to comprehend this saying; and have even supposed that Peter could not be alluding to the final day of the Lord, but to the judgment then coming upon the inhabitants of Jerusalem by the destruction of their place and nation. Yet, if we examine, we shall find nothing in his words which is not easily explained, and confirmed by the whole of Scripture.

For, first, surely it may be said of the righteous, that he is *scarcely saved,* when he is only saved by the blood of Christ shed for him on the cross: when such was his original corruption, and such his actual transgressions, that the infinite holiness and offended justice of God required this sacrifice. And this is the first principle of our faith. All Scripture leads to one point, that Christ is the only door of access to God or heaven: for that "all have sinned, and come short of the glory of God: being justified freely by his grace through the redemption that is in Christ Jesus."[2]

And in asserting this, Scripture does not contradict, but confirms the feeling of the righteous man himself. Looking to his own heart, he feels its weakness; looking to his works, he sees their unworthiness; whichever way he looks, he perceives his shortcomings. And reflecting on this, which is really his state before God, he will declare of himself, whatever others may judge

[1] *μολις*, with difficulty.

[2] Rom. iii. 23, 24.

concerning him, that he has no hope nor confidence but in the cross of the Redeemer.

Now, surely we may allow that a man is *scarcely saved*, when he is only saved by the mighty sacrifice of the Son of God, coming in his nature and dying for his sins.

This, then, is the first reason why the righteous *scarcely are saved.* And the second is, that they are not saved without constant diligence and labour.

Here, too, we are supported, as before, both by Scripture and experience. The words of Scripture are, "Strive to enter in at the strait gate. For many" (when it is too late) "shall seek to enter in, and shall not be able." "Not every one that saith unto me, Lord, Lord, shall enter into the kingdom of heaven: but he that doeth the will of my Father which is in heaven." Scripture also points out the necessity of watchfulness. "Watch and pray, that ye enter not into temptation." "Watch and pray always, that ye may be counted worthy to escape all those things that shall come to pass, and to stand before the Son of man." Scripture declares the necessity of self-denial. "If a man doth not take up his cross and follow me, he cannot be my disciple." "Work out your own salvation with fear and trembling." St. Paul says of himself, "I keep under my body, and bring it into subjection, lest by any means, when I have preached to others, I myself should become a castaway."

Surely, then, we may affirm, that a man is *scarcely saved,* who is not saved without habitual watchfulness, persevering labour, and patient self-denial.

Especially when the experience of every earnest

Christian proves, that all these means of holiness are absolutely required by him. The temper, the disposition, the graces or qualities which show a meetness for heaven, are clearly laid down: but no less certainly are these qualities foreign to the natural heart, and the natural heart averse from them; they must be cultivated, therefore, like plants which are not in their proper climate; cultivated with care: and if that care is relaxed, they will decline and wither. It needs but a short remission of prayer and vigilance, to give unchristian feelings, tempers, and desires an advantage over us. To forget that we are in a state of trial, that we have corrupt hearts, that we are watched by a spiritual enemy, would be ruin to the soul. There is no safety but to the man "who feareth always," and "taketh heed lest he fall."

Still there is nothing in the words of St. Peter which need dismay the righteous. The *righteous scarcely are saved:* are only saved with difficulty and exertion. This agrees with all the feelings and confessions of a disciple of Christ. It reminds him of the many hinderances which beset him both from within and from without in the way of salvation. It reminds him of the watchfulness in prayer, and the earnestness in labour, which are required to "make his calling and election sure." It reminds him of the prop, on which alone he dares to lean: and draws him closer to the rock on which alone his foundation must be laid. But having tried this, and being confident of its strength; though he is serious, he is without disturbance; though he is serious, he is not alarmed or apprehensive. He is *scarcely saved.* But still he *is* saved. "For there is no condemnation to them that are in Christ Jesus; who walk not after the flesh, but after the Spirit." Therefore he is able to *commit the keeping of his soul to God, as unto a faithful Creator*; and to trust that the "good work which hath been begun in him, will be performed unto the day of Jesus Christ," who is "able to keep him from falling, and to present him faultless before the presence of his glory with exceeding joy."

LXIX.

THE PERFECTION OF THE CHRISTIAN CHARACTER.

PHIL. iv. 8, 9.

8. *Finally, brethren, whatsoever things are true, whatsoever things are honest, whatsoever things are just, whatsoever things are pure, whatsoever things are lovely, whatsoever things are of good report; if there be any virtue and if there be any praise, think on these things.*

ST. PAUL has elsewhere described Christians as having "put off the old man with his deeds, and having put on the new man, which after God is created in righteousness and true holiness:"[1] renewed after the image of his Creator: that image in which he was originally formed, but which was soon defaced by Adam's transgression. So speaking, he describes, as we may say, a beautiful statue, which man is to resemble through the power of the Holy Ghost. But a beautiful statue is made up of separate limbs and features, which together form the whole admirable figure. These different parts are here detailed.

First, TRUTH. *Whatsoever things are true,* the Christian must study and follow. There must be in him that sincerity, that genuineness of character, which is the basis of all good. St. Paul gave an example of it in his trial before the council, when, as he opened his defence, "the high priest Ananias commanded them that stood by to smite him on the mouth." Stung by the injustice of such treatment, "Paul said unto him, God shall smite thee, thou whited wall: for sittest thou to judge me after the law, and commandest me to be smitten contrary to the law? And they that stood by said, Revilest thou God's high priest?" At once he acknowledged that he had been hasty, and incurred blame. "I wist not, brethren, that he was the high priest; for it is written, Thou shalt not speak evil of the ruler of thy people."[2]

The beauty of such sincerity is most plainly seen in contrast with the contrary character of falsehood

[1] See Ephes. iv. 22—24; Col. iii. 9—12. [2] Acts xxiii. 1—5.

or hypocrisy. As shown, for example, by Ananias; when he retained a part of his property, and claimed the merit of having given up the whole.[3] This was like the sin reproved in the Jews by their prophets: when they brought the lame, and the blind, and the refuse of their flock for sacrifice, and so "robbed God," at the moment when with their lips they honoured him.[4] Well might He say, who knew the heart, "Your sacrifice is an abomination to me."

Secondly, *Whatsoever things are honest*, the Christian must pursue: providing things honourable, respectable, consistent in the eyes of man. That a man *be* virtuous, is the first and main thing; but that he *appear so* likewise, and "let not his good be evil spoken of," is highly to be desired. He thus conciliates favour, which may lead the way to imitation. Our Lord performed a miracle, lest he should give occasion of offence by claiming to be free from tribute, on grounds which the Jews might not understand.[5] And St. Peter earnestly exhorts all men to adorn by their conduct the doctrine which they profess, so that they of the contrary part "may be ashamed, who falsely accuse their good conversation in Christ."

Justice, as well as truth, is a quality on which many pride themselves who do not look beyond the present world. The Christian, therefore, who does look beyond the present world, must especially study *whatsoever things are just.* Conduct, for instance, like

[3] Acts v. 1, 2. [4] Mal. i. 13; iii. 8. [5] Matt. xvii. 24—27.

that of Abraham must have struck with admiration the people who surrounded him, after the battle which he had been forced to wage in defence of Lot and his family.[6] When he had recovered the captive persons, and the goods, "the king of Sodom said unto Abram, Give me the persons, and take the goods to thyself." But Abram stedfastly refused. "And Abram said unto the king of Sodom, I have lift up my hand unto the Lord, the most high God, the possessor of heaven and earth, that I will not take from a thread even to a shoe-latchet, and that I will not take anything that is thine, lest thou shouldest say, I have made Abram rich: save only that which the young men have eaten, and the portion of the men that went with me, Aner, Eshcol, and Mamre, let them take their portion."

This conduct, in all its parts, was justice. It was just, that the prisoners who had been made captive should be recovered, and that the goods which had been seized should be restored. It was just that they should remain the property of those from whom they had been unlawfully taken; and that the king of Sodom should have his own again. But it was also just that the young men who had assisted in regaining the lost possessions, should be repaid for the time and cost which they had expended, and should receive "their portion." Thus the light of Abram's character shone brightly before the king of an ungodly people, and the God whom he feared was honoured in their eyes.

[6] Gen. xiv. 21, &c.

So likewise must be studied, *whatsoever things are pure.* The Christian is "the temple of the living God."[7] The Holy Spirit dwells in him. From the earthly temple at Jerusalem the Lord drove out "the money changers and them that bought and sold," that worldly dealings might not profane the "house of prayer."[8] With how much more reason should be cast out from the Christian's heart, devoted as it ought to be unto God, those evil thoughts and desires which defile it, and render it unworthy of the Divine presence? He who hath redeemed him, and hath called him to holiness, was without spot and undefiled; the Christian must strive to be "holy as he is holy," to "purify himself even as he is pure."

And not only in these important qualities, truth, consistency, justice, purity—on which the character of the man depends, and without which the signs of the new creation are wanting—but in all the excellences which adorn human nature, should the Christian be conspicuous. *Whatsoever things are lovely or of good report, if there be any virtue, or if there be any praise,* let him *think on these things:* so that men may look on him and say, This is the work of God. Human nature, ruined and corrupt in itself, is capable of being renewed, and "made partaker of the divine nature," being delivered from the evil that is in the world.

And St. Paul, in recommending these things, was able to exhibit to the Philippians a living example in which they had been seen.

[7] 1 Cor. vi. 19; 2 Cor. vi. 14. [8] Matt. xxi. 12.

9. *Those things, which ye have both learned, and received, and heard, and seen in me, do: and the God of peace shall be with you.*

He had sojourned with them at Philippi, long enough to show them what manner of man he was: that he did not advise them to walk in the light, whilst his own path was not light but darkness: like his Lord and Master, he had left them "an example that they should follow his steps"[9] in all holy and virtuous conversation. If any should plead human infirmity, an ensnaring world, a watchful adversary; he could bring forward a proof that the adversary may be resisted, the world overcome, and human infirmity changed for more than human strength. And therefore he says, *those things which ye have seen in me, do: and the God of peace shall be with you.*

The God of peace would certainly be with them whilst they thus lived; and even whilst they endeavoured to live thus. Could they be thus perfect, their *peace* would be perfect too. But perfection, either of peace or character, is not for this world: otherwise this world would be heaven. In proportion as they *thought on these things,* aimed at these things, advanced towards these things, *the God of peace would be with them* here, and admit them to perfect peace and perfect happiness among "the spirits made perfect" in the everlasting kingdom of our God and Saviour.

[9] 1 Pet. ii. 21.

LXX.

THE HEIRS OF THE KINGDOM.

MATT. xx. 23.

Jesus answered and said, To sit on my right hand and on my left is not mine to give, but it shall be given to them for whom it is prepared of my Father.

THOSE who are nearest in power and greatness to an earthly king, sit on his right hand and on his left. The mother of the two disciples, James and John, asked this distinction for her sons, not doubting that "the throne of David," on which the Lord was to sit, was a throne of this present world.

The answer which our Lord returned, at first, takes us by surprise. *To sit on my right hand, and on my left, is not mine to give, but it shall be given to them for whom it is prepared of my Father.* The matter in our Lord's mind, as he spoke, was, no doubt, his heavenly kingdom. It might not be in the apostles' mind, but it was in his mind. And how are we to explain his meaning, when he says, *It is not mine to give?* To whom then should we go? Especially when he has elsewhere asserted: "The Father judgeth no man, but hath delivered all judgment to the Son." "All things are delivered unto me of my Father." "I go to prepare a place for you, that where I am, there ye may be also." All these sentences prove, that, in one sense, the kingdom of heaven *is* our Lord's giving, and only his giving.

How then do they agree with the clause, which says, it shall only *be given to them for whom it is prepared of the Father?* A little consideration will explain.

It has pleased God, in the gospel covenant, to promise eternal life to such as shall possess a certain character, or answer a certain description. He does not assign it to particular persons, but to a particular description of persons. Not to this or that individual, but to every individual in whom that character is found.

HE knows, indeed, who they are, whom he "has decreed to deliver from curse and damnation, and to bring by Christ to everlasting salvation, as vessels made to honour." But all that he reveals, or enables us to know of them, is their character. They "are called by his Spirit working in due season; they through grace obey the calling; they are made like the image of his Son; they walk religiously in good works: and at length, by God's mercy, they attain to everlasting felicity."[1] And beyond these; to others than these; and not of this class;—it is not in the power even of our Lord to give an entrance into his kingdom. The request was, that he should dispose of it differently: that he should assign it to persons, without respect to character. *Grant to these my two sons, that they may sit, the one on thy right hand, and the other on the left, in thy kingdom.* Just as in the world situations of trust are sometimes bestowed, not because the individuals are fit for them, but because they desire them. And this unjust request draws forth the memorable reply: *It is not mine to give, but to them for whom it is prepared of my*

[1] See Articles of Religion, xvii.

Father.[2] Not from want of authority in him, "who is over all, God blessed for ever;" but for want of fitness in the person. In the same sense as we say, It is impossible for God to be false to his word: in that sense it is impossible for Christ himself to give his kingdom to others than those for whom God has prepared it.

It cannot, therefore, be designed for any who do not believe in him by whom it was purchased, and through whom it is bestowed.

First, because "eternal life is the gift of God through Jesus Christ:" "No man cometh unto the Father, but by him."

Secondly, because these alone direct their lives, discipline their hearts, and order their conversation, according to the rules of his kingdom. They "receive him," not only as the "author of eternal salvation," but as the author of a law in which they should walk towards it. This is a very peculiar path; very unlike that which we should follow of our own accord; very unlike that in which those are travelling, who have not the kingdom of God before their eyes. He in whom they are trusting, and to whom they have surrendered themselves, gradually prepares them for the state to which they look forward: withdraws them from the works of the flesh, and brings forth in them the fruits of the Spirit.

It would be contrary to the nature of things, it

[2] So the sentence would be rendered more clearly, and more exactly represent the original, omitting the words, it *shall be given*, with which our translators have filled up the sentence; ἀλλα, but, is equivalent to ἐι μη, except.

would be contrary to the perfect righteousness of God, if this kingdom were granted to others. There must be some agreement between the kingdom, and the characters belonging to it. To take a sinful creature, with lusts unconquered, with temper unbroken, with pride unsubdued, with a heart never bent before God in prostration of self-abasement, or raised towards him in the aspiration of piety and love; to place such an one in the presence of God and his angels, and bid him dwell in the realms of holiness; this would be contrary to all our reasonable notions of what is right and suitable. Our own understanding teaches us, (may we never be condemned by the acknowledgment!) that they must be "pure in heart," who are admitted to "see God;" they must be "meek," who "inherit the land" where all is peace: they must be "merciful," who obtain mercy. They must "hunger and thirst after righteousness," who are to inhabit "a new heaven and a new earth, wherein dwelleth righteousness." These are they for whom the kingdom is prepared of the Father. And as the Father and his Christ are one, it is not Christ's to give to any *except those for whom it is prepared of the Father*. But, to them, it is *his to give,* and his alone. As will be seen, "when the Son of man shall come in his glory, and all the holy angels with him, and shall sit on the throne of his glory." And we are clearly told *to whom it shall be given.* No one who reads the Scriptures with a humble desire to be instructed by them, can have a doubt respecting the characters of those to whom "the King shall say, Come, ye blessed of my Father, receive the kingdom prepared for you from the foundation of the world."[3]

Happy indeed are they who can discern that character in their own hearts and lives: in their hearts, for they "have believed in the only begotten Son of God;" and in their lives, for they have fashioned them according to his will.

LXXI.

THE SPIRITUAL RESURRECTION.

COL. iii. 1—4.

1. *If ye then be risen with Christ, seek those things which are above, where Christ sitteth on the right hand of God.*
2. *Set your affection on things above, not on things on the earth.*
3. *For ye are dead, and your life is hid with Christ in God.*

Risen with Christ. That, then, was the state of the Colossian Christians. But to have *risen with*

[3] Matt. xxv. 34.

Christ, they must first have died. St. Paul here says that they had died. *For ye are dead.* He often uses this figure, to denote the change of heart which takes place in the Christian: to express his frame of mind in regard to this present world: the world for which he no longer lives:[1] the world to which he is dead; for *his life is hid with Christ in God.*

We can understand the phrase. Upon one who is dead, the world has no effect: makes no impression. To one who is dead, whatever may have been the case before, sin offers no temptation. And one who takes on himself the faith of Christ, and is baptized in his name, is "buried with Christ" from the sinful affections of the flesh and of the mind: his baptism implies that he is dead with Christ from "the rudiments of the world;" he is "crucified to the world," and the world to him.

In this sense is the Christian *dead:* but in no other. His baptism, whilst it is "a death unto sin," is "a new birth unto righteousness." For as Christ only submitted to death, that he might rise triumphant from the grave; so the Christian dies to sin, that he may "walk in newness of life:" dies to this world, that *his life may be hid with God.* He is "buried with Christ in baptism," that like the seed, which, after perishing in the ground, becomes a luxuriant tree, he may *rise with Christ* to a better life than that which he has laid down, a life of holiness and righteousness. He is "dead indeed unto sin, but alive unto God, through Jesus Christ our Lord."[2]

The apostle, therefore, proceeds to the conduct

[1] See Rom. vi. 3, &c.

[2] Rom. vi. 11.

which befits their altered state. *If ye then be risen with Christ, seek those things which are above, where Christ sitteth on the right hand of God.* Seek the things where he is, and not the things which he has left, and you also must soon leave. *Set your affections on things above, not on things on the earth.* What *the things above* are, we partly know, though now we see as through a glass, darkly. They are the things which God has prepared for them that love him: the things that are "at his right hand, where is fulness of joy, and pleasures for evermore." They are the glorious company, to which, even now, Christians are said to "have come," and to which they belong;[3] "the city of the living God, the heavenly Jerusalem, an innumerable company of angels, the general assembly and church of the first-born, God the Judge of all, the spirits of just men made perfect, Jesus the mediator of the new covenant." These are *the things which are above,* the things of which the apostle says, *Seek them. Set your affections on them.* Be not like the guests in the parable, whom the king invited to his banquet; "and they all with one consent began to make excuse. The first said unto him, I have bought a piece of ground, and I must needs go and see it: I pray thee have me excused. And another said, I have bought five yoke of oxen, and I go to prove them: I pray thee have me excused. And another said, I have married a wife, and therefore I cannot come."[4] Perhaps if these persons had been asked, whether the things of heaven, or the things of the earth were to be held first in value, they would

[3] Heb. xii.

[4] Luke xiv. 16, &c.

have answered, The things of heaven. So many would, who are not seeking them. But we should be aware that they deceived themselves. We could never believe that the spendthrift, who lavishes his money on every trifle which is presented to him, values wealth, and makes it his chief business to increase it. We could never believe that the miser, who is constantly adding to his store, with no regard to the wants which are around him, is loving his neighbour as himself, or looking to other interests than his own. And so we can never believe that they are "seeking first the kingdom of God and his righteousness," who are pursuing the vanities and follies of this present world; or that they are *setting their affections on things above*, who neglect the precepts of the gospel, and indulge, perhaps, the very sins of which we are assured that "they which do such things, have no inheritance in the kingdom of Christ and of God."[5]

On the other hand, we read of some who made it plain, what they were seeking. We read, for instance, of one of the disciples, named Joses, "who having land, sold it, and brought the money, and laid it at the apostles' feet."[6] We read of the apostles, who were imprisoned, and beaten, and threatened, if they dared to "preach at all or teach in the name of Jesus." But they persisted, saying, "We ought to obey God rather than man;" and "departed from the council, rejoicing that they were counted worthy to suffer shame for his name."[7] These, therefore, were *seeking the things that are above*. And so, no less, are they, who though not called to the same proof of their devoted-

[5] Gal. v. 21. [6] Acts iv. 36, 37. [7] Acts v. 29, &c.

ness, are "giving all diligence, that they may add to their faith, virtue, and knowledge, and temperance, and patience, and godliness, and charity:"[8] who, "denying ungodliness and worldly lusts, are walking soberly, righteously, and godly in the world," looking for the appearance of their Lord in glory.[9] To be following "whatsoever things are honourable, and just, and pure, and lovely;" to be shunning whatever is contrary to these things; to be continually "pressing on towards the prize of our high calling, not as though we had already attained, either were already perfect:" this is to have withdrawn the affections from things of the earth, and to have set them on the things that are above.

Can it be said of any who do less than this, that the words of St. Paul are fulfilled in them, and *their life is hid with Christ in God?* Yet they are words which we can easily comprehend. Our life is, where our heart is. If we have greatly loved an earthly object, and that object is distant from us: where is our life? Where was the life of the patriarch Jacob, when tidings were brought him of the death of his favourite Joseph? "And Jacob rent his clothes, and put sackcloth upon his loins, and mourned for his son many days. And all his sons and all his daughters rose up to comfort him: but he refused to be comforted, and said, For I will go down into the grave unto my son mourning."[1] Thus Jacob's life was not with his family around him, nor with the place where he was drawing breath. Jacob's life was with his son Joseph in the grave where he supposed him to be laid. This is the apostle's

[8] 2 Pet. i. 5—7. [9] Tit. ii. 12—16. [1] Gen. xxxvii. 34, 35.

meaning—*Your life is hid with Christ in God.* Your body is here in this present world, where ye are thankful for its comforts, tasting of its refreshments, and fulfilling its duties: "not slothful in business, but fervent in spirit, serving the Lord." But *your life*, your heart, *is hid with Christ:* laid up there, where he is preparing a place for you, and from whence in his own good time he will come again and take you to himself. Because he is there, ye are there also: already there in spirit; and looking onward to "the glorious appearing of the great God and our Saviour Jesus Christ," and to the fulfilment of "that blessed hope," which he permits his true disciples to enjoy.[2]

For this is the result to which the Christian looks.

4. *When Christ, who is our life, shall appear, then shall ye also appear with him in glory.*

This is the "reason which we should be ready to give of the hope that is in us."[3] Such a reason we must have. One who is continually climbing, must be urged onward by some impulse. One who is always striving against a stream, must have a cause to impel him. The apostles asked for such a motive; saying to the Lord, "Lo, we have left all, and followed thee: what shall we have therefore? And Jesus said unto them, Verily I say unto you, That every one who hath forsaken houses, or brethren, or sisters, or father, or mother, or wife, or children, or lands, for my name's sake, shall receive a hundredfold, and shall inherit everlasting life."[4] For "the Son of man shall come in

[2] Tit. ii. 13. [3] 1 Pet. iii. 15. [4] Matt. xix. 27—29.

the glory of his Father with his angels; and then he shall reward every man according to his works."[5] And then they who have been "dead with him" on earth, shall rise to live with him above. They who have shared his sufferings, shall also *appear with him in glory*. He shall "change their vile body, that it may be made like unto his glorious body:" this "corruptible shall put on incorruption; this mortal shall put on immortality." The very place of their future habitation was disclosed in a vision to St. John, who writes: "I saw a new heaven and a new earth, for the first heaven and the first earth were passed away. And I heard a great voice from heaven, saying, Behold, the tabernacle of God is with men; and he shall dwell with them, and they shall be his people. God himself shall be with them, and be their God. And God shall wipe away all tears from their eyes; and there shall be no more death, neither sorrow nor crying; for the former things are passed away."[6]

These are *the things which are above:* the things of which St. Paul says, *Set your affections on them:* the things to which he says, we *are risen:* risen in thought, and desire, and title: the things upon which our heart should be fixed, and among which our life, "our conversation"[7] should be even now; for where our heart is, there will our life be also.

This, then, is the proper attitude of every Christian man. His residence here; his home, above; his tone of mind, his habits of living such, as to show that his affections are set on heavenly things. Nothing less, is to answer the purpose of our redemption, by which

[5] Matt. xvi. 27. [6] Rev. xxi. 1—4. [7] Phil. iii. 20.

we are "delivered from this present evil world." Nothing less can answer the requirements of our baptism, in which we engaged to renounce all worldly pomps and vanities. Nothing less, is to "walk worthy of Christ, who has called us to his kingdom and glory." Nothing less will enable us, *when he shall appear,* to "have confidence, and not be ashamed before him at his coming."[8]

LXXII.

HEAVEN THE ABODE OF RIGHTEOUSNESS.

2 Peter iii. 13.

We, according to his promise, look for new heavens and a new earth, wherein dwelleth righteousness.

St. Peter gives this short, but emphatic, description of the heavenly kingdom, which the Christian is permitted to look for, when all things which now are "shall be dissolved." He does not speak of it as a place "where is fulness of joy, and pleasures for evermore:" he does not attempt to represent its glories,

[8] 1 John ii. 28.

by figuring to our minds gates of pearl, and streets of gold: he does not even make mention of the absence of all sorrow, "where they shall hunger no more, nor thirst any more, neither shall there be any more pain:"[1] —but he simply speaks of a new world *wherein dwelleth righteousness.* He states this, and this alone, as if this were all, and this all-sufficient.

And truly, speaking thus, he speaks as one who had gone through the ranks of mankind, and the abodes of human nature, and had learnt what causes misery, and what real happiness consists in. He speaks as one who had entered into the recesses of his own heart, and had discovered what was needful to its peace: and then he describes heaven as a place *wherein dwelleth righteousness.*

This world would have been free from all calamity, if there had been no unrighteousness. If the heart of man had remained uncorrupt, all things else would have remained as they were at first pronounced by their Creator, who surveyed the works of his hands, "and behold they were very good." With sin came death; came all the pain and woe that leads to death, and attends it. With sin came that blight upon the earth, from which labour and indigence and privation spring. And yet it is not in these—not in the severity of labour nor in the straits of poverty that real unhappiness consists: indeed under all the calamities and trials of life the pious and godly mind may be upheld: moral evil is the thorn which rankles in the side, and causes the wound which cannot be remedied or mitigated, till its source is removed.

[1] See Rev. vii. and xxi.

I look (for example) to the history of the patriarch Jacob,[2] and find one who is leaving his country and his home, his whole fortune and his sole companion, being the staff on which he leaned; a mother too, who loved him but too well, is forced to conquer nature and hasten his departure. This is one of the sore distresses of life: the separation of those who are dear to each other: the departure from the home we have known, and the country we have loved. If we trace this case of unhappiness to its cause, it arises from sin. It arises from the practice of deceit in one, and in the indulgence of revenge in another. Jacob is forced to fly, because he has supplanted his brother of his birthright: because Esau is waiting for an opportunity to slay him.

I look again to the history of the kings of Israel,[3] and find the picture of a monarch who "comes home to his house heavy and displeased, and lays him down upon his bed, and turns away his face, and will eat no bread." Here too is unhappiness. And here too is sin under another form: the form of covetousness. Ahab has been disappointed in his desire to possess Naboth's vineyard.

Again, I turn to the thirty-eighth Psalm and read these words: "O Lord, rebuke me not in thy wrath, neither chasten me in thy hot displeasure. For thine arrows stick fast in me, and thy hand presseth me sore. There is no soundness in my flesh by reason of thine anger: neither is there any rest in my bones because of my sin. For mine iniquities are gone over my head; as a heavy burthen, they are too heavy for me."

[2] Gen. xxvii.

[3] 1 Kings xxi.

The complaint is from David. It is not pain, it is not poverty, it is not the loss of those dear to him, which cause these mournful words: he is grieving, because he acknowledges his transgressions, and his sin is ever before him. And what would these, and such as these, require, that their sorrow may be turned into joy, their mourning changed for peace? A nature which shall not sin: a nature which shall not be overcome by evil desires: a nature which shall not covet what God has not permitted: a nature which shall not be capable of envy, hatred, malice, and uncharitableness: a nature where the flesh shall not lust against the spirit, or a law in the members war against the law of the mind: a nature, in short, wherein *dwelleth righteousness:* dwelleth, not as now, a guest brought in, admitted into the heart, yet often finding itself a stranger, as one not in its native home: not as now, even at the best, soon disturbed as a bird from the resting-place it has chosen, and forced to flee away; but where righteousness dwells as in its own birthplace.

Neither is it a man's own sinfulness alone which brings him unhappiness in this world. How much of what is suffered comes from the sin of others! How many families are made miserable from the conduct of those who ought to be their stay and comfort! What wretchedness did Jacob suffer from the wickedness of his children! David, too; was there any sorrow like the sorrow which he felt for Absalom? St. Peter, like all the early Christians, knew much of this: so that if, as St. Paul writes, "in this world only they had hope, they were of all men most miserable:" reproached by their friends, cast off by their relations, despoiled of their goods, reviled, defamed, imprisoned, tormented: and this for the Gospel's sake; because they would be faithful to their God and Saviour. Who can wonder that Peter, who had suffered all this, and was writing to those who suffered it, should represent heaven as the place wherein none are persecuted for righteousness' sake, for therein *dwelleth righteousness:* "there the wicked cease from troubling, and the weary are at rest."

This, says the apostle, is what *we look for*. We look for it according to divine promise. Even if there were no promise, we might look for it with hope: for whilst we see around us a vast multitude who do even as they list, neither fearing God nor regarding man; yet we also see others, who follow after holiness, and set God before them: and our reason forbids us to believe, that the righteous should be as the wicked: that God should make no "difference between those who serve him, and those who serve him not."[1] But we have still firmer ground to stand upon: we have the assurance of the Son of God himself, that "whosoever heareth his words, and doeth them, shall have eternal life:" and that "eye hath not seen, nor ear heard, neither hath it entered into the heart of man to conceive such things as God has prepared for them that love him."

One reflection grows out of these words. Heaven is represented as the scene and abode of righteousness. In proportion, therefore, as we cultivate righteousness here, we anticipate the happiness of heaven. Heaven

[1] Mal. iii.

cannot be perfected here, because righteousness cannot be here perfect. But the nearer we approach to righteousnes, the nearer we approach to that *new heaven and new earth wherein dwelleth righteousness*.

FINIS.

CPSIA information can be obtained
at www.ICGtesting.com
Printed in the USA
LVHW040840100123
736786LV00001B/171